Praise for *Hand In The Till:*

"Continued brilliance, the characters still make you laugh and cry and fume the entire time you're reading," Colin Quinn

"Another excellent piece from Hansen. Darkly comic, I laughed out loud. Hansen brings the personal side of the continuing divisions in Derry with the dynamic interplay of his wonderful characters." Kate Rigby, *Little Guide to Unhip, Lost the Plot, Seaview Terrace,* among others

"Little and not so little brats from Hell, brilliantly staged, a surreal feat, gloriously dark and comically tragic. It's compulsive reading," Ashen Venema, *Course of Mirrors*

"Consummate black humor, skillfully crafted characters, inventive descriptions and a smart plot," Iva Polansky, *Fame and Infamy*

"Humor, the greatest weapon known to man when it comes to tackling institutional bigotry or social inequality. And Hansen takes that weapon and uses it like a pallet knife on this excellent canvas," James McPherson, *Lucifer and Auld Lang Syne*

"Bitingly, bitterly humorous. A strong voice and flowing prose, with a good pace and an idiosyncratic take on a bleak world," J.S. Watts, *A Darker Moon*

"The dialogue simply sparkles. Brilliantly funny even while a tad disturbing," John O'Brien, *Other Face*

"An absolute pleasure to read. The dialogue is spot-on, and the imagery stark and vivid. Shifts gears from the tragic to the hilarious with ease," R.A. Baker, *Rayna of Nightwind*

"Hansen has mastered the art of believable colloquial dialogue and his descriptive narrative puts you right there in the scene. The characters jump off the page and the read entertains. Yet another example of his excellent work," Delcan Conner, *Russian Brides*

"A black comedy indeed. A gift for dialogue and the ability to weave an intriguing tale," Katy Christie, *No Man No Cry*

"Puts you right there in that world with a masterly confidence, and the characters and setting are sketched with deft economy," NSL Lee, *Chosen*

"A masterful piece of work that deserves as much praise as can be piled upon it. A supreme writer with talent in buckets, buckets of talent and a gift that can never be achieved, only owned," Andrew Skaife, *God, the Son and the Holy Dwarf*

Praise for the ABNA 2010 Semifinalist *An Embarrassment of Riches:*

"A masterpiece," Colin Quinn

"As absorbing as it is hysterical," Publishers Weekly

"Wildly amusing…a cross between a roller-coaster and a carousel," Olivera Baumgartner-Jackson. Readerviews.com

"Clearly the work of a craftsman! (The characters) career around Derry with the grace of a drunken and horny bull," Chris Gerrib, Podpeople.com

"Classic, I-can't-stop-reading literature," Jonathan Henderson, Jonhenderscon.com

"Absolutely hilarious," Jessica Roberts, Bookpleasures.com

"Comedy as pitch-black as the moors of the Emerald Island itself," Riot, BurningLeaves.com

"Riotous entertainment," P.P.O Kane, CompulsiveReader.com

FLEEING THE JURISDICTION

Gerald Hansen

Mint Books
New York

FLEEING THE JURISDICTON
Gerald Hansen
Copyright © Gerald Hansen 2012
Published by Mint Books

To Lorna Matcham, and Mom and Dad

In Loving Memory of Aunt Nancy Beachboard and Great Aunt
Phoebe Doherty

"Whoever has will be given more and he will have an abundance. Whoever does not have, even what he does have will be taken away."
Matthew 13.2

ACKNOWLEDGMENTS

Many, many thanks to all who helped me with this book. I could never have written it without you. HyeJeong Park, the cover is amazing! Thanks so much! Gosia Kurek, what would I have done without your editing, and, of course, the special additions. Special thanks to Haddou Mahjoubi for showing me Morocco, Alfredo DeQuesada and Lydia Aquino for showing me Puerto Rico, and Lawrence Martinetion for getting me to these amazing locales in the first place; to Sandro Carra for police information, Octavia Melian for legal advice, Mark Gondelman for the title, "T" for cruise liner information, and Paula Costa of Dragon's Kitchen, home to her fantastic *Titanic* Dinner Project. For various other bits and pieces that make the book click, my hearty thanks to Aldercy Flores (you're a treasure trove of Dymphna inspiration!), Steven MacEnrue, Jeferson Medeiros, Erin Lynch, Yvonne Sherwell, Robash Sandhu, Jeana Barenboim, Mike Falotico, Fabrizio Caso and of course my photographer supreme, Marcin Kaliski. Thanks also for continued support to Bonita Vander and all the students at Manhattan Language School, Noam Dworman and everyone at the Olive Tree Cafe and Comedy Cellar, and Archie A. Special thanks, also, to the kind people at Authonomy, Margaret Brown, editor of the fantastic Shelf Unbound ezine for her kindness, the wonderful ladies, 'piggies,' I believe they like to be called, of The Cheap, Andrew Wessel of Digital Book Today for his continued support, Greg Doublet of Ereaeder News Today, and Sharon Rosen of Pixel of Ink. Sharon, my career as a writer started with you! Colin Quinn, the man himself, you are amazing, and I am continually shocked at your support of my work. Thanks so much. And, of course, I am most grateful to all the readers who were willing to give me a chance...and actually liked what they were reading! Thanks so, so much all of you!

HOW TO PRONOUNCE THE NAMES (by popular demand):

Ursula: **Uhr**-suh-lah
Finnonuala: Fin-**noo**-lah
Dymphna: **Dimf**-nah
Siofra: **Shee**-frah
Eoin: Owen

CHAPTER ONE—WISCONSIN

When she heard the sirens, Louella Barnett was in Dunkin Donuts counting out the 87 cents needed to complete her purchase.

Her brother-in-law Jed had dropped her off, then gone next door to the pharmacy to stock up on their prescriptions: Celebrex and Oxycontin (Jed's benign colon polyps and his 'pains'), Prinivil and Xanax (Ursula's high blood pressure and anxiety), Lipitor, Orlistat and Zocor (Slim's high cholesterol, obesity and acid reflux), and Fosamax and Claritin (Louella's osteoporosis and allergies). They'd need two weeks' worth for the time they'd be on the run. Inside the donut store, Louella wanted to down a handful of Ursula's Xanax. It was no wonder: there were fifteen registers and two cashiers. At numbers 1 and 15.

"There's two lines! You gotta choose a line and stay in it! " the harried cashiers kept calling out.

"Like hell we will!" seemed to be the response. They were like surly ping pong players on speed, the hunger gnawing at them, ready to pounce on whichever cashier became available first. Louella had wasted the last fourteen minutes fiercely defending her position. She had sharp elbows and put them to good use at all angles.

Louella eyed in panic the precious seconds trickling away on her watch. Her fingernails dug into the pleather of her purse. She whimpered inwardly as she inched forward to nab the supplies meant to fill their four stomachs on the way to the airport, unable to stop the thoughts that her purchase was more important than any of these beasts'. Her manners and strict Lutheran upbringing wouldn't allow her to tell them so. She suffered in silence instead, the sweat trickling down her armpits, though she had given them a few extra rolls of the Lady Speed Stick that morning; she knew this day would be a trial. Her eyes shot wildly around the bright and happy tiles, seeking some distraction to calm her. The Black Eyed Peas from the speakers wasn't helping. There was a 'Visitor' sticker on the chunky sweater of the girl to her left that her elbows had yet to alienate. Louella leaned in toward her.

"Who was you off visiting, hon?" Louella asked, just to make conversation and compress time. She was shocked her voice could sound conversational.

The girl looked down and fingered in surprise the sticker she had forgotten to peel off.

"My dear old mama."Louella parted her lips, then whispered fearfully: "...Prison?" It was the only thing on her mind, and from the girl's stringy hair and crystal meth eyes, likely.

"Hospital!"

Louella turned away from the daggers the girl shot her. She saw Jed pacing outside in the parking lot, already clutching the jumbo bag from the pharmacy and sucking an unfiltered Camel; Ursula had forbidden him from smoking in his own car. He was doing a scratch card, and the sleet was spitting down on the cowboy hat that never seemed to leave his head. Ursula and Jed had lived next to her and Slim for two years, and Louella still didn't know what the color of Jed's hair was. Maybe he had none. More troubling now, though, was if the sleet would turn to snow and ground the plane. If that happened, she and Ursula were sure to find themselves banged up in the women's wing of the Waupun State Penitentiary.

Register #15 was free. Louella scuttled forward, took a deep breath and rattled her order into the old-school braces and acne scars of the girl at the till: "Four bacon and egg croissants, two French crullers, an apple fritter, a double cocoa fritter, two chocolate chip muffins, four hash browns, a Boston crème, 16 Munchkins in assorted flavors, a Box O' Joe, an iced hot chocolate and a tea. Please."

Panicked as she was, Louella still noticed the special seasonal pomegranate jelly stick on the promotional poster above the cashier's bobbing cap. She added four to the order, her taste buds tingling in anticipation.

"Large family?" The braces smiled.

"None of your beeswax!" Louella longed to snap. But she just grinned, her jaw muscles aching with the exertion of it, and gave a slight nod of the head. Her mouth didn't tell the lie, so it wasn't actually sinning. But if the cashier saw the size of Louella's husband Slim, she'd understand why Louella was always buying in bulk. Louella's fingernails clacked on the counter as the girl rang up the order. The girl couldn't meet her eyes as she said the total. Louella unshackled her wallet and reluctantly handed over the bills. But she couldn't hand over an extra dollar for the 87 cents. She pulled out her change purse.

"52...53...58..." Louella murmured through her grimace, fingers scrabbling. The cashier ground her molars, and those still to order roared their protest, but to Louella, even as rushed as she was, a penny saved was a dollar—

The sirens ripped through the sleet-slick air outside, her keen Doppler effect telling Louella they were heading towards the Dunkin

Donuts, not away. She screeched and, as pennies spewed in the air, her heart sank. Watching the change rain down upon the cashier's cap, Louella reflected she had brought it on herself: worrying so much about the police arresting them just before they escaped, she had *willed* it to happen. The fluorescent strips on the ceiling suddenly spotlighted her, every line on her face a crack. She had to get out.

"Gimme my food, please! Now!" Louella begged. The cashier hastened to comply. Louella heaved up the many bags and pushed through the angry masses to the exit.

Her creaky heart hammered into her breastplate. She shouldn't be putting it through this pressure, not at her age, 59. She was clawing the depths of her purse for sunglasses, and cursing sleet for being translucent because it was difficult to hide behind, when she saw the teen addict wracked in spasms next to a garbage can that overflowed with losing scratch cards. Jed and a few onlookers in parkas were inspecting him. The sirens that pierced the air probably belonged to an ambulance, but Louella still had the urge of flight. At once. Jed smiled as she approached.

"Look at that poor guy, he just collapsed on the—"

"A real tragedy, yeah," Louella agreed. Her fingernails clawed into the flesh of Jed's sagging bicep as a fixed grin insinuated itself on her face. "C'mon Jed, the Lord'll help him, and now we've got to help ourselves."

She tugged him toward the station wagon.

"What's the big rush?" Jed wondered, neck turned and eyes ogling the twitching body beyond his Buddy Holly glasses.

"The snow, the snow!" Louella dithered. "Let's get out of here before we get stuck. We're gonna miss our flight at this rate. And you don't wanna spoil Ursula's entire *anniversary surprise,* do you? Let's get outta town."

They were indeed 'in town,' the one block of it, but 'in town' was miles from where they lived. They still had to travel through twenty minutes of nothingness to Jed's and Ursula's house, pick up their spouses, who had hopefully finished unloading Louella and Slim's luggage from the pickup truck Slim had left in Jed's garage, safe from the impending blizzard. They would throw the luggage into the station wagon, head off to the airport, and when the flight attendant was showing them how to attach the oxygen masks to their faces, only then would Louella's heart still. As the station wagon lurched out of the parking lot, sideswiping the oncoming ambulance, Louella shrieked.

"Relax," Jed told her. "I've got air bags."

It wasn't Jed's driving, more the cop cruiser lights flashing into her eyes as they sped inches past it. As Louella heaved nervous gasps and slipped the pomegranate jelly sticks from the bag to her purse, in her mind's eye, she was back in Detective Scarrey's interrogation room like three weeks ago. With its chipped table and the metal chair that dug into her spine and the lone light bulb without a shade, his eyes boring into hers, like he was trying to pierce her brain and read the thoughts within, his promise as he dismissed her that he would want to speak to her again and his order that she and Ursula not to leave the jurisdiction. She fondled the airline ticket in her pocket, and praised the Lord that Scarrey hadn't taken their passports. That showed how weak the police's case was against them, but this was faint comfort to Louella.

Jed slipped a Tammy Wynette CD into the player, and Louella cringed as she heard Tammy croon '*Our D.I.V.O.R.C.E...becomes final...today.*' It wasn't because she hated Tammy Wynette. In fact, she had a set of swanky Tammy Wynette cloth dinner napkins with matching wooden George Jones holders she put on the place mats every Thanksgiving and Flag Day. Rather, she wondered what her husband and Ursula might have gotten up to while she and Jed were collecting the travel supplies. She wondered if she might be singing the very same words in the future.

As Jed hummed and tapped along on the steering wheel, Louella shot him little glances every time his eyes went to the rear view mirror. She wondered if he suspected as well. Not only why they were fleeing the country, but what his wife might be doing behind his back with his brother. She didn't think so. She didn't know what the pleasantries were that always seemed to be going on under the brim of his cowboy hat, but Jed seemed content. Louella envied him.

Arriving at the nothingness in which the Barnetts lived, Jed and Louella exited the car. Louella took one of the Dunkin Donuts bags inside in case immediate sustenance was needed. They made their way down the hallway, past the hanging collection of ceramic heads of people of different ethnicities from all around the world that Ursula was so proud of, and headed towards the kitchen. Louella stuck her hand out as she stopped in her tracks.

"Wait!" she warned Jed. "Hush a minute and listen!"

Jed cocked his head and did as he was told. From the kitchen, they heard excited squawks and groans and the flapping of what sounded like flesh against flesh, even the clanking of a buckle.

"Merciful Lord in Heaven! It's massive, so it is!" Louella and Jed, to their horror, heard Ursula moan through the door. "Och! *Ach!* I'm having terrible trouble fitting it all in. Push, would ye, Slim? *Push!*"

"I'm trying, chipmunk," Slim panted in return, "But at this angle *grunt!* there's only so much I can *pant!* do. If you move your leg a bit to the left—"

"God bless us and save us, quit yer yammering and shove it in, just!"

Jed was frozen in confusion, Louella incandescent with rage. She flashed Jed a look which said, "I *knew* it!" and her hand shot to the doorknob.

Jed stopped her.

"Should we at least knock?" he wondered.

Louella's hand hung like a noodle in the air before the knob, and her second look at Jed said, "Man up!"

Then she remembered the sirens she had just heard, the cop car inches from her face, and she was hit by a vision of a slab of concrete for a bed and a toilet with no seat. She pursed her schoolmarm lips and, praying ice cubes weren't involved, pried open the door. Jed ground his eyes shut.

Mid-thrust, Slim and Ursula greeted them in alarm, sweat lashing down the Twister-poses of their bodies on the tiles. Ursula raked fingers through her disheveled eggplant-colored bob and giggled sheepishly. Muffins the poodle yipped at their contorted heels.

"Oh!"

Jed must have felt Louella deflating with relief, because he pried apart his lids to view whatever monstrosity might befall his eye.

"Oh!"

"You're packing," Louella said. "Thank God! But...in the kitchen? Who packs in the kitchen, for crying out loud?"

Her eyes glinted with suspicion still.

"Yer flimmin bag exploded," Ursula explained. "Talk about overpacking! We was taking them from the garage into the hallway, and the lock on this one gave way, so it did, and these clothes of yers flew all

5

over the place. Go on and give us a hand shoving this tuxedo of Slim's into the bag, would ye? The size of it!"

The four of them pushed away at the straining suitcase like human compactors. As Louella pushed, she suspected that Ursula and Slim had somehow known they were outside the door and orchestrated the scene for her and Jed to see.

"That's it finally all in," Ursula announced as the locks were clicked shut and the masking tape was wound around.

"Would somebody please tell me where the hell we're going?" Slim implored. One hand wiped the sweat from his bald head, the other polished his bifocals with his lumberjack shirt.

Louella and Ursula froze for a second, eyes agog, then yipped in chorus:

"Hurry, would ye!" "Time's a-wasting!" "We've to get Muffins in her cage still!"

"Would you tell us what we are running *from?*"Jed put in, finally.

"Get them bags out to the car, just," Ursula snipped. "I don't want to tell ye now and spoil *the anniversary surprise.*" She said it as if quoting from a script, badly. 'Louella, let's make wer way from the scullery and ensure all the plugs of the appliances and such is pulled outta the walls."

"Surely." Louella's smile was strained. Ursula's alien Irish vocabulary—who on the planet called a kitchen a 'scullery,' for Pete's sake?—rankled her just as much as the thought of Ursula making whoopie with Slim. But, partners in crime as they were now, racing to avoid arrest, she would have to put up with her strangeness. They left Jed and Slim to the manly haulage and hurried towards the living room sockets.

"Ach, ye've got some breakfast for us, have ye?"

Louella handed the bag over the top of the sofa to Ursula, and Muffins leaped towards it.

"And I've to lock this one up in her cage to drop her off at the doggy hotel." Ursula groaned as she scooped Muffins into her arms. "Who's a good boy? Whooo's a good boy?" she said in a deep silly pet-owner voice to the dog. It squirmed against the lifesized palm leaves of her pantsuit with the flared legs as if trying to escape from the fashion faux pas. Ursula stuck her hand in the bag. Louella tugged plug after plug out of socket after socket. Ursula followed her, talking and chewing. "What if the plane be's grounded, Louella, and we be's stuck here in the States? That's us banged up as sure as the Pope be's a Catholic. The guilt, Louella, the guilt of what we did all them years ago, it be's gnawing a hole in me stomach. And them coppers, the hands of them be's like tentacles of a deep sea creature, reaching out to get us as the time passes, the suction cups coming closer and closer to us and...Ye know what I'm on about, aye? I wouldn't mind, but yer woman went and died anyroad. And what was the meaning of that look ye gave me as ye was coming into the scullery just now? Ye fairly took the gloss offa me eyeballs with the daggers ye was shooting me way!"

Louella's skeletal fingers slipped into her purse.

Ursula turned—

and screamed at the gun in Louella's fist.

CHAPTER TWO—DERRY, NORTHERN IRELAND

Fionnuala Flood opened the door to the pub and felt her breasts were in sudden danger. She shot a hand protectively to the bright flowers of her sopping shirt, the other slammed shut the door. She heaved the wicker basket up and dragged her startled husband down the cobblestones.

"What's up with ye, woman?" Paddy asked, his breath heavy with the stench of cheap drink. "Was the pub full of Proddies?"

"I never thought me mouth would ever utter it, but a pub of Protestant bastards would have been more welcome."

She peered around the corner of the city walls and took a tentative step under the Mountains of Mourne Gate towards the drunken roars and screams and sounds of breaking glass. Night was encroaching through the buckets of rain, and with it the usual danger of their neighborhood, the Moorside, next to the city center, but Fionnuala would rather be threatened by a hopped-up hooligan's sharpened screwdriver than...*that!* She shuddered her disgust and rage, the image of the unseemly mannish women leering at her still burned on the backs of her corneas. She turned, picked up a rock and made to fling it at the pub window. Paddy rushed over.

"Are ye soft in the head?" he yelled, grabbing the flying flesh of her underarm and hauling it back.

"Lemme at the sinful beasts!" Fionnuala snarled into his greasy stubble. "Lemme smash that flimmin window!"

Paddy wouldn't. Fionnuala tried to launch the rock as best her fingers, struggling inside Paddy's fist, could. It toppled to the ground and trundled two inches. Fionnuala's eyes bored their rage into Paddy's like two icepicks.

"Ach, ye're a gobshite, so ye are!"

"Flinging rocks at yer age!" he tutted. "Ye headbin! Do ye want the Filth after ye?"

Fionnuala shook the rain from her bleached ponytails and considered. She had been a spotty, gawky teen when she had last flung a rock; the target had been a British land rover barreling down the street of her childhood, and, yes, a member of the Royal Ulster Constabulary, as the police had been called in those days, had hauled her in to the Filth Shop. She had gotten off with a warning, and hadn't even spent time in a holding cell—they had propped her up in the corridor against a beware-of-unattended-parcels poster—but thirty years later she still winced at the memory of the walloping her mother Maureen had given her arse with the fireplace poker; the extreme punishment had been less for attempting to harm British soldiers than spotlighting the family to the Protestant police. Nowadays, the Filth were called the Police Service of Northern Ireland—the PSNI—and a few Catholics had joined their ranks, but they were still to be avoided like Pet Shop Boys CDs. And lesbians, for that matter.

"Wall-to-wall with unseemly *bean-flickers* that flimming pub was. I blame the Yanks, so I do."

Paddy stared wistfully behind him.

"Shall we not count how much we've collected for them bills before we make wer way to the next pub?" he suggested.

Paddy reached to the basket dangling from her elbow. Bills were indeed long overdue, and they had been going pub to pub to earn what they could; except for the packs of Eastern-bloc cigarettes, there hadn't been many takers. Few in Derry seemed to have use for the urinal cakes, fake Fabergé eggs and jam jars filled with homemade toothpaste Fionnuala thought would be must-haves. She had noticed toothpaste had gotten expensive at the Derry branch of the Top Yer Trolly superstore and had gone creative in the family kitchen with baking soda, salt, a few drops of water and the spice rack; she had not only spearmint and cinnamon flavored for sale, but also nutmeg and paprika. The enterprise stank of desperation, and that's because it was.

A trio of surly teens with shaved heads rounded the corner, fists curled, ready for post-pub violence, the more casual and senseless the better. They eyed the basket.

"On the scrounge, are youse?" one asked over the techno music blaring from the headphones around his neck.

Fionnuala yelped as the basket was wrenched from her arm, almost dislocating her elbow.

"Let's see what ye have there, gran."

They pounced on the basket. Fionnuala screamed her rage and anguish as they broke the jars of toothpaste against the wall and stamped on the eggs. A third shoved Paddy to the ground as he tried to intervene.

"Outta wer way, gramps."

"Would youse look at that, hi? Free fags!" one 'marveled' from his hood, scooping up the remaining packs of cigarettes. "Ta for the fags, youse."

"The rest be's useless shite, but," the third said. As Paddy struggled to prise himself from the slivers of egg, he pushed him back down and spat his contempt all down the front of his lapels.

And then they were gone. Paddy roared abuse at their disappearing backs and, looking down at the spittle, figured the rain would wash it away. Alternately saddened and furious at the sight of all her hard work dripping down the walls in mint and spice globs, Fionnuala gathered up the now-soaked urinal cakes.

A gaggle of roaring, lager-infused girls, feeding on styrofoam containers of soggy chips and looking to inflict pain on anyone who looked at them the wrong way with the heels of their stilettos, swam past, casting Fionnuala looks as if she were a hooker and Paddy a john trolling on a budget. The girls erupted with the cruel laughter of the young.

"Would ye look at the state of yer woman's hair? Piggin wile-looking, so it is!"

"I wouldn't let me granny step foot in the street dressed like me, so I wouldn't."

"Has she no mirrors in her house, hi?"

"Aye, and yer man the wannabe Elvis with her."

"Shakin Stevens, do ye not mean?"

Their hoots of mirth echoed as they rounded the corner, singing and clapping along to "Green Door." Paddy and Fionnuala looked at each other. While Paddy wondered how the girls knew of the UK #1 by the rockabilly artist of the early 80's, let alone the lyrics, another thread of his jumbled thoughts made him think his drink intake was causing him to hallucinate. In the dim yellow of the lamppost yards away, and even with the raindrops spattering his wife's face, Paddy thought he could make out tears rolling down her cheeks. He stood in shock. Fionnuala was usually unflappable.

He knew the city center was a magnet for the youth of the day, but there hadn't been such violence and contempt from youngsters when Paddy had been one three decades earlier. He and Fionnuala were hardly the aged, after all!

"Let's make wer way to the city walls," Paddy suggested with a pat on her shivering shoulders, "for a wee bit of privacy."

They had been avoiding the Moorside stretch of the City Walls on their selling spree, as they wanted to avoid the twin dangers of slipping on stale vomit and maneuvering through lakes of fresh urine. But now they seemed a refuge. After the Free Derry wall, the world-famous icon of a violent past, the city's historic Walls were the second stop on a disappointed tourist's itinerary; the third stop was usually a pub. Winding around the inner city and resplendent with bastions and bulwarks, battlements and parapets, an artillery of cannons poking out, they were built in the 1600s to protect against invaders. During the Troubles, they had been a no-go zone imposed by the invading British troops as they were a marvelous vantage point for snipers, festooned with barbed wire in the 70s, razor wire in the 80s. Since the Peace Process of the mid-90s, when the hated British troops had gone home, the walls had been restored and polished, and now rose proud and masterful to carry on the tradition of protecting their citizens. They were now open for public use, not only historic and beautiful, but also functional, and put them to use the public did with a vengeance. While in other areas of the city they were fine, here in the hardened and deprived Moorside they were a delightful, romantic location for the ingestion of recreational drugs and underage drinking, and excellent for muggings. And in some corners the use was more pubic than public.

Mounting the ancient steps and climbing up the ramp, Paddy and Fionnuala wound their way through droppings they hoped were dog, not human, and declined the wares of the two drug dealers that approached them from the darkness in quick succession. Fionnuala headed to the cannon against which she had lost her virginity decades earlier, and around which other acned, drunk and sopping teens were now in various stages of doing the same.

Fionnuala sat on the cannon and cried into the urinal cakes, huge alarming sobs that seemed better suited exiting the jowls of an injured animal of large stature. Paddy stared at some slate. He didn't know how to comfort his wife. She wasn't one for coddling or cuddling. His fingers reached out nevertheless through the rain towards her shivering shoulder. She smacked them away and wrapped her drenched cardigan around her. She reached into her stocking for the money hidden there and counted it. Her sadness dissolved to anger.

"Seventeen pound fifty-eight pee. We're never gonny make them bills. And now we've nothing left to sell. What didn't help us, Paddy, was that every pub we went in, ye ran over to the bar and bought yerself a pint. Slipping through wer fingers, the money be's."

Paddy wavered back and forth before her.

"What was I meant to do? Stand there with nothing in me hand?"

"Aye!"

Fionnuala didn't fault her husband for being drunk; many people she knew often were. But he could've controlled himself in places where the markup of lager was so high, and should've taken along a flask of whiskey or waited until he got home to the cheaper beer sitting in the family fridge.

"Ach, Paddy, what's become of wer town? " Fionnuala moaned, sucking back the mucus that trickled from her nostrils. After the flicker of rage, the sadness was back. Finally, it seemed, the fight had gone out of her, the misery of life evident on her overbite. Paddy tried to focus on her face below him, his black hair slicked back with grease and rain. A raindrop fell from his nose. Fionnuala fondled some wicker as she continued: "The holes in me tights be's repaired with nail polish, we've the gas and electric and phone and telly people breathing down wer necks every hour God sends. And Lorcan and Eoin showing up at the same time like that. They could've had the decency to stagger their releases. It be's as if the prison service be's making fun of me, wer two sons suddenly materializing in me house like that, strangers to us all after their time locked up at her Majesty's pleasure."

The older, 21-year-old Lorcan, had been sent down for grievous bodily harm, and the former altar boy Eoin, 18, had turned drug dealer. When they were fresh convicts, their mother had been all for visiting them in prison, but the novelty had quickly worn off. And then she had been barred for smuggling Vicodin in for Lorcan to either use or sell. She thought she'd be pleased, excited even, to have them back home. But, no.

"Unemployable, them eejits be's, and I kyanny believe the bloody size of em both after their stints banged up. And we've the other three wanes and me mother thrown into the mix and all, crammed into them two beds, sleeping heads against toes. And when they're awake, stomachs insatiable, jaws gaping wide, ready for mounds of food to be thrown down em. And expecting us to provide for the lot of em! Yer paycheck from the fish packing plant can stretch only so far."

Fionnuala thought for a second, trying to add up how many teeth

Seamus, 6, Siofra, 9, and Padraig, 12, had between them in those mouths of theirs, then realized she'd have to subtract her mother's from the total, as they were fake, and then add the teeth of Lorcan and Eoin also. She gave up. Her eyes flashed with anger.

"That hateful sister of yers, Ursula, be's to blame for wer current woes!"

Paddy blinked. He couldn't think how his older sister was responsible for anything now, especially after Fionnuala had persecuted Ursula so much she had fled with her American husband to his homeland the year before. "...Ursula?"

"Aye! The cunt! Torturing me across the miles! I had time to go through it in me mind the other day while out hanging up the washing. Wer lives have been spiraling ever downward since she won that lotto years back—"

"It was Jed that won the lotto. And do I have to remind ye, they paid wer mortgage off for us, then gave us the family house and all—"

"Aye, that's what I'm on about. A false sense of security, her lotto win gave us. And moving all the wanes into 5 Murphy Crescent around the corner got me and you used to the luxury of living two to a house. I wouldn't have forced me mammy to up sticks and move into the extra house to look after the wanes if we hadn't been given it, like. And when the house burned down, back they all tramped, me mother included, into space we'd gotten used to living in alone! If ye hadn't let them insurance payments lapse, we might've got a windfall out of the accident. Naw, but—"

As she babbled on and on further details about the injustice of Ursula not handing over all the Barnett's lotto winnings to her and how useless he was to her as a husband, how useless he had been for the 23 years they had been wed, Paddy reflected on the year before, when Fionnuala demanded he pass the picket line and become a scab at the fish packing plant where he worked. He still had no mates in Derry because of it, and the men on the factory floor—they had come back to work after three weeks on strike without any of their demands being met—still put salt in his tea, sugar in his sandwiches in the canteen, and elbowed him in the ribs when he passed them to get to a mixing and grinding machine. They had dyed his work overalls pink, and his locker was sprayed with anti-Paddy graffiti. But that was preferable to the persecution Fionnuala would have put him through if he hadn't crossed the picket line. He had seen what his wife put his sister Ursula through.

Paddy suddenly knew what to do. It was the alcohol affecting his judgment, he was somehow aware, and he knew he would regret it in the harsh bright light of sobriety when he woke the next afternoon, but it was time a few home truths were told: Fionnuala tainted everything she touched and everyone she met. And he had had 23 years of wedded hell to analyze her and knew why the lotto win had rankled as it had. Fionnuala was always aware in the back of her mind that she was disadvantaged. The lotto win had spotlighted it. And, as a family member, even though she was only an in-law, she figured she was entitled to a piece of the action. She insisted on a life she would never have, an entitlement to which she was not born, the Heggarty clan of thugs and petty criminals, always feeling in her mind she would claw her way from abject poverty to the glossy spreads of the lifestyle magazines she loved so. Not only that, she needed to put herself on a workout regime as well. The Lord alone knew he had difficulty keeping down the sick when the pull of his libido demanded he take her at night. He parted his lips to tell her everything.

CHAPTER THREE

Ursula squashed the fritter in fright as the gun inched towards her nose. She backed into the china cabinet. Muffins leaned forward and licked the barrel.

"W-what have I ever done to ye?" Ursula blubbered, a look on her face as if she were struggling to comprehend why Louella would want to shoot her point blank, so she would die there in the living room on the verge of their getaway. "Are ye soft in the head?"

Louella clacked her teeth in scorn, though part of her brain knew exactly why she might want to shoot Ursula, her husband's secret paramour. "I'm not shooting you, sweetie. I'm just showing you the weapon I'm bringing along, protection for our trip. I was thinking more of shooting out the tires if a cruiser started chasing us down the highway. To give us more time to get away sort of thing. I ordered it online from the store's suppliers when Slim and Jed weren't looking."

They were partners of a store, Sinkers, Scorchers, Shooters and Beef Jerky, which sold fish tackle and bait, hot sauce, guns and, of course, beef jerky (a recent addition). The gun was a feminine, slimline pistol that no macho hunter would be caught dead with.

"Och," Ursula spat, softening her grip on the fritter and Muffins' paws. "Don't be daft. It's crimes of the *past* that be's giving us such grief, and now ye be's wanting to engage in *new* crimes the coppers can persecute us for? The clicking of time be's wer only chance of escape. And, anyroad, ye've only half a brain if ye think we can smuggle that past all them security checks at the airport."

Louella's face fell; she quite liked the heft of it in her hand. And the fright it had given Ursula.

"And," Ursula continued, pulling out the plug of the Ionic Breeze air purifier, "if that was yer plan, ye could've had a lend of the Glock Jed got for me last year. Ye mind he give it me when I thought that madwoman from the casino was stalking me?"

"Come on, girls!" Slim called from the hallway. "The car's loaded."

Ursula grabbed the pistol from Louella and plopped it inside a replica Ming vase. She shoved Muffins in his cage, then the two raced into the hallway, where Ursula paused to grab her keys, her purse, the bags from Dunkin Donuts and her well-thumbed copy of *Lotto Balls of Shame*. And they were out the door.

15

Fumes plumed from the station wagon's exhaust pipe. Jed and Slim had heaved up the suitcases and suffered through the sleet to the station wagon, yelping at the icy bits pelting their faces. Jed had had to chase after his cowboy hat when it blew into the circle of garden gnomes Ursula had demanded he install.

Louella shoved aside the mound of beef jerky Jed kept in the back seat for emergencies and shoehorned herself beside Ursula and Jed. Slim would have to drive as it was always best to give him the room his mass required. Louella still bristled over having to buy him two airline seats. She yelped as the car sped off.

Under the brim of Jed's cowboy hat, there were currently no pleasantries going on. Jed had heard that you couldn't bullshit a bullshitter, and although he was no bullshitter, he didn't appreciate Ursula's duplicity towards him. The first he suspected of his wife and sister-in-law's crime was the week before, when he happened upon Ursula's pink laptop in the conservatory. He had brushed aside the cookie crumbs on the keyboard, and seen the browser window open to the YouAskEmWeAnswerEm website. 'Statue of Limitations' Ursula had typed, and beside the mouse was her notepad with the butterflies of the tropical world on each page. Ursula had written in her rounded, very Irish handwriting MISDEMENOR OR <u>FELONY</u>?? Class A?? Two days later, she had barged in from a trip to the supermarket for blizzard supplies and told them they had to leave immediately. It was an anniversary surprise she claimed, but not only was their anniversary two months away, the 35th anniversary gift was meant to be jade not travel (Jed had looked it up), so Jed tended not to believe her. Unless, of course, they were traveling to Indonesia to mine some jade. Jed had checked his credit card statement online later, and knew her 'anniversary surprise' had cost him $5000.

He didn't know if they'd be going someplace where cigarettes were cheaper, how long the trip might last, if gambling was legal there or why it required formal wear. Ursula had insisted he and Slim bring tuxedos. Jed even had a red cummerbund in his suitcase. One part of him didn't care, as he knew from Ursula's insistence on passports they were off to somewhere abroad, and he had domestic online gaming worries he wanted to distance himself from. And although it was annoying not knowing *where* they were going, Jed was more worried about the *why*. Ursula and Louella had never been particularly thick as thieves; Ursula didn't like Louella cheating at their weekly cribbage games. But maybe the 'thieves' part was true. Or...worse?

As they rounded a corner and sped past the AIRPORT 237 MILES sign, and though Ursula had gotten a manicure the day before, Jed kept checking his wife's fingernails that gripped into the leather of the seat beside him for signs of blood. *What had she and Louella done?*

CHAPTER FOUR

"Could ye help us out there, muckers?"

Paddy and Fionnuala jumped at the filthy hand that materialized under their noses from the dark. A drunk wet tramp had shuffled up to them for coins for drink, the other still clutching the dregs left in a bottle of generic whiskey.

"Naw!" Fionnuala roared into his battered face. "We kyanny help werselves, sure! Away with ye!" As he toppled off, Fionnuala fixed a pony tail with an air of superiority: "What was ye on the verge of telling me?"

"It's gone." Paddy shrugged his drunken shoulders. "But I told ye last year that Ursula doesn't be responsible for all the evils of the world."

It was as if Fionnuala hadn't heard him. Rant over, she sighed against the cascabel (the knob at the back of the cannon). "Ach, Paddy, I haven't a clue what we're meant to do. Them flimmin hooligans with no sense of respect for their elders! I've realized, but, that I'm relieved ye stopped me from flinging that rock at the pub window. Could ye imagine if the Filth came and hauled me in?"

The cuffs of the Filth around her wrists would mirror the lack of escape she felt in her heart.

Fionnuala continued: "Should we not ask Dymphna's fancy man for a sub of some money to get us through the week? Or his mother? She be's minted. Shall we not go pay Dymphna a visit at the fish and chip van? It be's parked outside the Seabound Cockleshells this time of night."

"Does the hunger be gnawing a hole in yer stomach?"

Paddy knew only the lure of free curry chips and a fish finger or two—and a possible loan—would make Fionnuala gladly visit the shame that was her daughter. Dymphna, 20, was living in the Protestant Waterside with her fiancé, an engagement that had dragged on as their litter of half-Orange bastards grew.

Fionnuala's love for her children was conditional, and very conditional at that. Paddy had seen her many times lounging on the couch with a notepad and pencil, compiling a list of who she loved most. Dymphna always came last, except for those three years after they had realized the eldest daughter, Moira, was a lesbian and had written an exposé about the family. But *Lotto Balls of Shame* hadn't sold many copies, and the traitor lesbo perv was away in Malta, and absence had apparently made the heart grow fonder, and, even with the group in the pub causing her such anger, Fionnuala had told him once that she suspected in her heart of hearts lesbianism really didn't exist, and so Dymphna had moved back to the bottom of the list.

"I am a bit peckish, aye," Fionnuala admitted.

Paddy's pay-as-you-go cellphone rang. As if she had known they were discussing her, it was Dymphna on the other end. "Daddy! Pass the phone to Mammy! Quick!" Dymphna said.

"She wants to speak to you," Paddy said. Fionnuala took the phone as if he were handing her an infection.

"Mammy, Mammy!" Fionnuala heard through the wailing of the two infants in the background. She ground her teeth in annoyance.

"I kyanny hear ye with them wanes of yers screaming bloody murder."

"One moment there."

The children suddenly went silent, and Fionnuala didn't want to know how that happened. Dymphna came back to the phone: "Could ye tell me the name of the only black man on the *Titanic?*"

Fionnuala stared in disbelief at the phone, shook it a few times, then pressed angry lips to the little slit people were supposed to talk through.

"Are ye taking the mick outta me, wee girl?" she warned.

"Naw, Mammy! I've not the time to explain now...ye're the only person what knows more about the *Titanic* than anyone else, but. Tell me now, just!"

"I swear to the heavenly Father, if you be's..." but even while she chided her daughter, Fionnuala's synapses flipped through the useless information stored in her cranium. Two caverns in her brain were devoted to *Titanic* trivia: one for the 1995 movie, one for 1912 reality. No, not caverns. Magical grottos that sparkled and glowed in a brain under siege from the depression and negativity of her real world.

"Joseph Philippe Lemercier Laroche." She said it proudly.

"And now name me the seventh course on the dinner menu the night the boat sank."

"First, second or third class are ye on about?"

"First."

"Roast squid with wilted cress and salon of beef with château potatoes, whatever the bloody hell them be's. And creamed carrots with boiled rice."

"Ta. Cheerio."

As her mother stared at the phone that had suddenly gone dead in her hand, Dymphna quickly redialed the number of the radio station scribbled on her hand from inside the chip van where she was sat. Surrounded by frozen fish fingers, congealing patties of beef and rancid potato peels, filthy dishrags and greasy bottles of sauces, the sweat lashing down the back of her from the heat of the grill, the front of her shivering from the rain spitting in from the order hatch, she had hit rock bottom.

Dymphna was working there to tend favor with her future mother-in-law, Zoë Riddell, who had bought the van at an auction months before. Dymphna hoped Zoë would allow her to marry her son, Rory, even though she was Catholic and had already given birth to her two grandchildren. Dymphna was grateful Beeyonsay had finally been wrenched out of her by the doctor's tongs a few weeks earlier; the more pregnant she had become, the less space she had had in the van. Now Beeyonsay slumbered in a stroller next to the spitting oil of the chip vat beside her older brother Keanu, the secret 'special treat' she had given them both having worked. Not even the rain hammering on the roof inches above Dymphna's red curls could wake them.

"Ach, hurry up, would ye, ye eejits," she muttered at the ring tone of the phone, then yelped at an almighty thump next to the service hatch. Shards of glass sprinkled through her hoop earrings and across the counter. Keanu and Beeyonsay erupted into shrieks. Dymphna raced up and poked her head out into the rain. Two children were laughing and running away backwards, flipping her off as they went. As if the bottle smashed against the van wasn't enough!

"Hey, missus!" one called out. "Are ye carting around anoller Orange mongrel bastard in yer stomach?"

"Clear off outta here before I clatter seven shades of shite outta ye!" Dymphna growled.

But they were already gone. Wiping away the broken bottle bits with the hand not clutching the still-ringing phone, Dymphna wondered, *Will themmuns never tire of their horrid wee games?* Three quarters of the town regarded Keanu and Beeyonsay more as creatures than infants due to their Catholic mother and Protestant father. And Dymphna herself was no stranger to rocks hurled in her direction as well when she went down the town for a manicure or a pop magazine or what have you.

"Hello?! Hello??" she squealed into the phone.

"Right ye are, love. Ye're caller number ten! Have ye got the answers?"

"I have, aye!" Dymphna said breathlessly, feeling her heart pound, the blood percolating in her temples, the slight damp in her knickers. She looked down at the napkin she had written her mother's answers on and read them out in a reedy, careful voice. As if her life depended on it. There was silence at the other end. And then—

"Brace yerself...Spot on! Congrats! Right girl ye are! Ye've won the special centennial *Titanic* commemorative cruise for four!"

"*YYIIIPPEEEEEEEEEEEE!!!*" Dymphna screamed, tears of joy running down the acne due to spitting grease on her once flawless face. "Ach, ye've not a clue what this means to me! Me mammy's gonny love me—er, the trip, I meant to say."

"So ye're gonny take yer mammy on the cruise?"

"Aye. Ye see, *Titanic* be's her number one fave film of all time. She can quote from it and all, ye understand."

"And who else will ye be taking?"

"Is that me voice I hear on the radio behind me?"

"Aye, we be's broadcasting this live."

"Och, of course. I hear callers winning things all the time. I never thought, but, that one day it would be me! I'll be taking along me daddy as well, of course. Perhaps me wee sister Siofra. She be's one of me favorites. Could ye tell me, but, if wee infants counts as people or does they be more like articles of luggage?"

After a few more pleasantries, the DJ put Dymphna on hold and, while the radio played Celine Dion's "My Heart Will Go On," he came back on the line and took her details. The moment she hung up, she called her father. "Daddy! Daddy! Put Mammy back on!"

Paddy did.

"What is it now, wee girl?" Fionnuala sighed into the phone.

"I've won us a special 100-year *Titanic* cruise!"

"Och, what are ye on about? Anyone'd be dead before the end of a hundred year cruise, sure."

"Naw, I mean..." And she explained what had happened.

Five minutes later, Fionnuala galloped down the steps of the City Walls, the joy screaming out of her lips. It was as if a free trip somehow made the bills disappear. Paddy was close behind. She rushed to the lesbian pub energized, a woman renewed. She reached down and grabbed a rock nestling under fake Fabergé egg remains.

"Take that, youse! Take that, youse filthy creatures!"

She took careful aim and launched the rock at the window. This one gave a satisfying crack. Fionnuala clapped her hands with glee.

"We're clearing outta this hellhole!"

Even as they raced from the approaching police, Paddy couldn't help but smile. His old Fionnuala was back.

"C'mere, Paddy, where are we meant to buy passports from?" Fionnuala panted as they ran from the sirens. "Me cousin Una told me she bagged some cheap the other month at the Mountains of Mourne Gate market. The stall next to the one what sells knockoff football scarves. And what two wanes should we take with us on wer cruise? I'm thinking wer Lorcan and Eoin. Them lads be's in desperate need of a holiday, so they do, and them lads has always been such lovely wee boys, not a trouble have themmuns given their dear aul mammy..."

CHAPTER FIVE—SOUTHAMPTON PORT, UK

Ursula realized she had been indulging in too many of Louella's potato pancakes when she slipped the evening gown over her head and found herself trapped in it. Her lips and nostrils gasped for air against the bodice. One hand, more a useless paw caught half-way down the fabric of the arm, flapped blindly around the restroom stall, trying to locate something horizontal for balance. It found the paper toilet seat dispenser and clung on. The pantyhosed toes of one foot scrabbled against the curvature of the toilet bowl for support. Her head appeared to have grown as well, as she couldn't shove it through the neckline. The string of pearls strangled her inside the swathes of red silk, and her whimpers were drowned by the flushing and reflushing of the automatic toilet.

Dear Lord, give me strength! was her frenzied thought, the other hand clawing up her back, trying to locate the dangly bit of the zipper to tug it further so the fabric could inch down the newly pudgy rolls of her body. She cursed Louella's home cooking, and she cursed the others for already having changed in the restrooms of Heathrow airport three hours earlier. She had had to keep guard over their carts of luggage and, when her time came, the restrooms were closed for cleaning.

That meant riding on the train from London to the port of Southampton in her leisure suit, wrinkled and grungy from three quarters of a day's intercontinental travel, while Jed, Slim and Louella sat beside her, the men smart in their tuxedos and splashes of Aqua-Velvet, Louella resplendent in sparkly emerald and a spritz of Elizabeth Taylor's White Diamonds. But Ursula did notice it was those three receiving odd looks from the other passengers.

Why, she wondered as she grew dizzy and panic gripped her and little moans and grunts escaped her, had they even bothered with formal wear to board the ship? Only because that's how she and Louella had imagined it: the thrill and sophistication of a grand entrance up the gangway of the ocean liner they hoped was their vehicle to avoid imprisonment.

She and Louella had revealed the "anniversary surprise" to the boys at last on the train as the English countryside trundled by: they were booked on a 12-day cruise, Operas of the Earth, with stops in ports of Germany, Portugal, Spain, France and Italy. Each night they would go ashore and watch an opera. Ursula reeled off some of the names: *Aida, La Bohème, Carmen, La Traviata, Madame Butterfly, Der Ring des Nibelungen* and *Die Zauberflöte*, though she wasn't sure of the pronunciation of the last two. Jed and Slim had looked stricken, and for a moment it seemed their eyes were searching for emergency breaks that could be pulled. But when Louella mentioned the recreational facilities on board, casually slipping in the casino, plus the $500 on board spending credit, between the splash pool and the golf simulator, they had nudged each other and their eyes had glistened with glee.

Louella'a advice to Ursula after they had both been hauled in for questioning about the missing $100,000 from almost six years ago was simple: the best way to avoid the police for such an old crime was to get out of the country until they passed that—statue-thing, whatever it was, the thing that they couldn't arrest Nazi war criminals for anymore. Now they were only persons of interest and hadn't been officially charged, so it was their only chance of freedom. Ursula was a bit confused about British law, and American law was even more alien to her. But, Louella reasoned, they may as well have fun while they were on the lam, as Louella had termed it, and as they both enjoyed opera—

Ursula finally cranked down the zipper a few teeth and freed precious millimeters of space. She wriggled a few inches of silk over her mounds. And yelped at a curt knock on the stall door.

"Ma'am?"

Ursula froze, neckhole digging diagonally into her face, one eye still sightless, hemline prisoner at her hips, panties exposed. The voice was pure efficiency, not a trace of compassion. And *British*. Perhaps due to the collective consciousness of many Irish worldwide, even with a dose of Xanax, the synapses crackled across the surface of Ursula's cerebrum like mini-fireworks from the sound of the accent.

"Ma'am!"

Ursula crouched against the toilet seat dispenser, hoping the woman would just go away.

"Police here!"

Her heart jumped. Had Detective Scarrey made some international phone calls and located her?! She gulped whimpers of fear down past the pearls that dug into her neck. They should have never, ever flown into Britain. Wasn't it known as the land of CCTV footage? A nation under surveillance? How stupid had she and Louella been? They could have booked the flight to Belfast and boarded the cruise there, the first port of call; in Northern Ireland, she had read somewhere, there were fewer cameras per capita, whatever that meant. But, no. The thought of stepping foot in her homeland had caused her stomach to churn; with her family hating her after the lottery win, in Northern Ireland Ursula felt under surveillance of another kind. She realized now how silly that was.

"We know you're in there! We can see your feet! Answer us!"

We? There were more of them perched outside? Ready to clamp on the handcuffs and haul her off to some miserable room with peeling paint and a lone light bulb...?

The toilet flushed.

"...I'm in here," Ursula managed through the swathes of silk pressed against her lips and the roar of water down the bowl.

"We're simply checking you're in no harm. A woman heard the noises you were making in there and informed us. I must ask if everything's okay."

Ursula grit her teeth, panic dissolving into annoyance. No, everything was not okay. The British police were no-nonsense toerags desperate to fill quotas, promotion-obsessed, and the woman who had reported her, whoever the daft simpleton was, was a nosy parker, sticking her nose in where it didn't belong. And she had a ship to catch.

"A-aye."

There was a moment of silence. Then, harsher, suspicious:

"Ma'am, unlock the door and step outside."

Not a 'please' to be heard. *Disgraceful!* Fuming, Ursula realized what her mistake had been: 'aye.' The IRA had been decommissioned decades earlier, the Peace Process now a Peace Accomplished, but memories were long and bitter. She should've Americanized her language. Her tongue and vocal chords found it impossible to rid themselves of the accent that caused so much suspicion to the British forces, military or police. Or parking attendants and airport security guards, for that matter. She had noticed their wands lingered longer on her limbs than they had on Jed and Louella's, and her patdown had been particularly invasive. She should have said 'yes' instead of 'aye.' Better, she should've just slid her American passport under the door. They would've left her in peace.

Trembling with rage, Ursula popped her head through the neckline and thrust herself into the gown. Still barefoot, her hair like Einstein's but purple, she unlocked the door like a child about to be reprimanded for stealing from the cookie jar. She yelped again. There a hard-faced member of the British police stood, barely out of Huggies, checked cap on head, whippy-baton thing ready to strike, and behind her two more, men—*boys!*—with pepper spray aimed at her eyeballs, faces alight with the thrill of capturing an Irish terrorist and receiving a promotion. A third seemed to serve no function, as far as Ursula could tell, except to stand in the distance and look grim.

"I was just changing me outfit. If ye don't mind," she said in a stilted voice, trying as best she could to keep her anger in check and a shred of dignity in her. She knew if she told this slip of a girl everything she thought about her, she would be hauled in and detained hours for questioning and they would miss their getaway liner.

The WPC peered into the toilet stall, even shone a flashlight in for a few seconds, sweeping it around the interior, though lights were blazing from the ceiling. *Who does she think she be's,* Ursula wondered narkily, adjusting her bra strap, *yer woman outta* Prime Suspect, *DCI Jane Tennison?*

The girl turned to her backup, and they deflated, pepper spray falling to their sides. Ursula was happy to disappoint.

"It's very dangerous, ma'am, to change in the stalls of a public lavatory," the girl chided.

Ursula's nails dug into her palms and she fought the urge to scream at her she didn't need her advice and where else could she change in a busy port terminal, an aisle of the duty free? They all exchanged a look which said *Our Work Is Done Here. Unfortunately.* The three men turned and the WPC graced Ursula with a curt nod, apparently giving her the permission to continue her life unhindered.

"As you were," she said. And then they were gone.

Not even a *"Sorry!"* As Ursula pounded her feet into the high heels, she wanted to call the WPC back to zip her up in the back. But didn't want to give the jumped up creature the satisfaction of having been of help. She'd have Jed do it when she met the others outside security.

She crammed her leisure suit and sensible traveling shoes into her bag and exited the restroom. As she pushed through the throngs of laughing, chatting, excited vacationers, she was relieved to hear very few nails-on-a-chalkboard British accents around her. England had become even more multicultural since the last time she had been there; in Northern Ireland this was less true. Nobody in England seemed to speak English anymore.

But as she gazed up at a sign, desperate to locate an arrow that pointed her in the direction of Security, two police officers raced purposefully past her, one clipping her elbow, on their way to break up a drunken brawl at the Now Voyager Lounge. Ursula twitched again with worry and grief. She and Louella were racing from the law, but as scary as Scarrey was, Ursula knew he was only a Yank detective. Compared to their British counterparts, she thought of the US police as somewhat bumbling. Not as ruthless, heartless, cold and *effective*. Heathrow had been teeming with coppers, and Ursula had made a show of clutching her US passport so everyone could view it, grateful she had taken the plunge and converted to Americanism years earlier to pacify Jed. As an older woman, there was none of this The-US-Is-The-World-Aggressor-And-The-UK-Has-Become-Its-51st-State nonsense that annoyed the British youth of the day so. She always had a vision of Reagan and Thatcher exiting a limo together on their way to some international conference or another, wondering if they had spent a night of passion together, always aware of the 'special relationship' between the US and the UK, the world leaders, the benefits and benefits of the doubt they passed to each of their citizens in consulates worldwide. They were one. So, if she kept her mouth shut, she was safe. If she kept her mouth shut.

Unless Detective Scarrey really did have friends in the British police service. Or Interpol. Knowing she was Irish, and seeing their house empty, might he think she had gone home to Ireland and contact his foreign friends and set them after her? It was quite easy to do nowadays, what with the Internet and surveillance satellites circling the Earth as they did.

Finally chancing upon security (the arrows had been no help; she relied on female intuition), Jed hurried over to her, the corners of his goatee bent with concern.

"Are you okay?"

"I had trouble fitting into me gown," Ursula said. "Do me zipper up, would ye?"

"I remember this dress from the Petty Officer's Christmas party in 1987," Jed said as he zipped. "You look great."

Ursula suspected she probably didn't, but smiled.

"Where's Slim?" she asked.

Louella barged up.

"Those darn fools in security thought his samples of hot sauce were bomb-making chemicals!" she roared. "They dragged him off somewhere with their dogs sniffing all around him. Why he had to bring them with him—"

"They're all less than 3 ounces," Jed put in. "We're trying to get customers for our online business—"

"Darn foolish idea!" Louella inspected her watch, willing the seconds to pass more slowly. "We're gonna be stranded here if they don't let him out soon." Then she inspected Ursula. "What's up with that dress? Your arms are bulging out of the seams like a bodybuilder."

"I-I must've put on a few pounds since the last time I wore it," Ursula explained.

Louella marched to their luggage cart and dug through a bag.

"Slip this on, I brought it for me, but it's too darned hot in this terminal."

Ursula and Jed stared in horror at what Louella was handing her. But Ursula slipped it on nevertheless. They jumped at a disembodied voice.

"...is the final boarding announcement. All passengers for the *Queen of Crabs*, please make your way to the check-in counter. Now. The ship will embark in forty-five minutes. Those who have not already checked in may be refused boarding. And will not receive a refund. Quickly, please."

"The *Queen of Crabs*? Doesn't that be us?" Ursula asked, nibbling nervously on her lip.

"No refund?" screamed Louella, as if someone had just stabbed her in the heart with a rusty implement.

"Aye, did ye not read the—"

"Forget Slim!" Louella said. "We gotta go now—oh! Here he is at last!"

Up he waddled, a man shattered, one hand flapping at lips like those of a bargain bin hustler who had spent the last three hours on his knees. The case of hot sauce now hung unloved at his side.

"Those idiots had me taste every last one of our hot sauces to be sure they weren't chemicals or poisons or some stupid thing," Slim panted. "Even the Liquid Death triple X. I need milk, water, bread..."

"Later!" Louella barked, grabbing his arm. "Let's go!"

Jed grabbed one cart, Slim found the handle of the other through eyes that still watered and stung, and they stared up at the signs, trying to find the check-in arrow.

"There it is!" Jed said, pointing. They hurried through the masses.

"Och," Ursula said, "it clear slipped me mind to do me business when I was in the loo. Me bladder's on the verge of bursting. I'll catch youse up." She paused a second, thinking of facing another Brit in a uniform at the check-in desk. "Take you me passport with ye, Louella, in case themmuns at the desk needs it."

She handed it over, a weight off her mind. Louella snatched it, then barked: "We'll meet you at the desk. Make it quick, darnit!"

CHAPTER SIX

With each thrust of the toilet brush, Fionnuala imagined the bowl was Dymphna's throat. She still couldn't believe the cheek—the *gall!*—of her daughter: refusing to give up her ticket to allow one of her older and more deserving brothers to go. Not that Lorcan or Eoin had seemed particularly bothered or even interested, but that wasn't the point. Fionnuala was the one who loved all things *Titanic*, so she should be the one to choose who would accompany her on the adventure of her lifetime. And, as Fionnuala had spared no breath letting Dymphna know, if Fionnuala hadn't given birth to her, Dymphna wouldn't even be a human now and wouldn't have the fingers to dial the radio station to win the tickets, nor that which allowed her to claim the prize on the mobile phone: vocal chords. Which brought her back to Dymphna's throat. Fionnuala wielded the brush like a spear and pounded it down the filthy depths.

Bam! Bam!

Fionnuala flushed. She wiped her brow, got up off her knees before the aged porcelain and, yellow rubber gloves dripping, moved to the equally squalid sink, where a glance made a well of despair rise in her. It looked like it hadn't seen a spritz of bleach since Margaret Thatcher's reign. And she was another selfish bitch and all, Fionnuala reflected, attacking the porcelain with a filthy rag. In the next room, her 9-year old daughter Siofra was warbling what seemed to be some godawful pop tune of the day, each syllable of which was a like a rusty nail in Fionnuala's cerebral cortex.

"Swagger Jagger, Swagger Jagger...!"

"Shut yer trap, wee girl!" Fionnuala barked, abandoning the rag and reaching into her bucket of cleaning supplies for a pad with scrubby bits to remove the mold and congealed toothpaste and God alone knew what else which clung to the ceramic. As she scrubbed, she eyed the closed shower curtain with dread, wondering what horrors lay beyond.

"Swagger Jagger, Swagger Jagger...!"

"Dear God, give me strength!" Were there no other words to the fecking song? Or was her daughter too soft in the head to remember them? "Och, would ye shut yer flimmin bake or I'll shut it for ye, ye tonedeaf cunt, ye!"

There was silence, and then, "Aye, mammy," Fionnuala heard. Like

30

butter wouldn't melt. But Fionnuala knew well the dark heart that beat under the sparkles of her daughter's pink top. Siofra'd taken to hanging around with—Fionnuala attacked the sink with fury as she thought about it—that horrid *Protestant* creature Victoria Skivvins as of late. And with Dymphna engaged to an Orange bastard as well, Fionnuala didn't know where to look when she walked down the streets of the neighborhood any longer, the eyes of Mrs. Connelly and Mrs. Connors and Mrs. O'Connelley inspecting her over the hedges with suspicion. As if it were she herself cavorting with the enemy! The whole world had gone mad, if even those who had entered the world from between her very own spread legs—her own *offspring!*—were being brainwashed by liberal teachers to believe that they could befriend the Enemy. What was the world coming to when God-fearing Catholics could prance about town, arms linked with Protestants, and not a dot of shame on their faces? What chance did others without a good, moral upbringing like her children have? She feared a knock on the door late one evening, the neighbors all pinched lips and throats bulging with hatred and rage when she opened it, a bucket of tar and a bag of feathers ready to make an example of the entire family in the back garden, tarring and feathering them all next to her rhubarb patch and the broken suntan bed there had been no room for in the sitting room since the arrival of the karaoke machine, now broken as well.

"I'll be inspecting them bedsheets for wrinkles, wee girl!" Fionnuala warned. "Mind ye do em as ye were showed!"

Siofra poked her head into the bathroom. Her usual pale face was pink with exertion, her twiglet arms unable to keep up with the work Fionnuala insisted they do, the purple butterfly barrette clung to her sweaty strands of black hair at an odd angle.

"Mammy?"

"Och, ye've me head cracking, wane. Don't distract me," Fionnuala warned, sweat prickling her brow from all the scrubbing.

"Me tummy's wile sore, so it is. I try to stop it, but it keeps on grumbling with hunger."

"I told ye not to bring it up again! Me own stomach thinks me throat's been cut, I'm hollow with starvation as well, ye don't hear me yammering on about it, but!"

"Yer body be's miles bigger, but, and with all them extra—"

Siofra yelped as the rubber glove sliced through the air and splat against her face, the filth from it dribbling down her cheeks. She scurried for safety out of the bathroom, and Fionnuala was in hot pursuit. Siofra's eyes gurgled with tears as she massaged her smarting cheek, spreading the dinge further into her pores.

"Yer mammy's a fat cow, are ye saying?" Fionnuala gave an imploring look upwards. "Why was wer Siofra chosen, heavenly Father? *Why?!*" she asked of the Lord, but He had more pressing questions to answer elsewhere. Fionnuala was stuck staring up at a bulb that needed changing. By her.

"Naw, I meant...I meant...What time are we eating, but?" Siofra still wanted to know through the tears.

"Don't ask me again, ye simple gack! Ye were telt the rules same as me, sure, we kyanny eat until them what has paid has had their fill and what does that be sticking outta yer pocket, wee girl?"

"N-nothing," Siofra lied through the waterworks, lower lip trembling. She backed against the wall as her mother approached.

"I seen the glint of gems and gold coming from yer pocket! Have ye been thieving? *Thieving?!*"

"Naw, Mammy, naw!"

Fionnuala towered over her and tugged off the glove; she hadn't been proud of the previous slap. She needed the satisfaction of flesh on flesh.

Smack! Smack!

As Siofra reeled from the force of the blows, there was a boom of thunder, and lightning cackled through the sky outside the window. Siofra eyed the bolts as if she didn't know what was worse: Mammy or Mammy Nature. Fionnuala pinned her daughter's fighting arms against the wall with one hand, and dug with the other into the pocket of the girl's mini-jeans embroidered with unicorns and dolphins.

"I was gonny give it ye!" Siofra squealed as she squirmed against the evacuation notice. "I was gonny give it ye!"

As she wound her fingers around the jewelry in Siofra's pocket, it seemed to Fionnuala the floor beneath them began to shift and wobble, like that House of Fun she went through at the seashore in Buncrana every summer, the one with the mirrors that made her look odd. Lightning spat more angrily through the air outside. Around them, the room started to tremble and sway.

"Jesus, Mary and Joseph and a wee donkey!" Fionnuala screamed over a new roar of thunder.

The thing in Siofra's pocket flew from her, and Fionnuala clawed at the fringes of the lampshade for support. They weren't much use, slipping through her grasping fingers. Siofra scooped up the brooch and screamed in fear as her little legs buckled. Her body lurched into her mother's legs. She clung on tightly, yelping into the meaty thighs that bulged under the white stockings. Siora's fear angered Fionnuala, and the weight of the girl against her meant Fionnuala toppled toward the bed. The corner pounded into her spine. She screamed in pain. They tumbled to the carpet as the floor gave way under them, the room slanting and gravity no longer a friend. Brochures slid from the desk, bottles of cologne toppled over and the suits in the wardrobe swung like vines in a tropical storm. The minibar door flew open and little bottles rolled down the slanting carpet Siofra had just vacuumed. And then rolled up the carpet as they were pitched in the opposite direction. Fionnuala's head cracked against a leg of the bed, and Siofra flew up her mother's body.

"We're capsizing, Mammy! *Capsizing!*" Siofra whimpered into her mother's ear, now inches from her mouth.

As Fionnuala fought for balance and to get the girl off her, one part of her brain wanted to smack her again for using such big language. But Siofra was right: they were capsizing! Until the next peal of thunder seemed knots away, lightning crackled weakly, the floor suddenly settled and it was obvious they weren't. It had been a tiny flash storm and a big wave, was all. In the abrupt stillness, they heard whoops of passengers from the hallway, excited they had survived their first bout of sea turbulence.

"God bless us and save us! Me life flashed before me eyes! I saw meself all the way to yer daddy and mines wedding! The state of me hair then! Disgraceful! C'mere, are we meant to endure eleven more days of being tossed about like that?" Fionnuala clamped a cigarette between her trembling lips, lit up and puffed away.

Siofra crossed her arms.

"Mammy, ye were telt the rules and all. There's to be no smoking inside the ship."

Fionnuala blew smoke in her face just to annoy her. Calamity over, she motioned to Siofra.

"Lemme see what ye've nicked!"

Siofra, still shaken, unfurled her fist. In her sticky little palm sat a golden brooch. Fionnuala pried it loose and inspected it. She suspected the craftsman who had fashioned it wanted it to be a pelican, but its body was so misshapen it resembled more a dodo, with eyes that sparkled with ruby rhinestones, and little purple, green and orange gems that ran up and down its feathers. Its webbed feet were covered in amber.

"I'm all for thieving, ye know that. Ye want us thrown overboard, but? Ye spastic! That Yootha telt us there's to be surprise inspections of wer living quarters for things what we might've nicked from the passengers' cabins, and wer lockers and all. Where did ye get it, ye wee thug?"

"I found it under the cushion of that chair over there. It kyanny belong to them what has the room now, as I can tell from the clothing they be's two men. So it kyanny be thieving. It be's *finding!*"

Fionnuala's lips curled with pure disgust as she thought back to the tube of KY Jelly she had discovered poking out of the Ralph Lauren Dopp kit on the back of the toilet. She felt ill at the thought what of the two 'men' sharing this cabin did on the bedsheets Siofra's fingers had just folded. And she had just grabbed.

"And ye see, Mammy? It be's manky aul person's jewelry, grown-up jewelry! Minging and useless and pig-ugly! I wouldn't be caught dead on the playground with such shite, sure. It was me special surprise gift for ye, Mammy! I was gonny give it ye after dessert. When we ever gets to eat."

Fionnuala had to admit that even her own mother would find the brooch too old-aged-pensioner. For once, her daughter wasn't lying: it was hideous. But somewhere in a cranny of her mind she realized Siofra had been doing something nice for her.

"Och, ye're a wee dote, so ye are!" she said finally, swaddling Siofra in her breasts and tugging out a Snickers she had been secretly munching on between scrubs.

"Ye've earned yerself a bite. A wee one, mind."

Siofra bared her little teeth and took a nibble. Fionnuala bit the pelican's beak and the hard texture of the metal on her molars let her know it wasn't even gold-plated. Her face crumpled with disappointment. She slipped the brooch in a pocket of her housekeeping apron and looked around the disheveled cabin.

34

"Och, this room be's a tip. We've no time to tidy up again, but. Them arse bandits what be's in the room'll think it was the storm what did the damage anyroad. We've to move to the next cabin or that hard-faced toerag Yootha's gonny somehow ensure we get no food at all."

She gathered up her bucket of cleaning supplies and they left the cabin, and the thought of how many more cabins they had yet to clean made her hate Dymphna even more. Fionnuala simmered over the humiliation at the port in Belfast two days before, while Siofra secretly slipped her hand into her pocket, making sure the five Euro note she had also found under the cushion was still there. It was.

CHAPTER SEVEN—SOUTHAMPTON PORT, TEN MINUTES EARLIER

"...Quickly, please."

Anthea Planck, the check-in agent for Econo-Lux Cruiselines, flicked off the PA microphone and turned to her co-worker Scully, but the lazy chancer had already skipped away to the staff room, leaving her to fend for herself at the counter. She couldn't fault him; they had spent a morning's worth of lying through their smiles to passenger after furious passenger about the 'special new cruise' that had been arranged after the sudden cancellation of the one they had booked. The victims seemed to think there was nothing special or new about the 100 Years of Misery: the *Titanic* Memorial Cruise. And speaking of misery, something was coming up on Anthea's left heel...a blister? a boil? a weeping sore?

If she just slipped her foot out of the high heels Econo-Lux insisted she wear and somehow shimmied down her pantyhose, she could inspect it right there behind the counter. But with all the passengers milling around her, and the occasional patrolling police officers, she realized she'd better wait and whip her pantyhose off in the staff room. When she ever made it there.

Cursing Scully, and checking the computer, she saw there were still four passengers, the Barnetts, who had yet to make their way from security. They were probably puttering around in the gift shops for overpriced Union Jack pencil sharpeners when they only had fifteen minutes before the gangway was locked. Fifteen minutes before she unpinned her name tag. Visions of choking a Silk Cut Extra Mild down to the butt, then collapsing before a cup of tea and a chocolate biscuit at the staff room table danced in her mind. She could almost taste the chamomile, feel the fingers massaging the tortured and cracked flesh of her heels, inspecting the growth...

Hoping she wouldn't have to lance, Anthea thought back to the long line of faces twisted with confusion and rage when she and Scully had handed them the change in theme and itinerary, and, on the next page, their no stringent refund policy. Econo-Lux was on the brink of financial ruin, and helping inch it closer to Chapter 13 were the weak sales of five themed cruises that season, the gambling one, the action/adventure one, the Experience the Exotic Creatures of the

36

World one, the hip-hop one and the—Anthea shuddered—the *opera* one; she couldn't think of anything more oppressive than being locked in a ship with no escape from the Pavarotti piped into the hallways and cabins 24/7. Some idiot higher up had canceled all the cruises just the week before, and the few booked passengers were all bundled together on one cruise that the same idiot quickly rebranded, in a vain attempt to cash in on the fever that was gripping the industry that year, an enchanting *Titanic* cruise. If the rage directed at her and Scully all morning long was anything to go by, few were enchanted. She tried gamely to explain over their roars that they could get their gambling and action/adventure and exotic creatures and hip-hop and opera, somehow, on the *Titanic* cruise as well!

Those who had handed over thousands a pop were not encouraged by the sad selection of on board *Titanic* activities Anthea pointed out— the lifeboat reenactment, the mandatory hours of memorial silence ship-wide from 11:40 PM April 14th to 2:20 AM (from iceberg to final submersion), the put-your-hand-in-a-bag-and-choose-a-real-*Titanic*-passenger-and-find-out-if-you-lived-or-died-at-the-end-of-the-cruise.
Anthea hoped whoever was in charge of these less than diverting diversions would soon be handed their pink slip. Nor were they happy about the peculiar route the ship was taking. Two weeks before, Econo-Lux had had to sell routes to better established cruise lines, and that meant slim pickings around the world for Econo-Lux passengers. How could she and Scully explain to the screaming faces a *Titanic* cruise that wasn't following the route of the *Titanic?* Instead of the North Atlantic, they would head south from the UK, but not even to the paradise of Madeira. The first stop would be the uninhabitable Savage Islands, all 1.05 square miles of them, off the coast of Morocco. And after that, a variety of ports chosen in haste and desperation that were less tourist destinations and more just *places.* Worse, how could she and Scully reveal the company wasn't even sure of the itinerary towards the end of the cruise? "And a variety of mystery destinations," they had ended each explanation to face after startled face. And kept pointing out they had been informed by email and kept pointing to the no refund clause. It would give Anthea sleepless nights that she was lying about the emails.

Anthea was privy to even sadder truths as the disgruntled passengers boarded like lambs to the slaughter: due to the ongoing industrial action by the mostly Scandinavian crew, the entire staff had been fired and replaced by barely-trained peons willing to work for pennies on the pound, but when twenty had called in sick with food poisoning, the Econo-Lux HR department had had to devise a disingenuous plan to fill the slots with unwitting scabs! Also, it was the *Queen of Crab*'s last voyage, she would be junked at the end. Econo-Lux had invested in a cosmetic overhaul as it was cheaper than fixing mechanical problems, which meant the ship was all fur coat and no knickers. The passage of time had made the hull delicate, leaks spouting everywhere, the boiler constantly on the blink, and a wide array of electrical malfunctions and pistons in need of a corrosion expert.

Anthea would've been blissfully unaware of all this unwanted information if it weren't for the fact she was the regional manager's bit on the side, and he had gone on and on about it that morning as she had pulled her nightdress on and made him a boiled egg. Which the git hadn't bothered to eat, such was his distress about the plans for the disaster cruise which was to be the *Queen of Crabs*. Just a chomp of a slice of toast and a peck on the cheek and he was out the door. Pounding on the computer as if each key were one of his eyeballs, she resolved to make her way to another lover and another job.

Anthea glanced at her watch. There were now an unlucky thirteen minutes left for the Barnetts to board the bucket of rusty bolts that might be sending them all to their deaths. Perhaps *Titanic* wasn't such an idiotic choice of theme after all. She wrenched up the PA mic again and growled into it.

"This is the final boarding announcement for passengers Jed, Ursula, Louella and Bruce Barnett. Please make your way, now—!"

"Hold on! Wait! We're here! *We're here, darnit!*"

Anthea turned to see who we was. A woman marched purposefully towards her: a brittle, bossy-looking thing with a gray flip and red round glasses which made her eyes look like those of a tasier, and a sparkly emerald evening gown, an acrylic blend Anthea noticed, which hung on her like a bathmat on a rake.

"Please, God, tell us we didn't miss it!" Rake Woman said, panic-stricken, shoving a selection of passports at her.

"No, but—"

The tasier-eyes peered past her.

"What are all them signs about the *Titanic*? Am I at the wrong desk?"

Anthea's teeth shone their best customer-service smile.

"I can see from your attire you were expecting the—"

"Yep! Operas of the Earth! I got it right here." The woman dug into her purse, tugged out a brochure and squinted at the tag line. "12 Arias in 12 Areas, it says."

"We sent an email. That cruise has been canceled, lack of interest, but fret not. We've another thrilling sea excursion planned instead. But you really must hurry. They're about to raise the gangway. Where are the others in your group?"

She inspected the passports.

"Jed's right behind me with the luggage, and my husband, but he can't walk so quickly. When you see the size of him, you'll understand. They detained him at the security, that's why we're late. And Ursula's on the commode."

Anthea took a step back.

"Security?"

A man in a cowboy hat, Buddy-Holly glasses, a tuxedo and a cummerbund that looked like it was doing damage to his inner organs raced up. He was rolling a luggage cart laden with half-closed suitcases seeping clothing, a shirt sleeve dangling here, a bra strap there. The masking tape that apparently had kept them closed flapped in the wind. Cowboy Hat looked sheepish, and Anthea suspected the tuxedo was to blame. No doubt Rake Woman had insisted he wear it.

Anthea took a step forward as he handed her a business card.

"If you're ever in Wisconsin, and need some place to spend your dollars," he said.

Anthea smiled. They seemed like such nice, older, vaguely affluent Americans who could have no qualms about the current World Order and therefore no need to dabble in terrorism. Why had security given them such a hard time? She inspected the card from his business, apparently called Shooters, Sinkers and Scorchers (and Beef Jerky). *Get your guns 'n' more at our family store* it read at the bottom. Her smile soured. She took a step back.

"...I heard they done it with mothers and their babies' formula, but I never thought I'd be put through something like that. Okay, I'm here. Have we missed it?"

An obese bald man with a walrus-type mustache joined the others, trailing another luggage cart behind him. He was poured into a tuxedo in need of ironing, and close to apoplexy. His bright red face and the sweat that poured from it seemed to come from more than the physical exertion of rushing compounded with his girth would suggest.

"You really must hurry," Anthea said, her eyes settling everywhere except on this new arrival. "Non-smoking cabins?"

"Over my dead body," Cowboy Hat said.

Anthea smiled as best she could, her fingers pecking away at the keyboard. "I was just explaining to your, er, friend, we've had to change the cruise, and it's now a *Titanic* cruise. I'm sure you approve," and here she nodded her head and beamed brightly as she had been instructed, "after all, $1,843,201,268-worth of people world-wide loved the movie *Titanic*. I'm sure you do, as well."

"Who in their right mind would want to celebrate the sinking of a ship on a *ship?*" Cowboy Hat wondered.

"Rod Stewart, for one." This was Anthea's ace-up-the-sleeve. She gave a triumphant smile.

Cowboy Hat and Sweaty Red Walrus exchanged a blank look. Rake Woman pushed forward, eyes shining.

"On our cruise?"

"No," Anthea admitted. "On **a** *Titanic* cruise. It's quite a competitive market this year. Which is another reason why you should count yourselves lucky to be included."

"Will we still have chambermaids?" Rake Woman asked.

"Cabin attendants, yes."

"Are tips still included?" she demanded fiercely.

"Yes."

"And will the ship keep us out of American waters?"

"You certainly have the questions!" Anthea marveled, while her brain wondered not only how she would answer this question, the "mystery destinations" at the tail end of the cruise considered, but also why Rake Woman would be interested. "You really must hurry quickly. They'll bar you from boarding the ship in," she glanced at the clock on the computer, "three minutes. Where is your fourth?"

They peered through the throngs, and Anthea's eyes joined theirs.

"There she is!"

"Ursula! Over here! *Ursula!*"

"Hurry! Quickly!"

They pointed eagerly at a frazzled eggplant-colored bob making its way through the crowd. The woman who owned it raced toward her, and Anthea gasped at the fox stole around her neck, one of those creepy ones that had dangling paws and beady eyes and chomped on its own tail.

"C'mere a wee moment, have we missed wer ship?"

Anthea took another step back in shock, and it wasn't from Fox Woman's breath. This strange new arrival was maybe trying to affect an American twang, but Anthea wasn't fooled. The accent underneath was Northern Irish, Londonderry, if she wasn't mistaken, breeding ground for generations of IRA operatives. Anthea's lips disappeared. *Now* she understood perfectly security's problem with them.

"Have we missed it?" Fox Woman asked breathlessly.

"Almost, but no."

"We've got to get on board now."

As Anthea printed out their boarding passes, she did the math in her mind: an inability to meet her eyes + a Northern Ireland accent + access to arms =

It wasn't rocket science, especially as she had come in third in her terrorist-detection class.

"Here are your boarding passes. The gate's over there."

As they grabbed them and headed off, tugging the luggage carts with them, Anthea considered slipping her finger under the counter and pressing the button to alert the ship's security that People of Interest were boarding. But then her heel twitched with pain, her lungs were in need of nicotine, and she wasn't long for this job in any event. She flicked off the computer and the PA system. Besides, she considered, she had heard rumors that MI-5, or was it MI-6, one of the branches of the British Secret Service anyway, was on board due to a heightened alert of some sort. They could deal with Terrorist Fox Woman if need be. She made her way toward the staff room, humming *Maggie May* as she went.

CHAPTER EIGHT

Fionnuala hated being made a fool of, and that's what Dymphna had done to the entire family. She shuddered as she thought back to them all trembling with excitement as they marched to the counter of the port in Belfast to board the complimentary *Titanic* cruise. They had been dressed in what passed for their Sunday best (Fionnuala had unearthed her special hat festooned with exotic bird feathers last seen at Siofra's first holy communion), and bundled in duffel coats and hurriedly shoplifted scarves, suitcases packed with winter gear as they assumed they would be following the route of the *Titanic*, which was akin to traveling to the Arctic Circle. Fionnuala had long ago researched the route and committed it to memory. And, indeed, at 6:00 AM on April 2nd, 1912, the *Titanic* had set off from Belfast, where it had been built, a never ending source of Fionnuala's Irish pride, and from there it had plowed masterfully through the waves of the Irish Sea to Southampton in England, then to Cherbourg in France, then back to Queenstown, Cork in Ireland, its final port of call, and afterward...nowhere, really. It just trundled through the dreary waters of the Northern Atlantic until it sank. Fionnuala hoped there were plenty of activities on board, as otherwise she would go mad with boredom.

"Should I at least have brought me swimming gear?" Dymphna had asked as they stood in line, inching closer and closer to the counter for the trip of a lifetime. Paddy and Siofra were at the duty free and the mini-mart; they needed toothpaste as Fionnuala's homemade jar had been confiscated at security, the cinnamon one which gave her teeth an extra little *zing*.

Fionnuala scoffed and took a sip of tea, the price of which still stung. "Naw. Miserable, the weather will be. It was an *iceberg* themmuns collided with, if ye recall. And I still kyanny believe what a selfish bitch ye be's, not allowing yer brothers along on the trip. Lorcan and Eoin spent the past two years locked up at her Majesty's pleasure in minging dark cells with pervy hands grasping their arses, and now they've finally been released and can walk around the Earth like normal beings, ye deny them this chance to see the world outside the nick."

Dymphna had given her a glare like one she had never seen before that, almost, made Fionnuala shrink back.

"Mammy, it was *me* what won them tickets, so of course I'm taking meself. Can ye imagine the grief I've had offa Rory for not choosing him? He be's me fiancé, after all. And his mammy pretended she wasn't bothered about being chosen. I saw it in Zoë's eyes, but, and can only imagine what an even more miserable bitch she's gonny be to me when I get back. She can afford her own cruise, but, the pounds bulging in her bank account as they be's. If ye want, I can take them tickets offa ye and me daddy, and Lorcan and Eoin can take yer place. As I telt Rory and his mammy, but, ye're mad for the *Titanic,* and ye'd disown me if I didn't take ye along. Are ye saying now ye're disowning me anyroad?"

"I kyanny understand why ye chose wer Siofra, in that case."

Dymphna took a deep breath. "After ye and me and me daddy, there was only one place left. I couldn't take Eoin and not Lorcan, or Lorcan and not Eoin."

"Ye could've taken me mammy, yer granny Heggarty."

"Aye, but then we'd have to cart her up and down the ramps and what have ye day and night, what with her walking stick and all."

"And what of them wanes of yers?" Fionnuala eyed Keanu and Beeyonsay, screaming in their stroller that really wasn't made for two, but somehow Dymphna had made them both fit. "What madness brings them here with us?"

"They be's almost freebies, like extra luggage. I've to pay a nominal fee for the two of them, and I worked extra hours all last week at the chip van to afford to take them along with me. And ye kyanny tell me ye'd pass up a bargain like that."

"Ungrateful wee cunt!" Fionnuala seethed into the feathers of her hat. But they took another step closer to the counter and, caught up in the excitement, she brightened as she turned back to her daughter. "We're getting werselves to the captain's table for dinner one night come hell or high water. Let's see if we kyanny get ye a real fiancé and all. This be's the chance of a lifetime, the swanky ones we're to be lounging next to during the floor shows. Ye kyanny seriously expect ye'll be satisfied with a Proddy bastard student as a husband for the rest of yer life. Ye know marriage is final, as the Church won't let ye divorce. Ye must think carefully, and I know thinking doesn't be one of yer strengths, so I'll do yer thinking for ye. I'm happy that Rory's mammy doesn't allow ye outta the house with the engagement ring round yer finger no more. There's sure to be loads of minted aul men on board, desperate for a young, fertile slip of a thing the likes of ye. Religion's to be the second thing ye find out, after how minted he be's. The world be's peopled with pagans and heathens and madmen we don't see the likes of in Derry, make sure he be's a Catholic."

"What about Keanu and Beeyonsay? Two wanes from the todger of another fella might put em off, hi."

"Och, we'll tell him they be's mines, sure."

When Dymphna looked anywhere but at her, Fionnuala muttered, "Or Siofra's."

"She be's but nine years of age."

"It happens all the time in Africa!" Fionnuala snapped. "I seen a BBC special on it!"

She turned her attention to counting the gadgets that helped the others shuffle toward the counter: one wheelchair, one walker, two canes and an oxygen tank on wheels. Then she counted all the heads. Only 22 heads more and then it was their turn...! Never had she thought she'd be standing in a line like this. Fionnuala was shocked at a wave of emotion that coursed from whatever organs it was stored in, and a sudden tear that fell from an eye. She leaned in toward her daughter.

"Och, Dymphna, love, forget yer aul mammy whinging on," she whispered conspiratorially over the infants' shrieks. She touched her daughter's elbow. "Not a word to a soul, mind, but I'm grateful ye've given me this opportunity. Ye've got me feeling like Lady Astor, rubbing shoulders with them what be's above the hoi-palloi, we're to be, parading in the luxury of olden times, the world bobbing by as we get wer nails done on the seas, dining on plates of fine china. Yer daddy and me could work for years and never be able to afford the likes of a trip like this. Ta, love." She touched her elbow again, in a different place this time.

Fionnuala was startled at the look of gratitude that came over Dymphna's face. As if she never received words of gratitude from her mother all the time! In Fionnuala's mind, she dealt them out like sheets of paper towels after a spill.

"Ta, mammy."

Dymphna gave her mother an awkward little hug, and for the second it lasted, Fionnuala whipped her head around to ensure nobody had seen. She felt uncomfortable and moved her body further down the line so Dymphna's hands would have to leave her personal space.

"Och, here's yer daddy and wer Siofra," Fionnuala said gratefully, "with the drink and the cheap fags. Looks like yer daddy's already begun the celebrations."

From his bloodshot eyes, Fionnuala suspected Paddy had already guzzled down as they had been making their way back to them.

"Did ye get me me Tanqueray?"

"Aye," Paddy said.

"Slip a wee bit into me tea here, would ye?"

She held out the cup, and as Paddy reached into the bag, Fionnuala's fingernails gouged into the flabby flesh of his arm with unbridled glee.

"Would ye look at that? Themmuns is handing out free credit cards to all the passengers!"

They peered past the canes to the counter.

"I think them be's cabin keys, Mammy," Dymphna said.

"Och, would ye wise up, wee girl?" Fionnuala snorted her derision and, in the back of her mind, filed away Paddy's nod of agreement. She'd get him back for that at a later date. "I've been using keys all me life, and I never seen—"

She stopped as she remembered those times she *had* used credit cards to gain unauthorized access into places, but she couldn't believe the cruise company would lower the tone by handing out tools from a criminal's bags of tricks to their well-heeled passengers. Also lowering the tone, she noticed, was the headless and charred Barbie Siofra clutched in her hand. She nudged the girl.

"Go you over there and play with that thing away from us," she said, nodding in the general direction of anywhere else in the port.

Siofra skipped off. They took little sips of alcohol from the bags and, finally, their turn at the counter arrived. Fionnuala marched up, adjusting the feathers of her hat.

"We'd like a cabin next to Rod Stewart's, if one be's still available, that is. And could ye tell me, are we to take one of them mini-submarines down to see the wreck on Remembrance Day?"

"What wreck?"

"Are ye daft in the head? The *Titanic!*"

"May I have your passports, please?"

Fionnuala wanted to smack the look off the woman's face, but felt Paddy's hand on her elbow. She handed over the passports in a gesture grand and proud. They were the first in both the Floods' and Heggartys' combined family trees to have gotten passports for the purpose of pleasure instead of finding work abroad. The man at the Mountains of Mourne market usually had a choice of UK or Irish, and Fionnuala knew which one she would choose: Irish (not only would she never be caught dead with a UK passport—as if she were really a British subject!—they were fifty pence cheaper *and* safer for a trip around the world). But all he had been out of the Irish ones. It had rankled Fionnuala, holding a UK passport, but she would toss it after the cruise, in any event. After a family outing to the photo booth at the Top-Yer-Trolley superstore in the city center, they were ready to go.

"Ah." The woman at the counter smiled. "I'm happy to tell you that all your criminal checks came back negative, so you are indeed welcome on the *Queen of Crabs*."

Although Fionnuala was startled at this sentence, she wondered how her criminal check could ever come back negative, especially after her troubles with Inspector McLaughlin the year before. She couldn't know that Dymphna, who had filled out the forms, thought her mother's name was spelled FINOOLA.

"C'mere," Paddy asked, leaning on the counter, male pride making him angered. "Why was we subjected to a criminal check? Is is because of they way we look? Or wer accents?"

"Because of the nature of the tickets."

Fionnuala nodded. "Och, I understand, sure. Because of the luxurious nature of the cruise, mixing as we'll be with the crème de la crème, ye've to ferret out the schemers and chancers."

The woman stared at her oddly.

"Something tells me you haven't read the disclaimers in the information pack we sent with the tickets, nor the waivers you signed and faxed back to us."

Paddy and Fionnuala looked at Dymphna.

"Did ye receive that information pack?" Paddy asked.

Dymphna nodded.

"Did ye sign and fax the waivers?"

Another nod.

"Where in the name of God did ye come across a fax machine?" Fionnuala wanted to know.

"There be's a wee machine at the Top-Yer-Trolly next to the organic vegetables," Dymphna explained. "Two pounds fifty pee a page, it cost me."

Fionnuala struggled to think of the layout of the store, but she had never ventured to that corner before. The woman behind the counter sighed deeply and tried her best to smile.

"The promotion we sent to the media was for a *working* holiday."

There was silence as the Floods struggled to understand this sentence. Keanu and Beeyonsay wailed in the background.

"Ye mean we're meant to...?" Paddy finally gasped.

"Yes, work your passage."

The woman flipped through some printouts and started to read aloud. They saw her lips move and they heard words exit, but none of them could grasp the full meaning: "....non-compliance...threat of action both criminal and civil...obligated...up to ?10,000 fine...mandatory safety and evacuation training session...10-hour workday...overtime not negotiable..."

The information was still settling, bit by horrible bit, into the crannies of their brains.

"Ye're having us on!" Paddy finally roared.

"Please keep your voice to a civil level, sir." Her eyes glinted with suspicion. "Do I smell alcohol?"

Dymphna sidled up to the counter: "Are we at least to be paid for wer services?"

The woman's smile grew thinner.

"I should think, given your economic status, entrance to the ship is payment enough. Don't forget, you'll get to see a bit of the world as well." She paused. "You might be happy to hear you *do* receive vouchers for food. Provided the tasks you have been assigned are completed in a timely and satisfactory manner."

"But...the captain's table...?" Fionnuala asked weakly, her shoulders drooping as the sparkling grottos of her mind dimmed.

There was a vehement shake of the head over the counter. "Meals will be had in the staff canteen in the hull."

"Ye're taking the piss, surely!" Paddy, again.

"I can assure you I'm not." She waved the papers with glee that was almost devilish. "It's all in here."

"But, the events, the on board activities, the amenities...?"

"You must, actually, participate in the day of silence on the anniversary of the sinking itself. But as for the shuffleboard and casino and spas and pool and what have you, those are the domain of the paying passengers. You are forbidden entry into the common areas of the ship. Except, of course, when you're working."

"Where are we meant to smoke?" Paddy asked.

Her arms were a sudden fortress around her chest.

"There is a gangway used for loading cargo that's left half-open. You will get a bit wet, but it's a filthy habit you members of the...disadvantaged...seem reluctant to break. There are people—real *passengers*—waiting to check in behind you. As I've said, you were informed of all of this in the information packet we sent. You have already agreed to the terms of the contract and must board. Shall I give you your assigned duties now? If not, I'm sure you see those police officers over there. They will be happy to escort you to the police station."

They looked at each other, knowing they had nothing to go back to in Derry but misery. They all nodded haltingly, still stunned. As Siofra skipped up to the counter, the woman rifled through more papers.

"You, Ms. Flood, will work in our crèche. I see you have two infants with you, so that's fitting. You, Mr. Flood, will be working in the galley."

Three sets of eyes stared at her.

"There be's art on the ship?" Paddy finally inquired.

"The galley is the kitchen," the woman explained. "A dishwasher, potato peeler or somesuch you'll be. And you, Mrs. Flood, will be a cabin attendant. I suppose the young girl there can tag along with you."

Fionnuala fixed her ponytails. It might be work, but it sounded quite posh. Dymphna nudged her. "Mammy, it's housekeeping."

Still Fionnuala smiled.

"A maid."

As Fionnuala's face caved in, tickets and papers were shoved into their hands.

"Make your way down that corridor over there, no, not that one, the unpainted one. Quickly, if you please. And I'm afraid Rod Stewart isn't on this cruise."

They were shown their hot and airless living quarters next to the boiler room, with light bulbs the wattage of which were more suitable to a surgical theater than a place to rest their heads at night. The only things missing in the room seemed to be the shackles and oars. And a functioning light switch.

And now, their second day afloat, Fionnuala had cleaned more cabins than she cared to remember, cabins peopled by the overpriviledged and overentitled. Siofra scampered into the next cabin, and Fionnuala struggled to fit her bucket through. The door across the corridor opened, and, as Fionnuala heard Siofra begin the vacuuming inside, a cleaning cart poked out, a plump black woman in its wake. She wore a white cleaning outfit and an expression as if people were peeling durians in her vicinity. Fionnuala had seen her at the safety and evacuation procedures training session, and remembered her because, when the instructor told them they didn't have time for the sensitivity training, she had said, quite loudly, Fionnuala thought, "Thank fuck for that." She was wearing pink cowboy boots with rhinestones on them, and her left hand scratched her forearm incessantly. Her fingernails fascinated Fionnuala. They were huge, clawlike things painted purple and blue, covered with glitter and stenciled with Gothic lettering. The right index fingernail was pierced, and a little golden ring dangled from it. Her nametag said Aquanetta. Fionnuala nodded a greeting as she passed. Aquanetta grunted.

"I see their scam roped you in too," she said. "Working on this shitty ship of fools."

Fionnuala stared. The Floods had circled the wagons, not speaking to any of the other employees in the staff quarters, first because they all seemed to be foreign, and second because they were mortified and wanted to keep it in the family. Were there others like them who had been duped? Fionnuala attempted a smile.

"C'mere a wee moment..." she said shyly.

"Can't hear you. Speak up," Aquanetta grunted.

"...Could ye teach me how to do me nails like themmuns ye've on yer fingers?"

Aquanetta peered at her.

"You got a speech imprediment?"

"It's me accent."

"English?"

"Aye, that's me language."

"No, I mean, you from England?"

"Naw!" Fionnuala spat. "Ireland."

Aquanetta shrugged. "Same diff'rence."

"I can assure ye it's not."

Aquanetta put her hand on her hip and seemed to consider. Finally, she said, "What you want on em?"

"Och, ye know I'm terrible religious, so something religious, something like..." Fionnuala's horsey teeth curled into a smile, "like Mary, Mother of God."

Aquanetta snorted her scorn.

"How many fingers you think you got? It gotta be something with ten letters."

"M-A-R-Y M-O-T-H—" Fionnuala was halfway through her second hand before she realized that either she didn't have enough fingers or there were indeed too many letters. " Or perhaps J-E-S-U-S S-A-V-E-S," she continued, wondering if she had the appropriate number of fingers.

"Yeah, that'll fit. I'll show you how. Your crib with the rest of us, next to the boiler room?"

Fionnuala nodded, then looked around the hallway for signs of Yootha or other management staff. The hallway hummed with silence.

"C'mere another wee moment til I ask yer advice about something," Fionnuala whispered, reaching into her pocket and pulling out the pelican/dodo. "What do ye think of us lifting this brooch from Room 432? Will that Yootha bitch find us out, do ye think?"

Aquanetta's face broke out into what Fionnuala suspected was a rarely-glimpsed grin. She reached her hand into the corresponding pocket of her own apron and tugged out a fistful of bills from a wide array of lands. "Only perk of the job. Just make sure you don't take too much so's the passengers notice."

"Ye mean...?"

"No iPads or full bottles of liquor. No whole jewelry boxes. And don't break into the safes. A little from here, a little from there. Don't want them setting the pigs after you. I know what I'm talking 'bout. Got two sons locked up in the penitentry."

Fionnuala nodded eagerly.

"Aye, me and all!" she said; Lorcan and Eoin had been released, but she was too embarrassed to mention this. "What does yers be in for?"

"Murder and rape. Yours?"

Fionnuala was again too embarrassed to reveal. She cursed Lorcan and Eoin for committing crimes as pansified as drug dealing and grievous bodily harm, reflecting she should've beaten them more to turn them into harder men.

"Er...burglary and, um, arson. What does them nails of yers read?"

Aquanetta proudly shoved her hands out and wriggled her talons under Fionnuala's eyes. R-I-P D-' said one hand, K-W-O-N, the other.

"In mem'rance of my youngest, D'Kwon. Died of an overdose."

"Moira, me eldest, be's a bean-flicker," Fionnuala countered, sure she was trumping the woman in the tragedy stakes.

"What the fuck that?"

"Ye know, one of them females what...lays down sinfully with other females. Tempting the wrath of God, if ye get me drift."

"A dyke?"

Fionnuala nodded haltingly, not sure of the vocabulary. Aquanetta's face scrunched with disgust, and Fionnuala knew they had found even more common ground. She shivered slightly, wondering if a friendship were forming. Aquanetta looked at her watch. Fionnuala wondered if she had stolen it.

"Better get a move on," Aquanetta said. "Don't want that Yootha busting my balls. I'll see you back at the crib and show you how to do your nails. Need to let em grow a bit."

And she was gone, the wheels of her cleaning cart squeaking down the hallway. Fionnuala entered the cabin elated but also strangely guilty. She had never encountered a black person before—they didn't really have them in Derry—and chatting with one had reminded her of how she felt listening to George Michael songs. She would hum along and even shimmy a little at the kitchen sink, but afterwards, knowing his sexual orientation, she always felt unclean afterwards, as if she had enjoyed something she shouldn't have. She slipped the brooch in her apron and reflected that, the next time she and Aquanetta met, she should ask where to hide the items she stole so they didn't get found during the surprise inspections. Now, each cabin she entered would no longer be a series of horizontal and vertical and curved surfaces that needed scrubbing and sanitizing, but a treasure trove of opportunity.

"Siofraaa!" she trilled with glee. "Yer mammy's got a fun wee game planned for the rest of the trip! Like a treasure hunt, so it is, love!"

Fionnuala tripped over the hose of the vacuum cleaner that was flapping around the carpet, unattended, like a lunatic snake. She spat a stream of curses as her head cracked against the corner of the desk. She looked angrily around the room. There was no Swagger Jagger, no twiglet arms or babbling on about hunger. Only the hum of the ship's generator and the caw of a seagull outside the porthole.

"Siofra!"

There were only two places she could be: the closet or the bathroom. Fionnuala popped her head inside both. She saw only furniture and dirt. Her confusion dissolved into anger.

"Quit them flimmin foolish shenanigans, would ye?" she fumed, searching under the bed, in the drawers. "Show yerself now or ye'll feel the force of me hand on yer bony wee arse!"

She heard a *crack!* under her left heel, and stooped to pick up something next to the trash can. It was a purple butterfly barrette.

"Siofra?" Fearfully, this time.

She searched under a pillow on the bed, but no matter where she looked and how hard she stared, her brain still struggled to comprehend what her eyes were telling her: Siofra was gone.

CHAPTER NINE—HEADING TO THE SAVAGE ISLANDS
"That was some meal!"

As Jed said it, his hands fiddled under the table. Ursula hoped to God he was just letting his belt out a few notches. She watched Louella pick at her teeth with a matchbook cover. The three sat around chipped china plates that moments before had groaned under mounds of 'gourmet' food but were now just bits of gristle and whatnot. Slim was on safari at the buffet again.

Jed's hands surfaced, and he downed some Bailey's from a champagne flute. He stuck his pinkie out as he drank, a nod perhaps to the fact that he was on a cruise ship. He leaned back and inspected the women under the brim of his hat. Ursula took a sip of tea.

"I don't know what we're on this cruise for," Jed said, "but I'm sure glad we came. Everything's great. Well, except the non-smoking areas but, hey, at least the casino's all smoking. And," he moved aside a bowl and pointed to the wrinkled tablecloth, "if these old cigarette burns are anything to go by, there used to be smoking here in the dining room too."

Louella smiled and looked down at the Jell-O fruit salad she was too full to touch.

"I'm glad you're enjoying it."

"Best time of my life! Getting out of Wisconsin for a while is going to do us a world of good. And you know I love the sea. Devoted my life to it in the Navy. And I hear there's some deep sea fishing we can do too while we're here. I can't wait! Just relaxing on the waves and enjoying the good life."

Ursula faced him with a fixed grin. She swished the tepid tea around her teeth and wondered if her husband was drunk, had misinterpreted the words 'the good life,' was entering an early dotage, or was somehow on a different cruise. She knew Jed was prone to optimism, and she knew he wasn't a fugitive on the run like her, but she struggled to match his view of this supposed pleasure cruise with her own.

On the first day, the *Queen of Crabs* had ferried through the English Channel like a taxi, loading up more victims at Cherbourg, France and Cork, Ireland. Ursula and Jed, Louella and Slim clutched the hand rails of the gangway for support, the waves heaving under them. But they were denied the opportunity to step foot on land and, as they stared wistfully at the shores, they couldn't know it was the only concession to the route of the *Titanic* EconoLux could afford.

They decided to check out the on board amenities, and perhaps this was where Jed's love for her hell on the waves began. He and Slim found the casino, and the women spectated with folded arms while the men crammed bills into the penny slots. They watched the men's heads tilt to the left and sway to the right. Jed won a bonus round and got fifteen free spins. The rum and cokes clutched in their hands spilled over their thumbs then their pinkies, and their shoes were rooted to the carpet for balance. Jed's bonus total was $1.16. Ursula's fox-shoulders slumped.

"Och," she tutted, "these men and their endless obsession with gambling. We're better than that, aren't we now, Louella?"

She turned, but Louella was already, eyes agog, on her third spin of Texas Hold Em two aisles over.

Ursula tugged her out of the casino, and the two staggered down the shape-shifting hallways and clutched each other like John Travolta and Olivia Newton-John on the undulating funhouse platform at the end of *Grease*. They poked their eggplant bob and gray flip into the movie theater (showing *Snakes On A Plane*), the desolate shuffleboard area, and the pool which was empty was being dredged. They tried the disco—Phun, the sign said—but were told they were too old for it, and that the more age-appropriate ballroom opened every night at eight on Deck C and that they could sing karaoke there if they couldn't dance.

The less than enchanting amenities and activities wasn't the only cause for Ursula's concern. Next to door that led to the mountain-climbing, she tripped over a bucket some staff member had placed on the floor to catch the water leaking from the ceiling. Ursula found it disturbing, and kept scanning the walls of the decks for fissures and leaks.

And she was filled with a vague sense of foreboding from the golden-toothed staff. Ursula would have imagined them to be freshly bathed, their uniforms laundered and pressed to perfection for the maiden days of the voyage at least. But, no. Every baggy pair of jeans, every teardrop tattoo on an unwashed face, every filthy fingernail, every Eastern European with a shaved head and menace in the eyes, the type who, it always seemed to her, spent time in remote wooded areas shooting snuff films for fun, each one she and Louella encountered as they rounded a corner made Ursula shackle her purse against the brass buttons of her turquoise jacket. She suspected many had recently been released from a variety of penal institutions the world over, similar to the one that might lay in her and Louella's future. Some seemed from former Soviet satellites, others from the Indian subcontinent, or Biafra, or Ursula didn't know where.

And there seemed to be precious few Operas Of The World passengers to commiserate about the staff with, and a disproportionate amount who had been rerouted from the hip-hop cruise that she had heard about. Ursula wasn't a racist as far as she could tell; she loved Lionel Richie's "Hello," after all, and did have her collection of the ceramic heads of people of different enthnicities in the hallway back home. It had taken her years to gather them all together, especially the limited edition Azerbaijani. On the north wall of her house, the people of the world were growing and living in harmony, but now in Urusla's life they seemed to be living in anything but. (The heads were expensive, but after tossing the Frisian and the Tutsi at a home intruder once, she realized they were money well spent: not only decorative and informational but functional as well.) But, back to the passengers, she couldn't comprehend those who chose to greet their fellow cruisemates on the decks with a swagger of menace instead of a smile.

By the time the ballroom opened, she and Louella had passed out in their cabin from nervous exhaustion. Slim and Jed staggered in from the casino at what time Ursula didn't know, but she hoped, as she thrust her head further under the pillow and wished she had taken an extra Lunesta, they hadn't lost big.

The next morning, the Barnetts found the ship had bypassed the sunshine and fun of the Canary Islands and was making its way glumly towards the largest of the uninhabitable Savage Islands. Ursula jostled through the throngs before the activities bulletin board and signed them up for the onshore excursion that afternoon; if these were her last days of freedom, they may as well make them fun. The dining room had been closed for renovation on day one (they had had to scavenge at the machines in the mini-mart for Snickers and Puff Doodles past their sell-by date), so they were delighted to see a scribbled note that said it would be open for lunch. And that's where they were now. Having lunch.

And this dining room was more like a mess hall, Ursula thought;

she should know, having eaten at many military bases across the globe as Jed's dependent. She looked around, but what renovations they they had made she couldn't detect. Ursula always thought these cruise lines had master chefs, but the *Queen of Crab's* must've phoned in sick. Shrimp was on offer, it was true, but neither shelled nor devined so they had to do all the dirty work themselves, éclairs, yes, but frozen. And the leaden mashed potatoes she had forced down her throat still had the eyes in them! They sat in her stomach now like cannon balls. Ursula wondered who she might speak with to have a word with whatever imbecile in the kitchen had peeled them. She could teach him a thing or two.

Slim arrived, his plate straining to hold a third helping of burnt ribs and bratwurst and soggy sauerkraut and runny macaroni and cheese and egg rolls and Kung Pao chicken and fried chicken and shepherd's pie and onion rings and tirimisu that looked like they had been flash-thawed.

"Hey, you guys!" he said. "They're handing out the fantasy *Titanic* boarding passes over by the ice cream machine. I got our four passengers. I had to put my hand into a bag."

He gave them their slips of paper.

"I'm the Countess of Rothes, Lucy Noël Martha Leslie!" Ursula squealed. "The countess *and* her servant, Miss Cissy Maioni."

"I'm Mabel Skoog." Jed scrunched his scrap of paper.

Louella eagerly unfolded hers. She flinched.

"You gotta be kidding! *Yousif Wazli?!* I'm a foreigner, for crying out loud! And..." Her eyes became mere slits beyond the red circles of her glasses, and she whispered like a man revealing erectile dysfunction. "...an *Arab!* I didn't even know they had them back then!"

"I'm a woman," countered Jed.

"If youse've not got a Mr. or Mrs. or a Major before yer names, youse must be two of them third-class passengers. Ye'll probably die. Wasn't most of them what couldn't get in the lifeboats the poor people? The non-Americans and non-English? And...Irish...?"

They stared at Ursula, wondering where she got her information from.

"Open your paper, Slim," Louella urged. "Let's see who you are."

The three leaned in eagerly.

"Pista Ilmakangas," Slim revealed.

While they were consoling him, a thug-type youth slouched

through the chewing passengers towards them. Louella bit short a scream of fear.

"This for you," he said.

He handed Ursula an elaborately embossed envelope. Louella held out her hand, expecting one as well. But all she saw was three-quarters of his ratty underwear as he slouched away.

Ursula slipped the envelope open with her fingernail, tugged out the parchment and read a few lines. She squealed as if she had just been told to Come On Down on *The Price Is Right*. Slim almost speared his tongue with the fork.

"It be's a special surprise invitation! They talked about em in the brochure, do ye mind?"

She grappled Jed's arm with excitement.

"Och, Jed, Jed, *Jed!* We've been invited to the captain's table for dinner!"

Jed stared around the tablecloths, startled.

"Now?"

"Naw, on the seventh night, sure. What will we wear, do ye think?"

Louella's eyes flashed across the rumpled napkins.

"And what about me? And Slim?"

Ursula checked the invitation again.

"I'm sorry, Mr. Wazli," Ursula said. "Ye've not been included."

Secretly, Ursula felt bad as she slipped the envelope in the special pocket of her purse, but she suspected Louella and Slim hadn't been invited because Slim wouldn't fit at the table. She didn't want to embarrass him by bringing this up; Slim's obesity was always the elephant in the room.

Jed cleared his throat.

"Now that the fun and games for the afternoon are over..."

His frank tone cast a sudden cloud over the table. Ursula knew that tone from years of marriage, and the look on his face as well. He seemed to be on the verge of asking many questions, formulating them in his mind beforehand the way Ursula had seen Detective Scarrey do. (She had seen that look, for example, after she had accidentally filled the family car with diesel instead of regular once in 1979, and again the morning after she had, on a whim, dyed her hair platinum blonde while he was sleeping in 1972. She still remembered after all these years the exact tone of his scream when he woke up.) She bent her head as if she were sipping tea from the cup she grappled, but considering the taste, it was the last thing her mouth wanted. She was hiding her eyes from her husband.

She felt the panic and shame fill her again and clutched Louella's knee under the table. It was bony.

"Now that me and Slim know what the anniversary surprise is," Jed continued, "now that we're *on* it, and we're definitely away from the States, isn't it about time you two fessed up? What are you two running away from?"

To look busy, Louella picked up a fork, Ursula thought maybe it was the fish one, and crammed fruit salad into her mouth. Ursula rearranged the salt and pepper shakers.

"Don't think I haven't seen the looks you give each other. Ursula, you were fidgety for a week before you started telling me all about this surprise. And our anniversary isn't for months."

"Ursula's always been a fidgety-gidget," Louella said. She forced down a pineapple chunk.

"And I seen you, too, Lou," Slim said through a leg of chicken. "Jumping every time the doorbell rang, hiding in your garden. Watching *Law and Order* and *Cold Case* reruns at night as if your life depended on it. As if you were doing research. Don't deny it."

Jed gawped.

"You mean the *cops* are somehow involved?"

Ursula and Louella threw their napkins on the table in tandem.

"The meatloaf!" Louella barked, making as if she had just remembered it. "It wouldn't fit on my plate!"

"And I want some of them asparagus spears!" Ursula squealed. "We've to make wer way to the buffet again."

They grabbed their handbags; they weren't going to leave them unattended, what with the staff. They scuttled away. Jed drank and Slim chewed in suspicion at their retreating backs.

Ursula grabbed an empty plate, and her eyes looked as if they were examining the the food before her, but she saw nothing. Her handbag dangled from her elbow over the cauliflower as the plate hovered aimlessly.

"Och, Louella," she whimpered. "This cruise be's turning out to be a misery, so it is. Me brain be's on the verge of exploding, and I kyanny keep deceiving Jed no longer. The fear be's gnawing a hole in me soul, pure and simple. I've to keep me eyes peeled for coppers every corner I round, every room I enter. And there be's loads of rooms on the ship. I keep shoveling them tablets, them Xanax, down me throat, hoping for to calm me nerves. Them tablets doesn't be helping, but. I've to find a church on board Did ye see one in the brochure?"

"A *church?*"

Louella stared over by what looked like a selection of pork rinds. She gingerly placed three on her plate.

"Aye," Ursula said, her handbag swaying above the wasabi and California rolls. "The guilt be's gnawing at me. I'm of the mind that if I confess me sins, or *wer* sins, I should say, it'll give me head and heart peace."

"I don't think you're going to find a confessional on board But," and Louella grabbed Ursula's arm so hard she filched and almost dropped her plate. She hissed so vehemently Ursula saw spittle spray the length of the rack of lamb, "don't you dare rat us out. You're in this with me. We made a pact."

"Louella, but," Ursula said, hating the tremble she heard in her voice, the tears she felt collecting in her ducts, and the fact she couldn't locate the asparagus, "we made a pact, aye, but if ye recall I hadn't a clue what ye were up to with them church funds. Ye roped me in and all. And I wouldn't mind so much, but ye've not been rightly civil to me for weeks now. I kyanny comprehend it. Ye looked like ye were smiling when ye pointed that gun at me, like ye were enjoying me fear. What have I ever done to ye?"

Ursula shrank at the look Louella passed her over the selection of salsas.

"Anyroad, priests be's bound by the silence of the confessional. And ye hurt me arm. And where in the name of all that be's sacred be's them flimmin asparagus spears?"

She looked over the counter for help, and was surprised to see the staff, a group of three youths, smiling for once, smiling and laughing over one thing or another in their mother tongue.

"There they are," Louella said, pointing.

Ursula rushed over to the asparagus gratefully, but stopped short.

"How am I meant to transfer em to me plate? Where's some tongs or a big fork or the like?"

She looked the length of the counter. She could take that spoon out of the egg drop soup, but...

"Wee boy!" she called across the asparagus to the staff member with the mole. "Wee boy!"

 Something suddenly caused them great hilarity. Ursula hoped it wasn't her. She fumed at Louella, "Themmuns is behaving like I doesn't be standing here."

She should be used to it, the contempt and impatience the youth of the day had in those over 25, but it angered her how companies worldwide seemed to be hiring younger and younger people the older she got; the people she was forced out of necessity to conduct purchases on a daily basis with were those who seemed plucked from a hiring process where only the annoyingly perky, the shrill and those who felt certain aging would never happen to them were deemed fit by management. She had spent the past ten years struggling to maintain a sense of dignity and wishing she belonged to an Asian culture where, and she had seen an episode of *60 Minutes on* it, elders were revered and treated with respect and even had a special celebration day during harvest time in the fall where womenfolk gathered in circles and sang songs and ate crescent-shaped rice cakes stuffed with sesame seeds. She had long ago given up expecting a smile at McDonald's, but she had paid $5000 for customer service on this ship.

"Am I invisible? *Am I invisible, youse?*" Ursula roared.

She looked for support from her fellow passengers, but all at once around her were only spines and backs of heads; even Louella's face had shut down. The smiling and laughing of the trio ceased. Mole boy came over. His face was Soviet-era.

"What your problem?" he asked.

"Me problem? Me *problem?*"

He tsked.

"I mean, what *the* problem."

"Naw ye didn't, ye cheeky wee—"

Her plate fell to the floor. Her purse straps whipped down her arm. She grabbed tight. The purse flew through the air and cracked against his forehead. And rained down on his skull again and again.

"Ye wee shite ye!" Ursula roared, her purse battering against his raised hands, the wasabi from the bottom spattering his palms, the buckle biting into his flesh. "That's sure to wipe the sarky wee grin offa yer hateful face!"

While those around her turned to spectate like a multi-eyed creature with many gaping jaws, she burst into tears, her assault waning. She clutched her purse, and pushed through the sea of widened eyes. She shoved past Louella's arms, now outstretched, she noticed, and ran from the dining room.

CHAPTER 10

Fionnuala thought first about perverts and white slavers—or were they called human traffickers nowadays?—and even about Somalian pirates; her mother Maureen had forced her to sit through a documentary about them one unfortunate evening. Running the vacuum a few strokes around the carpet, she also considered briefly David Copperfield-style magic tricks where a member of the audience disappeared from a box on the stage.

But as she flicked off the vacuum and wrapped the cord around it as if she were strangling it, she decided it was just her little bitch of a daughter playing up, skipping off and forcing her mother to scour the cabins herself while Siofra...did what? They were forbidden access to the exciting decks of the ship, forced to lurk in the darkened corridors of the underbelly like pariahs, except for these cleaning excursions. Siofra had disappeared out of pure badness. Fionnuala plumped pillows with a palm more accustomed to smacking her offspring's faces and became increasingly upset. As in angry. When Siofra resurfaced, Fionnuala wouldn't give the wee bitch the satisfaction of caring she had run off. She'd put her palm to better use.

She arranged the chocolates on the pillows and felt a niggling doubt. Weren't mothers supposed to care about their missing daughters? Didn't she watch shows on the tv about it all the time? She stared at the chocolates lounging on the softness of the pillowcases with the resentment of a hollow stomach. Yootha kept count, so she couldn't eat one. But, Fionnuala thought, there's nowhere Siofra could be but on this ship! The girl was at no risk...except from the walloping Fionnuala would give her when she resurfaced. If she resurfaced...?

Fionnuala cursed the moment of weakness where she had given Siofra a portion of her Snickers. How had her crafty cunt of a daughter had shown her gratitude? By running away. Fionnuala could stand the hunger no longer. It was making her unable to think clearly. She reached into the pocket of her smock, tugged out the map of the ship, and ran her finger over the route that would take her to the galley on Deck D. She snapped off the light, threw the cleaning supplies into the maintenance room next door and made her way towards Deck D to see if she couldn't bag some free food from Paddy in the kitchen.

CHAPTER 11

Dymphna peeled the diaper off the shrieking infant. She looked down and shrieked herself.

What in the name of God did this flimmin wane eat? she wondered.

Dry-heaving, she tried to keep the runny mess off the infant's twisting back and the changing table. She failed. Holding the creature captive on the table with one hand, she grabbed a fistful of wipes with the other to clean up the filth. In the corner, Keanu and Beeyonsay gurgled through their pacifiers in the confines of the one-size-didn't-fit-all-but Dymphna-had-made-it-happen stroller and seemed to be inspecting her with either disdain or contempt.

"Ach, can youse do a better job, hi?" she yelled at them over yet another Katy Perry song blaring from the speakers. Was there no other singer on the planet? Besides Rihanna?

Dymphna's body throbbed with pain. A purplish bruise snaked up her left forearm, and through the latex she could see scrapes gouged into the knuckles of her right hand. She hadn't a clue how she had sustained these injuries; the end of the night before was a mystery, and her head still throbbed from the remnants of alcohol abuse.

This infant with the soiled and bulging Huggy was the sixth that had been thrust into those aching arms that shift. Each shriek was like a knife gouging her ear canals. She recognized this baby; she had changed him three times so far. She couldn't understand why they just didn't have a trough in the nursery the staff could place the infants into, where they could relieve themselves to their hearts' content, and then the staff could simply hose them down before they were returned to their parents. Their parents, Dymphna thought grimly as she scoured the kicking legs, swanning around the luxury corridors of the ship, sipping Courvoisier from snifters and cosmopolitans from martini glasses, tinkling with laughter and gazing at the waves and sunsets, not a care in the world, as they had diaper-changing-machine Dymphna to do their dirty work. And it was dirty.

The diaper-changing stint was the worst part of her shift, a shift that contained many bad parts. Econolux had forbidden the carer's flesh from touching the children for fear of lawsuits (some strange American laws were creeping around the world), so Dymphna had to change the diapers while wearing gloves, the fingers of which were caked with baby powder that became doughy from baby oil and watery feces.

When they weren't in the diaper changing cubicle, the nursery staff had to wear fluffy outfits with heads, and Dymphna's was a cucumber with swivelly eyes and a beret and arms that had to wave and legs that had to dance and a lipstick-painted mouth that had to sing for the entertainment of the children, all under eight. The French Cucumber outfit made it difficult to breathe and to teach the screaming brats dance steps to the likes of "Cha Cha Slide" and "The Macarena," as they had to do. There was apparently to be a presentation of syncopated dancing for the parents on the last night of the cruise. How that was to happen when the majority couldn't even walk Dymphna didn't know.

Dymphna finished the diaper change—she was getting quite good at it, she thought—set the infant on the floor and, making sure there were no witnesses, gave it a push. It scrabbled, gurgling contentedly, over the floor of the cubicle and crawled onto the brightly-colored tiles of the creche where it would have to fend for itself amongst the stamping Jellies and mini-Crocs. The moment it rounded the corner, the diaper popped off, one grip stuck to a tiny calf and trailing behind the infant on the floor.

Inside, Dymphna sensed another shadow in the doorway and scowled. That pink-dinosaur-with-the-lime-green-polka-dots bitch already had another soiled shrieker to hand over?

"Deempanah!"

Dymphna looked up in alarm at the deep voice. She gasped. A bronze god stood before her, arms outstretched, a bottle of whiskey lodged in his armpit.

"Deempanah!" he said again as she stared blankly at him, wondering what he was saying. It dawned on her it was meant to be her name. His accent was Italian. "Pink dinosaur tell me you here."

He took a step to embrace her, saw the state of her gloves and faltered. Dymphna ran her eyes over him, over his quarterback shoulders and spade-like hands, his disheveled curls of jet-black hair and dark eager eyes brimming with sexual hunger, and she felt her lust pot tremble. She fluttered her eyelashes and smiled as she stripped the fetid gloves from her hands. *How do I know him, but?* she wondered. But she briefly praised the Lord for her consistent good taste.

They embraced against a jumbo box of sanitary wipes. The belt buckle under his puffy and grease-stained zippered EconoLux workman's overalls pressed against her pelvis, and also, beneath, she felt a monstrous warmth. The puzzle of her most invasive pain was solved, at least.

As he pounded his tongue down Dymphna's throat and she wondered how to trick his name from him, it all came back to her like slides set at the highest speed on the carousel flashing onto the backs of her eyelids: pipes spewing steam overhead and the rumbling of some industrial machine deep in the hull of the ship, his washboard abs thrusting against her yearning flesh, the bolts pressing into her back, the guttural moans of alien words muttered feverishly into her ear canal...

...and, before that, her mother and father and sister sleeping in exhaustion atop the bunk beds around her, she slipping out of the threadbare covers and prying open the door that warned: NO STAFF BEYOND THIS POINT, sneaking into Phun, sauntering in, casual-like, as if she had ever right to be there. Guzzling down shots of peppermint schnapps and flagons of cider and keeping a watchful eye through the flashing dots of the disco ball for Yootha or one of her henchmen. Not quite trusting herself to approach any of the guys there, as they seemed to be either rich Yank tourists or a bit too young for her. And this Italian stallion sidling up and, with a few basic techniques of the mime, conveying to her that they should leave this party and mate.

And they had. Somewhere in the depths of the ship where passengers were forbidden to tread.

"You have break, no?" he asked. "You say last night one o'clock."

Dymphna looked up at the clock. It was indeed break time. She was allotted forty minutes. She reached under the counter and grabbed her purse, which contained two Cup-O-Soups she bought with work tokens from the staff mini-mart for her lunch. She felt slight dismay she'd probably have to share one with him, as she didn't see any food in his hands.

She ran her fingers through her red curls, found a replacement for the changing room—the alligator with the bendy tail—and led him to the beanbags piled up in the reading area where no child dared to go.

They made a pretense of civility, engaging in conversation as normal people were meant to do over meals, when all they really hungered for was mindless physical instantaneous gratification. They greedily guzzled whiskey from the bottle. Their libidos simmered as they babbled on, Dymphna's face strained from trying to understand, about the current pop hits of the day, the sad state of the ship's engines, and his strange obsession with serial killers. His favorite was British harridan Myra Hindley, who, with her lover Ian Brady, had abducted, abused and murdered at least five children in the early 1960s, and whom he talked about at great length and with an intense gleam in his eyes that unsettled Dymphna but also set her quim more atingle. She slurped her Cup-O-Soup. It was chicken noodle, he had a cream of mushroom one. He fiddled with a few of the barely-perceptible little gray granules that were meant to be mushrooms.

"Not mushrooms!" he said contemptuously, looking down at three granules on the tip of his finger. "Not like Grandmama pick and serve when I child. Big and fresh. She make special rice dish with them always. Grandmama Homemade Mushroom Risotto, she call it."

"Eh?" Dymphna called through the roaring of children outside, the Katy Perry and the alcohol churning through her brain. "What are ye on about? What did else did Myra do?" She was one conversation behind.

He smiled and shook his head and slurped another spoonful. He waited for the shrieking to die down, then said, more loudly:

"She go to wooded area behind our house every weekend for look for them."

Dymphna stared.

"Behind yer house? She lived close to ye? Ye *knew* her?"

"It'sa my grandmama I tell about. You not can hear?"

"Yer...granny...?" Dymphna felt weak. This gorgeous hunk's grandmother was infamous serial killer Myra Hindley, for decades the most evil and, indeed, the most hated woman in the United Kingdom. To Dymphna, she was ancient history, but she recalled her mother tutting and spitting at the screen every time the actress playing Myra on a tv mini-series the year before appeared. And apparently this deranged murderer had found more little victims in the back yard of this hottie's family home in Italy! Had Myra Hindley even lived there? Dymphna hadn't seen it on the tv show, but she supposed they couldn't show everything.

He went on: "Grandmama, she find many under trees always, but Grandmama wanna special ones, she wanna..." He struggled with either the vocabulary or the morality of it, Dymphna couldn't decide which. "She wanna ones with...big *heads* and fat *bodies. Capisce?*"

Dymphna shivered from the chill up her spine.

"She havea the eyes of eagle, that mean is she find them always and she pick them up, and she wrap inna plastica and she take home."

"P-plastic?"

He nodded eagerly, and sidled closer to her as if revealing something not many people knew: "*Sì, sì.* Mama say put in basket, but Grandmama not listen. The plastica, she say, it make them...how you say...?" He paused to find the right English word. "...more softer."

Dymphna stared in horror. He got more excited, his hands flying around with Italian gestures. "Grandmama take them inna kitchen, rinse with water."

Dymphna struggled to comprehend.

"Why in the name of God would she do that?"

He snorted with derision.

"You not know? Very dirty. Then she chop them up, and put them inna pan with the butter, the garlic, and sauté, put on plates with rice for alla family to eat."

Dymphna gasped. She could barely get the words out at his face, which was beaming with pride and memory: "Ye're telling me...youse...youse *ate* em?"

He gave her a strange look.

"*Certamente!* That'sa why the good Lord put them onna this earth, for us to *mangia!*" He smacked his lips. "Grandmama make with the pasta and with shrimps and with spinach and for the Christmas, she stuff with hard bread bits and romano and little mint trees. Alla family eat like, how you say?...wolf. *Delizioso!*"

"Stop! Stop!" Dymphna implored, fingers in ears.

He pouted. "You not like grandmama story?" he asked, but his was a pout that could make many women's knickers drop, and, if the liberal left were to be believed, 10 percent of men's boxers. He shrugged, tossed aside his plastic spoon and enveloped her in his arms. "What is the talk anyway? Now we make the love!"

It was difficult, but Dymphna shoved away in a compartment of her brain for reflection later on the horror and sympathy she felt for Myra's gobbled-up little victims and spread her lips. Their bodies pressed against whatever is inside beanbag chairs. His sausage-like fingers grappled those parts of her body that were exclusively female, and they did make the love. And in which compartment of Dymphna's brain were thoughts of her fiancé Rory Riddell, whose spermatozoa was responsible for Beeyonsay and, ostensibly, Keanu? In a compartment that only sobriety and a return to Derry would pry open.

CHAPTER 12

Ursula wished she had thought to bring Muffins along for company. Growing up in a family with nine brothers and sisters as she had, she used to long to be alone, and now that she was, she found herself consumed with loneliness. She adjusted the fox-stole on her shoulders and made her way to the promenade. She could just make out the setting sun on the horizon through a bank of menacing clouds. Her group would take the excursion to the Savage Islands soon, then in two days the ship would be in Morocco. Exotic Africa. If she blocked out the pounding hip-hop bass from Phun and a variety of cabins which caused the ship to shudder slightly, and if she squinted her eyes to obscure the garbage that swirled on the promenade and the couple behind the deck chairs who seemed in the throes of offspring-making, and if she ignored the humidity that seemed to increase as the knots passed and made the sweat trickle more furiously under her armpits the closer they got to Africa, and if she shoved the reason they were on this ship into some hidden corner of her brain, she could just about let herself get swept away in the romance and excitement of this trip. She compelled her ears and eyes and armpits and brain to do what she wanted. As the ocean spray sprinkled her face, she felt the decades slipping away, and she was indeed stood on the promenade of the most glamorous liner of the day,

She was safe. She held her hand up to her mouth and breathed into it. She needed a TicTac. She opened her purse and clawed through the depths, and was startled at the sight of urgent flashing lights from her cellphone. Perplexed, she hauled it out and stared at it. She was surprised. She didn't know she had a plan that allowed her phone to function internationally. She didn't know anything about ariel towers and signals, but it seemed a miracle that her cellphone could function miles from civilization. Was it the hand of God? She had 17 voicemails. She scrolled down the calls received list, and saw one from Muffin's kennel and 16 from a number she recognized with a sudden weak heart as Detective Scarrey.

She wondered if, with each subsequent message she hadn't answered, she and Louella were moving further from being "people of interest" to being formally charged with the crime. She was about to pound the keys to listen to the messages, but couldn't.

She continued looking at the display as if she had just discovered a handful of human teeth. Ursula bent over to the railing and, ensuring nobody was looking, tossed the phone into the ocean. She tearfully swallowed a TicTac, then dug into the compartments of her purse again, found a Xanax, and threw that down her throat as well. She needed to find a confessional.

CHAPTER 13

"Dear God in Heaven above," Paddy muttered into the potato peels, "strike me down now and put me outta me misery."

He thought twenty-three years in the fish packing plant was hard graft, but that was before the *Queen of Crabs*. Overstaffed and underspaced, the galley had him exhausted. His calves ached from anchoring himself on the swaying floor, his fingers were scalded from grabbing pots that teetered from their burners, his backbone and shins were elbowed and kicked by the staff who jabbered away in tongues he couldn't understand and with whom he had to use an array of gestures to explain his most basic needs, the sweat was lashing down his face from the industrial blaze in which his limbs were expected to labor, his hair clung in sopping clumps to his sweaty scalp, prisoner in his hairnet. Grease clung to his flesh, even though he wasn't allowed near the excitement of the many grills and deep fryers.

And they had been laboring ten hours daily. Potatoes Paddy knew and ate and understood, but he had spent the past few days slicing and dicing mostly bizarre produce with peculiar kitchen tools, both of which he would be hard-pressed to describe afterwards. Being a meat, spuds and two veg man, he couldn't understand the majority of the pansified foreign food they were preparing for the minted cunts in the dining room. But thankfully, Yootha steered clear from the galley, which meant the staff felt free to break the regulations and chain smoke, smoldering butt ends clinging to their lips as they hovered over the bubbling pots. They had arranged industrial-sized fans to keep the smoke from billowing into the dining room. And thanks to strange recopies Paddy had read on the recipe bulletin board called 'beouf bouguignon' and 'coq au vin,' the name of which made him giggle, there was alcohol aplenty, though it was wine, which he had always thought of as women's drink. But he understood now it did the job as well as whiskey and a few pints of lager.

Paddy took a drag of a cigarette and a gulp from the bottle he kept by his right boot as he gouged the peeler into another potato. He wasn't doing a good job; those he tossed into the water of the 'peeled' vat were misshapen and dingy, and for this he blamed not only his general incompetence in any kitchen —surely the domain of wives, and why they had men doing women's work on this ship, he didn't know—but

71

also the Band-aids wrapped around fingers that had been sliced by the peeler and a variety of knives; Band-aids that were now sopping from the stint debearding mussels he had just taken a break from. He would have to get back to the mussels eventually that shift, but shuddered at the thought, bushing off the barnacles, prying the shells open with his grimy fingers, the creatures inside the shells wriggling like living tongues, pulling out the little bellies and squeezing out their shit into the slop bucket.

Another half-peeled spud fell into the vat, and Paddy reached into the sack for yet another. He raised his head, and flinched at Fionnuala's ponytails inches from his nose.

"Fionnuala! What in the name of all that's sacred brings ye here?"

"It's like me stomach be's wriggling with tapeworms begging for sustenance."

She shoved past him to get at the sack of oats to his left, plopped herself down on a case of canned tomato sauce and delved into the sack. He watched in horror as she shoveled handfuls of oats between her gaping lips. She gulped, shuddered for a second, then leaped up.

"How are ye?" she asked.

"Grand."

His eyes flickered to the space under her left elbow where he expected Siofra to be. All he saw were the crotches and buttocks of the staff in their yellowed aprons as they hurried past them in the mist of cigarette smoke.

"Where's wer Siofra?"

"Ach," Fionnuala spat through flakes of oats, "run off, so the wee bitch has. Left me to scour all them minging cabins by meself."

Paddy gripped the peeler in panic.

"Gone missing?"

"Can ye imagine? I can fairly see the bones of me fingers through the flesh, all the work I've had to do on me lonesome."

She grabbed a mango off a counter—"What the bloody feck be's this?"—and chomped her teeth into it. Paddy struggled to get his head around what she had said. Unease made its way up his spine.

"Should we not contact the security on the ship? What if a pedo perv has grabbed her? Be's interfering with the poor wee wane even as we speak?"

"Ach," Fionnuala snorted, "catch yerself on. Them things only happen on the telly, like. Tasteless shite."

She spat out the mango peel and scooped some chili into her maw.

"Anyroad, the only pervs I've caught wind of on this boat be's nancy boys, and arse bandits doesn't be interested in interfering with the private parts of wee girls."

She wiped a bean from her chin and popped it into her mouth.

"She might be injured, but, lying somewheres with the blood pouring outta her wee limbs, like. Ye've seen the state of the machines and whatnot in the engine room, haven't ye woman, spiky things poking out and all sorts. Should we not at least make wer way to the crèche and ask Dymphna if she's clamped eyes on her?"

Fionnuala had been scanning the surroundings for more nourishment, but Paddy now withered against the potato sack as daggers shot from her eyes, ablaze with sudden fury.

"Have ye not a clue what a crafty wee bitch wer Siofra be's? Have the years spent living with her not taught ye anything of the depths the lazy chancer won't stoop to to get herself outta hard graft? Naw, ye've not a clue, as ye be's at home only to pass out in a drunken stupor after yer shifts at that packing plant. Legless, ye be's more nights than not when ye stagger into wer family sitting room, the stench of aul fish and stale drink and accidental wee rising offa ye, overpowering, it be's, so we've to choke back the urge to spew when we make wer way round yer splayed legs to change the channels on the telly. Why do ye think ye know wer wanes better than the likes of me, the mother who bore em? Ye've not had a hand in the upbringing of any of the wee cunts. That's all been down to me, so it has. Who was it that cleaned their shite-filled nappies? Shoved the pureed carrots down their gaping throats? Dragged them outta bed for school every morning? Not that learning did any of em any good, the miserable lives they all lead now. I've difficulty figuring out which of em be's the biggest loser, so I do. Even the youngest, wer Seamus, I've a suspicion he be's a mindless simpleton. Afeared we're gonny get his first test results and have to shove him into a madhouse, so I'm are. Drool on himself to his heart's content he can do there. Aye, I see by the look on yer face now ye hadn't a clue. And I'm sure ye've no idea when their birthdays be's. Tell me one birthday. Tell me!"

After a few seconds of silence, she whooped triumphantly.

"Ye see? I told ye ye've not a clue what be's going on with wer wanes. I'm their mammy, and I know em through and through. I know all their birthdays and all."

As the length of her rant increased so did the volume of her voice; it was now shrill and threatening to overpower the blare from the blenders. The eyes of his co-workers inspected them, and there was some sniggering and pointing of fingers. Paddy simmered with quiet anger back at her. He leaped up.

"Are ye a mad woman yerself?" he whispered into her face. "Showing me up in front of me workmates like this?"

He knew Fionnuala was aware of the shame of airing dirty laundry in public, the importance of putting on the front of a happy married life for their Moorside neighbors. She was always harping on about what 'themmuns next door must think.'

"Mates? Ha! Anyroad, none of themmuns speaks a word of English, if I trust the babbling nonsense I be's hearing, so themmuns hasn't a clue what we be's saying. And ye think I give a shite what them foreign bastards thinks anyroad? Barely real people, they be's. I'm telling ye, but, no harm's come to wer Siofra. The lazy wee cunt will be back when she's hungry enough. Enough of this silly shite! I've filled me stomach to the bursting point, and now I want to bag meself a wee juke at the dining room." Irritation crossed her brow. "Where I thought I was to be dining most nights. More fool me."

"We kyanny go into the dining room. It's against the rules."

Fionnuala snorted and glared her husband down.

"Are ye a man or a mouse?"

Paddy was a man, he knew that, but he also knew he had to tread carefully where Fionnuala was concerned. After his dalliance with a Polish fish packing plant scab the year before, and suspecting his son Padraig, now 11 and thankfully at home in Derry, had told his wife what he had seen, he had to defer to her every whim. Perhaps this explained why he hadn't rattled out the home truths to her that night in Derry on the canons as he had been dying to. Frustration jangled him, but once again fear of Fionnuala made him relent.

He guided her over the buckets of mussels and cartons of canned goods, and she gripped his arm, dug her claws right into his flesh, and dragged him towards the doors that warned NO STAFF BEYOND THIS POINT.

The door creaked open, and his hairnet and her ponytails poked through. They crouched, one on either side of the crack, and peered into the dining room.

"Ach, Paddy..." Paddy feared his wife had contracted a sudden eye infection, but was shocked to realize it was her eyes filling with tears. "All them walls glittering with gold, and them red sashes hanging from them huge windows looking out onto the sea, velvet or suede they must be. And would ye look at them plates they be's dining off of, pure bone china. And all them knives and forks and spoons they've to choose from."

Sadness wracked her.

"When wer Dymphna won this trip, I thought for once in me life I'd be sitting in splendor like themmuns there, but instead we've been shoved off in the hull of the ship as if we was the victims of leprosy, saddled with views of gray pipes and peeling paint. Ye know I've always loved the glamor of the *Titanic,* ye know I made ye take me to up to Belfast for that Celine Dion concert for her My Heart Will Go On tour in '97. It was the only thing I wanted for wer fifteenth anniversary."

Her right hand felt around the top of her shoulder, then made like it was grasping for something hanging to the right of her breast, reaching for something that wasn't there.

"Ach, Paddy, ye mind me *Titanic* satchel?"

How could he forget? It had been Fionnuala's second prized possession (after her Kenny Rogers' *The Gambler* teaset). He had bought it after the concert in Belfast from a souvenir stand. He was still shocked at the cost of it. On one side, Celine Dion sang into a microphone, and on the other, there was a replica of the *Titanic,* and a special mechanism made the ship tilt when something was placed in the bag. When the bag was full, the ship 'sank.' The hours Fionnuala had spent on journeys on the mini-bus to and from town, the sinking *Titanic* displayed proudly on her sweaty lap.

"...and it was terrible handy for shoplifting and all," Fionnuala was reminiscing. "And then it was snatched off me shoulder by them drunken stokes last year. Just like me basket of eggs and toothpaste right before we left Derry, mind? How many packs of thugs, outta their minds on drink and drugs, be's trolling the streets of Derry, thieving anything they can get their hands on, roaring abuse at anyone they pass, fists at the ready? Och, Paddy, I kyanny get me head around the state of wer beloved town. Twenty years we spent with the bombs exploding around us, the paratroopers tramping with machine guns through wer front gardens, the pram searches at the doors of the Top-Yer-Trolly, dodging rubber bullets on wer way to the shops and the pubs, gagging from the tear gas on wer way back home. Pure misery, wer lives were, and though we had the love of wer families, we had a black and white telly, a larder instead of a fridge, the milk always going sour, no phone— ye mind we had to go round the corner to use Mrs. O'Grady's? Ten pence a call we had to place in the little box on her phone stand? Stingy bitch, and how she had a phone I'll never know. I think there was a Protestant in her family. Gray, it all seems in me mind when I think back to them times. The rain always seemed to be pelting down. Does them days seems like that in yer mind as well? Finally, but, when them Brit soldier bastards pulled out a few years ago, it was as if we'd won the lotto as a town together. I was of the mind we'd be able to make a better life for werselves and wer wanes. Now we've a color telly, a fridge, the wanes has their mobile phones, we've a VCR, though I hear they've all moved on to them DVDs nowadays, and we've even that tanning machine and the karaoke, though them be's both broken now, but we've got em anyroad. But wer lives is still as gray as the telly screens back in the days of the Troubles. And, speaking of the lottery, why wasn't it us that won, Paddy? Why for the love of God was it Ursula? She already had her swank Yank husband with a bulging bank account. It should've been us, God-fearing churchgoers as we be, never a foot put wrong in wer lives. Why, Paddy?" She whispered her despair into his hairnet. "*Why wasn't it us?*"

The ship shifted. Mangos rolled off the counter and splat on the floor. The Floods still crouched and peered in silence at the opulence before them. The jabbering of the foreigners, the blare of the blenders, the spitting of the grease continued behind them. Paddy softly touched her shoulder blades with his sopping Band-aids

"Och, well—"

"God bless us and save us! Would ye look at the bloody size of yer man over there!" She pointed into the dining room.

"Where?"

"Next to yer man in the flimmin daft useless article of a cowboy hat."

"Where?"

"Och! As big as a house, he be's! How could ye miss him? Ye see the spastic in the cowboy hat? In the checked shirt? Him with his back to us? Beside him."

Paddy finally saw and felt the same revulsion as his wife.

"Must be a Yank."

He closed the door. They got to their feet and turned away from the dining room, thankful they were European.

"Two men dining together," Fionnuala sniffed knowingly. "Arse bandits, themmuns must be and all."

She wiped her eyes, and then there appeared a creature Paddy laid eyes on only on the rarest of occasions: a smiling Fionnuala.

CHAPTER 14—THE SAVAGE ISLANDS

The captain of the *Queen of Crabs* anchored the ship at 29° 35' N, 16° 50' W. The day was glum, Industrial-Revolution-type clouds pressing down. The ship would idle until those few passengers who had signed up for the three-hour excursion to the Savage Islands returned. Then it would cruise south-west at an angle of 12 degrees until it reached the port city of Sidit Ifnin in Morocco the morning after next. It didn't take that long, but there was nowhere else to go. EconoLux had planned for the ship to dock in Casablanca, but those routes were full. There was nothing much to delight an inquisitive tourist in Sidit Ifnin, but it was better than more sea.

Captain Hoe was interrupted from his lunchtime nap by a call from the radio room. When he got there, the chief radio officer pointed to a blip on the radar.

"It's been following us since Cherbourg," he explained. "Always keeping its distance, quite a few miles behind, which would make it just barely visible to us on the horizon."

"How big is it?"

"From what I can tell, rather big."

Captain Hoe's lips disappeared as if pulled by a string.

"And you've tried to make contact?"

"Certainly. But no reply."

"The military?"

"They would never let us know."

"Pirates?"

"...Off Northern Africa? Not since the 19th Century, the Barbary Coast and all that. Nowadays, they seem to always be off the coast of Somalia. There's always the possibility to time travel, I suppose...?"

Captain Hoe glared.

"Just a joke, sir," the radio officer said with a cringing expression on his face.

Deep in thought, Captain Hoe left the radio room. Outside on the bridge, over miles of slate gray waves, his naked eye detected a speck. He trained his binoculars on it. There were no visible markings on the ship to let him know who it might belong to, if it were a friendly fishing trawler or a foe of some sort. The ship was equipped with a helipad, helicopter at the ready. He lowered the binoculars. He chewed on his lower lip. And he wondered. He'd have to make a few phone calls to see if he couldn't put his mind to rest.

The glass-bottom boat flung through the waves. They clutched the rails for dear life, heads snapping on necks, tongues in danger of being bitten off. The fury of the ocean churned inches under their buttocks, sphincters clenched in fear atop the orange benches. Untamed sea spray drenched them, Hawaiian shirts clinging to their flesh, hair like the seaweed the boat stank of. Some clung in fear at their sunglasses, but these accessories were affectations as the day was grim. Ursula lifted her jerking head to the one beam of sunlight and prayed for Providence. She tugged the cords of the plastic rain cap so it clung to her scalp and longingly eyed the single orange life ring flapping from the canopy.

Their bobble-heads seemed to be nodding in manic approval as the tour guide yelled over the engine in an indiscriminate accent she could only classify as 'foreign' what they would find on Selvagem Grande, but what he said didn't instill confidence of a pleasurable day out. It sounded atrocious.

"Calcareous faults! Basaltic rock! Volcanic ash!"

He unfolded a pamphlet that whipped in the wind and poked his finger at photos of the indigenous creatures they would encounter on the largest of the Savage Islands archipelago. There seemed to be a gecko, some snails, a brown rat and a small array of beetles. The only wildlife Ursula showed interest in now, even as the fear of accidental death coursed through her, was the British cougar who seemed to be making Jed her prey, though he was at least forty years beyond boy toy status.

The boat could only hold 20 passengers, and there had been initial confusion as to whether Slim was considered one or two. It didn't matter in the end, as only seven others had signed up, including this British harridan. She must have been rerouted from the opera cruise. Her French-manicured hands—which, Ursula had noticed while boarding, always seemed to reach for Jed's elbow or arm when going up a ramp or tripping on a rope—poked out of an expensively tailored pantsuit that screamed Harvey Nichols, the upmarket British emporium for the rich and the doors of which Ursula wouldn't have trusted herself to venture through, even after those heady days after the lotto win, even if Derry had a branch, which it didn't. The type of clothes the Floods assumed she wore, but which Ursula had never been able to afford.

The woman crouched now beside the bilge pump, dangerously close to Jed, tossing her hair seductively, and, as the boat was ejected over the waves, grabbing him and erupting with throaty laughter. She seemed to be the only one enjoying herself. The others were whimpering in fear. Ursula ground her teeth. The woman obviously had the cash to defy her age, but Ursula's eagle eyes saw they were contemporaries. She had a vaguely aristocratic face, jet black hair and bangs, and kohl mascara which shrouded shrew blue eyes. She clung to a rather formal handbag.

Ursula forced a mask of friendliness onto her face as she tempted fate and sloshed through the sewer-like seawater, arms like a tightrope walker, to shove herself between Jed and the tart. Ursula made a show of grappling Jed's shoulder for support, then grabbed his hand and fiddled with the wedding band held captive on the finger time had bloated. The woman folded one bared Sharon-Stone-esque leg against the bilge pump and played with the camera function of her iPhone. Ursula marveled at her being able to strike that pose, shunting to and fro as they all were.

"Marine biodiversity!" the tour guide squawked.

He pointed down in great excitement at what he insisted was a 'barred hogfish' and a 'sea spider.' Their cameras clicked what they could of the underwater creatures whizzing by through the filth of the glass under their sodden flip flops.

"Migratory species!" He pointed into the air. They clutched the rails and looked up. They focused their lenses on, apparently, a 'White-faced Storm Petrel,' a 'Yellow-Legged Gull' and a 'Berthelot's Pipit.' Ursula wondered briefly as she clicked away who she would show the photos of the Pipit to. Probably herself. She had always dreamed of pressing photos of a lifetime trip into an album and showing them off to those she loved most. But the Floods would never want to see them, not now, so what, really, was the point of going on trips in the first place?

She placed her sudden sadness, her anger at the cougar, and her fear of drowning to the side of her mind for the moment and focused on Providence. She crossed herself. She felt closer to the Lord now. Now that she had finally confessed.

After she had run out of the dining room a few hours earlier, still gasping huge sobs of shame from assaulting the buffet boy, she had made a beeline for the information booth. The woman there seemed to be imprisoned behind what looked like bullet-proof glass, with a slot at the bottom she had to poke her lips towards in order for what she said to be heard. One sign behind her said Beware of Pickpockets, another Our Staff Won't Tolerate Drunken Abuse, Threatened or Actual Violence, and a third Enjoy Your Trip.

"Can I help you?" she had asked, her voice from some godless ex-Soviet satellite and chirpy, though how Ursula couldn't understand, as she must have to lean over all shift long to be heard through the slot. Perhaps she took drugs; much of the staff seemed unsteady on their feet, and Ursula was beginning to suspect the flow of the ocean wasn't to blame.

"Have youse a church on board?"

The girl's lips tightened with disapproval.

"We have something," she admitted with reluctance, eyes goggling the slot, "on Deck F, between dispensary and...Death Room."

Ursula blinked.

"Death Room?"

"Yes. It happens, you know, on cruise. Hundred of passenger every year need Death Room. Not on this one ship, you must understand. In general."

"And just for me own information, could ye tell me what goes on in there?"

"If you must know, there is body bag there and...refrigerated container? Erm, coffin? To store unlucky passenger until arrangement to meet up with funeral boat made. But now I tell you what you ask. We call it Faith Center." She picked up a brochure and read uncertainly. "'A place of meditation, prayer and reflection for all faith tradition,' it say here."

She made it clear she found this exchange distasteful.

"Ye mean, like a church-lite? A diet house of the Lord? Does there be a priest on duty there? I'm a Roman Catholic and need to confess me sins. Quickly."

It was as if the girl behind the glass had paid too much attention during the liberal sensitivity training portion of her customer service course. On this secular cruise, all sins seemed to be tolerated, celebrated and perhaps even catered for; the only perversion seemed to be practicing an organized religion. She screwed up her face as she continued to read.

"There is part-time multi-demoninational minister who drops by occasionally. Maybe you lucky and see him."

"A priest?"

"We call Faith Man."

Ursula hurried off to Deck F. She didn't like the sound of the Faith Man, but short of one side of her brain confessing to the other, she would have to give him a chance. She found the dispensary, heard drunken roars of protest from inside, hoped it was from passengers admitted and not the nurses, and stared at the simple black door of what she guessed was the Death Room.

She opened the door to the Faith Center. There was no statue of the Virgin Mary, no stations of the cross, not even a cross, no incense, no holy water font, no kneelers on the pews, no pews, not a Bible in sight, certainly no Latin anywhere. But there were rainbows and balloons and even unicorns aplenty painted on the walls. She sensed patchouli and a faint whiff of marijuana. The Faith Man was sitting on a bean bag chair. He wore no familiar white square on a black collar, but he *was* wearing jeans, and torn ones at that, an Amy Grant 'Heart In Motion' World Tour 1991 t-shirt, had a beard and was strumming an acoustic guitar. He smiled at her.

Ursula inspected him with crossed arms. He had raced to a cosmetic dentist if his perfect white American teeth were anything to go by, but she was sure he hadn't gone through the theological training of the Holy Roman Catholic church, nor attended one of their many worldwide seminaries. He was someone, she thought, who obviously couldn't be bothered to make a vow of celibacy. She felt she was closer to God than this charlatan; she would be better off revealing her sins to herself. He approached her, guitar pick in hand.

"Hi, there. My name's Frank, and I'm here to help."

She wondered why he were affecting an American accent. He was obviously British, teeth notwithstanding. She put that thought to the side, and realized she half-expected Frank the Faith Man to press a tambourine in her palm and lead her along in an impromptu rendition of "He's Got The Whole World In His Hands," "I'd Like To Teach The World To Sing," or a selection from *Godspell*. These non-traditional/folk services always seemed to be locked in the 1970s or even the 1960s, as if society hadn't progressed culturally since, and not the black-and-white, Swinging London 60s of mini-skirts, hoop earrings and knee length white patent leather boots, but the unbathed, scraggly haired, barefooted, LDS-infused, songs without choruses tail end of the decade. But there was kindness in Frank's eyes, and that's what Ursula needed at the moment.

"I'm a Roman Catholic, and I need to confess."

He seemed genuinely pained.

"Oh, I'm so sorry," he pressed a hand into her forearm, "but I don't have that special prerogative. What's your name, by the way? Let's get to know each other."

"What are ye trying to say?"

"I don't do confessions."

"Ye don't do confessions, or ye've not the training?"

"I can't do confessions."

Ursula surprised herself by collapsing into him with huge, wracking sobs.

"Ye got to help me! Perhaps ye're not a man of God, but ye're a man of faith, sure! Ye're the Faith Man! Ye've to hear me confession! Please!"

Frank tried to soothe her bob, running fingers and the pick through the tangled purple strands.

"There, there," he cooed. "I can listen. Like a confidant or a shrink. I can help you get whatever troubles you might have off your mind. But I'm not a trained professional of the priesthood. I can't absolve you of whatever sins you think you might have committed. I'm not a go-between for you and your Lord."

"Ye must, Father! Ye must give me Penance so I can clear me soul of all me sins!"

She sobbed down the list of cities on Amy Grant's tour. The Faith Man unclamped her fingers from his shoulder blades and guided her to the beanbag chair.

"Can I ask you a question?"

"A-aye," Ursula said, reaching into her purse and tugging out tissues she pressed to her nose.

"Why didn't you confess these sins at your local church before you came on the ship?" A sudden thought came to him, and his eyes seemed to flicker towards an emergency button which would call security to the

Faith Room. "Or have you done something here on the ship?"

"Naw!" Ursula sobbed. "Most of the money, ye see, came from me own congregation, and that's why I kyanny confess there. Och, the sleepless nights I've had! Me brain's about to explode from the torture of it all. And now the coppers be's after me and all. That's why I'm on this cruise, to bide me time till the statue runs out on that limitations thing. Half me mind, but, thinks I deserve to be persecuted and crucified by the coppers. Strung up and made an example of for all to see, I should be!"

Frank's smile had long since disappeared.

"Would you like to tell me about it?"

"Are ye gonny abide by the confidentiality of the confessional, but?"

"If you've slaughtered someone," he said it as if it happened often on the ship, "I—"

"Naw! That doesn't be it."

Frank had relaxed somewhat.

"In that case, I *am* a trained psychologist, and anything you tell me will be protected by patient confidentiality. That's almost as good as the confidentiality of the confessional, isn't it?"

Ursula nodded into her tissue. Her mind was made up. She would tell him everything.

"Could ye do me a wee favor, but?"

"Whatever you want. Get it all off your chest."

"Could ye sit as if ye was the priest in the confessional? Sideways to me, like. And don't look at me."

In the confessional, Ursula had always taken comfort in the mystery of eyes glinting beyond the grille, the disembodied voice soothing her in the hush of the darkened booth for her sins.

Frank shrugged.

"It's highly irregular, but...well, I *am* here to help. So, okay."

He arranged himself as she had instructed on the beanbag opposite. Ursula grabbed a box of scented candles and knelt on it. She rummaged in her purse, retrieved her rosary beads and clutched them for support. She folded her hands in prayer and took a deep breath. She had a lot to confess.

"Bless me, Father, for I have sinned. It's been a year since me last confession." She struggled to push her crime from her brain to her lips.

"I know I told ye I haven't been to speak to me priest in Wisconsin, but I went on holiday to me hometown of Derry last year, and I went to confession while I was there. I couldn't tell Father Hogan about me dead terrible sins, but, as he knows the sound of me voice. So I've six-year-old sins to reveal to ye now. And six years ago it all started.

"I was living in Derry back then, and me husband had taken me to Wisconsin to finally meet his family. Louella, that's his sister-in-law, came to me one day and told me it was her turn to set up the annual charity bake sale for her church. She asked me to help her. I was uncomfortable, as she be's one of them Lutherans. Better than pagans or heathens, I thought finally, but. Now, I'm useless in the kitchen, me, but yer woman, that's that sleekit wee sister-in-law of mine, told me it was to be for a special charity for a new orphanage and home for unwed mothers they was planning to set up on the edge of town. Me and Louella was to be the organizers of the bake sale, and though we got all the papers signed from all the churches together, Louella told me she would deal with the finances. All I had to do was bake. And bake I did. Och, I must tell ye now, I was raging at her, so I was. I know that's a sin, so I want to stick that one in and all, but please don't judge me, as ye've no idea the hours I put in, toiling and sweating over a hot oven. And Louella's always been tight-fisted with the money. Told me she hadn't the overheads for luxury cupcakes and brownies and whatnot, so we went to a discount store and bought eggs past their sell by date, so there I was, separating the yolks from the white, surrounded by fumes of sulfur, and me gagging all the while I whisked the expired eggs. I just threw in extra confectioner's sugar until the smell disappeared, but.

"Me and Jed, that's me husband, flew back to Derry two days after the bake sale. I heard, but, that many were almost on their deathbeds from wer bad eggs, with foul liquid spewing from both their holes, if ye know what I mean and—*don't look at me, I've already told ye!*"

Frank's head fell back down, so he was left staring back at his knees, which were clutched together.

"The sleepless nights it's caused me, Father, causing all that misery to so many. Mortified, I've been, about it. Anyroad, if ye leave that aside, the bake sale was a roaring success. Over $100,000 we raised, and I was proud to help the church and the orphanage out, and even the unwed mothers. $500 we got for one cupcake, and one woman, Mrs. Prattertine, was hoping to adopt the first orphan, so she paid $10,000 for me red velvet cake. And for that she had to spend two nights in hospital!

"Weeks passed, and I heard all the rest of this now from Louella. And from Detective Scarrey, the copper who's hell bent on locking us up. Yer woman who wanted the child, Mrs. Prattertine, wondered what was going on with the orphanage. Over in Derry, I wondered and all. With $100,000, I supposed they would build a nice one. I wanted to get me photo taken in front of it the next time I went to Wisconsin to visit, with me arms around one or two of the orphans. And perhaps I'd allow one of them unwed mothers to stand in the background and all."

The Faith Man twisted before her on the beanbag chair as if he could feel the passage of time on his face and body as the confession went on.

"Anyroad, the weeks turned into months, and still yer woman Mrs. Pratterine—oach, how I kyanny stick even the sound of her name!—tried to Google the orphanage and its progress, but nothing ever came up on the Internet about it. I think she even drove out to where it was supposed to be built, but she saw nothing but grass. She finally phoned Louella, who gave her excuse after excuse, first there was problems with planning permission, then with the licensing, then construction problems as the price of lumber and concrete had gone up. The months turned into years, and finally yer woman, that Mrs. Prattertine, went to the coppers and asked them to investigate.

"I hadn't a clue of any of this. And, a year ago, me and Jed moved to Wisconsin, and I don't have the time here to tell ye why we moved from Ireland. Suffice it to say wer lotto win caused problems between me and me family and moving to Wisconsin was the best thing to do, though I'll let in on a wee secret and tell ye I'll go to me grave a happy woman if I never lock eyes on another snow plow or jar of salt.

"Anyroad, I saw the look of shock in Louella's eyes when we stepped into her house for the first time; we live down the road from themmuns, and me husband and his brother, Slim, that's Louella's man, started a shop together. I'm sure ye don't want to hear about that, but. Now I understand the look of shock. Louella thought I'd be out of the country forever. I was her lapdog, her dupe, so I was. One night a few months ago, we was watching the finals of *Dancing With The Stars*, we never miss it, and Louella was knocking the gin and tonics down her bake and I was indulging in a few glasses of rose and all, I don't mind admitting. She told me, with her eyes all goggled, there had been a knock on her door, and she had been hauled down to the police station by Detective Scarrey for questioning about the disappearing $100,000. Not only had Mrs. Prattertine complained but, ye see, it was supposed to be church funds for the church to do with as it saw fit, to whatever charity they chose. The church had a new accountant as the old one had finally died, and he went digging through the records and receipts and what have you. I think the old accountant must have been in cahoots with Louella. The new one contacted the coppers and all. A case was starting to form. But they didn't have enough evidence to arrest Louella. But she told me Detective Scarrey was looking at me and all, and would soon be knocking on me door as well. Can you imagine me shock? I was her partner in crime, and I hadn't a clue! She told me I would get as much prison time as her, collison, I think it's called. It's taken every ounce of me Christian compassion to forgive her, but I had to. Me family back in Ireland already kyanny stomach the sight of me, so I didn't want to get off on the wrong foot with me new family, start as we mean to go on sort of thing. Where did the money go, but, I wanted to know. She told me it was really for an operation for one of her oldest mates, someone called Daisy Flynster. She was dying of some disease of the lungs, something to do with asbestos poisoning, she said it was. M-M...?"

"Mesothelioma?"

"Aye, that's the one. Anyroad, if yer woman didn't get this operation, she would die. Why didn't ye just make her the subject of the charity? I asked Louella. And she told me a real charity be's wile difficult to set up, there be's loads of paperwork, and that that disease, that meso-whatever wasn't, and I'm quoting Louella, a sexy enough disease, and that nobody would be interested because of that. And mainly because nobody in the town could stomach the sight of Daisy except her. A sleekit nosy parker, by all accounts. I stole from the church, and what greater sin could there be, Father?" He winced every time she said it. "And not just from the Catholic church in wer parish, from all the churches in town. And I know all them other religions, the Lutherans and the Pentecostals and what not, they doesn't be real religions, more like fancy fake ones made up by people who couldn't be accepted into the real Holy Roman Catholic church, like, because they've lower moral standards, ye must know what I mean, having to deal with them yerself all the time, like, but I snatched the money outta their hands like food from their wane's mouths. And there ye have it, father, the sins I've committed."

Ursula deflated. She was shaking, but she felt pounds lighter. Even without the promise of absolution. Frank was staring off into the distance. Ursula wasn't finished. She rattled off her Act of Contrition.

"Oh, my God, I am heartily sorry for all my sins, because they offend Thee..."

She had been happy enough then, but Ursula gazed now upon the dull brown cliff approaching with a sense of resignation. The sight of the island didn't make her want to spring from the boat in excitement.

"I wonder if there's a McDonald's on it," Slim said. But they could see no buildings or, indeed, signs of human life on the sodden rocks.

The motor of the boat sputtered to a stop at the rocky wall reaching up into the clouds. They craned their necks. How were they ever supposed to get to the top?

"And now," the tour guide said with a sudden devilish smile. "We climb!"

They stood in shock and silence.

"He's having us on!" Ursula finally scoffed. She appealed to the other with arms open, hoping someone with more muscles than she would overpower the tour guide and make him see sense. "He's having us on!" she repeated.

He wasn't. He pointed to a pile of helmets next to the motor, and then, to their collective horror, delved into a box and pulled out a tangled mass of cords and pulleys and hook-things of many different sizes that Ursula had seen bikers and lesbians hanging their keys from. There were many people who lived on the fringes of society in their little town in Wisconsin, and Ursula had inspected their bricolage, their appropriation of common objects for their own use, with an interested yet disapproving eye. The guide kept reaching into the box, and pushed into their confused hands belt-type items with legs loops and buckles and chest straps and many more of the metal contraption hook things dangling from the waist bands.

"These harnesses. Must put on. One leg through each loop, over the shoulder and around the waist. They help."

With what, they weren't sure. They inspected them, turning them around gingerly in their hands in confusion and fear, the hooks clanging.

"Are we properly insured for this?" an elderly woman in a drooping sunhat called out, peering fearfully over the top of her oversized sunglasses at him.

"No panic. Is top roping. Very simple. Only pull yourself upstairs on rope. Rope already there, fixed to top of cliff. Made earlier. We do every month. Very simple. Child can do. Fun. Put on harnesses. I show how." He turned to Ursula. "You first."

Terror filled her as he approached with a helmet and a malevolent grin that said 'stupid tourists.'

"Hey, wait a minute!" Jed protested, squelching across sea detritus in the boat toward his wife. "Do it to me first."

The guide shook his head vehemently and held Jed at bay with a filthy palm.

"She first I say. Easy for you, hard for her. I must show. You stand back."

Jed looked on helplessly as Ursula's bob disappeared under the helmet the guide from Hell thrust on her head. Jed's fists curled as the guide demanded she sit, legs outstretched, so he could demonstrate the complex harnessing procedure. As she took up the position, Ursula felt Providence slipping away.

The hoops slipped up her calves, and her squeals of protest drowned out, in the distance, the thwak-thwak-thwak of helicopter blades slicing through the air, coming closer and closer...

CHAPTER 15

As she scuttled down the hallways, keeping an eye peeled for Yootha, Fionnuala was relieved Paddy hadn't called her bluff: she hadn't a clue of any of her seven children's birth dates, they always sprang up unannounced, and seemed to be celebrated different days every year, the children choosing dates on a whim.

When she had entered the kitchen, she had a quick look around the staff for a lascivious young thing that might lead her husband astray. She had learned her lesson from the Polish scab at his factory the year before (and was lying in wait to exact her revenge at some stage in the future). She was relieved to see Paddy was working with, as her mind termed it, 'flimmin loads of chinks and pakis and coons.' She was sure he would never touch the likes of any of them. Then, remembering her recent encounter with Aquanetta and how she hoped the woman would be her exotic and exciting new friend, Fionnuala felt guilty about the moniker 'coons,' and changed it to 'darkies.' She slipped her all-access card key into the lock of cabin 342, shoulders slumped at the thought of the endless scrubbing and scouring that stretched before her until she dragged herself to her bunk and its threadbare bedsheet that evening.

She was smacking the dust rag on the nightstand beside the bed with its 1000-thread count sheets when she felt her stomach lurch. It must be the oats. To her horror, she suddenly recalled a phone-in food show on the radio, and she had been chained to the kitchen sink with a mountain of dishes needing to be washed, but even so she couldn't understand why she had been listening in—she must have been desperate for the company—where a caller had said some people might find digesting raw oats more difficult than cooked ones. Although raw oats weren't unhealthy or dangerous, the caller had wittered on, people should avoid eating them if they caused gastrointestinal distress such as constipation, excess gas, stomach cramps, nausea and difficulty passing stool. Fionnuala felt like she had all five. She gripped the nightstand, and the rosary beads and books there clattered to the floor. Woozy, she groaned as she configured her body to pick them up.

Who would bring rosary beads along on a cruise? she wondered, tossing them back on the nightstand. She grabbed the books. *Twenty Steps To Winning Every Argument*, claimed one, the *Bible* was the second, and— Fionnuala's fevered brain suddenly froze—*Lotto Balls of Shame* was the title of the third. This one was well-thumbed. The oats bulldozed a path through Fionnuala's internal organs, but the pain in her frozen brain was more an anguish. Nobody, but nobody had bought eldest daughter and family traitor—and filthy lesbian to boot!—Moira's book. Fionnuala opened the book gingerly and flipped through the pages. To her growing alarm, she saw passages underlined in pencil, adjectives circled.

"To call Nelly Frood an obese layabout would be an understatement. Although she had given birth to nine children in a row, that's where her labor stopped. Her sister-in-law, Una Bartlett, however, couldn't have been cut from a more different cloth. Civic-minded, loyal and industrious, the classy lady of Derry City rightfully deserved the multi-million pound win on the lottery which had given her a swanky new home with a view of the River Foyle, a chauffeur for her BMW, and an upscale nail salon to which she was the sole proprietor."

The existence of a copy of Moira's family exposé with such marks in this cabin of a ship trundling towards the coast of Northern Africa could only mean one thing. Clutching the distended mass of her rumbling stomach, Fionnuala—Nelly Frood!—made her way on knees that quaked with illness and rage toward the closet. She flung open the doors and rifled through the clothes on the hangers. The aqua pantsuit, the mauve top with the frills down the front, the flowing daisy skirt...something seemed familiar about them all. Fionnuala was thrown a bit by the fox stole, but the leisure suit with the lifesized palm leaves certainly looked like something Ursula Barnett would buy. It was her style, and, as she held it out before her, the girth was appropriate for Ursula's body. Fionnuala had never seen it on that body because, her enraged brain knew, she had never encountered Ursula in any climate other than Derry's relentless cold rain. She seethed at the thought of people who could afford to splash out on special clothing that didn't fit their natural habitat or that didn't fit occasions of a mundane daily life, clothing to be worn on a fancy vacation in strange weather and then hung, unused and forgotten, in the depths of a closet once they got home. It was a waste of good money, and a very Protestant thing to do.

Then Fionnuala thought back to the man in the cowboy hat in the dining room. She had been gripped with unease at the sight of him, yet couldn't understand why as she loved Kenny Rogers. But now it was all too clear.

Ursula and Jed Barnett were on the ship! And she a chambermaid! *Their* chambermaid! She had just vacuumed Ursula's floor, scraped her toothpaste from the sink, scrubbed out her toilet bowl, for the love of God! Mortification and fury and despair vied for attention in her mind, and she didn't know which to attend to first. The obvious thing to do, of course, was take a dump on Ursula's bed; she knew it was what all the kids of the day did when they broke into houses—adding insult to the injury of a robbery—and she knew from the books on the nightstand which side Ursula slept on, but Yootha would know from the cleaning schedule she was responsible.

Fionnuala slammed the closet shut as if doing so would teleport Ursula back to Wisconsin. An inhuman whimper rose from her larynx and exited her lips as an enraged growl. She pressed the upheaval in her bowels to the back of her mind for the moment. She ran for the cabin door, hands clawing the air, caged in her work smock, imprisoned in her ancillary life and nametag, while Ursula swanned around the world in the clothing of the free. She yelped as she slipped and fell. Struggling to lift her rusty limbs, she saw she had slipped on an embossed envelope that had fallen with the books. She tore it open and read. And yowled. An invitation to the captain's table! Was there nothing that wasn't handed to the jammy bitch on a silver platter?

Tears stinging her eyes, Fionnuala wrenched open the door and leaned against the evacuation procedures poster. The frame dug into her skull. She heaved deep breaths. Her stomach told her to find a bathroom fast. She would never use Ursula's toilet, even as desperate as the need was. She slipped her card key into the next cabin, did what she needed to as she sobbed anguished tears, dried her eyes with some toilet paper, then exited.

In the hallway, Aquanetta ran towards her. Still shaken, Fionnuala fashioned her lips into what for her was a smile. Aquanetta's face was as stricken as Fionnuala's had been moments earlier. Alarmed, Fionnuala looked behind her in the hallway. There was nothing there. Her heart fell. She hadn't found a friend after all. Aquanetta was racing towards her with something like rage on her face.

"That dinosaur with wings!" Aquanetta barked.

Fionnuala pointed at herself in confusion. Aquanetta snorted.

"I mean, that jewelry you snatched from 432."

"I think it's meant to be a pel—"

"Whatever the damn thing is! Dump that shit! Now!"

Suspicion trickled through Fionnuala's brain.

"Am I right in thinking ye're expecting me to hand it over to ye?" she demanded, hand on hip. She snorted. "I know the scam. We've it in Ireland and all, ye know."

But Aquanetta appeared to be capable of out-hand-on-hipping her, and while she was doing it, muttered something inaudible about a crazy assed white bitch.

"I was taking a break in the broom closet, and I overheard Yootha talking bout some old fart went on the last cruise and left it in her cabin. Called up to complain to EconoLux. Yelled some shit on a phone bout a lawsuit if she don't get it back. Heard something bout her taking it to Judge Joe Brown if need be. Yootha mad as shit. Gonna go through all our lockers till she find it. Gotta go to my locker now and hide my gear, my pipe. Fell off the wagon a bit. And you better dump that nasty piece of shit overboard if you know what's good for you."

Fionnuala looked down and was surprised to see her arms were folded. It wasn't the correct stance for inviting friendship. She couldn't just whip her arms down, so she made as if she were swatting away a fantasy fly or mosquito.

"Ta for thinking of me, like." She did her best to smile in gratitude, reminding herself that smiling was just like riding a bike, and even reached out and touched the black woman's elbow. Aquanetta grunted.

"Guess you got no shit to clear outta your locker?"

Fionnuala shook her head, and Aquanetta was down the hallway and around the corner. As she bathed in the glow of a newfound friendship, Fionnuala's brain cells trundled. She was now only too aware of the weight of the pelican brooch in the pocket of her work smock First she cursed Siofra for having found it, second she blamed her daughter for giving it to her, and then she thought of the chocolates she herself placed every day on the pillows in each cabin she cleaned. She thought of the five days until Ursula sat herself down at the splendor of the captain's table. And finally she entered the Barnett's cabin again.

She ripped a blank sheet from the back of the *Arguments* book, felt in her pockets for a writing tool, but realized she had never had any use for them. She went to the vanity, found Ursula's eyebrow pencil and scrawled on the paper, "Please wear the special gifts we will place on your pillouw every night instead of the choklites to the captains table."

She propped the note against the books, placed the pelican on the pillow, popped the Ferrero Rocher in her mouth and scuttled out of the cabin with a giggle much younger than her years.

CHAPTER 16

Their heads rocked from side to side in a semi-circle around Ursula. She smacked away the guide's dirty hands which sought to force the increasingly strained elastic of the hoops around her pelvis. "God bless us and save us, naw! Violated, ye're making me feel."

"And you ain't shoving one of those things up my netherregions, neither," Louella fumed, arms crossed. "And you ain't getting me up that mountain. I wanna see my grandkids again."

A chorus of agreement arose from the others. The guide's patience had long since fled.

"Don't fret! Is only six meters tall!"

They didn't know what that meant, but their eyes could gauge that the wall was about twenty feet high. Twenty vertical feet of wilting sprigs of plants sticking out of very hard rock. The cougar smiled and raised her hand like she was trying to get a teacher's attention.

"I'd quite like to have a go up the cliff. It looks great fun! I can't understand this reluctance everyone seems to be feeling. Surely we're on this cruise for new and exciting experiences? You can do me up first."

The guide turned to face the woman, grateful. Ursula trailed the hoops out of his palms.

"Ye told me I was to be first!" she barked as if betrayed, squelching her flesh through the mesh and forcing it around her pelvic bone. She thrust the straps over her shoulders, stood, and snapped the belt around her waist. She stuck a pose for all as she wavered from side to side, hooks clanking around her hips. "Does that be how ye want us all?"

The guide nodded, and there was much clunking of belts and buckles and hooks as everyone harnessed up, shooting daggers at Miss Gung-Ho Brit. But as terrifying as everyone thought clawing at vertical rock would be for their own brittle bones and long-dormant muscles, each was secretly more concerned about how Slim would hoist his tonnage up the cliff before them. The guide put their minds at rest. He singled Slim out with a filthy finger.

"No harness for you. You are belayer. Your job, sit in boat, hold rope, keep straight. Very important job."

Slim seemed disappointed, stood there in his plaid shirt paired with checkered shorts as he was, ready for action. He slid out of the hoops he had struggled to get past even his ankles.

"My hair!" Louella complained as she struggled into her helmet.

"It'll be great fun," Ursula countered. "And," she said to the guide, "I want to be the first to go up and all and Jed I'm not taking naw for an answer." She eyed the cougar as she said it.

"Then I'm going second," Louella said, suddenly resolute.

Ursula looked at her in surprise.

The guide nodded, his eagerness increasing. "I show you all how. You follow me."

He now had his own harness on, ropes threaded through the pulley around his waist. He instructed Slim to sit at the back of the boat and hold the main rope tight with both hands. He explained that his great weight was perfect leverage, and that everyone should have no trouble getting to the top as long as Slim remained committed to the task at hand. But he didn't use that vocabulary. Slim scowled as he slouched next to the bilge pump and grappled the rope. The guide pranced over the glass bottom towards Ursula. "You will see I pull on bottom rope only. Pull on top rope, you crash and die."

He tugged at the bottom rope. His skinny butt shimmied up the cliff like Lionel Richie in the *Dancing On The Ceiling* video. In seconds, he had scrabbled to the top. He stuck his head over the cliff, cackled, and motioned to Ursula.

"Come! Climb!"

Ursula wound her frail hands around the girth of the rope attached to the pulley which disappeared over the top of the cliff. The others' brains were more concerned with Ursula's life-or-death climb to give much thought to the sound of the helicopter blades steadily approaching. Ursula wiped the fear from her face and replaced it with a steely resolve. Jed put a hand on her shoulder harness.

"You don't have to do this, you know, honey."

She shrugged his hand off.

"Aye, dear," Her eyes flashed, "I do."

A groan erupted from deep within her as she tugged on the rope. Her feet lifted from the safety of the boat floor. She hauled herself further and further up the rope. Already her wrists, fingers and shoulders ached. But she wouldn't give Louella and British Adventure Woman the satisfaction of seeing any discomfort. Especially the Brit.

She let out a fun-filled "Wheeee!" when all she wanted to scream. Her body spun in the air above their heads. She squealed as her eyelashes prickled dangerously close to the slate wall before them. Her feet scrabbled for little bits of rock to attach themselves to, her ankles ached, her heart raced with fear, her eyes welled with tears, and her mind offered feverish prayers of safety to the Lord, His Son, the Virgin Mary and she threw in another to the Holy Ghost for good measure. *This here be's me true penance for me sins,* she whimpered in her brain as she inched up the rock, *and if I plummet to me death, that's as the Lord wants it. So be it.*

Those in the boat craned their necks up at Ursula's spinning rump, the harness straps prisoner in the crevices of her bulging, stretching pants suit slacks, the effects of potato pancakes painfully evident. Her handbag swung from her right elbow. It was a sight their brains would never be able to erase.

Jed's face was twisted with concern and fear. His fingernails dug into his palms. He felt British breath on his neck. The attention that had excited him so before now was beginning to rankle.

"I hope she makes it," she whispered into his ear.

Jed glared.

"She will. She's my wife."

Ten feet above them, Ursula's shrieks pierced the air as her toes slipped and pebbles and dust rained down on them. They gasped as a unit as her body pirouetted on the spinning rope. Her girth bounced against the rock. Her fingernails scrabbled up the rope and fought for control. Louella pointed her pink Vivitar Clipshot upwards. She gleefully snapped a few pics as around her the others clutched whoever was beside them. Jed had the floppy/sunglasses woman. Ursula's helmet toppled to his feet. Then a flip flop.

Ursula's fingernails finally clawed the clumps of muck at the edge of the cliff. She hauled herself over the horizon with as much dignity as she could muster, sweat lashing down the panting, heaving mass of her aching torso.

The guide slapped her back. The applause from below warmed her heart. She crossed herself, thanked the Lord, then looked down, a hand rummaging through the mess of her bob.

"I made it, youse!" Her voice was weak. "Come on up!"

Louella grimaced up as, around her, everyone eyed her expectantly.

"Seeing you in action, you've gone and given me the jitters," she called to Ursula. The photos she had taken weren't funny anymore, as she realized anyone in the boat could now do the same to her. Brit K-2 Champ took a step towards the rope.

"Ach, catch yerself on, Louella!" Ursula called down. "Wile fun, a great craic, so it is!" She'd have to go to confession again for sinning.

Louella grabbed the rope from the Brit and heaved her body upwards. *More dang Irish slang,* she thought. She wouldn't know how to configure her arms to 'catch herself on' if she tried. From what she gathered, it meant something like 'don't be a dork.'

Even as she feared for her life, feared her twig-arms might snap, as she mounted the cliff and glared at every passing sprig, she wondered what it must be like living inside Ursula's head—all that strange vocabulary floating around, looking at common household objects and having a different name for them, all around her people speaking in a different tongue while she pushed her minority language into the living space of others and expected them to understand her.

Louella felt her glasses slide down the sweaty slope of her nose. They perched precariously on the tip. She didn't trust herself to unwrap her fingers from the rope to— She yelped as the top rope suddenly wilted before her. Gravity attacked her, and her bones jerked down the slate, her knees clacking.

"Dang blammit! Keep the rope straight, Slim! If I die, I'll kill you!"

"Sorry, hon!" she heard way below.

The rope straightened, and Louella clawed her way back up, adrenaline shooting through her veins, quaking in her battered knees and elbows, and on her thoughts raced as she glared up at Ursula's happy face beaming down upon her. Ursula was one of those exotic foreign people. But, because she was Irish, when you looked at her, she could pass for a real person like Louella and Slim. If you overlooked the peculiar color of her hair. It was only when Ursula opened her mouth that people in Wisconsin took a step back, and the woman before them was magically transformed into something exciting and unfamiliar, like a siren, a mermaid or a Klingon...and Slim was a big *Star Trek* fan.

"Ach, ye're almost there, Louella!" Ursula squealed, clapping her hands in glee.

Louella's molars ground as if they were tearing into some of Slim and Jed's beef jerky. Yes, Ursula had paid for the cruise, and yes, she was grateful for the sacrifice Ursula had made—for her sake—five years, eleven months and twenty-four days ago, and, yes, she understood the danger she had put Ursula in, and, yes, foreigners were always welcome in Louella's life and in her home (as long as they didn't use her toilet). But she didn't like that she couldn't understand what Ursula was saying half the time, and that Ursula always caught her cheating at cribbage—she had tallied up that Ursula had caused her to lose over $300 with her eagle-eye—and, most importantly, Louella couldn't erase from her mind the photo she had come across in Slim's wallet when he was in the shower the day before they left Wisconsin— she had been going through it for a 30% off coupon she knew he had from Wal-Mart.

She hadn't found the coupon, but she *had* found a photo of Ursula, staring longingly—seductively?—into the camera. Louella could tell the picture was from the 1980s, what with Ursula's Bonnie Tyler hairdo— feathered blonde highlights captive in an air tunnel—the majestic shoulder pads, and the scene from *Dallas* frozen on the tv in the background. The TV that used to be in her and Slim's living room. How long had it gone on for? Was it still going on? Who had made the first move? And what had Slim bought with the 30% off coupon? These were her questions. Confined to the cruise ship, the two suspects sitting ducks for the next ten days, she was determined to find out. With each pull of her body up the rope, resolve grew on her wrinkles. If she plummeted now to her death, she would be standing at the pearly gates being handed her wings and harp by St. Peter, none the wiser. She made her mind up. She would confront Ursula as soon as she could.

There was more applause as Louella heaved herself onto the island. Ursula wrapped her arms around her as Louella shook the dirt away. Louella accepted the hug, but her eyes crackled with anger. And when the hug was over, she pointed a shuddering twig-finger into the guide's chest. "I'll sue the foreign pants off of you if we have to climb back down!"

Fifteen minutes later, they had all heaved themselves onto the island, except Slim. He was rooting through all their bags, looking for something to eat. Being a belayer built up an appetite. Gasping for air and armpits dripping sweat, they followed the guide.

Cooped up together on the ship as they all were, and even more cooped up on the glass bottom boat as they had been, they felt like rushing off in individual directions of the island, but there wasn't enough room on it to do that. If the entire 2200 on this ship had decided to go, they wouldn't have fit.

They scaled the mud and clawed at the rubble. The tour guide skipped nimbly before them across the lunar landscape like a mountain goat. He pointed out the local animal species scrabbling around the sullen lunar landscape. They snapped photos of the brown rat, the three species of beetle, the gecko and the snail.

The guide babbled on, shouting to make himself heard above the crashing of the waves below, about the local fauna (a few creeping plants and bushes), and they all began to fidget. Ursula and Louella wondered if prison might be preferable to this excursion. They felt a whipping of the wind around them. Their hems and cuffs flapped furiously. Floppy Sunhat and Jed grabbed their hats in tandem.

"Excuse me, where's that sudden breeze coming from and what's that noi—?!"

Thwak-thwak-thwak!

They started, alarmed, as the chuntering blades of a helicopter materialized over the cliff.

"Is this another of your surprises?" Louella demanded of the tour guide. But he, too, was backing away in fear.

The blades gave way to the helicopter itself, big and black and scarily official, rising like a mechanical beast and bearing down on them. They screamed and scattered like an elderly herd of gazelle on the Serengeti. Fearing machine guns or chemical sprays or they didn't know what, they lunged for bushes and boulders for protection. What little a few branches or a few inches of mineral might give.

"Dear Lord," Ursula hissed to Louella through a fern, "what's it doing all the way out here in the..."

"Butthole of nowhere?"

"Louella...do ye be thinking the same as me?" Ursula could barely get the words out through the frond, so terrified was she.

"Do you mean...?"

"Aye! That copter be's sent by Detective Scarrey! I feel it in me bones! Don't ye? Don't ye feel it in yer bones and all? *Don't ye?*"

She clamped her hand on Louella's fist. Louella's fist struggled through the dirt to free itself.

The chopper whooped over the prone bodies of all trapped on the island. They clamped shut their eyes from the dust and dirt it churned up and spat into their faces. They tensed their bodies against rocks and twigs for whatever harm might attack them. And then, just as suddenly as it had appeared, the helicopter flew over the cliff and was gone.

As the unfortunate excursion goers struggled to raise themselves on already-exhausted limbs, their questions rang out:

"Who was that?"

"What was the point?"

"I'm gonna sue EconoLux!"

Locked together in a crevice, Jed and the Brit faced each other with shaking heads. Jed was about to rush off to Ursula to make sure she was okay. The woman grabbed his elbow and pulled him back.

"Pardon me, but are you ex-military by any chance?"

Jed puffed up his chest.

"Thirty years of service," he said. "Master chief petty officer."

He thought he saw a flicker of surprise pass her face, but if he did it had been repressed in a second. She leaned toward him with a smile and a pout of the lips, "I thought as much." but the question asked itself in a corner of his mind: if she hadn't thought he was ex-military, why did she ask the question?

"I see you're living your retirement to the fullest, dressed down as you could never be during your years in uniform. But I detected somewhere a steely military interior under that fetching cowboy hat of yours."

Jed had been trained in hand-to-hand combat, but the only thing he had ever tackled was a pile of requisition forms in war zones throughout the world.

"I see you are here in a party of four. You've told me one is your wife. And the others...?"

"My brother and sister-in-law. But what—?"

She shook her head and motioned to the others, in a circle perhaps inspecting each other for signs of chemical poisoning.

"Not here, not now. But that helicopter...I think it might have something to do with me. Let's just say..." She lowered her voice, though there really was no need with all the yelling and babbling going on, "I'm not who I might appear. I'm currently on an *assignment*. I've got a partner with me, but we need more help. I wonder if I might engage your assistance? Ex-military is excellent. Very, very excellent. Will you help us?"

Jed was still eying her with a bemused smile and confused eyes.

"Just a little nod yes. And I will be in touch. No need for you to contact me."

Jed gave a halting little nod.

"Perfect." She whispered it. She squeezed his flaccid bicep and was gone, staggering over the rocks and pebbles to the others. Jed followed behind.

Louella was feigning a sudden bout of nausea and begging the guide if he could just take them back to the ship. Please.

Back on board, the others stood around Louella in a circle and praised her ingenuity, including the British tourist who, it didn't escape Ursula's eye or rage, pressed her hand against Jed's back as she reached through the circle to pat Louella on the shoulder. Ursula's fist strangled the creeping plant she had picked from the island as a souvenir She shifted her foot and found the toe of her shoe against the woman's calf. The woman turned to face her.

"Terribly sorry," she apologized, as if her calf had been in the wrong place.

"Aye, so ye will be if ye lay another finger on me man," Ursula longed to say. She gave a less-than-convincing smile at the tart instead and, marking her territory, wrapped her arm around Jed's flaccid bicep.

But it was half-hearted attempt at possessiveness. She squinted as a lone sunbeam found her face through the damp clouds and singled her out. Her brain was in a frenzy over the helicopter and what appeared to be the longer-than-she-thought arms of the law snaking across the Atlantic to snatch her and Louella. As she stood there on the deck, a smile on her lips for the outer world, Jed at her side, she feverishly counted off how many days they would have to endure until she could breathe the crystal air of freedom. Eight...? No, nine. Nine long days stretching endlessly before her...

All at once, she was consumed with a lethargy of the body and mind greater than any she had ever felt before. She felt old.

"I'm away off to wer cabin," she muttered to Jed. She turned and headed down the deck, clutching the handrail for support. She was surprised that, all at once, she cared little about what advances the British woman might make on her man. The only bright spot she could think of as she made her halting way past the happy vacationers was what new treasure she might find on her pillow when she got to cabin 342 on this voyage of the damned.

CHAPTER 17—SIDIT IFNIN, MOROCCO

"Allahu Akbar Allahu Akbar Allaaaaah-aaah-aaah-aaah-aaah-aaah-aaaah-aaaah-aaaaaaahu Akbar Ash Hadu an lAaaaaaaaaaaaaaa ilAha illaallAaahhh-aaaah-aaah-aahhh-aaaaah!"

Fionnuala lurched from her bunk bed with a shriek of alarm, then one of pain as her head cracked against the bed springs above. The Arab man roared at her though the porthole. Her hand shot to her chest, and she was on the verge of crying rape. Her worst nightmare was coming true, and at the hands of a filthy pagan beast at that!

Keanu and Beeyonsay shrieked from the stroller corner. The light flicked on. Paddy and Dymphna's heads poked out in a similar state of shock. The Arab voice continued to scream at nightclub levels, but through the infants' wails, Fionnuala realized it was less screaming and more chanting, praying even.

"Ach, I read about this," Paddy grumbled opposite her, wiping sleep from his eyes. "We must've pulled into port in Morocco That caterwauling be's the call to prayer, so it does. It be's broadcast every morning at five thirty."

"God bless us and save us!" Dymphna moaned from above, her voice thick with hangover. "Does he be calling everyone the length and breadth of the entire country to mass? The noise of it!"

The roaring prayer seemed to end. The babies gurgled. The grown-up Floods lay tensed between the sheets, hopeful. Seconds ticked by. Sweat trickled down their spent limbs. The silence continued. Dymphna snuggled her sweaty, scraggly red ringlets into the hardness of her pillow.

"I guess he's called them all to their heathen churches now and we can bag some sleep," Paddy muttered.

His head disappeared, and as Fionnuala wrapped the thin sheet around her, she wondered what Paddy had been doing reading. It was an alien activity in their household, newspapers bought only for the horse racing results and a glance at the little suns or the clouds spitting rain which indicated the weather.

The alien prayer rang out again, and a collective moan arose from the Floods. This different man was in need of a good dose of cough syrup, his hacking coughs interrupting the flow of the *'aaaaahhhh*'s.

"Could yer man there not have called in sick for the day?"

Dymphna wondered.

Apparently not; the urge to call all his countryfolk in to hear the word of Allah was too strong. On and on he went, so they had no choice but rouse themselves out of their bunks and sit, hunched and haggard-eyed, in the furnace of their cabin. They delved into their cigarette packs as a unit, lit up, and puffed away. The smoke detector had been disconnected the moment they first stepped through the door, and Fionnuala had swiped a can of lavender air freshener from the staff mini-mart that she put to use as often as necessary, which was often.

The cosmetic makeover the *Queen of Crabs* hadn't extended to the staff living quarters. Where the Floods were held captive had a 'porthole,' true, but it was cracked and caked with grime of the ages, rusty wire bars to keep others out or to lock them in, they weren't sure. Four dour bunk beds stretched up toward a bare light bulb hanging from a ceiling that dripped brownish condensation on their already sweaty bodies. The constant rumbling of the engines, the thrust of the nearby pistons, the shuddering walls of peeling gray paint and the exposed industrial-sized bolts that poked from the walls and grazed their flesh, this was their reality when they weren't working their fingers to the bone. The community showers and lavatories were down a very long hall, together with the lockers which held their uniforms and what little toiletries they had and were subject to rigorous searches by Yootha and her henchmen.

They were thankful their clothing was elsewhere, as they were only left in the cabin with two feet by seven feet of empty space in which to perform their daily actions. Their elbows were constantly by their sides when at 'home,' and one square foot was taken up with the stroller corner.

Dymphna climbed down and headed there now to spoon some pureed apricots down their throats.

"And this torture," Paddy moaned, "them screaming their prayers outta them at levels that cause permanent hearing loss, is to be repeated five times a day."

"Dear God, and this is the land Yootha be's allowing us to visit?" Dymphna asked.

Fionnuala snorted and sneered knowingly. "I knew there was some catch. She be's a sleekit bitch, that Yootha! We should nab some earplugs from the staff mini-mart before we step foot off the ship. And you there!" Paddy jumped. "Aye, you clever clogs! Zip it!" Fionnuala was fuming, Paddy showing off his knowledge unbidden like that.

As penance, she sent him off to the staff kitchen in his wife-beater and shorts to bag boiling water for their instant coffee and Cup-O-Noodles, some sugar and a knife. She also told him to go to their lockers and grab a handful of clothes. They had packed for Northern Atlantic weather (actually, 98% of their clothes were suited to this weather, considering their natural habitat of Derry), but the further they traveled, the hotter it was becoming. And now that Yootha had shocked the staff with the announcement they had earned two hours of shore leave at the first port of call, Fionnuala wanted to make sure they at least had short-sleeved sweaters. Hence the knife. He staggered out. He seemed to be nursing his own hangover also.

The call to prayer ended. Dymphna twisted shut the jars of baby food, feeding time over, and tried to find a way to fill the silence she and her mother now sat in. In some distant corner of her brain, the girl knew she should be excited about going ashore—she was actually going to set foot on soil that wasn't Irish for the first time in her life!—but was more concerned about the whiskey sledgehammer that seemed to have attacked her cerebrum, and the unmade bed where Siofra should have been.

"Don't ye think, Mammy, we ought to alert the security that wer Siofra's missing? It's been three days, sure. It could be some filthy perv what's taken her and be's doing all sorts to her poor wee body even as we speak."

"Speaking of doing all sorts with bodies, what was ye up to til all hours of the morning?" Fionnuala demanded accusingly instead. "I had to tend to them wailing wanes of yers all night. Only two hours ago did I hear the door open. Ye came in, spewed up, passed out."

"Ye told me to nab meself a man, didn't ye? To replace Rory?"

Dymphna got up, maneuvered past her mother's knees, and went back to the stroller corner. She countered her mother's lack of maternal instincts by making a show of her own, though under normal circumstances, these were lacking, sorely. But other than adjusting the angles of the pacifiers in the infants' mouths, she wasn't sure what else she should do. She licked her thumb and smoothed down the thread-like hairs of Beeyonsay's fringe. She was relieved when her father came back in with the goods.

"Christ, I was in need of a slash!" he said. "Ye shoulda seen the size of the queue for the urinals! And the showers be's closed for repair."

They shrugged at that.

"Now that ye mention it, but, I'm bursting for a wee and all," Dymphna said. She scuttled out and down the long corridor.

When she came back, Fionnuala had been industrious for once, sitting on the bunk, black coffee at one side, tomato Cup-O-Noodles at the other, hacking away at their sweaters and jeans.

"Right!" Fionnuala said, wiping a noodle from her chin. "Yer holiday gear be's ready!"

She held them up as high as she could in the bunk bed for their approval. Their eyes goggled at the masses of frayed cotton and wool.

"Dear God, what've ye gone and done to me good jeans, woman?" Paddy seethed. "Men that doesn't be Yanks doesn't wear shorts! Themmuns is only fit for school boys, so they are. A laughing stock, I'll be out there onshore, a grown man in kit like that."

"Ye'll thank me when ye're out baking in that heat."

Fionnuala set them aside and, knife glinting in her hand, started to fashion a bikini top out of two mittens and some shoelaces.

"This be's for you, Dymphna. It be's yer special treat for winning us this cruise. I got these mittens at the Mountains of Mourne market before we left, pure Icelandic wool, they be's. Ye see, yer mammy thinks of ye," she babbled on, while Dymphna wondered what they fed the sheep in Iceland to make them grow acrylic wool. "And I'm going to make sure ye wear it when Yootha allows us to use the pool on the ship. I think we're to be getting half an hour next Thursday, after the lifeboat reenactment."

Dymphna was horrified. She had formerly been a young woman who loved showing off her body, perhaps too much so, her beer-fueled memories of bared breasts in the pub at closing time taken into account, but after two surprise births, the thought of struggling into a bathing suit, and especially one like that, filled her now with dread.

"Did I not tell ye, Dymphna," Fionnuala wittered on as she fiddled with the shoelaces, "yer Auntie Ursula be's on the boat with us? Och, the mortification of cleaning her cabin! Priceless, it's gonny be, but, when Her Ladyship be's sat at the captain's table, feeling all lah-di-dah, and all the while weighed down with the bits and bobs I've stolen from the cabins and duped her into wearing! Especially as Yootha's sure to be informed of each theft, and she eats at the captain's table most nights!" She threw back her head, roared with horsey laughter, then clutched at her gut. "Och, me stomach be's aching with the hilarity of it all!"

Dymphna was immune to her mother's transports of delight at the expense of her kindhearted Auntie Ursula.

"Aye, Mammy, we're hearing nothing but. Again."

Dymphna hovered once more over her babies and attempted to be seen to be doing maternal-looking things with their squawking little bodies, doing her best to hide the edge in her voice. The year before, Ursula Barnett had come to Derry to visit, had saved the Top-Yer-Trolley from being blown up by a terrorist bomb, and even that hadn't softened her mother's heart towards her long-suffering aunt. Indeed, Ursula's bravery had Paddy and Dymphna on the verge of calling a truce to the family feud that had begun when the Barnetts won the lotto years earlier, when they had wised up, realizing Ursula would soon leave for the US and they would be stuck with Fionnuala fuming at them daily. But Paddy had manned up and, at least, demanded Fionnuala thank Ursula for the check she had given to Dymphna for Keanu's upbringing. Fionnuala had done so. Reluctantly.

The alarm rang to tell them they could leave the ship. They had all struggled into the sad emergency summer clothing. Fionnuala had her peacock feather hat on.

"C'mon, let's get this over with, hi," Dymphna said.

Her mother gaped as she reached for the arms of the stroller.

"Ye're not seriously considering taking them shrieking wanes with us and all?"

It is true that if Siofra had been safely with the family there, Dymphna would've suggested just locking Keanu and Beeyonsay in the cabin; they couldn't come to any harm locked in the cabin, could they, and they wouldn't remember anything of Morocco they saw, would they? But now that she was trying to out-mammy her mammy, she had to look affronted at the presumption she might leave them behind.

"Of course!" she snapped. "C'mere you, da, and help me get this pram up them steps. Och, natural daylight we're finally to be seeing for the first time in a week!"

They gulped down the carcinogens as they stepped onto the blaring

107

sunshine of the deck, a group of gray-skinned people, shocked eyes like they just arisen from their coffins. The sunbeams bored into their sensitive flesh and seared their eyeballs. Fionnuala collided with a pole.

Dymphna noticed the real passengers were laughing and trilling their glee as they made toward the gangway, and they were all wearing that most American of accessories, sunglasses. It was what they needed more than short sleeves and pant legs, but they didn't have the funds for them, and what use would they be when they got back to Derry, anyway?

"C'mon, mammy, daddy."

Dymphna didn't know why, but it seemed as if her mother was afraid to leave the ship, to explore the world beyond Derry. She was inspecting the lifeboat next to them, having lifted up the canvas that covered it and was staring inside, doing something on her fingers, delaying the inevitable.

"What are ye up to, Mammy?"

"Counting the lifeboats and how much they seat."

"Why would ye do that?"

"Have ye not a clue that the original *Titanic* only had enough for the first class passengers?" She said it as if everyone knew. "Naw, ye've not a clue, have ye?"

She tossed her daughter a look that implied she didn't have a clue about anything at all.

"Hold on a wee moment while I count to make sure they've enough seats for the staff and all."

Fionnuala hurried off down the promenade. Father and daughter stared at her retreating back in disbelief.

"C'mere," Paddy said, surprised, "the stench of shite out here on the deck be's right overpowering. I'm finding it difficult to fight back the urge to boke, so I'm are. Ye'd think that Yootha would tell off the cleaning staff for—"

"Och, that be's Keanu and Beeyonsay, sure," Dymphna said; with a sniff she could tell her own infants' distinctive bathroom odor. In the back of her mind, she wondered if that's why her mother had decided to count the lifeboat seats. "Go on a give us a hand changing their nappies, would ye?"

She registered the shock on her father's face and took a step back in alarm as he grabbed the handrail and dry-heaved into the front of his sweater for a moment, tears welling.

"Aye, I know it be's woman's work, help me, just."

She hauled the struggling babies onto the lifeboat cover, stripped them and threw their soiled diapers overboard. The streams of passengers stared at her curiously as they passed. She had long since run out of disposable diapers, and was afraid to steal any from the nursery in case Yootha found out. She had lifted some hand towels from the linen closet instead. She passed her father one now, and a roll of tape.

"Ye work on Keanu, and I'll take Beeyonsay." They set to work, Paddy's face green. "Daddy, ye're to have a word with Mammy. All that about Auntie Ursula. I was right with her at the beginning, after them Barnetts won the lotto and wouldn't share the loot. But after all the years that has passed, and Auntie Ursula saving wer lives and all, and now Mammy not caring about—*what the flimmin feck are ye looking at?*," she yelled at a particularly inquisitive passerby. "*Fecking nosy parker!* Daddy, when I moved to the Waterside with the Riddells, I realized the wee pink suitcase I packed me smalls in was a gift from Auntie Ursula. One of many she's given us over the years. Sure, every morning ye perch yer arse on that padded toilet seat with the daffodils on it she give ye!"

"Whose this boyo Fabrizio I heard ye on about? *Och, for the love of— Bejesus!*" Paddy scraped his palm down the side of the boat to remove Keanu's mess from his fingers.

"Don't try to change the subject. If ye're not up for it, I'll be the one to start getting wer family back into Auntie Ursula's good books. All the wanes, wer Lorcan and Eoin and Padraig, and even wer wee Seamus who be's but five and can barely speak or think, they all be's up for it, even wer granny Heggarty. Quit struggling, would ye, Beeyonsay? Och, that's a good girl. And wer Moira wrote that book about the lotto win, so we know she jumped ship long ago. I don't give a cold shite in Hell about how mammy will react. She couldn't hate me any more than she already flimmin does."

"Och, go on away a that! Yer mammy loves ye, so she does."

Dymphna wondered if all the booze her father threw back had attacked his powers of perception. She taped up Beeyonsay's fresh clean 'diaper' and propped her upright against a pole.

"She didn't even want me along on this cruise, and I won it for her! She wanted to take wer Lorcan and wer Eoin. Give you me Keanu. I'll finish him off."

Paddy gratefully handed over the chaotic jumble of towel to Dymphna, and the half-attached baby. He lit another cigarette and puffed hungrily.

"Ye kyanny fault yer mammy for that. Yer brothers had just been released from the nick and she wanted to give em a special wee treat, is all."

Disappointment and betrayal crossed Dymphna's face as she held down Keanu's kicking legs with one hand and wiped down the yellowish-brown juices spattered across the canvas with the other.

"Not you and all!"

"Naw! I understand yer mammy's way of thinking, but. Yonks, I've been married to the woman. And," he looked around furtively, "it's not been all wine and roses, mind. Wine, aye, and loads of it. Roses, but..." He held his hands up in a gesture of defeat.

"I kyanny comprehend why ye kyanny...why ye kyanny...*What's with yer gaping jaw? What are ye waiting for? A bloody communion wafer?*"

The curious passenger's head shot down, and she scurried off down the gangway. Keanu was finally snug in his diaper.

"Out with it, wee girl," Paddy demanded.

Dymphna deposited Keanu in the stroller and screwed a pacifier into his mouth. She didn't want to point out any aberration in Paddy's character. She was her father's daughter, after all. But perhaps it was time she finally did.

"I kyanny comprehend why ye kyanny put yer foot down." "Down mammy's gaping bake," she longed to add, but she turned for Beeyonsay instead. The infant had toppled over and was gnawing at one of the lifeboat ropes. Dymphna pried her head off the rope and squeezed her into the stroller next to her brother. "Now that I'm living at the Riddells, away from wer family, like, I see Mammy differently, and it doesn't be because I'm like a jumped up Proddy bitch what's used to more than four channels on the telly now. Zoë Riddell be's a right sarky cunt, I'm well aware, so I know they have them over there on the Waterside and all. The way she calls them two dots over her name an *umlaut*, and uses the real German pronunciation when she says it makes me wanny spew. Mammy, but, she be's deranged, like a wane herself."

"Ye're a stronger man than I if ye think ye can take a stance against yer mammy, love."

"Is she not done counting them lifeboat seats yet? She be's demented with all this *Titanic* palaver. Unnatural, so it be's. The mind of a wane, I've telt ye. Och, here she comes now. Quick, give me yer answer, you. Are ye with me or not, Daddy?"

Fionnuala scurried up to them, face scrunched with the effort of counting. They could see the total of lifeboat seats must have been a surprise to her.

"Looks like ship companies thinks we be's worth saving nowadays," she said.

"Afeared of compensation lawsuits nowadays, more like." Paddy put in.

"Let's get wersevles onshore." Dymphna grabbed the stroller and trundled it over the deck towards the gangway. Her parents followed.

Fionnuala shielded her eyes with her hand and peered across at the shore dotted with palm trees and cranes, the construction ones, not the birds.

"What I wanny know is...Where be's all them swank casinos? And do youse think we might be lucky enough to get a wee juke at Princess Grace and all?"

"She be's long dead. And we doesn't be in Monaco, Mammy. We be's in Morocco."

"Where the bloody hell...?"

"Africa."

"Och, catch yerself on, ye mindless gobshite. Themmuns there on the shore doesn't be coo—darkies, so they're not."

"It be's North Africa, Mammy, and themmuns be's Muslims."

Fionnuala looked around fearfully.

"Ye mean...*Arabs?*...like 9/11?!"

They nodded, and it was as if it were the two of them on one side and Fionnuala on another.

"Ye're joking!"

"Anyroad," Paddy said, massaging the frayed wool clinging to Fionnuala's shoulder, "we've no fear of the Arabs. We be's Irish, mind. With wer history of the IRA and exploding bombs right, left and center, I'm sure they sees us as brothers in arms, if ye get me drift."

"Why did the eejit at the market have no Irish passports left? We be's saddled with bastard UK ones now, and them Brits be's oppressors of the world just like the Yanks. Kidnapped and tortured, we're to be, if they get a glance at them passports. I'm not stepping foot on that godforsaken soil." Fionnuala's breasts disappeared under her suddenly folded arms.

"Aye, ye are," Paddy said. "I haven't been slaving away in that scullery for nothing. I want to see the world. Off ye go, love."

He gave her a little push off the deck and onto the gangway, turned to Dymphna and gave a halting nod. "I'm with ye," he mouthed.

Dymphna slipped her arm through his, and they shared a secret little father-daughter smile as Fionnuala grappled the handrail and clattered clumsily down the gangway, peacock feather lurching. It was almost unheard of for Derry families, and they felt the collective guilt of the generations before them warning against it, but Dymphna and Paddy were circling the wagons within the nuclear family itself, leaving matriarch Fionnuala out with the rolling tumbleweeds and rattlesnakes with fangs bared to fend for herself. A bit of *the Good, the Bad and the Ugly*, indeed.

CHAPTER 18

Jed was in the casino on the hunt for a hot penny slot machine.

The ship was docked in Sidit Ifnin, but he had had no desire to go ashore. Morocco was an Arab country after all, and although George Bush had added it to the list of Non-NATO Major Allies in 2004, the thought of doing touristy things there made ex-Navy Jed uncomfortable. It would be like having an affair behind Ursula's back, and that was something he would never do (at least, he didn't think so). She herself was in the cabin with an icepack on her head and Xanax in her veins. Slim and Louella were in Morocco. They said when they got back they would show them pictures of the mosque which broadcasted the prayers that had made them all lurch from their beds at 5:30. Jed wouldn't bother looking at them.

He grabbed a passing cocktail waitress.

"Another Bailey's, please."

She smiled and nodded and scurried off through the groups of children shrieking and chasing each other through the rows of blinking, chiming machines. Jed got the two dollar bills for her tip ready—he didn't know if she could spend them where she came from, but he felt sure US dollars were still desired all around the world. He jumped to the next slot machine. He felt the seat. It was cold. He nodded and sat down.

Jed had a system for winning on the penny slots, and it required a lot of moving from machine to machine, which was a form of exercise, he justified to himself, so he was keeping fit as he won money. And he was actually winning; he figured he was about $10 up. His system hadn't failed him yet, except for that visit to Vegas the year before that Ursula still spoke about, and the riverboat cruise on the Mississippi last February, and those two dreadful years after the big lotto win in Derry when he went gambling mad, tens of thousands of pounds slipping from his fingers at the bookies and dog track and bringing them dangerously close to bankruptcy, from rags to riches and back to a second mortgage again.

His winning system was based on two simple Jed-truths: Only a 'hot' machine would pay out, and a big win would come within the first three spins. For a machine to be hot, he had to be the first one to play it in a while; if someone had been on it for hours, it was exhausted paying out and therefore cold. That's why he felt the seats before he sat down. A hot seat meant a cold machine. And a machine could be cold for minutes, hours, days, weeks, or even months; you never knew how long, so even if a seat was cold, you still had to find out if the machine was hot. To discover this, he bet three times on it. If he didn't win big, he would move on to the next. And if he won big, he withdrew his money and moved on, in search of the next hot machine.

That session, after a brief spurt of hot machine after hot machine, Jed had slid into a cold patch. He had already wasted three spins—and put a dent in his winnings—on a wide array of slots he had abandoned in quick succession: the one with the nymphs and extending wild ferns, the one with the jackals, scarabs and Cleopatra scatters, the jumping lemmings one, the buxom female warrior one, the Wild West one, the one with the ladybugs, and the caterpillars that were supposed to turn into wild butterflies when he hit the bonus, but he never hit the bonus.

He was now on a patriotic one, an American patriotic one, he was pleased to see, with George Washington scatters and bald eagles and some strange plant-like wilds he eventually figured were 'amber waves of grain.'

"There you go," the waitress said.

Jed smiled and grunted and took the Bailey's. She took the two dollars with a grateful smile; maybe she was used to quarters. He stuck a $1.25 coupon in the slot, chose all lines times one, and pressed the button. The eagles and stalks of grain spun before his glassy eyes. The machine had a conniption, bells clanking, lights flashing, a disco-fied *Star Spangled Banner* ringing out. Jed felt the room growing larger, the screen of the machine receding from him. His eyes rounded. Seven George Washington scatters! One hundred and fifty free spins!

His heart froze in excitement and fear. So many free spins was like the machine telling him, "Get set for riches!" He had never loved the national anthem or George Washington's face more. He grabbed his cowboy hat, chucked down some Bailey's and, fighting off the weakness in his heart and the sudden tears in his eyes, moved his trembling finger toward the Spin button. He had done it again! After the big lotto win in Ireland years ago, everyone told him he would never win big again. He was about to prove them wrong.

Tensed on the seat, gripping the edge of the machine for support, Jed pressed Spin. He won nothing on the first spin. That was fine. He had 149 more. The second spin, nothing but a scattering of symbols in no order whatsoever. The third spin, the same. Jed stared in anger at the machine. Time passed.

Spin 25. $4.08.

The blaring of *The Star Spangled Banner* was beginning to grate. Jed tapped his pack of Marlboros against the machine and tugged out a smoke.

Spin 27. $4.08.

He lit up. He didn't know what country this ship was registered to, but from the smoking and the children allowed on the gambling floor, it wasn't the USA. In the Navy, he had spent his lifetime fighting for freedom in a variety of US military bases around the world, all the while hankering to return home to Wisconsin. But he had promised Ursula the night before their wedding in Derry that, when he retired, they would return to Northern Ireland and live there for the rest of their days.

He had bided his time in Ireland to get back to the US, relieved when they finally moved back there due to the persecution Ursula's family had put them through. But while he was gone, the country he had been serving, had been fighting for, had changed.

Jed glared at the spinning wheels. George Washington's wooden teeth seemed to be jeering at him. Back in the USA, he was greeted with a wide array of regulations he couldn't understand, and many that didn't make sense: health code regulations, safety code regulations, fire code regulations, mandatory car seats for children, bicycle helmets, carding adults in their forties and beyond, the term 'sexual harassment,' outlawing trans-fats (which he loved), excessive salt (ditto), sugary drinks in schools. Some schools had banned peanut butter and jelly sandwiches, for Christ's sake! The worst for him was no smoking in public places, and he had heard of entire towns in California where you couldn't smoke anywhere. Even in your own dwelling. He suspected lawyers and fear of liability/lawsuits was somehow to blame.

Jed was sickened at the sight of the machine by now. Those damn bald eagles! Coming from Ireland, where everything seemed to be allowed everywhere, he was startled at what the USA, the land of the free, had become. Everywhere he looked, there were signs posted with large red diagonal stripes: no, you can't to this, no, you can't do that. How was this freedom? The modern US he had returned to wasn't one he would feel comfortable fighting for anymore. Everyone talked about Singapore, but was, for example, Cincinnati any more free? The nanny government of the USA was treating its citizens as imbeciles. He was no longer shocked when he read recently that Mayor Bloomberg in New York City wanted to limit alcohol drinking. Wasn't this the nation that had learned its lesson from Prohibition, and was now fighting for civil rights so that people in Muslim countries had the choice to down a beer if they wanted, but was on the verge of denying its citizens the same 'liberty?'

He thought of all the hoops of red tape he had had to jump through for the sake of the store, the regulators that stormed in like demi-gods and barked out what things need to be changed, hand sanitizers that needed to be installed, the hot sauce and beef jerky attached to thermometers and kept at a precise degree of temperature that was basic room temperature...

Spin 74. $8.12.

He still remembered his and Ursula's shock when the US government tried to take steps to outlaw the use of MSG in food. Ursula used to sprinkle it on everything she cooked to make it taste better, and considering her cooking skills this was a much-needed ingredient. And, worst of all, the year before, online gambling was forbidden to US citizens by the government. Jed had figured out a clever way to reroute the IP address of the store's computer so that it seemed he was actually betting and playing in South Africa. Then, two weeks ago, the store had received a visit from some federal agents who demanded he erase his account, and they had given him a warning. He was forbidden from gambling online in the land of the free, while the rest of the world was on Youbetem.com playing craps to their delight. All this, when half the politicians on Capitol Hill wanted to legalize marijuana! Where had the country he loved gone?

If Ursula had also broken one of the USA's many many laws, and he suspected she had, he was secretly pleased. Good for her.

His jaw ached, and Jed realized he had been grinding his teeth for the past twenty spins. He sat, disgusted at the Americana on the spinning wheels. The machine was actually dull, dead, barren, empty, *cold*.

"Having fun?"

Jed stifled a squeal. The British woman was peering at him over the top of the machine by the service button. Usually during bonus spins, Jed hated any type of interruption; he waved away cocktail waitresses even if his glass was empty. Though in the back of his mind he still held out hope of one surprise big millionaire spin this bonus, he welcomed the intrusion.

"Oh, hi, again."

She struggled to pull a seat from the adjacent machine over to him. She perched her shapely legs on it and sat a Zero Halliburton aluminum briefcase beside them. Jed wondered what was inside. Her face was filled with vim and derring-do, and she was smiling, but he detected a glint in her kohl eyes which showed she didn't suffer fools gladly.

"I told you I would find you."

Her smile widened, he guessed to alleviate any threat he might feel.

"By the way," Jed said, "I meant to ask the other day, what's your name?"

She seemed to debate this in her mind, which he found damn odd.

"You are Jed Barnett, yes?"

Jed was shocked.

"Yeah, but how do you know?"

She looked around.

"We have vast databases."

Jed looked around too, but couldn't see the we. He looked at the machine instead, but it was still disappointing.

"Who is we?"

She leaned forward and perched her lips next to his earlobe.

"MI-6."

She leaned back and waited for the look on his face. It was just confusion.

"M...?" he asked.

Her flicker of irritation was replaced at once with a smile.

"The British secret intelligence service, similar to your CIA. And now I can introduce myself. Matcham. *Agent* Matcham."

The hairs on the back of his neck tingled. He gripped the edge of the George Washington penny slot and threw the rest of the Bailey's down his throat.

"You mean...the people James Bond works with?"

As his heartbeat increased, a bemused smile played on her lips.

"If cable car fights and speedboat chases and being pushed out of airplanes without a parachute and ripping off your scuba diving gear to reveal a white tux underneath are what you have in mind, I'm afraid you could be rather disappointed. The reality is a bit more mundane. There's a lot more paperwork involved than the movies would make you think. Most of the time I'm chained to a computer. And, well, I realize we're meeting in one now, but there are fewer casinos involved, and a dearth of high-tech gadgets. Even MI-6 has been experiencing budget cuts in their research department. And I'm afraid, on this mission, I'm the closest thing to a Bond Girl you will encounter. A Bond Spinster, perhaps?"

"Oh, don't call yourself that," Jed said, his head still reeling and, somehow, refusing to believe this classy woman's job was as boring as she made it; his experience with Brits was that they tended to be a self-deprecating lot.

"I hope I haven't put you off, as the assignment I'm on now *is* proving to be a rather thrilling one. It reminds me of the reason I joined MI-6 in the first place. Which brings me to why I am speaking to you now. We're finding ourselves at a bit of a loose end at the moment. Some of our operatives were waylaid in Cherbourg at the beginning of the cruise. My partner and I are now the only two on board, and we are in need of additional manpower."

"That helicopter on the island...?"

"It was an EH-1 Merlin, transporting our backup, but I gave them a subtle sign as they flew overhead to let them know it wouldn't be necessary to rappel further agents down to us. I had already discovered you on board I much prefer working with someone mature, someone with experience, better than some amateur culled from," she gave a little snort of derision, "today's thrusting young secret service force. But we do need someone's help. I hope that someone will be you."

Jed sputtered. He took off his glasses and cleaned the lenses with the hem of his shirt. Agent Matcham avoided looking at the revealed flesh. He put them back on, glanced at the machine, then up at her.

"I don't understand. I think I know how the CIA works, and they would never just approach strangers to ask them to help them."

"Remember, Jed Aaron Barnett, born in Wisconsin, USA, Master Chief Petty Officer, proprietor of Sinkers, Scorchers, Shooters and Beef Jerky, you are not a stranger. We vet those we feel might be suitable as auxiliary agents. When we realized we were a bit short-staffed, we did extensive research on all the passengers aboard. Your record was the most exemplary and fitted out needs the most, all those medals from the US Navy, and also your store which sells arms, showing you're no stranger to ammunition."

Jed was excited. He was also a bit scared.

"Can you tell me what the...*mission* is?" He felt silly saying it like that in real life.

She shook her head.

"Not without you signing some," she gave a little laugh and clasped her briefcase to her knees, "paperwork. You see, I told you? Although one of the pages *is* the Official Secrets Act, which I suppose you might find exciting. Already now, you mustn't breathe a word of any of this to anyone, not even the fact that I approached you for recruitment. This includes your wife and your brother and sister-in-law. I'm sure you understand the sensitivity of it all."

"Sort of like, if I tell them, you have to kill them?"

She trilled a little laugh, then grew deathly serious.

"Just so."

They sat for a moment, looking at each other. Finally, Agent Matcham spoke again, and it seemed to be against her better judgment.

"I suppose I won't be giving too much away if I tell you the gist. We are after a group of individuals who boarded in France, a group of individuals who despise the West and all it stands for."

"A...cell, you mean? A terrorist cell?"

Agent Matcham gave an eager smile.

"I see you've been keeping yourself abreast of all the terrorist argot."

"I watch that show on BBC America about English spies. But...I thought it was called *MI-5*?"

This seemed to worry Agent Matcham for some reason, but she pushed a smile back onto her face as she answered.

"Yes, that's our sister organization, Military Intelligence, responsible for internal strife. We deal with international matters. And, in the UK, we call that BBC program *Spooks.*"

The horror of the un-PCness of the title shone through the streaks of Jed's greasy lenses.

"I see why they changed the name for Americans,"

"Never mind that. This group of individuals have an insidious plot to—" She cut herself off and smoothed the lap of her dress. "I daren't reveal too much without you officially agreeing and signing all the paperwork."

She motioned to her briefcase. If the *Star Spangled Banner* hadn't been ringing out, and the children hadn't been shrieking around them, and if the waves hadn't been roaring, silence would have surrounded them as Jed thought hard.

"I suppose if you're too scared, the cruiser is still waiting for us a few nautical miles behind. I can always get one of the other agents. But I hope it will be you." She placed her hand on his and gave it a tender squeeze. Jed thought it strange she was wearing gloves. "So, what do you think? Are you on board?"

The Donna Summer tune that had been blaring from the speakers cut out mid-shriek. The Americana machine lights and the chandeliers in the casino blinked, waned and died. A shuddering rocked the lead carcass of the ship. The *Queen of Crabs* moaned as if it were some monstrous lumbering creature in the final throes of mechanical death. Jed squawked along with all the others shrieking around them, and he clutched for Agent Matcham's arm in the blackness. The chill of the air-conditioning sputtered and was gone. The whimpering of fear surrounded them.

"What's—?"

Jed had no time to finish. There was a roaring deep within the bowels of the ship, a jolt that threw them sideways in the dark, heads clanking against slot machines and children thrown to the ground. The lights around them flickered from an eerie yellow to their usual blindingness, the AC blasted upon their goose-pimpled flesh, and the humming of the ship returned to normal. Around them, squeals and exclamations arose, along with those bodies flung to the floor. Jed was still clutching Agent Matcham's arm in fear. If he had seen a glimmer of fear in her eyes, it was now replaced with steel.

"The generators," Agent Matcham said, "have kicked in. Perhaps this ship is in need of some basic upkeep. Or perhaps the cell has already begun its evil deeds. What's it to be, Jed? Are you with us or not? Do you want to help in the fight for freedom or not? Deal or no deal?"

Freedom! And he had just been cursing the lack of it. But everything was relative, he understood in a second, and some freedom was better than fundamentalist tyranny. God Bless America, he suddenly thought, and God Save The Queen he added as an afterthought. He was raring to go.

"Sign me up!"

She nodded as if she had expected nothing less. She clicked open the briefcase, slipped her hand inside and withdrew a sheet of paper and a pen. She clicked the top of the pen, Jed saw it was a Mark Cross. The clicking sounds were as efficient as she herself. Agent Matcham's apparent efficiency comforted him.

"As I said, we know all about your brave past, but before we swear you in as an agent, we need to put you through a few little tests to ensure, physically, you're up to the task at hand. Testing your reflexes and what have you. You must sign a disclaimer disavowing MI-6 of any responsibility should you come to any harm during these tests. Do you feel comfortable signing?"

Jed grabbed the pen. He had no time to consider if he should be alarmed at the disclaimer, the speed with which she snatched it out of his hand the moment his signature had ended.

"Fine," Agent Matcham said, slipping the paper back into her briefcase. "Now, please follow me. And after the physical tests, you may sign the Official Secrets Act."

She got up. Jed glanced at the slot machine. The 150 free spins had won him $11.32. Jed didn't care, he realized as he tugged the sad coupon from the machine and followed Agent Matcham's swinging shiny briefcase and her stiletto Louboutins as they clacked over the cigarette burns and strange stains on the carpet. He was now winning in different ways.

CHAPTER 19

The perspiration was finally lifting from their spent bodies. In a grotty hotel room off a busy motorway, Anthea Planck, ticket agent for Econo-Lux, lay on the damp patch in the middle of the bed. She curled up against her lover's legs, unfulfilled. She ran a finger up his spine and wondered when his less-than-riveting performances in bed would be relegated to some horrible memory she would find herself hard pressed to believe she had actually been privy to. She wondered how desperate for a man she was. Let alone the fact that Richard Bright, southwest regional manager of the cruise line, was married, in the back of her mind, Anthea was realizing that Richard was really a bit of a dick.

At a loss for something to talk about and wanting to quell the animal-like grunts coming from him—could her fingers on his spine really be causing such rapture?—she wracked her brain feverishly for anything, anything at *all*, to talk about.

"Remember those rumors of MI-5 on the *Queen of Crabs*, Richard, dear? What ever happened? What were they doing there?"

He threw back his head and hooted with laughter.

"You've been reading too many Tom Clancy novels. And I didn't even think women read them! *Haw, haw, haw!* MI-5? *Haw, haw, haw!* Where did you hear this?"

She launched a pillow at him. Richard the dick was now a condescending prick.

"In the staff canteen if you must know. Clara from accounts told me she heard it from the one who brings the toner for the photocopier. Or maybe it was MI-6?"

"And Clara from accounts knows everything, does she? I've never heard anything so ridiculous. She needs to get herself a life. You know I'd tell you myself if something like that was true. I've told you all about the ship's boiler problems, and that she probably will never pull into her final port, which is still a bit of a mystery to us. Perhaps Puerto Rico, we're working on it now. But, dear, I can assure you," he nibbled on her neck as he fought the urge to laugh. "There's nothing cloak and dagger about the *Queen of Crabs*, no MI-5. *Haw! Haw! Haw!* Or MI-6 for that matter. *Haw! Haw! Haw! Hilarious!*"

She hit him with another pillow to stop his horsey laughter. Then they made love again, Anthea this time, definitely, finally, against her better instincts.

CHAPTER 20—SIDIT IFNIN, MOROCCO

The Floods clutched each other's hands in fear, a buddy system set up from the terror of being sideswiped by the clunky scooters and rusty, dust-encrusted cars from the 70s that came at their bodies from all angles. There were no traffic lights in sight, and absolutely no pedestrian crossings. Dymphna had to be quick with the stroller as one wheel always stuck in the endless expanse of crumbling, rutted muck that passed for their sidewalks and roads. The stroller bucked and jostled as if Dymphna kept tossing it down flights of stairs. The babies shrieked like they were being slaughtered. The adults ignored the noise and craned their necks for snake charmers, belly dancers and men with monkeys on their shoulders. They couldn't find any.

They tramped through wilting palm trees and traffic cones with the roar of pneumatic drills skewering their brains and the dust flying up, and they clamored over broken bricks and barriers and homemade bridges of planks of wood set up to get the indigenous population over the many ditches. They paused for breath in a circle of cement mixers, the sweat lashing down their wool-clad bodies. Even Dymphna, who was partial to the heat of the tanning bed at home before it got broken, was finding it hard going, finding it difficult to force air into her lungs. She didn't know if this was due to the hellish heat or the dust that gave the air a brownish tinge. She wondered if she should have worn the bikini her mother had made after all.

Paddy wiped his brow with a well-soiled handkerchief and shoved it back in his pocket. He thought he had entered the land of the insane, men in long dresses mincing by as if it were the natural state of things, and a traitor Arab McDonalds and a matching KFC with their signs in strange foreign letters instead of the real ones. He knew they were McDonalds and KFC by the golden arches and the Colonel's face. Why the people of this land didn't use letters like normal people Paddy couldn't comprehend, and there didn't seem to be a way to distinguish a big letter, a capital, from a small one.

Paddy raised his hands imploringly to the sunbolt-ridden air ripe with filth above him. "Why the bleeding hell do they think we'd want to tour the city if it doesn't be fully built yet?"

There were plenty of hard hats, but they only saw two fezes; indeed, Dymphna grabbed her daddy's arm and pointed at them, but they belonged to the doormen of the Sheraton that they didn't dare enter, and which seemed to have the only sidewalk of the city in front of it. Leaving the pavement, they stumbled, literally, into a market next to a row of overflowing dumpsters that smelled like they were stuffed with rotting body parts.

They pushed past stalls bearing fruit and vegetables they had never seen the likes of in the Derry Top-Yer-Trolley produce section. Fionnuala's lips curled. Her brain wavered between repulsion and fear. She shackled her handbag to her hipbone. She didn't like this new land. The natives that jostled her to get at look at the bizarre wares were unbathed and unbaptized, their teeth disgusting (!). Vendors thrust items at her she didn't know were use or ornament. She was well out of her comfort zone in a place she loved, a market, as the scams pulled on this side of the globe were unknown to her. She was away from home with what was sure to be a confusing exchange rate. Math hadn't been her strongest subject in school, just like spelling, biology, home economics, physical education and making friends, so she was unsure what were bargains and what were rip-offs, unaware how to get in on the action herself. Plus, she had none of the local Monopoly money. Paddy had bagged a tenner of the local currency from one of the kitchen staff, and she didn't know if it would buy one souvenir or fifty. Though why she might want a reminder of this bedlam of sinners on the fireplace mantel at home next to her good Christian knickknacks like the little bottle of holy water from Knock and the plaster statue of the Virgin Mary from Lourdes she couldn't now fathom.

"C'mere youse," Dymphna said, "there's a café over there, hi! Let's have tea outside on the verandah, shall we?"

"Tea?" Paddy asked. "In this heat? Ye're mad, you!"

"Verandah?" Fionnuala stared at her daughter.

"There be's a special way they pour it. Fabrizio told me."

The parents reluctantly followed their daughter through the wrought-iron barrier onto the terrace where a few men sat, each at a table alone, and all wearing sunglasses and staring at newspapers, an espresso cup at their elbows. How could they read their strange script, and with sunglasses? The tepid breeze from the overhead fans and the ashtray on the table comforted them. Dymphna wheeled the stroller of shrieks to a table by a potted palm tree and they sat down. Fionnuala fanned herself with her hand.

A grown man dressed in what looked like women's silk embroidered pajamas approached them with what they assumed were menus. Paddy tried to hide a factory-floor culture snigger.

"Tea for three," Dymphna said, smiling brightly.

The waiter disappeared. They lit up and smoked in what silence they could as they swiped fat flies from their flesh. The men at the tables kept glancing at the screaming stroller, annoyed. Dymphna scrabbled in the stroller to locate two pacifiers and forced them between Keanu and Beeyonsay's lips. The waiter reappeared and placed an ornate silver tray before them, on it a teapot with a massive spout even Granny Heggarty's best tea service didn't have. He placed one thin and pagan-looking teacup and saucer in one hand, held the teapot over his right shoulder, and poured. The tea flowed like a waterfall into the cup.

"Moroccan way," he said.

Dymphna found it sexy. And the waiter too. She loved the look of 'natural eyeliner' his eyes seemed to have, and the slicked back jet black hair. She arranged her breasts as seductively as she could in their tattered woolen strands and puckered her lips in a suggestive smile, but, as he poured the final cup, she couldn't meet his eyes to exchange a look which said 'let's meet in a darkened corridor out the back away from me parents and me wanes,' as his eyes seemed to be watering up. Dymphna also detected the familiar almighty stench rising again off the babies as the rest of the family stewed in the heat and reached for the dainty handles of their teacups. The waiter scurried off indoors.

Fionnuala slipped the disposable camera out of the purse she gripped as if it might fly away any second. She twisted the Quick Snap nervously in her fingers, trying to choose which passing native she might trust to take the family vacation snapshot. It would have to be someone with one foot in the grave, preferably with a walking aide of some sort, as there was no way the infirm would make off with it down the 'street' without Fionnuala not catching up with them. She took a sip of tea and considered.

She didn't trust any of the men, it seemed like they were all wearing eyeliner—she remembered when your man, Phil Oakey, from the Human League had worn it on Top of the Pops on the telly while singing 'Don't You Want Me'—she couldn't believe it was the Christmas Number One of 1981, when there were loads of songs about sleigh rides and mistletoe out there. Disgraceful!—and she had ejected a handful of Brussels sprouts (she had been clearing the dinner table at her mother's house) at the screen and yelled 'poofter' at him. And she shuddered when she thought of his New Wave hairdo at the time, long on one side and short on the other. What had he been thinking?!

And the women were even stranger, no not the two tatty dancing slags from the Human League, but the ones parading before her now in Morocco. The female foreign heathens passed them on the dirt sidewalk with napkins wrapped around their heads, and not those cheap flimsy kinds they handed over the counter of Kebabalicious in Derry with such reluctance, but the fancy cloth kind her mother used to have in the family home in Creggan Heights and brought out with such pride for christenings and prison releases and other special family occasions But what use were the napkins wrapped around their heads? Fionnuala wondered. They could hardly reach up and clean their mouths with them. If any of them had any sense of decent Christian cleanliness. Of which she doubted they had any.

"I've to use the loo," Fionnuala suddenly decided.

Her husband and daughter looked stricken.

"Here?!" Dymphna squealed.

She withered under her mother's glare and inspected the liquid in her teacup.

"Ye should've gone before ye left the ship, love," Paddy said, a pat on her hand.

Fionnuala snapped it away and stood, fuming at the insensitivity of her husband and Dymphna. It was a natural bodily function that needed to be performed when necessary, after all. She made her way through darkened corridors searching for a door that looked like it might contain toilet bowls. She adjusted her peacock feathers. She found a likely door, but it was locked. She stood in misery for a few minutes. The door finally unlocked, but when she saw who came out, she was afraid to go in. She decided to wait until she got back on the ship. The glimpse of a dark hole on the floor she was meant to squat over didn't help. She was horrified. Back on the terrace, she plastered a look of content on her face as if she had done her business.

"C'mere til I tell youse," she said, the content now a sneer. She sat back down on her chair at an angle, the urge still desperate between her legs. "Themmuns have misspelled all their English, so they have. Foolish fecking foreign cunts. Ye should've seen how they've spelled toilets, for the love of God! T-O-I-L-E-T-T-E-S. Eejits! *Eejits*, I tell youse, and what the bloody feck does them SORTIE signs be's pointing to with arrows all over the place? I kept going through them SORTIE doors to see what sorties be's, but themmuns only leads outside!"

Dymphna remembered something from history class, old Mr. O'Leary babbling on and on about Chapter 15, called The Age of Colonialism and Empiricism, in the coma-inducing textbook, about Morocco belonging to the French in the past. The only thing of use she had learned from the chapter, and it still rankled, was that Derry was somehow caught up in history...*still!* due to a crumbling British Empire. And though she had flunked French twice, she knew that *sortie* meant 'exit' and *toilette* was 'toilet,'obviously.

They screamed and spilled their tea as a unit as three natives clambered past the wrought iron that kept the Floods pent in safely. One seemed to be selling shoe shines, another, a box hanging around his neck, a supply of tissues, imitation designer watches and belts and scents and sunglasses, travel kits with toenail clippers and Q-Tips. The third pointed eagerly at a camel chewing in the heat. The Floods were three pale people with arms clasped around them. The men smiled down at them.

"I am Haddou."

"I am Youssef."

"I am Abderrahmane. I am Berber from Agadir."

"And what the bleeding feck is that meant to mean?" Fionnuala wanted to know. It was English she had never encountered before.

"I shine your shoes," Youssef said, pointing to the table under Paddy. "You need."

"Naw, ye're alright, mate," Paddy said. He knew he needed, but he didn't know if the tenner would even cover the tea.

"You want Rolex, lovely young miss?" Abderrahmane asked Dymphna. "Or Calvin Klein One?"

Dymphna stared longingly, but knew she had no money.

"I give you camel ride?" Haddou asked Fionnuala.

"Are ye flimmin deranged? Riddled with diseases, that beast looks."

"Or tour of city? Best tour of city for best price. I promise. From my heart." Haddou beat his chest. *"Bismillah!"*

Paddy's ears perked at *Bismillah*. Queen's 'Bohemian Rhapsody' was one of his favorite songs, even after he had learned the shocking news the lead singer was an arse bandit. His arms fell to the table. He could tell his daughter fancied two of them, if her fluttering eyelashes and positioning of female parts was anything to go by. They seemed nice people, and a tour of the city on a camel would be exotic and fun. But he was too embarrassed to admit he didn't have the money for anything.

"Special price, city tour, three for one," Haddou said.

"How about swab for ear?" Abderrahmane asked.

He sidled up to Fionnuala, his box next to her cleavage.

"I know you want Elizabeth Taylor's White Diamonds."

"Och, sure, that's me mammy's fav—"

"Clear the feck off, ye cunts!" Fionnuala cut Dymphna off. Yes, White Diamonds was her favorite, but she was penniless in this land, and the anger of her destitution got the best of her. "I'll clatter the living shite outta youse if ye doesn't leave us in peace! *Waiter! Waiter! Themmuns is trying to grapple me private parts!*"

The merchants scattered, taking the camel with them. The men at the tables grunted and pulled their newspapers closer to their noses.

"What?!" Fionnuala admonished Paddy and Dymphna with a glare that make them cower. They glumly inspected their tea. "The only reason I haven't gone back to the safety of the ship long ago be's I know I've nothing there waiting for me but corridor after endless corridor of rooms to scour. By meself."

She saw next to the barrier a native girl the same age as traitor Siofra pawing the dirt with a stick, a form of play, she supposed.

"Away, away with ye! *Shoo!* Shoo yerself outta here!" Fionnuala waved her off like the mongrel she thought she was. The girl scampered away. Fionnuala turned to husband and daughter. "What does her mammy be thinking anyroad? Sending a wee wane out on the streets like that to scavage amongst the danger and the filth."

Dymphna's head shot up. She didn't know if it was the heat or the hangover or the fear her maidenly delights were waning. A relentless stream of dark male eyes had been inspecting her as they passed without even a lecherous grin. She had heard there was no alcohol in this land, but did the men also not have casual anonymous sex? Was that possible? Her brain couldn't comprehend what she was feeling. Should she cover herself up or strip off? So deranged were her thoughts at the moment, she challenged her mother.

"Ye mean just like ye do to wer Siofra? The poor wee 9-year-old

129

wane that should be here with us now, seeing the world? The daughter of yers who ye couldn't give a cold shite in Hell about?"

"I'm sick to me back teeth hearing ye yammering on about the clarty wee toerag!"

"I'm only looking out for ye, sure, Mammy. Child Protective Services, and all that."

"Look somewheres else."

As Paddy looked on, amazed, Dymphna tried to make her mother see the sense of alerting the authorities. Fionnuala was having none of it.

"Ye know the problems I have, we all have, speaking to them what has uniforms on. And I don't want to disturb the smarmy pricks, as after all their effort, after finding wer Siofra, the wee bitch just says she run off just to spite her mammy! I'll never live down the mortification, burning red for weeks me cheeks'll be. Everything that wee geebag does be's to spite me!"

"We could at least search for her."

"If ye think I'd get down on me hands and knees and crawl through pipes and bang me head on other innards of the ship searching for the mindless gobshite, ye've another think coming. Not after a hard day's graft scouring away the remnants of seasickness and irritable bowel syndrome from strangers' loos. I'm knackered. If ye want to find wer Siofra, look for her fecking yerself. But ye won't, will ye, and I'll tell ye why, shall I? Ye be's too busy spreading yer legs for any male of the species what comes near ye. Ye think I didn't see ye making eyes at wer waiter? And ye've not left that Fabrizio cunt's bed not half an hour since. God help any man that comes within ten feet of ye, Dymphna, as yer twat be's like a Venus fly-trap and them strangers todgers be's the flies ye ensnare, luring em in and snapping down on their bollocks. I've spent manys a night wondering about that Beeyonsay of yers. They says wanes born of weemin riddled with syphilis turns out to be spastics, and that Beeyonsay shows all the signs. I've not a clue what perverted winding road to Hell ye think ye're traveling I blame video games and the pop music of the day. I dread the day ye walk through the door of wer family home with yer arm draped around the arm of a filthy *coon*. Aye! I said it! I'm only saying out loud what we all be's thinking in private and kyanny say in public anymore!"

Dymphna thought of the siblings snatched away from her during her few years on Earth, two brothers to prison and one sister to the altar of Lesbos, her mother's delinquent child rearing and housekeeping somehow responsible for Lorcan and Eoin turning to crime and for Moira growing up into a pervert. Lorcan and Eoin had just been released, she knew, but they had been hauled off by the coppers as loveable boys and come back strange men. With nothing to do but visit the prison gymnasium, the young ones she had helped her mother raise had been transformed into a hulking, gargantuan creatures the likes of she had only seen on the telly every four years during the Olympics wrestling matches, and even then only from Hungary and Romania.

"I know ye despise me, and maybe ye've good call to, like. But ye're useless as a mother. Aye, useless! Wer Lorcan and Eoin were happy to go to prison. In they went like...like...praying mantises, and out they came as yaks! It's yer upbringing that to blame. The good Lord knows, ye didn't think to ask where *I* was out to at all hours of the night at 14, 15 or 17."

"Or 16," Paddy corrected.

"Daddy does nothing, aye, it's not his job, but." She swatted away a fly.

Paddy suspected he should have been the one to bring all of this up, not his daughter. But Dymphna was young and in the throes of a new love, no matter how misguided it would probably turn out, and her heart was softer; she wanted to right all the wrongs in the world. No matter what the consequences.

As Fionnuala gasped and spat, Paddy was amazed. His daughter was beautiful, that he knew; his dart team mates back in Derry, back when he had them, never tired of telling him when a night was winding down and too many beers had been drunk. Their lechery and their details of what they'd like to do to her had led to a few flying fists with cigarettes still lodged between fingers, had Paddy staggering home with an aching jaw and a fag burn on many a night. But Dymphna had never looked as lovely as she did right now, sticking up for her long-suffering young sister Siofra, even with her pupils like two raisins stuck in pools of bloodied snow, her hair like the tangle of cords and wired behind the telly stand at home, and the faint stench of a foreign stranger's spent jism on her tongue (Dymphna's, not Siofra's). He should stick up for her. He took a breath: "I agree with wer Dymphna."

Fionnuala shuddered with betrayal. Her face turned the color of rhubarb, and Paddy didn't know if it was the heat or the anger, as he couldn't read her face, so many emotions seemed to be vying for attention on it.

"Honestly, Paddy, I could swing for ye sometimes...!"

"But...ye *do!*"

Smack! Smack! Smack!

"Take that back now!" Fionnuala barked.

Paddy massaged his cheek, and the men inspecting him with bemusement over their papers angered him more than Fionnuala's slap had.

"And as for ye," Fionnuala snarled at Dymphna, "ye ungrateful wee slag...!"

Smack! Smack! Smack!

Dymphna didn't flinch, the flesh of her cheek so accustomed to feeling her mother's palm that the pain receptors located there scarcely bothered to register it any more. She stood up.

"I'm away off back to the ship."

Paddy scraped his chair against the floor.

"Aye, me and all. And you, love, are making yer own way back."

"Heartless cunt," Dymphna muttered under her breath as she flounced off. Paddy's hand instinctively raised to strike, as it had been taught to to deal with any insult of his wife (by Fionnuala herself), but realized there was now a New Flood World Order. He lowered his hand and wrapped it around his daughter's arm.

"Och, daddy, I've forgot the wanes," Dymphna whispered.

She turned and went to the terrace for the stroller, and was delighted to see five or six vendors had swooped down on her mother. All she saw were Fionnuala's hands grabbing the air around their shoulders. She quickly grabbed the stroller and carved a path through the dirt, racing off with her father.

"Traitors!" they heard Fionnuala wail. "Don't youse leave me here on me lonesome! There'll be hell to pay, I'm warning youse! Lemme at youse! Traitors! Bloody flimmin feckin *traitors! Don't leave me here with these foreign cunts on me own!"*

They didn't dare turn around at the sound of breaking glass, the tinkling of shards, and the sharp roar of anger in foreign tongues. They were leaving Fionnuala as she had left Siofra, in a strange and scary place, abandoned. Fionnuala's screams were soon drowned out as the call to prayer rang out again from the loudspeakers on the mosque as

Paddy and Dymphna and the stroller passed.
   "Allahu Akbar Allahu Akbar Allaaaaah-aaah-aaah..."

CHAPTER 21

"If you like em...painted up, powdered up, then you outta be glad...
"Cause your good girl's...gonna go bad!"

Slim and Louella finished off their massacre of the Tammy Wynette classic with little bows. There was a smattering of uninterested applause; it seemed that good old country music wasn't to the taste of the mostly hip-hop audience.

As Louella wiped the sweat of excitement from her face, Slim struggled to slip the microphone back in the stand. He ended up just handing it over to the clawlike hand of the bargain bin drag queen MC that reached out to snatch it back. Slim lumbered and Louella skipped off the stage. They squinted into the spotlights that bored into their liquored eyeballs, and managed, with some bumping and feeling around the blackness for horizontal features, to find their table and the drinks that awaited them.

"Woo hoo! That was great, Lou!" Slim chucked some beer down his throat. Louella fixed her hair and sipped her guava daiquiri, now watery.

It had been, Slim thought, a very copacetic day, and it was turning into a fun night. Except for the songs that every other passenger rapped instead of sang, the existence of a drag queen, and the strange malfunction that attacked the ship when they were on the gangway coming back; Louella had almost been thrown over the handrail. Steering clear of Ursula and Jed for once, they had taken the excursion to Sidit Ifnin, and were now in the ballroom. Out on the deck, they had clutched sweat-drenched palms (their hands, not the trees) and strolled the promenade in the romance of a moonlit night, the lure of exotic foreign fruit in the air, the sloshing of waves against the rotting hull of the ship as it drilled a path through the Atlantic Ocean.

"What a way to see the world, hey, hon?"

Slim nuzzled his jowls against the excessive perspiration of Louella's neck.

"Not in public!" she snapped in her Lutheran propriety, pushing away the advances that were more alcoholic than amorous. But, she had to admit, bubbly with rum, "I loved Morocco! All those palm trees everywhere you looked, and those guides were *so fantastic!* What were their names again? Haddou and Youssef and...?

"Something foreign."

"So friendly, and they knew everything about the city! And their American was great! I understood almost everything they said. That foreign church, that mesquite, or whatever they call it, all those pretty designs everywhere, and everyone in the market smiling at us. And they weren't like those ugly Arabs you see on the news after some terrorist arrest. Very handsome! The women, I couldn't tell, with those things on their heads. And I can't wait to hang all those fridge magnets I bought on the fridge back home, especially the one of the red pointy slippers. Pennies, they cost me. *Pennies!* Everyone that walks into our kitchen's gonna be jealous. And that big square, with the snake charmers and the dancing with tambourines and singing and clapping, and the monkeys dancing along! And the food! What was that mushy stuff that I loved so much?"

"Koo-koo."

"Yeah, the koo-koo. I want the recipe! And that camel ride! Oh, Slim, you shoulda gotten on it as well! Don't look at me like that, I don't mean at the same time as me, but afterwards. It was *so much fun*. When I finally got used to how the damn animal walked. And, you know what, Slim, I worked it out on my calculator when we got back. I thought those guys were ripping us off when they told us how much of their money they wanted us to pay. But that whole tour of the city only cost us *$7.50!* Can you believe it? What a bargain!"

"Maybe I shoulda tipped them more."

"Like hell you should've! Everything they need to buy's cheap in their country. What are they gonna do with extra money?"

She slurped the last of her daiquiri, grabbed a passing waitress and slurred for another.

"And get him another beer too. Put it on cabin 342's tab."

The waitress slouched off through the bass beats and second-rate rapping.

"Do you think we should be putting all this on Jed's tab?"

Louella waved drunken, dismissive fingers in the air.

"Aw, they can afford it. Plus, I'm teed off about all that jewelry Ursula keeps getting on her pillow every night. As if getting invited to the captain's table for dinner isn't enough! She already showed me a pelican brooch, a pearl earring, an amethyst choker and a damn weird Egyptian necklace. Why do I only get stupid dang chocolates? And mine from last night was squashed, and it shoulda been a chocolate-covered cherry, but the cherry was missing."

"Maybe we shoulda forced Ursula and Jed to come out with us tonight."

"What did you put her name first for?" Louella's voice was like an ax. Slim shrank slightly from the fierce glare. Her arms folded before her scanty bosom.

The waitress arrived with the drinks, thankfully, and Slim gulped down.

"If you wanna know," Louella said, her eyes trying hard to focus on his, "if you wanna know, I'm trying hard not to picture the two of you in bed together. I keep trying to get it outta my mind, but the picture keeps coming back."

She shuddered, her lips, curled with distaste, clamped around the straw and slurped greedily. Slim was shocked.

"Are you outta your mind? *Ursula* and me? You're nuts!"

"Don't think I don't know," Louella wiped guava bits from her chin, then pointed a drunken finger in what she thought was the location of his face, "I know what sinful shenanigans you two have been up to behind my back." It was a grunted whisper of revelation.

"Don't be ridicul—*ow!*" Slim winced with pain and his hand shot from the beer glass to somewhere behind his mass. *"Hell's bells!"*

The drunken finger still wavered accusingly below his nose.

"Don't try to change the subject."

"No, really, honey, there's something wrong. *Ow, ow!* The pain in my back's been killing me ever since that boat trip."

He would've doubled over if the table top weren't in his way. He whimpered like a forest animal caught in the metal claws of a trap. Louella's glazed eyes flickered to show she realized something serious was happening.

"Ain't there a hospital on board?" she asked, reaching out and massaging his shuddering shoulders. "There is. I remember on the floor plan. The dispensary, they call it. Oh, my poor Slim. My poor, poor Slim."

Her coos in his ear weren't going to cure him. His chair legs scraped across the carpet as he struggled to stand.

"We better get there."

"Can you walk?"

Slim's face was beet red and slick, but relief washed over it as all at once the shooting pains dissolved into a dull ache in his spine. He gripped the edge of the table and moaned with joy, but still his limbs were shuddering from the attack.

"It's gone," he said.

"I don't care. We're getting you to the doctor and getting you checked out. It was that belaying you had to do on the boat. Oh, Slim! If anything happens to you, I'll wring the neck of that scrawny tour guide! And if there's permanent damage, I'll scream blue murder and sue this ship for everything they have! Just see if I don't!"

"Get the case, hon, and let's go," Slim instructed. Louella picked up the little suitcase of samples with one hand. Slim had brought the hot sauce along to drum up some business, but there had been no takers. She picked up her daiquiri with the other hand.

"No sense letting this go to waste, after we paid for it."

She pulled a Ziploc bag from her purse, scooped the complimentary peanuts from the dish on the table into it, zipped it tight and forced his beer into his hand.

"And that'll dull the pain if it comes again."

She wrapped her arm around what she could of his waist, and he leaned in toward her as they made their way through the tables toward the exit.

They staggered down the corridor towards the ship floor plan, clutching the walls for support. Slim realized that, deep within the largeness of his body, the pain in his lower back had started the day after he had been forced to hold the rope for all the others climbing the cliff at the Savage Islands. It was constant, but sometimes flared up as it had just done. Alcohol should have dulled the pain, but it seemed to be making it worse. His bones in that area felt like they were scraping up against each other in places they weren't allowed to.

"I've felt a crick in my neck ever since climbing that cliff," Louella bellowed at his side. "I need to get it looked at too. It feels like my head's gonna snap right off my neck when I turn it to the left. Now where's this damn doctor?"

They pulled up to a map of the ship far too complicated for their eyes. They had difficultly locating the You Are Here dot amongst what looked like the original blueprints.

"I swear, the staff here's like taxis," Louella said, "Never one around when you nee—There! There is it! Next to the..." she snorted. "Mountain Climbing Room and the...Death Room? What the heck? Anyway, three decks down, and over...one, two, three, four, five doors."

En route to the elevator, Slim stopped and took a gulp of his beer.

"Lou, hon, I think I'm fine now. Really."

"No, ain't! You're gonna see the doctor if I have to drag you there myself. I've got my neck too, don't forget. And if we're gonna sue, we need official records." She gripped his arm in excitement. "Oh, Slim! If we sue and win, we'll be just like Jed and Ursula after they won the lotto! We could take it to *Judge Judy*. I wonder..." Her fingers dug deeper. "Do you think I'll have to do my own hair and makeup, or will they have someone there in a dressing room in the studio to do it for me? I'm sure they will. I'll have my own personal makeup team! Though they got a dang $5000 limit on the show..."

There was a *ping!* and the elevator doors opened. Louella hustled Slim inside. She couldn't press the button with the daiquiri sloshing over one hand, the case in the other, and a purse clanking from her elbow. Slim pressed it. It didn't take long. They peered down the hallway of the new floor.

"I can't tell, do we go right or left?" Louella asked.

"Left, I think."

They counted the doors, and wavered before a black one.

"This must be it," Louella said. She tried the handle. The door seemed locked. "You gotta be kidding me!"

"Let's just go back to the cabin. If the doctor's not there, there's nothing we can do."

"I know you men. Hating doctors. I think they're inside just taking a break. Lazy good-for-nothings. Probably laughing at us on the other side of the door while they leaf through magazines or play video games or something. But, Slim, if we miss this chance for a lawsuit, I'm never gonna forgive you. *Never.* You can forget ever eating my meatloaf again."

"Let me try the door."

He grappled the handle and put all his weight behind it. He grunted and shoved down. There was a strange clunk, and the handle buckled under the pressure. It hung at an odd angle. The door creaked open. They peered into the darkness. They took tiny steps inside. Slim felt up and down the length of the wall for a light switch. He couldn't find one.

Their nostrils clenched in unison at an acrid antiseptic stench mixed with that of unbathed tramp. Their goggled eyes detected the outlines of long metal boxes in rows before them.

"Hello?" Louella called into the metal and stench, her voice a weedy, shrill, rum-infused shriek. *"Hello?* Is the doctor there?"

"Let's go—"

"Hush! Did you hear that? Like a...a scurrying sound, it sounded like."

Slim strained to listen. He froze as he caught sight of something half-human, half-feral clawing along the inky blackness toward them. He clutched Louella's bony shoulder and screamed.

From the glow of the hallway lights behind them, they could make out more and more of the creature as it slithered its way towards them. Slim knew they should run. But he now understood why, in horror movies, the dumb kids at the campground didn't run as the slasher approached. They were rooted to the spot in terror.

It made its way to the edge of the triangle of light and struggled to get up on its hind legs. It whimpered and grabbed the edge of one of the metal boxes for support. And then it came towards them.

CHAPTER 22—FIVE HOURS EARLIER

Hot on the trail of Agent Matcham's clacking heels, Jed staggered towards the emergency exit door behind the poker table, the door that warned NO PASSENGERS BEYOND THIS POINT, the door beyond which he was sure he would find opportunity and excitement. An age-appropriate woman with legs up to her armpits, the promise of action and protecting a country he loved. It was a living, breathing Tom Clancy novel. What hot blooded male in the dusk of his years (and not a member of the Third Sex) could resist? It all seemed too good to be true, but Jed was ready to give it a chance; he was a gambling man, after all.

The further they moved from the casino, the more his nerves jangled. Here in the private areas of the ship the walls weren't brightly painted, hell, some weren't even painted at all, it was all tarnished metal with big bolts sticking out, no velvet or gold to be seen. Agent Matcham spoke as they descended into the depths, her voice crisp in the air that stank of sweat and oil and ancient filth:

'I'm sure, given your age, you spent the majority of your time fighting in the Cold War. So did I. Truth be told, I pine for the days when our adversary was the Soviet Union. Today it's all so...chaotic and, not to mince words, sordid. A rather DIY attempt at world domination, if you like. The Reds somehow seemed a more worthy adversary, with the might of the world-wide communist regime behind them; they were people in *uniform,* and very attractive ones at that."

The people or the uniforms? Jed wondered as he gripped a handrail and followed her down the steel steps.

"Take MI-6's new recruitment process, for example. Oh, I don't mean you, you're an exception, in fact, you hearken back to the old days. Since 9/11, it has switched from those Eton- and Cambridge-trained to coarse but racially correct youngsters in the know on the streets, and rather grim streets at that, streets of doner kebabs and chicken vindaloo. Recruits who are rather, how shall I put it? Declassé? Yes, that will do. Declassé."

They passed a door where the aroma of burnt grease made Jed woozy. A sign on the door said it was the galley.

"I blame the permissiveness of the Sixties, if you understand. Remember the split in society? Crew cuts and skinny ties on one side, long hair and kaftans on the other. This is why, actually, this mission is awakening in me some of my old...ah, here we are."

She strained to drag open a bank-vault type door of rust. Jed followed her inside and gulped. They were perched on a catwalk many floors above the engine room floor. It was a less glamorous meeting place than he had imagined. He suspected, UK government budget cuts notwithstanding, the Queen had put the agents up in a luxury cabin. He had wanted to compare it with the spartan cabin he shared with Ursula.

"I thought we'd be meeting at your place," Jed said. His voice competed with the rumbling of tens of mechanical thunks and wheezes and rumblings themselves competing with one another. Agent Matcham looked stricken.

"We daren't. We suspect we might be being..." she looked around the pipes and whispered, "listened in on."

"Bugged?" That's just what Jed's eyes did.

"Yes."

"So you think this terrorist cell...they might know who you really are?"

"Oh, I doubt it. We're professionals, after all. But one can never be too careful."

Jed peered down, and his head spun. Steel steps and handrails led down to the rumbling depths below, a cavernous room almost half the length of the ship with light bulbs swinging in little cages, pumps and pistons, banks of computers that stopped being state of the art many moons since with flashing buttons, huge rumbling tanks, huge container-type things with cords leading to pressure gauges on the walls, generators and purifiers and air reservoirs and compressors and bilge pumps and Christ knew what, things of the type he had only glimpsed under his car hood, but on a larger scale, the metal calcified with age and rust and slick with grease and oil and clumped with decades of filth, the stench of sweat and sewage rising from it.

"Not many people here," he said.

"The engine room staff have been given liberty, allowed to go ashore for a few hours. Left with a skeleton crew. We, of course, are kept abreast of all the minutiae of life on the ship."

"But that malfunction earlier? With nobody here, how did the ship fix itself?"

"Yes, the passengers were pretty much left to fend for themselves, but thankfully much is automated nowadays."

She perched herself on a barrel of oil. Her skirt ran up her legs. She smoothed it down. Her legs swung. She looked at her watch. Jed saw it was Cartier.

"We were due to meet my partner for the training, but as he appears to be tardy, I don't mind telling you a few details about the assignment. I know I shouldn't, but..."

Jed held his hands out in a stop-right-there gesture.

"If you tell me without me signing the papers, won't you have to...?"

"Yes, kill you. But I feel confident you'll pass the physical."

Jed waited, torn between desperate and dreading to know.

"A group has somehow secured a substance that is the holy grail of terrorists, something able to make high precision nuclear bombs, a super-conductive material that is the short-cut to the atom bomb. We at MI-6 long doubted its existence. We thought it was a hoax, started sometime in the 1980s with 'leaks' from the Soviet propaganda machine, but now, well, forget uranium! We now realize such an insidious death chemical compound, sadly, does exist. And five kilograms is now in the hands of ruthless men, and perhaps women, who are on this ship en route to the US to sell it on the open market to the highest bidder. And, I can assure you, five kilograms is more than enough to wreak destruction on a scale that will make Hiroshima and Nagasaki seem like child's play. I can see from your face you want to know what it is. Oh, I really shouldn't..."

Jed's goatee drooped in disappointment.

"Oh, let me go ahead, then. It is..." and here she lowered her voice even more, though there really was no need, what with all the bleeping and clanking around them, and the lack of other humans. Jed strained to hear the words. "...red mercury." She said it as if it had capital letters.

A chill ran up Jed's spine. He had heard of red mercury somewhere before, and associated it with cheap and easy—express—worldwide destruction. He struggled to think where, but he couldn't make his way through the tangled pathways of his memory.

"—Ah, there he is!"

Swaggering towards them on the metal holes of the catwalk was a wiry twenty-something in a sharp tight shiny gray suit, dark gelled hair with a perfect side part, and a smirk in his eyes. Jed felt instinctively something was wrong with him. He looked at Agent Matcham, but she was smiling. Jed didn't trust her partner, didn't like him on sight, but if Agent Matcham rated him...

"Here's our new recruit," Agent Matcham said to the upstart, "Jed Barnett. And Jed, this is—"

"Ben?" Jed asked.

The smirk faltered from the guy's eyes, then Agent Matcham noticed the label over her partner's handkerchief pocket. She tinkled with laughter.

"Oh, Ben Sherman, you mean," she said. "He wears nothing but. The best of the British. No, h—"

"Nigel," Nigel said. He didn't extend a hand. Agent Matcham removed herself from the oil barrel and looked at her watch again.

"We don't have much time," she said. "The rest of the crew will be back any minute. It's true we've got all areas access—"

"And a license to kill," Nigel added, smiling menacingly.

"But the clock is ticking." She pulled a notepad and pen out of her briefcase—Jed supposed to make notes of his progress in the training. She straightened her collar, which was askew, then eyed them with piercing precision. She leaned against the handrail. "Let the training begin."

Nigel laughed. It was not a pleasant sound. He approached Jed on the catwalk with teleporter speed.

"You want to know the assignment, innit?" he taunted, a fist percolating under Jed's chin.

"Don't be alarmed, Nigel, but I've already filled him in on a few things."

Nigel's eyes, millimeters from Jed's, bristled with a sudden rage. Jed felt puffs of angry breath on his nose. It smelled of stale hamburger.

"I-I've got short-term-memory problems!" Jed yelped.

"And I haven't revealed what his function is yet," Agent Matcham said in an attempt, Jed supposed, to placate her partner.

"Right!" Nigel growled. "Whatever! Lesson one!"

The cowboy hat popped off Jed's head and tumbled over the handrail. He yawped in pain and shock, doubled over. Nigel's right fist was in his stomach. Then his left fist, then the right again. The jerk sniggered as his knuckles pummeled the soft flesh of Jed's gut.

"Wh-wha—?" Jed gasped, his hands shooting out to protect

himself. They were useless against the machine-gun precision of Nigel's knuckles. Again and again they pounded into Jed. Jed grasped handfuls of air, unable to locate the fists of fury as they shot through his flesh, cracked against his ribs.

"Lesson two!" Nigel growled with a giggle.

Jed's mouth snapped open. He was shocked to find it filled with a fist. His glasses leaped from his nose as Nigel smacked his face. His head swiveled from one side to the other as the hard young palms clattered against his sagging cheeks.

"Not the face!" Jed heard Agent Matcham call out from somewhere in the haze of his vision. Nigel appeared not to hear. *Smack! Smack! Smack!*

"What sort of training is thi—?!" Jed wheezed.

"Nigel! Not his face!"

Jed groaned as Nigel grabbed his left shoulder for leverage and slugged his stomach with his right fist again and again, his punches lithe and painful like those of a featherweight boxing champion.

"You want to know your assignment? Fight back, old codger!" It was a taunt spat at Jed's stinging face. Coupled with manic laughter. Jed saw nothing but a blurry approximation of his snide, sneering face. The punches came quick and hard, an uppercut to the shoulder, a hook to the breastplate, a cross to the sternum, and a multi-punch combo to every part of his torso.

Jed was still frozen by the shock and ferocity of the attack. He tried to duck, to weave, but his lumbered limbs seemed captive in molasses. Pain wracked so many locations, he didn't know what hurt when.

Below, he heard the *crack!* as his foot landed on his glasses. And somewhere in the shock, the surprise, and all the pain, he felt deep within him the rumblings of anger, the remnants of combat training from a boot camp decades since, the strength of a thousand pushups in the pouring rain and the spattering mud with the drill sergeant yelling insults at them all in their fatigues, the nimbleness and reflexes he once had, a trained fighter for his country.

Jed lifted his aching arm and, an older man attempting a youngster's game, willed the vestiges of the strength and vim long relegated to the past to surge through his sinews and corpuscles. His fingers curled into a fist. A hard fist. And he thrust his knuckles into the bobbing, taunting body before him. They hit the air. Nigel hooted with laughter.

"Lesson three!" he threatened.

"You little shit!" Jed roared.

He grabbed Nigel's earlobes—they were big enough—and pounded his head into the punk's forehead. Nigel groaned, then roared with rage. Agent Matcham clapped with delight.

"That's it, Jed! Show him what you're made of!"

Nigel grabbed Jed's arms and held him captive against the handrail.

"Right! You're in for it now, you punching pensioner prat!" he roared into Jed's ear. Jed struggled to break free, his veins finally tingling with adrenaline.

"Not if I get you first, you—"

"What the flimmin—?! *Get you yer hands off me uncle Jed!*"

"Who..?!" Agent Matcham gasped. Her notepad clattered to the catwalk.

They smelled her before they saw her, and Jed with his myopia never even saw her. Barging up the steps was a child. A little girl, maybe five or six. Her black hair hung in matted strands against a death's mask of a face, streaked with grease and filth. Her dress had once been pink, and her purple leggings were spotted with ladders. She looked like a cross between an Ellis Island immigrant from 1882, a castaway and a raccoon. Her left arm hung at a strange angle, and in her right she held Jed's cowboy hat. Her face was creased with rage.

"Youse flimmin hooligans! Get offa him!"

"Security breach! Security breach!" Nigel squawked, fists still clutching the lapels of Jed's sports coat. Agent Matcham wittered strange noises.

The girl scrabbled over the catwalk toward the menacing stance of Nigel's thighs. She thrust out her foot, yelped in pain, but attacked his shins with tiny kicks. Still holding Jed tight, Nigel threw back his head as laughter spilled from his mouth. The girl's head shot forward, and, tiny teeth bared, she chomped down upon his upper thigh.

"You little bitch!"

Nigel's hand sliced through the air, but the little girl had apparently had practice aplenty jumping out of the way of hands zooming towards her. She raced across the catwalk and punched Agent Matcham's knees.

"Leave me uncle Jed be, ye hateful cunt! The clarty wee shite's let ye go, Uncle Jed! Run! Run for the door!"

Jed knew the vocabulary, suddenly knew the voice, and even as his brain registered the reality, it struggled to make sense of it.

"...Siofra...??! No, but, they're my frien—"

But she was gone, limping down the steps. As Nigel massaged his bitten thigh, tears in his eyes and mewing like a newborn kitty, and Agent Matcham worried about the run in her tights—the girls fingernails were like claws of the homeless!—and Jed moaned with pain as he bent down to retrieve his hat she had left for him, and as he checked his shirt for signs of blood or a tear or a lost button, and as he felt around the catwalk for his glasses and wondered what the state of them was, Jed was shocked to realize something. He was grateful to Siofra. But he hadn't wanted to be saved.

CHAPTER 23

Anthea removed the oven mitt and picked up the phone. She saw who was calling, and red flags waved. She couldn't rid the edge from her voice.

"Richard? What now?"

"Anthea, love, I'm so sorry, so so very sorry, but something's come up."

Her fingers strangled the phone. She *knew* it. *Why do I bother?* Her nostrils flared as she fought to conceal a heave of disgusted raged. "Do you know how many hours I've toiled over this stupid—"

"I know, beef wellington, my favorite, as I asked. But," it seemed he cupped his hand around his lips and the receiver, "I can't get away from the snarling beast. I'm behind the garden shed now, she thinks I'm having a quick fag break." Andrea assumed he meant his wife, as he had no pets she could recall. "I know you went to a lot of trouble and I was supposed to be there in ten minutes, but—"

"Richard! You insisted only the Gordon Ramsay recipe would do! Do you understand how complex, how many ingredients—"

"I know, love."

"And I had to make the puff pastry myself!" She glared over at the powdery mess on the counter top still, the clingflim strewn everywhere, the rolling pin she had slaved over for half an hour. Tears welled. "The egg wash on the pastry, and wrapping the damn Parma ham and beef in clingfilm and trying to configure them into the same shape and the brushing with mustard and..." She sniveled like a small beast.

"You could always heat it up for me at some later date. But *don't eat it yourself!* The last thing you need is to put on more pounds! *Haw, haw, haw!*"

She was on the verge of flinging the phone into the remnants of the pureed mushrooms.

"Oh, but before I hang up, I heard something yesterday that reminded me of you."

"Yes?!" Hope sprang eternal in Athena even as clingwrap melted on the grill. She tried to remove it with tongs. Perhaps he had heard a snippet of Sade's *No Ordinary Love* on a radio somewhere? Bette Midler's *Wind Beneath My Wings?* She knew what song reminded her of him: once, in the beginning, it had been Mariah Carey's *Hero*, now it was *Mr. Vain*.

'It's the *most* peculiar thing...remember you asked about MI-5 agents on the *Queen of Crabs?*"

Anthea slumped. A stiff 'yes' exited her. She stayed on the line only because speaking to the bastard was better than facing the shambles that was her kitchenette alone. She pierced the dough with the claws of her fingernails and dug deep, imagining it was his flabby stomach.

"Well, and I'm just getting word of this now, apparently there aren't any agents on board, as I told you—what a silly idea—*but* there's a mother and son scam team that *Interpol's* been trying to catch for eons; very famous, I believe they rank numbers 9 and 12 respectively on the Most Wanted list. Let me see if I can get this right. How did it go...? They pulled off some huge international art fraud scam, it was some Damien Hirst from the Tate Gallery. They made a fake of his The Physical Impossibility of Death In The Mind of Someone Liv—"

"You mean the shark in a tank?"

"Yes."

"Why didn't you just say that?"

"Anyway, it must have been quite a task. Who knows how they pulled it off. But they solicited a dead tiger shark from somewhere, filled a tank with formald—"

"I understand. But I think it would be quite easy to make a fake of that, would it not? It's not like a Van Gogh with brushstrokes you have to spend hours practicing before you let your brush touch the canvas. All you have to do is throw a shark in a tank of formaldehyde. I could do it myself. If I worked at an aquarium."

"And they posed as curators and sold it to the Louvre...for £8,000,000. It was their most audacious crime yet, and they escaped on one of *our* ships." He sounded quite proud. "When Interpol found out, they sent one of their cruisers, equipped with a helipad, to follow the *Queen of Crabs* a few nautical miles away."

"Why didn't they just swoop in and arrest them?"

Anthea fumed at his bark of laughter.

'Haw, haw, haw! Dear, dear Anthea; your innocence is one of the reasons I love you so. The *Queen of Crabs* is in international waters. Even Interpol have no jurisdiction. Plus, they're still gathering evidence. All they could do was make sure they didn't flee to any of the countries the ship visited, which, fortunately, wasn't many. I heard the woman got off at the Savage Islands, and they had to send the helicopter after her. But she got back on the ship, which I can understand, because I don't know how she could've survived on that godforsaken island with nothing on it but soil. God only knows what the passengers made of it, but... Anyway, once Interpol contacted us and we had figured out exactly where to send the ship, it *is* Puerto Rico, by the way, they sent their cruiser back to France and will just meet up with them there. They're quite ruthless, changing identities, conning people out of millions all across the EU. Computer savvy, hacking into people's personal accounts at will and making them think they know everything about them. What am I saying, making them think? They *do* know!"

"Interpol does this?"

"*Haw, haw, haw!* Don't be daft! The con artists! Interpol was able to freeze their assets, freeze the £8,000,000 they scammed, and all their online sources of income were cut off. Now they're on the *Queen of Crabs*, destitute and desperate. Most scam artists aren't dangerous, but this mother and son team, well, they're quite ruthless, and dangerous as well. The son is a mental case, an unhinged sadist by all accounts. Who knows how they're managing, and what havoc they might wreak on the ship. But we're forbidden from warning the passengers they're on board and might use their elaborate scams to take them to the cleaners."

"For heaven's sake! Why?"

"I thought that would be patently obvious. If we send out an alert, they will know we're on their tail."

"But the helicopter...? Hmgh! Anyway, Richard!" Her irritation made itself known. "All this information will help me how?"

"I just thought you'd like to know."

"Perhaps Clara in accounts knew what she was talking about after all?"

"Well, no, because Interpol and MI-5 are quite different. You see, one is—"

"Richard, I am now hanging up."

"And I've been too long out here in the garden anyway. I'll tell the creature I had two fags. But before you go, I think she's going out later tonight, her pilates class. I'm quite randy. Perhaps I can pop by for a quick shag?"

Anthea hung up. She dumped the half-cooked beef wellington in the garbage can, envisioning it was his severed head. It was misshapen and smelled rank anyway (the beef, not his head). She kicked the garbage can and went to her computer, typing DatezAplenty.com in a frenzy. She'd change her phone number too.

CHAPTER 24

When Ursula was growing up in Derry, she and the rest of her family—all seven of them!—shoehorned themselves in the tiny sitting room three times a week to watch an evening soap called *Coronation Street*.

It was a British production, so perhaps the Floods shouldn't have indulged, shouldn't have been watching the entertainment output of the oppressors and, worse, enjoying it. Maybe it was the lure of forbidden fruit, or because they found the show more exciting than its Irish counterparts, *The Riordans* and *Glenroe*. Although they would have vehemently denied it, the Floods in Northern Ireland were increasingly more socialized to the British way of life than that of their Southern cousins. *The Riordans* and *Glenroe*, Irish-made, -acted and -produced, were broadcast on Telefis Éireann from Dublin, miles away across the border, and the reception was always bad in the North. Plus, all the Floods' neighbors watched *Coronation Street*, and the parish priest as well—he sometimes discussed the moral implications of various storylines during his Sunday sermons—so the Floods rested easy in their Catholic minds that it wasn't a sin.

Ursula and her brothers and sisters grew from childhood to spotty teen to young adult, their boyfriends and girlfriends came and went, pop stars rose and fell, their parents got older and more infirm, life got more violent and the barbed wire was replaced by the newly invented razor wire, but the after-dinner ('tea') viewing of *Corrie*, as they called it, was the constant in their lives. Indeed, many of the characters and actors stayed the same and storylines were repeated with alarming regularity as the decades passed, so it was a constant that was very, very constant.

They would sprawl before a blazing fire in the hearth, all the family together, brothers Eric, Stewart and Paddy pulling Ursula's hair, she sniping with sisters Roisin and Cait, the grimy net curtains drawn to hide the pelting rain and patrolling paratroopers outside and the barricade of burnt out cars on the street outside their patch of front garden at 5 Murphy Crescent, their daddy Patrick lifting his head from his newspaper and whiskey to spit in disgust at every kiss on the screen, their mammy Eda on the edge of the settee enjoying a fag, clutched like it was her scepter, the kiddies in their bell bottoms on the threadbare carpet, clustered around cups of milky tea and bags that spilled sweets, Jelly Babies and Wine Gums, and packets of tomato- and sausage-

151

flavored potato 'crisps,' dodging the embers the fire shot at them as they watched the comedy-tinged drama on the screen; the fireguard needed replacing for years, but food was always a more urgent priority.

It was a time that, when Ursula visited it in her mind, and she did so often, the memories were all monochrome, as black and white as the tv that, well into the eighties, they watched characters Ken and Deirdre Barlow breaking up and making up on, memories obscured by a cloud of tear gas and framed with rusty barbed wire, punctuated with the screams of children shot with rubber bullets. But the steely edge of those hard times was softened by the feeling of belonging to a large, loving family. The Troubles were just that, but Ursula had had the love of her family. After the lotto win, her brothers and sisters had withdrawn from her life just as the British troops had from Derry after the Peace Process. Her brothers and sisters were friends no longer, there was a divide between them. Ursula Barnett was living a comfortable life, but she felt alone in the world.

Corrie was still wildly popular now decades later (there had been a big to-do when it celebrated its fiftieth anniversary), and Ursula had squealed with delight when Jed found a way a few years back to illegally download it—on the same day the episodes were broadcast in the UK! There were now five episodes a week, and they watched them together, hunched before his computer. The World Wide Web was bringing the global village into their bedroom (that's where Jed's computer was), and it made Ursula feel as if a bit of her was still in Derry. But Stewart and Cait and Roisin and Paddy, especially Paddy, weren't at her side, and she couldn't find Jelly Babies in Wisconsin, let alone tomato and sausage flavored potato chips. So she watched the show while glumly chomping on beef jerky with Jed at her side and, occasionally, Muffins.

In its 50-plus years on screen, there were quite a few times on *Corrie* when a child was sent upstairs to their bedroom (usually at the boring age of seven or eight, where after the storyline of shoplifting sweets from the corner store there was not much else to do with them). They would come down eight or nine years later, ready for the drugs/alcohol storyline...played by a different actor!

It made the Floods uncomfortable. They knew exactly who these new charlatans were meant to be—they were supposed to have the same personalities—but the new actors, usually more attractive and fit, made formerly beloved characters alien to them. It took a few episodes to get their minds around it and grudgingly accept them for who they were supposed to be.

On this cruise ship heaving over the waves to, seemingly, nowhere in her mad attempt to escape the law, that's how Ursula felt now, but in reverse. She looked the same, but she was now different inside. She had gone into her cabin days earlier, did nothing but fret and sleep, and now she had resurfaced, she thought...a new person.

It was time to come clean. Jed deserved to know why she and Louella had forced him and Slim on this trip. She wanted to come clean. Confessing to Frank the Faith Man hadn't been enough, and it wasn't just because he wasn't a real man of the cloth. Jed was her rock, he always stood by her. He didn't always tell things straight, especially when it came to his reckless gambling and drinking. But she loved his little lies, loved seeing through them all. She enjoyed the sense of shared purpose as they traveled through life together. But now she wasn't being a good wife, a good soulmate, a good lifetime partner. And this wasn't a little lie. It was a whopper.

But where was Jed? That afternoon, she had searched various entertainment venues and areas of the ship. She had tried the casino as a matter of course, and while there had even come across a glass with the remnants of Bailey's and an overflowing ashtray by the Amber Fields of Gold slot machine, knowing these were clues he had been sat there. But the waitressing on the ship left much to be desired, so they could have been there oxidizing for who knew how long. There was no Jed.

When she had come back from scouring the ship, empty-handed, she saw the cabin had been cleaned, though in a rather slap-dash manner; the mirror and portholes were streaky, the wastebasket hadn't been emptied, and she had screamed at a glance down the toilet bowl. But on her pillow was her new complimentary gift from EconoLux: a charm bracelet with little gold-plated animals dangling from it. A giraffe, a frog, a goose and two rodents of some sort. She was delighted, but in the back of her mind, she hoped housekeeping would eventually leave the second pearl earring so she would have a matching pair to wear to the captain's table on the night.

Ursula peered through the streaks of the porthole. There was nothing but ocean out there. Furious, violent ocean. She sighed and, for lack of anything better to do, approached her handbag. When compared to the shambles of her mind, Ursula's handbag was an orderly affair, especially when placed beside Louella's rather disreputable-looking bag.

Ursula had separate compartments for money items, first aid remedies—seasickness pills, band-aids, and gnat bite salve—makeup and sundries. She had a new compartment especially reserved for all the jewelry she had been steadily accruing thanks to EconoLux. She delved into it now and gathered them all together.

She went into the bathroom—clutching anything she could to balance herself—for a dress rehearsal for the captain's dinner. She slipped the necklace on, forced the pearl earring into her pierced left lobe, snapped the charm bracelet around her left wrist, the Egyptian-themed necklace with golden King Tut heads around the neckline and dangling scarab-type rubies down her décolletage, then the black velvet choker with the amethyst hanging bit around her neck. She pinned the strange pelican brooch onto her lapel. The gems clashed with the oversized palm leaves of the outfit, but she'd be wearing something different on the night.

She arrived at the mirror and peered at it almost fearfully. The jewels were a peculiar mish-mash of styles and looked bizarre together on one body. She looked like she had gone wild in a pawn shop, grabbing at anything in sight, then marching in madness to the cashier. But if EconoLux wanted her to wear them while basking in the privilege of dining with the captain...

She inspected her face in the unforgiving lights like those in a surgery that circled the mirror. *Am I not entitled to some dignity?* she asked herself, adding grudgingly, *at me age.*

Unable to look at herself any longer, her eyes shot down to the perfume bottles she had lined up on the edge of the sink. Her eyes rounded. Someone had been at her Elizabeth Taylor's White Diamonds!

Louella had insisted on marking the levels of Ursula's perfumes with a magic marker before they boarded, as she said all the housekeeping staff on these cruises were 'robbing jerks,' and as Ursula peered at the liquid under the line, it now appeared that that was true. A shiver crept up her spine. The only other person in the world she knew who also loved White Diamonds was Fionnuala Flood, but the idea of her nemesis having been in the cabin was so ludicrous she dismissed it from her mind. She snorted at her thought. It was ridiculous; she was seeing Fionnuala Flood everywhere.

Louella had told her once that, for all the grief Ursula claimed her family gave her, for how much they hated her, the Floods were the only people Ursula ever showed Louella photos of, "and there are damn plenty of them," she had said, though Ursula didn't know if she meant too many photos or too many Floods. Ursula thought back to all the presents she had showered on that particular cell of her family after the lotto win, the karaoke machine, the tanning bed, the padded toilet seat with the embroidered daffodils, the mortgage for the Flood's house they had paid off for them, and, in a last desperate attempt to win back their affection the year before, even bestowing on them 5 Murphy Crescent, the family home. Which had promptly burned down.

Fat lot of good it all did me she thought, forcing herself to complete the arduous task of inspecting her face, and stabbing at her lips with Revlon's Bed of Roses. *And here was me thinking it would bring me family closer. More fool me.*

Move on. Move on, her mind kept whispering as her lips transformed into a bed of roses, but it was difficult: the wounds of familial pariahness still lingered. But hadn't she woken a different person? Wasn't she full of resolve and action? Didn't she now no longer care about the past? She had people around her. Didn't she?

She wasn't physically alone, she knew that. But in Wisconsin, Slim's mass always seemed to be invading her private space, a roll of stomach here, a pudgy finger there. And he gave off an unpleasant smell, as if his clothes had been left overnight in the washer. And Louella...!

Oh, Louella, Louella, Louella... Ursula thought, snapping mascara onto her eyelashes, her feelings confused and ambivalent. It had taken every ounce of Christian compassion Ursula possessed to forgive her sister-in-law for getting her involved in the defrauding the Church, and for sending all those innocents to the emergency room, and now Louella, her only female friend in this life of solitude, was treating her like an adversary rather than a partner in crime while they were on the run. She couldn't comprehend why Louella was being so *mean* to her.

Louella was one of those strange Americans, and after almost two years of living among them, their mental processes still confounded Ursula. She had watched as many episodes of *Dr. Phil* as her eyes would allow in an attempt to understand Americans in general and Louella in specific. She still couldn't understand Louella's hobbies, needlepoint and extreme couponing, nor her excitement when confronted with a jumbo carton of Dunkin Donuts, especially her squeals of delight at the

Munchins. And she still didn't understand Louella's string bean salad with crunchy onion bits or her chicken casseroles, her soufflés made with Velveeta, her Clamato Bloody Marys or her Spam and mustard sandwiches. Louella had told her once she couldn't blame her: Ursula was one of those Irish people, after all, and couldn't be expected to understand real food and tv shows.

Ursula thought back to the sausage- and tomato-flavored crisps of her youth, and then the roast chicken ones, and the cheese and onion and, her favorite, prawn cocktail. She was stranded in a world where KFC was the real food, where *American Idol* was the real tv. Thanks to the Internet, she didn't miss Corrie, but she missed her own real food. It had been two years of no boiled spuds with a hefty dollop of salt for taste, no fish sauce, no shepherd's pie, no stew with loads of carrots and the special secret Bisto gravy sauce. When she had been in Derry last, she knew the wanes of the day were all mad for the 'new food,' KFC and its ilk, and vindaloo and kebabs in strange half-moon breads, but the classics of the Irish scullery were just that: classics.

But, no. She snapped her mascara back into its case and attempted a grin at her image in the mirror. She was an American now. Her passport said so. She knew the Pledge of Allegiance by heart, and all the presidents. And she had arisen from her bed a different person. She would tell Jed everything. And while she was at it, she thought with steely resolve, she must confront Louella as well. She couldn't find Jed, so she would now seek out Louella.

She marched out of the bathroom and strode purposefully across the badly-vacuumed carpet of the cabin. She flung open the door and peered down the hallway, though why she didn't know. Louella and Slim were at the karaoke, as far as she knew. They wouldn't be at their cabin now, and Louella certainly wouldn't be loitering in the hallway outside her door. There were screams of what Ursula hoped was joy coming from the cabin opposite, and the thunder of rap music. There was a housekeeping cart down the hall.

The lights flickered, and Ursula gripped the door jamb as the ship shuddered. That was the second time now. She wondered fearfully if the ship would make it to the end of its journey to their final port, if they were escaping arrest only to succumb to death on the ocean floor. She hoped the generator had an emergency generator. It seemed it did. After a mechanical rumbling enveloped her and everything around her, the ship seemed to right itself.

Ursula looked the other way down the hallway. A black woman in the white EconoLux housekeeping outfit was lumbering across the carpet in the opposite direction, thirty feet away. Ursula peered at her back with suspicion. She sniffed the air, trying to detect the scent of White Diamonds.

She almost called out to her. Then her eyes clamped down upon the woman's hands, swinging at her sides. Unease prickled on the nape of Ursula's neck. There was something familiar about the woman's fingernails. Ursula's eyesight wasn't spectacular, but she forced her optical nerves to zoom in on the nails. Long, menacing things, garishly painted, with Gothic lettering stenciled into them. A tiny ring dangling from the right forefinger. Ursula bit her knuckles and screamed silently into them as she backed into the hinges of the door in pure terror.

It was the woman from the Indian reservation casino! The woman who, Ursula thought, had threatened her in the ladies restroom when she didn't give her spare change, who Ursula mistakenly suspected had stolen her wallet and tried to break into their house to steal everything the lotto win had bought, and do even worse things to Ursula herself! It had all been a mistake, but Ursula had almost suffered a breakdown. And she had taken down the woman from Mali from her collection of ceramic heads and hidden it at the bottom of the dirty laundry basket in the laundry room.

How can this heartless creature be here? her mind, contorted with fear, wondered. *How is it flimmin possible? Why have ye sent her after me, Lord? What have I done to ye to deserve this?*

But she knew why. The Lord had 100,000 reasons why. She whimpered as her fingers fluttered again and again around the vicinity of the door handle, unable to perform the simple task of pressing it down. Finally, they succeeded.

Ursula slammed the door shut and heaved huge, shuddering breaths of disbelief and fear. She was a prisoner in her cabin of memories.

CHAPTER 25—TWENTY SEVEN MINUTES LATER

Dripping sweat, Fionnuala and Aquanetta forced their carts over the undulating floor past the cabin doors of the more-rich-and-famous-than-them towards the storage area. Wet mops poked out of their carts, the masses of blackened yarn smacking against the handles and spattering droplets of dingy water on their already sodden faces. Fionnuala rattled on and on, spitting with rage; Aquanetta seemed reflective.

"Would ye credit it? Kicked me outta their filthy foreign land, so they did, like a minder does to the alkies and druggies outside the doors of Starzzz. That's wer disco in Derry. Deported! *Me!* Of all people! Och, aye, surely it was me what damaged all them salesmen's wares, all them vases and clocks and whatnot themmuns was carting around, and them teapots of the grotty café and all. Them salesmen was shoving em under me nose, but, demanding I buy em. Not asking, like, *demanding!* They was worse than them from the Mountains of Mourne market. When they've a new load of nicked bits and bobs they need to offload sharpish, before the patrolling Filth catch a whiff, ye understand, they shove em under yer nose and doesn't take no for an answer. Well, they does with me, but with most people, naw. And me husband and daughter had fled, leaving me to fend for meself. Them minging aul pagans started shouting the odds, wanting me to pay for em all. The brass-necked *cheek!* And ye shoulda smelled the stench rising from the lot of em. But I had none of them filthy foreign coins on me anyroad, even if I wanted to pay, which I didn't, so themmuns alerted the authorities, called their foreign Filth on me, and off I was hauled into their cop shop. A mingin tip, it was, the stench of God alone knows what rising from all the desks and, oh, the mortification! They hauled me in to a dingy wee cell. Kicking and screaming, as ye can well imagine. Desperate for a wee, I was and all, and a shite, I don't mind admitting, while rodents and all sorts scurried around me feet and me arms. But wile horses wouldn'ta been able to drag me to perch me arse atop that filthy foreign loo of theirs, no matter how the load in me was begging to be set free. Couldn't clock no loo roll neither. Kept me and me passport captive for hours, so they did, then they stamped some papers and..."

They had reached the storage area. Aquanetta opened the door and they rolled their carts inside.

"Pure red in the face I was, being marched to the ship surrounded by bastards in uniform, the passengers leaning over the sides and pointing and laughing at me persecution. Crucified, I was, *me,* a good Christian, with a bishop in me family and all, and I'm kicked outta some godless shitehole, me life tainted with some foreign stamp on me passport no others kyanny understand! Ye know, me uncle be's a bishop, and I'm afreared having someone in the family what's been deported will get his strucken off the bishop's list. Excommunicated, he's gonny be. Can ye imagine how I be's feeling, er...?"

Fionnuala faltered. How was she supposed to say the woman's name? Although it was displayed there in plain view on her nametag, Fionnuala didn't trust herself to take a stab at pronouncing it, which was fine, as Aquanetta, since she had met her, had kept eying with a mixture of confusion and suspicion the bizarre selection of letters gathered together that spelled out Fionnuala's own. Fionnuala knew that, to the very few non-Irish aliens she had come into limited contact with, it was as if someone had plucked letters at random from the alphabet and strung them together in a drunken stupor to form a fantasy name.

"...love," Fionnuala decided.

"Happened to me, too, years ago," Aquanetta admitted, settling her rump on a barrel of bleach. "You ain't the only one. Can't step foot in Jamaica no more. When my son De'Kwon passed—drug overdose," she added in response to Fionnuala's eyebrows twitching more with curiosity than compassion, "I let myself slip. Now I been to rehab and got myself clean, I look back and see what a crazy-assed, looney-tunes bitch I was. Some nasty shit passing for recreational drugs out there. Tramping through the casinos near my house, high on whatever I could afford to buy. Digging my fingers into all the bottom tray things of the slot machines, hunting for slips people forgot. Searching the floor for dropped bills. Found some, too. Begging for handouts in the john. Who knows how many people I menaced. Can't remember a damn thing. Rehab sorted me out. I found the Lord again too. See?"

To Fionnuala's extreme alarm, she reached between the lapels of her outfit and began digging around in the chasm of her mountains. Aquanetta tugged out a little gold medal that hung from a chain that was prisoner in the folds of her neck flesh. She showed it to Fionnuala. There was a picture of God. It said Trust The Lord.

"I got my lesson learned. I got my eduction."

Fionnuala touched her elbow. Aquanetta moved it.

"Ye poor thing," Fionnuala twittered. "I never lost God. Right by me side, he's always been. I'm in the first pew every Sunday at St. Molaug's, and most Holy Days and all. C'mere, I've some leftover Tanqueray from the Duty Free in wer cabin, if ye fancy a wee tipple. We can have a right natter. I'm knackered, what with being locked up in that cell half the day and then coming back to the ship and hearing I had to do me shift after all. Twenty cabins in as many minutes, I musta did. I need to let me hair down and put me feet up. I think ye do and all. I want ye to join me."

Aquanetta looked worried, but then forced her head to nod, however uncertainly. She tilted her head. It seemed like a momentous decision had been reached.

"You ain't so bad," Aquanetta said. "I like you."

Fionnuala fizzled with excitement. Aquanetta closed the door to the storage room, and they headed to the stairs. They were forbidden from using the elevators to go down the nine decks to the staff quarters.

As they started their journey down, clutching the handrails as if their lives depended on it, and maybe they did, Aquanetta hummed what Fionnuala suspected was an R & B hit of yesteryear, perhaps "Oops Upside Your Head," or some such. She couldn't know it was a Mahalia Jackson gospel standard.

"And ye've to show me how to do me nails like yers and all. Jesus Saves, mind?"

Fionnuala's head bobbed before Aquanetta's as they went down and around, down further and around, her pony tails unable to swing, so slick with grease were they. Aquanetta sniffed the air. She emitted a noise that was halfway between a grunt and a snort.

"Smell like white folk round here." Fionnuala turned, looking stricken. Aquanetta seemed to realize Fionnuala's color. "*Rich* white folk, I'm talking bout. Not you. You one of us."

Fionnuala was affronted for a second, a hand to her breastplate, then understood this was meant to be a compliment. Her grin was strained and fixed as she turned back around and took more steps towards the bowels of the ship.

"Smell like that rich bitch Elizabeth Taylor."

"Erm...erm...that's me," Fionnuala admitted. "I found some of her scent in one of them cabins and gave meself a quick spritz."

"What you wanna make yourself smell like that for?"

Fionnuala thought guiltily back to her Burberry scarf somewhere in the house in Derry. She had cursed herself at not being able to find it, couldn't understand how she had misplaced the *pièce de resistance* accessory of all her outfits. But, considering the weather, she was relieved she hadn't found it and brought it along. And now...if she had it slung around her neck, she could only imagine what Aquanetta might think: she would be walking around with airs and graces. Like Ursula Barnett. She didn't want her new mate Aquanetta to think she was what Fionnuala thought Ursula was: a jumped up Lady of the Manor bitch. There was no greater sin. None. Her brain cells trundled more quickly than usual for a reply.

"There was still a terrible stench from them cells rising from me. I had to cover it up." Then, to assure Aquanetta she was indeed 'one of them,' she wittered on, "Och, me fingers be's falling offa me! I'm dead shattered, so I'm are! I haven't a clue if I be's going backwards or forwards, sure I haven't. I've hoovered that many floors, and all on me lonesome. That flimmin lazy layabout daughter of mines..."

Fionnuaula caught herself. It was a sin to spread gossip about family dissension, especially to this woman who was essentially a stranger. She struggled for other conversation.

"And, c'mere til I tell ye, I'm more used to taking loo roll outta strange toilets than putting it in, if ye catch me drift. Unnatural, so it be's, like condom machines in pub lavs."

They reached the cabin. Fionnuala ushered Aquanetta inside with a flourish of the hand. She was for the first time aware of the smell of them all in the cramped quarters, but Aquanetta didn't seem to mind. Fionnuala headed for the bottle of gin.

"Let's get that drink, shall we?" Fionnuala invited. She unscrewed the top and looked around for something to pour the liquid into. With all the detritus strewn around, it was amazing that the only thing Aquanetta's eyes zoomed in on was the DateJust Lady 31 Rolex lying on Fionnuala's bed, waiting to be put on Ursula's pillow the next morning.

"Hrmph! How you able to afford one of them? I seen them for upwards of 5 Gs on the Internet."

"Naw...ye're...ye're," Fionnuala stuttered, bottle in hand, "ye're misunderstanding. I lifted it from one of the cabins. And not for meself. For to give to me sis—och, it's terrible complicated to explain."

Aquanetta leaned against the wall and looked at her. It seemed suddenly chilly to Fionnuala in the cabin, which was ridiculous, in the hull next to the engine room and its many furnaces as they were. She tried to direct her attention to anything except the look Aquanetta was giving her, as if Fionnuala had just jumped up and thrust her tongue down her throat.

"Och, look at that, would ye! A note against me jar of headache tablets."

Fionnuala picked it up and read, her lips moving.

MAMMY! YOOTHA WANTS TO SEE US ALL IN HER OFFICE! IT SOUNDS DEAD URGENT! CAN YOU MAKE IT THERE IN 10 MINS? XOXO DYMPHNA

Forgotten was the Tanqueray. She stared at the words in confusion and then shock. Her eyes shot around wildly, searching for a timepiece of sorts. Then her nostrils flared in derision.

"Ten minutes from *when?* Daft cunt! Wer family's been given a summons from Gestapo Agent Yootha! What do ye think the slavemaster—" she caught herself again and eyed Aquanetta nervously "—wants with us all? And how the bloody hell am I meant to know if I'm early or late?"

"I'm guessing late."

Fionnuala gripped her arm.

"God bless us and save us! Ye don't think she's heard of me deportation, do ye? Or...or...?"

Fionnuala was suddenly spitting with rage at anyone but herself. Long and winding was her list of infractions of the ship's rules, but none of them were her fault. She blamed Siofra for running off, Ursula for being so much of a snide, selfish bitch that Fionnuala had to steal from the cabins to teach her a lesson, Dymphna for leaving the useless note.

"I've to make it down to yer woman's quarters sharpish. Would ye mind accompanying me?"

"I guess it good exercise for me."

Fionnuala squinted at the vagueness of her reflection in the mirror, plumping up her ponytails and quickly smeared on a line of lipstick. They left the cabin and hurried down the hallway towards the stairwell.

"Can ye be there in ten minutes!" she snorted. "C'mere til I tell ye, A-ak...woman, that daughter Dymphna of mines be's a right flimmin useless slapper! I should've smothered her with the pillow in the maternity ward when the sister's back was turned, so I should've. It's the God's honest truth, I felt terrible queer when she was clawing her way outta me."

Aquanetta's cornrows whipped around in alarm.

"Queer? Where the queers round here?"

"...Naw, peculiar, I meant, like."

Aquanetta still looked worried. Fionnuala, fearing she was losing her as a mate, quickly decided to break family rule number three and tell Aquanetta about Siofra. If she engaged Aquanetta in the decision-making process, perhaps her twin faux pas of luxury perfume and jewelry would be forgotten. She quickly explained about Siofra's disappearance. Aquanetta looked surprised. No, more. She looked shocked.

"What if Gestapo Woman's found out wer Siofra's not doing the quota of work laid out for her? What if one of the staff's found her, or if the wee bitch has gone and told Yootha herself I let her have the run of the ship!" Her face turned murderous. "I'll kick that manky geebag so hard up her arse, she'll have me toes for teeth!"

"You mean you ain't seen her for days now?" Fionnuala seemed not to hear the concern in Aquanetta's voice.

As they clawed the handrails leading up the steps to Deck C, Fionnuala babbled on, "And to add to me woes, wer Dymphna, she be's 20 years of age, and 20 years of terrible misery they've been for me and all."

"What she done?"

"Be herself. Och, I've something to reveal to ye. Not a word to a soul, mind."

Aquanetta raised her hand and swore to the Almighty as they rounded a corner.

"She doesn't be me daughter, not really," Fionnuala whispered.

"Adopted?"

"Och, naw, she came from between me legs, like. But her daddy doesn't be me betrothed, Paddy. And as the creature was conceived out of holy wedlock, I don't count her as one of me own. I see her more like a...a family pet of sorts, if ye catch me drift. Her father be's..." Fionnuala looked around the landing they had stopped on to catch their breath, but there were no eavesdroppers present, only a fire hose attached to a wall "...*the coal man!*"

Aquanetta's features scrunched with incomprehension.

"What the hell a cold man?"

The moved on upwards.

"Naw, *coal*. Wer coal delivery man."

"You mean like charcoal?"

"Aye."

"You got so many bar-b-ques in your country you gotta get your charcoal delivered?"

Fionnuala bawled with laughter. "Bar-b-ques! What are ye like?" She sobered quickly. "Naw, for the fireplace, like. To keep ye warm at night. And during the day, as well." Aquanetta took a step down, her eyes glinting with suspicion and betrayal. Fionnuala turned around and faltered on a step. Aquanetta folded her arms. Again. Fionnuala couldn't understand how she wouldn't know. "Have youse no fireplaces back at yers?"

Their house had since been modernized, but for years Fionnuala had been damned with dragging herself out of bed in the 6 AM chill to enter the sooty depths of the coal bin, shovel it up, start the fire with little blocks of wood and firelighters and the day before's newspaper placed against the gaping hole to get the fire raging; that and filling the hot water bottles nightly used to be the bane of her existence, when the rest of the industrialized world luxuriated in central heating. And she had been lying to Aquanetta: they never used the fireplace to heat the house at night. They filled hot water bottles.

"Got a hot tub, too?" Aquanetta snorted.

"Och, every house in Derry has fireplaces." Though now they were mainly for show and rodents' nests. "Had ye no clue?"

"I didn't even know if you had cars there. All I ever seen is photos of cows and sheep. And *Braveheart.*"

"That be's Scotland." Fionnuala couldn't hide the edge to her voice. "Och, this be's us, Deck C."

She wrenched open the door and scuttled off towards the door which was Yootha's lair. It was marked Staff Director. Her heart thumped close to her throat. Behind her, Aquanetta sawed at her nails with an emory board. And the look she gave to Fionnuala's back asked the question 'Why that rich white bitch slumming it? Pokin fun at us?'

CHAPTER 26

"Lou, we gotta tell somebody about that girl in there," Slim said as they passed the black door on their way back to the cabin. The passage of time had lifted the alcohol from their brains, and they were now merely woozy and infirm. "It's gotta be illegal for her to be holed up in that Dead Body Room like that all the time."

"You mean tell somebody like Jed and *Ursula?*" Louella spat her sister-in-law's name.

"Well, we can tell them too, but, no, I was thinking more like the authorities on the ship. A security guard or someone like that."

Louella regarded him in horror.

"Over my dead body!" she snapped. "We ain't going to no authorities! We wanna be as normal as we can be! Fly under the radar! I ain't speaking to nobody in a uniform!" Slim was startled at the vehemence. He watched as she wiped spittle from her lips. She stabbed and stabbed at the button for the elevator to take them up to their deck. Slim now understood hand sanitizer. They waited for the elevator to arrive.

"And now that we know you're not dying," Louella snarled, "tell me about you and *Ursula.*" She sneered the name and glared expectantly at him through those round red orbs that framed her face. Her lenses seemed to be steaming up with expectant rage.

They had been released from the dispensary, after an hour and a half in a waiting room where the only reading material was the staff's tattoos, and a ten minute audience each with the doctor proper. He had moved Louella's head from side to side and prodded the flesh around Slim's rump. The prognosis for each had been a relief. Louella's neck was suffering from mild hyperextension, Slim's back from gentle inflammation and nerve root impingement. He suggested Louella apply dry or moist heat, at her discretion, to the nape of her neck, and that Slim sleep on his side with a pillow between his knees. First he handed over some seasickness pills as, he said, he had it on good authority the ship would be traveling through increasingly rough terrain. Then he gave them both ibuprofen, advised them to behave themselves in a more age-appropriate manner in the future, no more rock climbing, and sent them away. He also advised Slim to go on a diet. Slim said he would be happy to when Hell froze over.

While they stared at the numbers above the elevator door, clutching each other to avoid toppling over, both couldn't help but thinking back to the strange little girl that had approached them from the dankness of the Death Room. They had been expecting something inhuman, but even as Slim and Louella had deflated with relief, they were alarmed at the disheveled sight of her.

"Are you a nurse?" Slim had asked, wondering about child labor laws on the ship. Away from the US, anything was possible.

The child had placed her right hand on her hip and glared up at them.

"Och, catch yerselves on! Do I look aul enough to be a flimmin nurse to youse?"

"I don't think we're at the doctor's, dear," Louella had whispered into Slim's ear. "I think this is the Death Room."

She had taken a tentative step towards the girl, who flinched backwards like a mutt used to regular beatings from its owner.

"Where's your mommy, sweetie pie?"

Slim thought 'sweaty pie' would have been more apt.

"Nosy aul parker!"

She had shouted it at them, but then, the armor she showed to the world seemed to fissure; she must have spent too long on her own without human contact. Her lower lip had started to tremble, and tears seemed to well in her eyes. She wiped her nostrils, which were flowing mucus. Louella had tried to reach out a hand, but Slim, fearful of disease, had pulled it back. The little girl sobbed before them, tugging on the sordid strands of hair that clung to her equally mucky cheeks.

"If youse must know, but, me mammy's to blame for me being here instead of with me family, as being with em be's a misery. Worse than when we be's back at home, so it be's. When me sister told me about wer holiday, I was of the mind it was gonny be wile fun, jumping rope with other wee girls from strange lands, playing snakes and ladders and even swimming in the sea and poking at the wee fish swimming by me, like. I seen on the Internet playrooms and all, full of playthings and loads of dolls and I don't know what. Nothing but a misery, it's been, but. I kyanny even see other wanes. All them what be's living and working with us be's ancient, and I was hearing wanes' voices from the hallways, and I wanted to join em, but me mammy told me I wasn't allowed to speak to em, like. Put me to work, so she did, clearing up rooms of minted flimmin gacks I never laid eyes on. I seen nothing but me mammy hovering over me and bedsheets and hoover bags. She had me toiling all the hours God sent."

"But...how did you get *here*, dear?" Louella had asked, concerned.

"When me mammy was out in the hallway nattering away to some strange woman, I got up on a chair and pried open one of them gratings what be's in the wall of the cabin. Took me down a metal tunnel of sorts, so it did. It was dead exciting. I saw wee animals scurrying before me, and could see into all the cabins I passed. Some things I saw I know I'm too young to see. I understand them peculiar spots on the sheets now. It was wile fun, but. And then I came to here. The grating on this wall was hanging half off. And I saw I would be alone, as there doesn't be anyone in here. I bumped me arm when I jumped down. Dead sore it was a few days ago. It be's getting better, but."

"A few *days*? How long have you been here?" Slim had asked, alarmed.

"I haven't a clue. It be's dark all the time."

"How are you eating? Or...*are* you eating?"

This question of Louella's had seemed to annoy the girl.

"Nosy aul parker!" she repeated.

"If you don't tell me, we're taking you with us to find your mother!"

Slim had looked at Louella sideways. It seemed she was now less concerned and, indeed, more a nosy parker. The girl bared her little teeth, then heaved a sigh. She seemed too exhausted to argue, which seemed to be her default setting.

"If ye must know...At night, when there be's nobody in the hallways, I go out and rummage through the rubbish bins. I found all sorts to eat. Bits of pizza and what have you, some mingin aul sweeties, but when I unwrapped them they looked and tasted like new. Some aul crisps I unearthed and all, but they was just ready salted. That doesn't even be a flavor. Now clear on outta here and leave me be, hi. What does youse be doing here, anyroad? Passengers doesn't be allowed here. Unless they be's dead. I seen what be's in them boxes."

"We're looking for the doctor's office," Slim had said.

"Two doors down, it be's. Maybe youse need an eye doctor and all."

"Are you sure you're alright?" Louella had asked. "Your arm, it—"

"Aye!" the girl snapped. "Clear on outta here or I'll be telling the staff ye touched me private parts!"

Slim had been taken aback. He had grabbed Louella's wrist and guided her towards the door.

"Come on, Lou. Let's get out of here."

Louella had seemed reluctant, but finally turned. They had closed the door and made their way past the Mountain Climbing Room.

"That girl," Louella had mused. "Why haven't her parents put out an alert for her? It shouldn't be too difficult to search the entire ship. What sort of irresponsible people would let...?"

She had shaken her head, anger and disgust at parental sloth on her face. They had found the dispensary and entered gladly.

"She sounded like...*Ursula,*" Louella said once the door closed behind them.

Ping! The elevator door opened before them. Inside, Louella looked at Slim expectantly.

"What about you and your secret paramour, your *floozie?*" she demanded to know. "What have you been up to with *Ursula?*"

"Did your neck turn you paranoid? I don't know what you're—" Slim gripped his side, where there was nothing. "Lou! Where are my hot sauce samples?"

"Don't try to change the subject! When did it start? Tell me now, Slim!"

"But, Lou! I had to sign all sorts of waivers and disclaimers or whatever to get them released into the general public. Some of those hot sauces are almost lethal. Amateurs can't handle them. They can only be sampled with a trained professional at their side. Me."

She beat with her little fists on the panorama of his shoulders.

"Open your wallet! Open it!" Louella shrieked.

"Ow! Watch my back! I don't know what you're talking about! Your brain ain't working right!"

Her little fists fell to her sides. Her eyes behind the owl-spectacles welled with tears. A finger slipped underneath the bright red frame to wipe them away. The glasses perched sideways on her face as her body was wracked with sobs. It was the longest elevator ride of Slim's life.

"Open your wallet," Louella sniveled. "And I'll show you the proof I found."

Slim felt like a fool, pandering to the deranged whims of a

madwoman. But, groaning as a twinge of pain shuddered up his back, he reached around to the dorsal side of his mass and tugged out his wallet. He wiped the grime off it and handed it over.

Ping! Slim escaped through the opening doors. Louella was hot on his heels. Slim took and step, yelped, and smacked into the wall.

"Ow! I keep putting my foot down where I think the floor is, but it keeps moving! This damn ship!"

She wrenched the wallet from him, dug into the depths and tore out the damning photo.

"There!" she said triumphantly. "I got ya, you cheating good-for-nothing! You got this picture of her staring at you, lips all puckered and ready for action. And you must keep it in your wallet all the time. I can tell it's been handled plenty of times. It's almost falling apart. I'm afraid to think of what you were doing while you were fingering it. There! I told you! I got proof!"

The surprise on Slim's perspiring face turned to hilarity. His head tilted slightly backwards on the folds of his neck flab, his version of throwing his head back, and he roared with laughter.

"You gotta be kidding! Oh, Lou! Lou!"

His laughter echoed down the hall. Louella's head shot around in anger.

"Shh!" she warned, still clinging the photo between fingers that were now configured into a less confident grip. It almost fluttered to the carpet. "What's gotten into you? What's in those pills the doctor gave you?"

"Lou, Lou, Lou...!"

As he wiped the tears, these of laughter, from his eyes, he approached her, arms outstretched. Louella backed into the fire extinguisher, uncertain.

"Back off!" she warned.

"Oh, chipmunk!"

"That's the name you used with *her!*" But he did seem to use it with any female.

"Take a look at that photo again."

Louella did with great reluctance. The sight of Ursula's pursed lips, the come-hither invitation in her eyes, made Louella's stomach churn.

"Look on the wall. In the background. Next to the tv."

She did.

"What am I looking at? The tail of a fish?"

"Not the tail of a fish! The tail of *the* fish!"

Louella suddenly understood. Now *she* felt like a damn fool. She handed the wallet back to her husband and, embarrassed, the photo.

"I plumb forgot all about that fish of yours," she said. "The 50-pound tiger muskellunge, the muskie, you caught in Lake Winnebago back in '84. You loved that fish. Loved it so much you had it stuffed and mounted. And then it started to rot on the wall."

"And we had to throw it out."

Louella remembered his tears at the time.

"And all I have left is this photo, and even then only of its tail. It was the only photo I had of my baby left. It was a damn shame I had to look at Ursula's face every time I wanted to see the muskie again, so I folded it over. You see the crease here on the photo?"

Louella didn't even have to look. That fish had been Slim's pride and joy. He had spoken of nothing but for three years. And after they had had to dispose of it, bury its stuffed carcass in the back garden next to the hydrangea, at times she felt she was competing with the ghost of the fish, the memory of it, for Slim's affection. That had taken a few years to pass.

Slim giggled. It was a startling noise coming from a man his size.

"Me and Ursula? You gotta be joking!"

Husband and wife shared an embrace against the fissure in the wall that was leaking water. And then they held hands as they walked down the hallway together, Louella's head resting against some part of Slim's body.

"Why's my back wet?" Slim wondered.

"Hey, Slim, we gotta sign up for the *Titanic* Lifeboat Jamboree. It's tomorrow at two. The prize is *ten percent off* our next cruise."

"You think I'm gonna go on another one of these?"

"That doesn't matter. Don't you see, we'll still have won the *ten percent off.*"

The look Slim gave her told her he didn't see, but it didn't matter. Her mind was set.

"Where did you hear about this?"

"There was a poster in the elevator. Didn't you see it?"

"In the ele—just now, you mean?"

"Sure."

"But how did you have time to read..." He didn't finish. He knew how. Her eyes could zone in on the words "ten percent off" from fifty yards away. "What's it all about anyway? This lifeboat jamboree?"

"I don't know, but they want teams of four. Me, you, Ursula and Jed. That's four."

Slim knew this without doing the math. He rubbed her left shoulder. She nuzzled against his chins. They reached their cabin. Slim unlocked the door and they stepped inside.

CHAPTER 27

Fionnuala rapped on the door; she knew that's what you should do before entering the boss' office; she had seen it in many films on the telly about people whose jobs were in multinational corporations, and EconoLux was a multinational corporation.

"Who is it?" Yootha called from inside. To Fionnuala, her voice was a brain-burrowing irritant. But she would use her best acting skills to suck up to the woman. She used them often when nattering across the clothesline in the back garden to the neighbors on either side, none of whom she could stomach much.

Fionnuala smoothed down her smock, adjusted the angle of her nametag, ran fingers through her ponytails and called out in a reedy voice: "Mrs. Fionnuala Flood."

"Come in."

As she entered the office, Fionnuala couldn't help blurting out: "That vicious wee shite only did it to provoke a reaction outta me!"

Heads shot up all around. The remnants of her family, traitors Paddy and Dymphna, were clustered around Yootha's desk. Paddy avoided her eye. The infants were gurgling in their stroller by the shredder. A gorgeous young man, but foreign—Fionnuala could tell from his skin, which looked like it had come from the womb needing a good scrub—stood beside the coffee machine, a swanky cappuccino one.

Yootha, hair like a tiki lampshade, inspected the new arrival over the pince-nez balanced on the bridge of her nose. She was a woman static cling seemed to love. Her fingers clamped around a pen. It advertised Viagra.

"What is the meaning of that bizarre outburst?" Yootha demanded. Her eyes were far from sparkling.

From the look Dymphna was shooting her mother, Fionnuala knew they hadn't peeped a word about the missing Siofra. Relieved, she took mincing little steps towards the desk where Gestapowoman was holding court.

"Erm, nothing...ma'am," Fionnuala said with a halting curtsey before the 'in' basket. "Ye don't mind me calling ye 'ma'am,' do ye, ma'am?"

"You weren't referring to some dereliction of duty, were you?"

"No, ma'am. Forget me outburst. I hadn't a clue what I was saying. Am I right in thinking ye summoned me and me family to yer office here? I'm terrible sorry for me tardiness, but I only caught word of it a few minutes ago. In fact, I had to finish off me duties after coming back on the ship. As ye well know."

Yootha looked at her watch.

"You seem to have overspent your time on Morocco. Insubordination cannot be tolerated. I gave the staff shore leave out of the kindness of my heart, as a reward for jobs well done. I don't expect to have my generosity thrown back in my face."

"And terrible grateful the lot of us be's and all for yer kind heart. Doesn't that be the God's honest truth, Paddy? Dymphna?" While their heads bobbed as a unit, Paddy and Dymphna stole glances at Fionnuala, wondering why her face looked so disfigured. Then they realized she had unleashed her smile. A smile as fake as the hue of her hair. Sucking up to Yootha as best she could. "I lost me way. Stuck in the mazes of one of their godless houses of God, so I was."

"Regardless." Yootha waved an irritated hand. "I've just explained to your family why I asked you to meet me. As you are probably aware, this is meant to be a Titanic centennial anniversary cruise—"

"41°43'57" North, 49°56'49" West!" Fionnuala barked. They all stared at her. "Them be's the numbers where the *Titanic* went down. The numbers that surround the earth, like."

And she struggled to remember her children's names!

Fionnuala's voice rang out, a woman confident: "The ship itself, I'll have ye know, ma'am, was constructed down the road from us, at the Harland and Wolff shipyard in Belfast. I take it as a source of personal pride that the film be's one of the most successful of all time. And that's why I'm so chuffed to be part of this celebratory cruise."

'Down the road,' when in reality it took her two hours by bus, usually with rave music blaring and no shock absorbers.

"Although nowadays, the sweat of manual laborers in Belfast is all but forgotten, and all the glory be's focused on them in Southampton what sent the ship on her way."

"I've a limited supply of interest in the minutia of the *Titanic*," Yootha revealed, "and that supply has just been depleted. I was just explaining to your husband and daughter and, er, the other, that tomorrow's Titanic activity has failed to capture the paying passengers' imaginations. It's called the *Titanic* Lifeboat Jamboree," her eyes rolled in all manner of ways, "though, personally, I think Lifeboat Free-For-All might be more apt. I wasn't in charge of arranging the activities, and more's the pity. We had planned on five teams to compete at the very least, but only three have signed up. There might be a late entry or two tomorrow on the day of, but we have to prepare. More teams is better than too few. Hence your family."

Dymphna bubbled with excitement, her hands performing little claps, her breasts jiggling. The filthy foreign beast next to the coffee machine bobbed his head as he followed their journey through space.

"We've been chosen, Mammy!"

"At random," Yootha shot back.

"And what does this lifeboat thingy be all about?"

"I've already told the others. Have them fill you in. You were late. I don't want to repeat myself." She was a dour woman of few words, none of them nice.

"And what's yer man in the corner there doing here? He doesn't belong to wer family, so he doesn't."

"It's Fabrizio, Mammy," Dymphna said proudly.

"Hello," Fabrizio said, with a little bow.

"So I gathered. Doesn't answer me question, but."

"Your daughter has apparently brought him along for moral support."

"But now," Dymphna piped in, "it's wicked he came with us, as we were one person down for wer team. He can be the fourth."

"Wicked, aye." Fionnuala perched herself on the edge of Yootha's desk and widened her creepy smile, to the woman's extreme alarm. "Will ye be there, ma'am, cheering us on, as representatives of EconoLux, like?"

"I'll have to miss it. I'll be preparing myself to dine at Captain Hoe's table later."

Fionnuala squirmed with excitement. So Yootha would have a front seat as Ursula swanned up to the table, groaning under the weight of the stolen jewelry.

"Have ye heard anything about all them gems what be's missing from the cabins?" Fionnuala asked eagerly. "Terrible alarming, so it is. Has any resurfaced, like?"

Yootha inspected her with her eyes.

"Please remove yourself from my desk."

Fionnuala's eyes glinted with rage, blood flooded the corpuscles of her face, but still the smile remained plastered on her face as her limbs gawkily sought to remove themselves from the horizontal surface with a shred of dignity. The ship hit a sudden wave, and Fionnuala's rump popped from the desk. She clawed the air before splatting on the floor. She sat there, legs akimbo, for a few seconds, shooting daggers at anyone who might have the nerve to laugh at her misfortune. She dragged herself up and ran her fingers through her ponytail with as much dignity as she could muster. She smiled.

There was no reaction from Yootha. It was as if, to her, this was the normal way a ship would behave.

"If that's all?" The way Yootha said it, they were being dismissed. She wanted them out of her office. "There's a peculiar...odor rising from those infants. If you could wheel them out of here please and take yourselves with them?"

This seemed to anger Paddy. He cleared his throat and took a tentative step towards her desk.

"I've a few questions for ye there," he said.

A slew of breath exited Yootha's mouth. Her eyes flashed with irritation.

"Yes?" It was pure ice.

"The weather be's getting worse every day we travel, and the boat be's terrible bumpy. And all them blackouts and whatnot. I fear for me safety and that of me family. Are ye sure we'll come to no harm on this boat? And wer hours of work be's terrible long. I no longer have the strength to put the tin opener to work most shifts."

Fionnuala regarded her husband in wonder. He was never one for standing up for himself or the family, especially to a figure of authority, but she was more than delighted to sit back and let him do all the angry bits for once. He probably knew she was going to claw the face off of him the moment they left the office for abandoning her in Morocco, and wanted to score some points with her beforehand to weaken the attack. Or maybe it was a rare attempt to show he was a man in front of the obvious masculinity that was Fabrizio. In that case, it was a lost cause; now that Dymphna's breasts were stagnant, the hunk seemed interested only in the buttons of the coffee machine. Yootha's eyes, though, widened with surprise, then glinted angrily.

"I've also a limited supply of sympathy," she said stiffly, rifling through papers that looked like their personal files. "From what I've read, you were given complimentary passage on this ship, and I've just now invited you to participate in one of the activities. Ungrateful springs to mind."

"Aye, that lifeboat activity, but. It seems dead violent... And surely ye only invited us outta desperation, like."

Fionnuala looked on in continual wonder. Paddy must be really terrified of her right now. Or Fabrizio more threatening to his sense of manhood than she suspected.

"I'm sensing a bit of, let me word it so you will understand, biting the hand that feeds it from you, Mr. Flood. If you don't wish to participate, I'm sure another group of four will be delighted to. Let me remind you, while you are playing, your colleagues will be working."

"And one more thing. Where's this boat off to next? We've a right to know, don't ye think?"

She forced a smile.

"How does Puerto Rico sound?"

"Foreign!" Fionnuala said.

"Go now."

Fionnuala's face crumpled the moment the door was shut. As rage erupted from her, in some corner of her mind she filed away in disappointment the fact that Aquanetta was nowhere to be seen.

"Fecking jumped up cunt, that Yootha! Every ounce of strength I possess, it took, to keep from reaching across them manila folders of hers and clawing the face offa her! And *youse!* Useless! A waste of space, the lot of youse! How dare youse leave me alone to fend for mesel—"

She stopped when she noticed the foreign stranger staring at her. She was making a show of herself to someone outside the family. She swallowed the insults and turned to Fabrizio with another fake smile. She had an unlimited supply.

"Nice to meet ye," she said.

Fabrizio nodded uncertainly. Dymphna wrapped her arm through his. Dymphna had brought Fabrizio along for moral support Yootha had said, but what sense that made Fionnuala didn't know, as her daughter didn't have any morals, and he was probably debasing her on a nightly basis.

He was an alien race, definitely an ex-con, probably a drug addict, and possibly quick with his fists where his female partners were concerned. But Fionnuala nodded approvingly. Better all that than a Protestant. And she was besotted with his biceps. Next to him, her catch-of-a-husband was a pitiful creature. She would postpone the bollocking. Her body trembled as she counted to five and forced a sigh from her body.

"Why does I be cursed with, what do they call it on the telly? An overdeveloped sense of duty," Fionnuala wondered.

Fabrizio was giving quick, shellshocked, glances at the squirming infants in the stroller. He seemed eager to leave.

"Now I must go."

"Aye, off ye go, love," Dymphna said. "See ye tomorrow at three down at the lifeboats."

The jealous sick rose in Fionnuala's throat as they exchanged a kiss. Fabrizio hurried down the hallway, stumbling into a handrail, and Fionnuala couldn't help but check out his arse as it rounded a corner. They made their way to the opposite stairwell, and Fionnuala was just about to roar abuse at Paddy and Dymphna when her daughter gripped her arm.

"Och, Mammy, Daddy! He's wile lovely, do ye not agree? But...But...I've been trying not to tell youse. But the closer me and yer man get, the more I kyanny keep it to meself. Not a word to a soul, mind, but his grandmammy be's...*Myra Hindley!*" She whispered the sinful name.

Paddy and Fionnuala exchanged a look of shock as Paddy opened the door. Keanu and Beeyonsay wailed as they were bumped down the steps.

"The most hated woman in the UK?!" Fionnuala gasped. "The wee wane murderess?!"

"Ye're having us on!" Paddy said.

"He be's from Italy, but!" Fionnuala said.

Dymphna shrugged as the stroller pounded down the stairs, and around.

Paddy coughed.

"Ye don't think, ye don't think...what if yer man there has them same sordid urges as his grandmammy Myra? Sexual and sadistic? Preying on defenseless wanes and abusing them like a pedo perv and then slaughtering them? And with wer Siofra gone missing...Do ye think yer fancy man there might've...?"

"Och, catch yerself on," Fionnuala snorted. "Dymphna's dragged home worse and let them have their filthy way with her, druggies and alkies and whatnot, and all wer wanes have lived to tell the tale. Protestants, she's let into wer house! Orange fecking bastards! Rory Riddell springs to mind. The father of them two half-human bastards, in the true sense of the word, I'm saddled with as me grandchildren. And mind that New Year's Day morning when a *beanflicker lesbo* surfaced from wer Moira's bedroom? Still makes me skin crawl. Aye, much, much worse we've had round ours."

As Paddy and Dymphna squirmed with disgust at the memory, as they clambered down deeper and deeper towards the hull, Fionnuala couldn't wait to get to the cabin to finally unleash her rage on them...

CHAPTER 28
"...ten percent off!"

"God bless us and save us! Are ye sure that's all we're meant to do? Sit werselves down in an empty lifeboat? Scraping the barrel with them activities, aren't they? Aye, it'll be a wile craic anyroad, so it will. We can take some photos of us in wer *Titanic*-type lifeboat. One for the photo album. See ye on the promenade at four, then. And ta for letting me know, Louella, love."

Feverish thoughts ricocheted through Jed's skull. Ursula's voice at the door roused himself from strange, disjointed dreams of swinging from the Burj Khalifa, diving through the fiery explosions of bombs, but instead of Agent Matcham at his side it was Ursula, grabbing his arm and twittering with fear. Ursula was trailing a kicking, squawking Siofra behind them.

He heard the door close. Then the bathroom door creaked open.

His organs groaned, more in pain than his wakening brain, his body being tossed from one end of the bed to the other as the ship carved its way through the protesting morass of the Atlantic towards the Caribbean. Jed wanted to firmly ensconce himself in the mattress and go back to sleep. But he had to drag himself out of bed. He had his first mission to perform that night as a brand spanking new member of MI-6! He tried to peel his eyelids open. They seemed glued to his eyeballs.

The toilet flushed.

On the backs of those eyelids he saw playing out—like a particularly unentertaining movie—his life before he had met Agent Matcham: bland, dull, plodding, decades spent going through the motions. He had had to enlist in the military, the government had given him no choice, but he had re-enlisted himself again and again for the excitement, the living in exotic locations, the smell of danger and excitement. The only time he had actually fired a gun was on the range during boot camp, he had rarely been on a destroyer, and never been in on the action on the ocean equivalent of the front line; he had been dressed in uniform, but he was a non-commissioned officer confined to an office. And a day spent typing was a day spent typing no matter how war-torn or exciting the location. He heard Ursula turn the shower on.

One of the reasons he had fallen in love with Ursula when he had been stationed on the Naval base in Derry was her exotic foreignness.

He certainly hadn't married her for her cooking! Every time she spoke in that strange accent of hers, the weird words she used to express the most mundane things, a thrill had coursed through him. This wasn't true any longer; he had grown used to her accent and her vocabulary. Though...he had to admit, the one exciting constant in his life was Ursula. Or it had been when they were in Derry, at any rate. Some new battle with her family always seemed to be brewing, from imagined slights erupting into drunken brawls to nephews being dragged off to prison, and so on.

Jed's organs moaned as the ship lurched over another massive wave. His bruises had bruises. He thought a rib or two might be bruised. The shower turned off.

His life in Wisconsin the past two years, figuring out what the hottest hot sauces were and ordering them for the store, stocking the shelves of ammunition, paying the bills, listening to Ursula babble on about her family although they were half the Earth away, everything was receding into the past. He thought back to the Indian reservation casinos he visited regularly, the penny slots, cold and hot, the complimentary alcohol, the illegal gambling online...

Perhaps gambling and drinking had been crutches to fill in the thing missing from his life: excitement? Sure, his heart had skipped a few beats when the federal government had made international gambling online illegal, and when they had sent him the notice that 'they knew' and would be visiting him soon; he had been happy to leave the country to let his ip address cool down a bit. But now he had no desire to gamble, no desire to drink; he had his mission to perform.

Ursula was gargling over the sink. She spat down the drain.

The nape of his neck also ached, but he realized this was due not to Nigel, but from the $1,200 he had hidden there. After Jed had passed Nigel's 'express guerrilla war-fighting test,' as they had termed it, Agent Matcham had pulled his copy of the Official Secrets Act out of her briefcase and Jed, fingers shuddering from pain or excitement, he didn't know, had signed it. Then Agent Matcham had reached again into her briefcase and handed over $1000. She said it was from 'Her Majesty's Treasury,' though Jed was a bit confused as to why the Queen was dealing in US dollars. He had had to sign a release form for the money. Agent Matcham said the assignment would take place the next night, but the money was for the trial run Jed would go through that afternoon. And if he passed this second test, she stressed, he would truly be one of them and be the star agent on the night, though of course a junior one.

There was a smell... He pried his left eye open. And shrieked. Ursula was hovering over him in her nightdress and damp eggplant hair, her eyes brimming with torture. She held out a cup of coffee for him. He was terrified of it scalding him.

"She's here! She's here!" Ursula hissed into his face.

Jed jerked from the pillow. His eyes shot around the cabin, trying to locate 'she.'

"Och, Jed, terrible heartscared, afeared, so I am are. All hours, ye was gone last night."

He grabbed the coffee. "What's wrong? *Who's* here?"

She perched herself beside him on the tousled sheets. He winced as her leg brushed against a bruised knee.

"Och, the show I made of meself back on that plane when I thought I caught sight of her, the persecution I put ye through then..."

Jed stared in shock.

"You mean...?"

"Aye! That madwoman from the casino in Wisconsin. Walking down the corridor plain as day, I saw her. In some maid outfit. How could she be here, Jed? *How?* I've scoffed down that many Xanax tablets, I'm clean out of me monthly supply. And we've a few more days left on this journey of wers. How me brain's meant to handle the stress, I haven't a clue."

"But—"

"Aye, I know. It sounds mad. It might be me mind seeing her only. Kyanny mistake them nails of hers, but, nor that tattoo of her dead son on her arm. Fearful for me life, I was last night. But now ye're here with me. I feel safe. And I really don't know if it be's her. Just make sure ye stay by me side, is all I ask. And that's the end of the discussion. I'll shut me bake about it now. I don't want ye hauling me off to the mental home, like. I just want ye to know what I thought me eyes clamped sight of."

Jed took a sip of scalding coffee, feeling disingenuous, and rubbed her fingers in a manner he hoped was comforting. She ran a hand through what was left of his hair. She leaned her face in towards his, and he could see the circles of her contacts.

"Och, Jed, ye're me rock. What would I do without ye, like?"

Jed blinked. He was a man torn. Ursula was relying on him, and wanted him to protect her from the nameless woman who had threatened her in a public restroom a year ago. While he knew her niece Siofra was also on the ship! And that could only mean the rest of her family, maybe even the entire Flood clan, was aboard. He shuddered at the thought. Ursula should know. Forewarned was forearmed. But if he told Ursula about Siofra, he would have to explain how the little girl had seen him getting the lumps knocked out of him by a sharply-dressed jerk in the engine room. And he couldn't; he had signed Official Secrets Act. Wouldn't he be arrested for treason? Even though he wasn't a British citizen? He didn't know. Oh, how his head ached, and for once it wasn't alcohol.

"Them slots must've been keeping ye busy, like. I couldn't wait no longer. I scoffed down some of them sleeping tablets and all and finally passed out. The chemicals that must be pumping through me bloodstream, there must be that many of them me body could be used for medical research. And I've something more to tell ye. I want to come clean. Ye need to know why me and Louella dragged ye on this cruise with us. Something terrible, we've done. On the run from the coppers, so we are. Sleepless nights, it's been causing me, not letting ye in on what we done."

Jed held his hand up. He now had secrets he could never reveal to his wife, so he didn't want to know hers. Quid pro quo, but in reverse.

"I understand why you didn't want to tell me. And I just want you to know, whatever you're running from, I'm behind you all the way."

He moved and winced. He suspected a third rib was bruised. He felt around on the nightstand for his glasses and put them on. Now he could see his wife clearly. Ursula looked a bit put out, her revelation waved away like that.

"What's up with them glasses of yers? They be's cracked."

Jed peered at her through the fissure in his left lens. She moved the sheet. His pajama top was hiked up over his stomach. She yelped at the sight.

"Where did ye get all them bruises from? Stumbling into the arms of the slot machines? C'mere, the weather's been dead terrible, but was it the sea or the drink? They look wile sore."

She put her fingers out to inspect them, but Jed waved her away.

"Don't touch! They hurt! Yes, I stumbled and fell into a slot machine. It's this damn ship. I can't walk correctly."

Ursula inspected his face with concern.

"It was the waves," Jed insisted. "And that's all I want to say about it."

Ursula considered for a second, then nodded. "Anyroad," she said. "Louella was just by. She's suddenly being wile civil to me, and I thank the Lord for that, and the Virgin Mary for that matter. I guess she and Slim had a good night last night. She's signed us up for some activity this afternoon. The *Titanic* Lifeboat Jamboree, it be's called. We're to get the four of us into an available lifeboat."

"How can that be an activity? How infirm do they think we are?"

"It's what she said. They need teams of four, so it be's the four of us."

"Seems easy enough. It'll be a cinch. What time is it at, though? I've signed myself up for the poker tournament tonight."

Ursula's eyes flickered with suspicion.

"Poker? I've only ever seen ye on the penny slots. And that one time on the roulette wheel."

"Yeah, um, I decided, uh, to mix it up a bit. See how good I am at it. I do know the rules."

The suspicion wouldn't leave Ursula's eyes.

"I swear to the heavenly Father, don't ye lay a finger on that $25,000 in wer special account! If I see ye hovering next to that ATM machine on board..!"

"Never. That's for our future."

He wished he could reveal the Queen of England was paying for his gambling. He had always wanted to share everything with Ursula. Theirs was a real marriage of love and sharing and *trust*, the rarity of two good people who committed themselves to each other before the eyes of God and stayed true to that promise in a world of fickle and secular hearts. But...that damn Official Secrets Act!

"And the tournament starts at ten."

"That's grand. The lifeboat thingy be's at four. And don't forget," she gripped his arm in excitement. Jed grit his teeth from the pain. "We're to be at the captain's dinner tonight at eight! Och, Jed, what a fine life we're leading now. If only it wasn't for that woman from the cas—och, I said I'd never utter her again."

183

"I've got to get in the shower," Jed said.

"Off ye go. Then we can have the breakfast buffet. I'll tell Louella and Slim to meet us in the dining room in half an hour, shall I? And I'll lay yer tuxedo on the bed for the dinner tonight. It's wile lucky we thought this was a black tie opera cruise, aye?"

"Yeah, and, yeah, you do that."

Under the steaming water, yelping as he ran the soap over his wounds, guilt gnawed at Jed. He felt he was deceiving Ursula. But if the Floods were indeed all aboard, and Ursula never ran into them, that would be the best. He tried to convince himself that there was no reason for Ursula to be unduly worried. It was a large ship, and ignorance was bliss. He forced the knowledge Siofra had seen him into a corner of his mind to think about later, and concentrated on the mission at hand. He scrubbed shampoo into his scalp.

As Agent Matcham had explained, each mission had to be specially tailored to suit the psychological makeup of the criminals involved, and after the home office profilers had conducted much research into the minds of the members of this particularly ruthless terrorist cell, they had identified gambling as their weakness. Either that or leather-clad sex, but Agent Matcham and Nigel (Jed supposed the little shit hadn't earned the title of 'Agent' yet, and he hoped he never would) had decided they would take advantage of the gambling weakness. Jed had been relieved. He lathered his armpits.

To that end, MI-6 had devised an elaborate, winding series of events, much like a *Mission: Impossible* plot, which had to unfold over the period of a few days on the ship. It would culminate in the terrorists handing over the red mercury to Agent Matcham, and for the three of them being responsible for making the world safe for democracy. They couldn't tell him who their adversaries were, couldn't show him photos. It would make Jed too nervous and unable to perform correctly. Plus, showing him the entire portfolio of all the cell members was too dangerous; such complete knowledge might get him killed, and he was only a junior agent at the moment, after all.

They also couldn't reveal the entire mission at the moment, they could only give him information piecemeal as time went by, 'in dribs and drabs,' was how Agent Matcham put it. But eventually he would understand their whole plan, and the reason that particular game during the poker tournament was important. Nigel had seemed to find this sentence wildly amusing for some strange reason.

Jed had been told he wouldn't know which of the cell members would be sat the table. At some stage during the game, Agent Matcham revealed, "After the cards are cut, Nigel will give you the sign. Oh, yes, you won't be scared. Nigel will be at the table with you. And I will be in the room as well, though in an ancillary capacity in the background. He will nod to let you know who you should try to let win the game. Obviously, we can only control so much, as there will be an element of chance due to the deal of the cards. The croupier is not a fellow agent. But Nigel will know, depending on how much the terrorists are winning or losing during a particular hand, how the important hand should play out. He will nod once if you are supposed to win, twice for the person to your left, three times for the person to your right, and so on. If he nods four times, you must let Nigel win." Agent Matcham laid a hand on Jed's thigh here. "Don't miscount. Such a mistake would be...egregious, and might have disastrous international consequences. And when Nigel fixes his tie, you must leave the table and cash out."

Conditioner stung Jed's eyes. He let the water wash it out. The assignment seemed wildly improbable and even ludicrous, but that was real life, wasn't it? If anyone tried to explain it to you, it wouldn't make much sense. But was an MI-6 operation really real life? Jed couldn't think straight. He turned off the water and gripped the shower stall as the ship thrust to the side, Jed realized he was excited, but also scared. Before this, winning the lottery had been the scariest experience in his life; he had been pale for weeks after the balls had landed.

But he had loved the trial run the night before. Jed and Nigel had sat at the poker table with 'one of the terrorists.' Agent Matcham had pointed out the woman with the floppy sunhat that had been on the Savage Islands with them. Jed was surprised; the old woman didn't seem like a terrorist. But Agent Matcham had told him that's why she had been on the Savage Islands excursion: to keep an eye on her. And then Nigel had done his nods.

Many times it had worked, they had folded when they should have bid higher or stayed, and the woman had won. And sometimes Nigel had won when he had nodded four times. And, best of all, the biggest hand, Nigel had nodded once, and Jed had won it all. Then Nigel had fixed his tie. And, as an added bonus, though he would receive a paycheck later, of course, Agent Matcham said, they had let Jed keep the winnings. He was up $200 on the $1000 they had given him. The Brit government was certainly very generous!

Still wondering what egregious meant, Jed toweled himself dry. He wrapped his bathrobe around him and left the bathroom.

Ursula was glaring at him, a fistful of hundreds in her hand.

"What," she demanded, "is the meaning of this? Where did ye get it from?"

"Wh-where did you—"

"I was plumping the pillows, as ye do, God knows the housekeeping never does, when I found stacks of money underneath! So help me, Jed, if ye've been dipping into wer special account...!"

"No, Ursula!" Jed said. "I swear I didn't. You can check it! Go to the ATM and see! I must've won it last night. I guess I had too many Bailey's. But now I seem to recall...I had a big jackpot on the Cleopatra Jones machine. Yeah, that's it. Cleopatra Jones."

"Sorry, love. I shouldn't've doubted ye."

Ursula looked guilty as she placed the money back on the sheets. And Jed felt guilty about her feeling guilty. He got dressed.

CHAPTER 29

"Deempahna!"

Fabrizio inspected Dymphna with his gorgeous heroin-addict-type eyes. His muscular arm was so close to her lips she could nibble it. And she wanted to. He was pointing at Keanu and Beeyonsay, who were squirming uncomfortably against each other in the stroller, a mass of tiny food-spattered limbs.

"Why you notta said to me befora about this..." he struggled with the vocabulary, "this *things?*"

With shards of rain biting into their flesh, droves of ocean water shooting over the side of the ship and drenching their calves, clutching handrails and pipes for support as the ship lurched like a drunk trying to make her way up Shipquay Street, they were waiting for the activity to begin. One of the teams had still to arrive.

Fionnuala looked on at the exchange between her daughter and her new victim, arms crossed. A good grandmother would have objected to her loved ones referred to as 'things.' A grandmother not saddled with half-Proddy bastards as grandchildren. She stifled a giggle. Dymphna stamped her foot, curls whipping through the violent air.

"Keanu and Beeyonsay doesn't be things! Themmuns be's *babies*. I'm sure you've heard of them before? Small human beings?"

Shoving through the throngs of spectators, Paddy clanked up to the group; at least they thought it was his face they detected beneath the helmet and grill of the face guard. At a look at the bulky shin guards, knee guards and football-style shoulder pads in which he was finding even the smallest movement a trial, Fionnuala and Dymphna threw back their heads and roared with laughter.

"What do ye look like, love?" Fionnuala wondered. "A daft eejit, that's what!"

"Aye, and so will youse and all," Paddy said through the steel cage against his face. "Yer man the moderator over there told me we're all to gear up."

He was trailing a bag. He dumped it at their feet.

"Yer uniforms be's in there. And then there's these doodads and all."

He tugged out poles, five foot long, with what looked like giant two foot marshmallows attached to each end.

"It seems this activity's to be more involved that we were lead to think by yer woman Yootha. We're to hit the other teams with these things. No hands, apparently. Oh, and the fifth team has just gone and arrived. So it won't be long til they blow the whistle now."

Dymphna and Fionnuala dug with horror into the bag and pulled out their own protective gear, holding it up to their limbs to see how it fit. Paddy saw Fabrizio staring down at the babies. His nostrils flared like an enraged bull.

"What's the matter with ye, man?" he demanded to know. "Are ye getting randy at the sight of them wee wanes' innocent bodies? Themmuns is me grandchildren, I'll have ye know!"

"Daddy!" Dymphna called out, mortified.

Paddy knocked away her hand.

"Naw! It needs to be said, like! Are ye eying them infants up now, man, thinking how ye're gonny interfere with them before ye...how did yer granny do it now? I kyanny recall. Was it strangulation? Putting yer hands round their wee necks while ye unleash yer revolting desires on em? Or was it stabbing? Anyroad, she was a filthy, disgusting perv!"

"Daddy, naw! Don't scare him off. He be's miles better than Rory!"

Fabrizio's eyebrows were raised. He turned to Dymphna.

"I not understand. Whata he say about?"

"Nothing for ye to worry yerself about."

Dymphna patted his sopping back and ran her hands through the luxury of his black curls, which were now plastered onto his sodden skull.

"Not to fear, Paddy," Fionnuala said, with a nod to Fabrizio. "Yer man there was eying them two revolting creatures more with fear in his eyes than hunger, and God luck to him, I say. Wer Dymphna's never gonny be able to keep her claws in him, more's the pity. Never. Gonny. Happen. I told her nobody in their right mind would gladly take on the thankless task of raising another man's offspring, and half-Proddy ones at that. He comes from Italy, ye know, and them wops be's all Holy Roman Catholic like we does, that's where the 'Roman' part comes from, ye understand from Rome in Italy, like, and I'm sure his mammy would be as mortified as I am about having tainted bastards in the family. How could she ever send out Christmas cards or enter a house of God on a regular basis with a clear conscience? Lords knows the struggles I've had with it, like. Wer Dymphna shoulda kept them wanes a secret until themmuns was steps from the altar. Or, better, the reception afterwards, after all the vows that kyanny be broken had been uttered."

"Mammy, would ye shut yer bake?" Dymphna roared.

"Och, he kyanny understand a word that comes outta me mouth, so he kyanny!"

After being enraged at his wife the day before, Paddy was now more inclined to let her spew her poisonous venom. Last night in the cabin, she had hiked up her tattered nightdress and allowed him access to her maidenly delights. He had been gagging for it.

Dymphna tugged out another set of gear from the bag for her fancy man, and they set about configuring their limbs where they ought to go after inspecting the confusing masses of straps and buckles. Fionnuala, struggling into her shoulder pads, checked out the clapping, shouting passengers who lined the deck, cameras ready, to watch the carnage.

They all looked American to her. She thought she could tell as they seemed, what with the medical procedures available in their land, as they had all been snatched by some black hole of eternal youth, and they all had exactly the same teeth. To Fionnuala, teeth gave people character, and cloned and bleached and straightened teeth stripped these people, these Yanks, of one dimension. They were two-dimensional beings. She grimaced as she forced the guards on her elbows. In their perfectly-toothed lives of content, she was sure, an outbreak of lice at the local school was considered a major catastrophe, and they had the luxury to treat the breaking of a drinking glass as a concern. Back in her hometown, she was used to windows being shattered by bombs. She hated them all.

She eyed the two teams on either side of her. They were slipping into their guards and helmets and trying out their poles, smacking each other with the pads on the ends, which, from the yowls of pain she heard, still seemed to hurt. These were Americans of a different sort, hip-hop ones. They were the type of people who, if they got on the mini-bus taking her down the town to do her weekly shopping in Derry, even Fionnuala would've gotten off and boarded the next.

The *Queen of Crabs* hit another massive wave, and Fabrizio toppled into her. Fionnuala barked at him to get off her.

The fourth team looked like a gang recently released from an

Eastern European prison, all shaved heads and menace in their eyes. She searched in vain for pierced earrings to yank during the game, hoping for blood. She couldn't see the fifth team, as they were way down the deck on the other side of the funnel.

"Welcome to the *Titanic* Lifeboat Jamboree!" the moderator, in an off-white seersucker jacket, yelled into a microphone. There was a roar of applause. And, speaking of Rome and Italy, Fionnuala suddenly had a vision of Christians being dragged into the Colosseum to be mauled for the entertainment of the masses. She cursed Yootha.

"Let me tell you all how this is going to play out. As I'm sure you've all seen, there are lifeboats lined up along both sides of the deck of the ship. Don't worry, everybody, unlike the *Titanic,* we at EconoLux pride ourselves in the fact that there *are* enough lifeboats for all in the unlikely event we have to put them to use. Some have holes, it is true, but there are enough for you all. Ha! Joke!"

Laughter was non-existent.

"Anyway, we've sealed off all the lifeboats, as you see, except for four on the other side of the deck. What the five teams of the Jamboree, one lucky team signed up this morning, what each team has to do is fight to get all their teammates onto one lifeboat. And, to make it more difficult, we will now reveal the exciting surprise. Everyone will be *blindfolded!*"

There was a confused silence from the assembled masses. The people on the sidelines looked at each other.

"How will we see if we're blindfolded?" someone called out.

"Ah, ha ha ha! No, I meant the *teams* will be blindfolded."

Fionnuala turned to Paddy.

"C'mere, that Yootha be's one pure cunt, so she does. The next time I'm called into her office, I'm gonny claw the fecking hair outta her skull."

"Aye, and I'll be tugging along with ye," Paddy muttered.

"You're joking!" someone from the adjacent team called out.

"No, I'm not. And, fear not, if one of you falls overboard, we've a diver down there in the ocean ready to rescue you!"

"Hellooo!" they all heard coming up at them from the side of the ship.

"The same can't be said for the pool, unfortunately, which, as you can all see, our fearless warriors will have to get to the other side of.

And now...introducing the teams! From Detroit, USA, we have *Team Detroit!*"

The hip-hop people to their left played to the uproarious applause.

"Dear God!" Fionnuala spat. "What does themmuns be playing at with their fingers? Contorting them in that foolish, goofy manner?"

"Them be's gang signs, Mammy," Dymphna explained. "I seen Snoop Dogg and other rappers do em in music videos, like. Eminem and all, if I'm not mistaken. It's their way of saying hello. Apparently."

Fionnuala knew, with Aquanetta as her new best mate, she should be more accepting, more tolerant, more inclusive of other cultures. She couldn't. To her, they were behaving like idiots. "Team Eejits, more like," Fionnuala muttered under her helmet.

"And *Team Cleveland!*"

More uproarious applause.

"And *Team Czech.*"

Less enthusiastic.

"And *Team Golden Oldies.*"

That must be the team beyond the funnel. There were a few half-hearted handclaps.

"And, finally, our own team devised of members specially chosen from your hard-working staff here on the *Queen of Crabs, Team EconoLux!*"

As Fionnuala was bowing, the boos rang out in their direction. She fumed under her face guard.

"Hateful bastards!" she snarled to herself.

"And we've one more surprise for our five brave teams...to make it even *more* exciting, we're going to scatter some ball bearings on the deck! Just a few, don't worry, but watch out!" He poured a bucket of them on the deck. They clattered and rolled around. "And let me unveil the prizes for the lucky team!"

He whipped away what looked like a tablecloth from the table beside him to reveal four little trophies, plastic, of a ship tilting. Presumably the *Titanic,* not the *Queen of Crabs.* It was anti-climatic. "And, of course, ten percent off their next EconoLux cruise! Jammy sods!"

The applause was disappointing.

"Where is the Lux in their name is what I wanna know!" Louella snorted on the other side of the funnel. "They should just call themselves Econo."

"Aw, come on! Gimme a break!" Slim said as he peered through the pelting rain to the other teams. They all looked young and fit, though he didn't know about Team EconoLux, as they were too far down the deck. "We may as well just give up now. How will we ever win?"

"Themmuns be's but wanes," Ursula said. "We've four lifetimes of experience on wer team and on wer side. And yer bulk and all, Slim. We can do it!"

"And, don't forget, the US hockey team beat the Soviet commie scum during the 1980 Winter Olympics at Lake Placid!" Louella said, startling them all with her knowledge of this.

Jed was shaking his helmeted head vehemently.

"No way. We're all gonna end up in the dispensary. There's gotta be some safety code violations going on here. I know this ain't the US and life is cheap out here in international waters, but—"

He was on the verge of pulling off his shin guards when Louella grabbed his hand.

"We are doing this, Jed," Louella spat through lips transfixed with determination. "It can be done."

And suddenly there were EconoLux staff members at their sides, instructing them to remove their helmets for a moment so they could tie the blindfolds around their eyes.

As the knot was tied behind Ursula's head, as she hid her sopping bob inside the helmet and felt around, sightless, for her battering ram, she prayed to the heavenly Father that asparagus buffet man wasn't on Team EconoLux or, worse, Casino Woman.

"Okay," she heard the moderator call out. "On your marks! Ready...steady...*go!*"

He blew the whistle, the crowd roared, lightning crackled in the sky, and the 'fun' began.

CHAPTER 30

Aquanetta, a face on her like she had just smelled shit, stood before Yootha's desk. Her big black arms were firmly crossed.

"I suppose you're wondering why I've called you to my office."

Better not've found my stash Aquanetta thought, though her lips were arranged in a smile. She had never seen a whiter face.

"Don't worry, you've done nothing wrong."

This didn't placate Aquanetta, especially as the woman said it as if to a mental retard.

"What's up?" she asked.

"Two of the waitstaff suffered serious burns during the particularly severe turbulence a few hours back. Do you recall? They were in the galley, and a boiling pot, potatoes, I believe it was, toppled from the stove and scalded them. We will be compensating them, of course," her lips stretched into a sick-inducing smile Aquanetta didn't trust for a second, "but now we're two people short for the five star service at the captain's table tonight. A meal, I don't mind sharing, I will be partaking of. Captain Hoe prefers waitresses. I know you're probably not well trained, indeed, perhaps you're not trained in fine dining at all, and I know you've worked your entire shift already today, but you and another woman from your section of the housekeeping division," she rifled through a file, "a Fionnuala Flood, you are the only two female staff members who don't speak English as a second, or, indeed, third language who spring to mind. You both speak English...of a sort. So I'm asking you to step in this evening and serve us. And I'm working from the presumption that you know this Flood woman?"

Aquanetta forced her head to nod, lips tightly pressed into their I'm-still-listening-so-get-on-with-it expression, one eye-brow raised in suspicion. The sounds the woman uttered as she said the name were different from how she said the name in her head, Feeohnoowallah, but it must be the woman with the bleached pony tails she had been thinking a lot about lately. Mistrusting a lot lately.

"She's currently taking part in the lifeboat activity on the deck, so I can't approach her. And I have my appointment at the salon, and then my spa treatment to attend to. For the dinner, you see. I trust you will be able to get word to her?"

Aquanetta nodded haltingly, but a look was blossoming on her face

193

as if someone had just taken an even larger dump in her vicinity. She hadn't even told the woman she'd do it herself! She knew what these women in a position of authority were like: never taking no for an answer from the staff. And that Irish woman! Aquanetta was realizing they could never be friends. She thought they were equally disadvantaged, having met in this sweatshop of a ship. She thought they had both suffered lives of misery. But she had a fireplace in what Aquanetta assumed was her swanky home in her foreign country, favored Liz Taylor perfume—she had said Liz instead of Elizabeth as if she knew her!—and owned a Rolex! Sure, she had tried to play it off as if she had stolen it. But Aquanetta didn't believe her. She felt betrayed. The look on her face grew darker, the lips pressed harder and the eyebrows were set for take off.

This seemed to alarm the woman across the desk, who said quickly, eyes flashing as her mind raced, "I can't demand that you work, certainly not, and I suppose it would be too much to ask for you to clip those talons of yours a bit, but needless to say, there will be dire consequences if you choose to pass on this opportunity. There are two vacancies for latrine duty if you would like to move from housekeeping to that. But I do have a reward to show my gratitude. If you agree to serve this evening, you both will get to go ashore in Puerto Rico for half an hour as a reward. We should reach there tonight, if I'm not mistaken."

Her beaming smile met dead eyes. Aquanetta clamped her hand to a hip.

"I want money too."

Yootha nibbled on a nail, and it seemed she was struggling to keep a torrent of rage in check. Indecision danced on her face. Finally, she nodded with reluctance.

"I'll give you each $10."

Aquanetta grunted her laughter.

"You think it 1985? Ten dollars don't buy shit no more!"

"Twenty, then."

Aquanetta muttered something into the jar of pens that sounded like, "Better off collecting food stamps," but she agreed with a nod. Yootha was immediately dismissive. She waved her away as if she couldn't wait for the Help to stop soiling the office with her presence.

"And you'll tell Flood as well?"

"Yeah. What time you want us there?"

"Here's a printout that will give you all the information, including your duties and the numbers of the lockers which contain the uniforms. If they don't have your size, you'll have to improvise. I have a second printout for the other woman as well."

She handed them over.

"...if she completes the lifeboat activity unscathed." Yootha suddenly looked worried, as if she were flipping through the manila folders in her mind for a third replacement if that were to be necessary. Yootha didn't give a shit if Feeohnoowallah toppled off the ship and was devoured by sharks. Maybe then Yootha would give her the entire $40. But then she thought not to mention the compen-SA-tion factor to the fancy lady with the fireplace and just keep all the cash for herself.

She looked Yootha square in the eye with hand outstretched and said, "Pay me the whole forty for the both of us up-front now, otherwise I say nothing to Feeohnoowallah or whatever you call her."

Yootha seemed pissed that this seemingly stupid housekeeping staff was so savvy. She paused a moment to recalculate and re-evaluate the situation and reluctantly reached for her bag from the locked drawer in her desk. "All I have is a fifty and a twenty," she informed Aquanetta.

"I'll take the fifty then," she said with a snarky smile, "and try to 'break it' before dinner is served. That cool with you, *ma'am?*"

Furious, Yootha handed over the fifty. Aquanetta took it from Yootha's paw with fingers daintily extended, leaned in and graciously said, "Thanks. Pleasure doing business with you." She flashed an enormous smile and left.

The office door slammed. Yootha collapsed with relief, then hurried off to her hairdressing appointment.

CHAPTER 31

"Effin magic!"

Siofra slipped through the grille of the air vent and dropped her grimy little body onto the carpet of Room 643, Deck E. She had found their cabin!

Her arm still hurt, and her tummy rumbled with hunger, but she had more important things to concern herself with. And she had grown used to hunger; it was now her body's default setting. Maybe, she thought, she had worms.

She looked around the cabin first for some dolls she could play with, but there were none. She searched the closets and the drawers. There was nothing but clothes. She scrabbled across the floor to the laptop that lay open on the desk. A screen saver of the British TV secret service spy show *Spooks* flickered on the screen.

She signed in to her email account, shot off an email to her best mate back in Derry, Grainne, WISH U WUR HERE XOXO, then went into the web browser history, as she had been taught by Miss McClurkin in school the year before. The most visited website seemed to be one for celebrity gossip; the woman who had been with her Uncle Jed apparently liked Lindsay Lohan and her ilk. Second were the links to horrible saucy websites featuring women in latex with strange studded collars on their necks. Siofra was fascinated and disgusted at the same time, wishing she could erase from her eyeballs the visions her too-young eyes had just clamped sight of. There was also a site called PrivateInfoForAPrice. Find Out Everything About Anyone, it promised. Finances, Criminal Records and Protection Orders Revealed! She didn't know what that was all about.

Then she scrolled further down the history, and saw that the BBC *Spooks* website had been visited many times, and also the How To Beat Em At Poker website. She clicked on most visited page of the *Spooks* website. It was an episode guide, and in Series 3 Episode 2, the secret service team had to stop 5 grams of red mercury, whatever that was, from getting into enemy hands. Useless information!

She perked up when she noticed a window that had been minimized to the bottom of the computer screen. She pressed it and it sprang, full-sized, on the screen. She shook her head. It was just some boring receipt for a villa, whatever that was, in some foreign place she'd never heard of. Bungalow #12, La Villa Boracha, La Isla Bonita, Puerto Rico. How was that English?

Her filthy little fingertips stopped clacking on the keys. Frustration overtook her. Tears welled in her eyes. This information told her nothing. She didn't know what else she could find that would tell her what the two horrid people were up to with her kind Uncle Jed. She was at a loss.

After she had escaped from the engine room, she had hidden in the stairwell in a closet filled with brooms and mops and scurvy-infested rats. She had the door pried open a bit so she could see when her Uncle Jed and the two horrible creatures left. Ages, they had been in the engine room. She had almost fallen asleep by the time they passed the door and headed up the stairs. She had followed them, they had gone to the casino, and she had waited outside the emergency exit, found some wilted, ketchup-sodden fries and a half-eaten banana in the garbage to help pass the time, then followed the two to their cabin after they had left the casino. Without Uncle Jed. That had been hours ago.

As if her hands were programmed for it, she dug into the trash can beside the desk. She tugged out screwed up bits of paper. There was a printout of the reservation, and then some scribbled notes. At first she didn't know what she was reading. But then her eyes widened. She knew what they were after! Her little face screwed with anger.

Siofra thought for a moment about taking all their clothes from the closets, all those shiny suits and plaid shirts and tattered jeans and women's two-pieces and rich skirts and laying them on the bed and peeing on them, maybe even doing a number two on them, but realized that was her mammy's way. She pocketed all the paper in her unicorn jeans, hauled the chair over to the grille and climbed the wall to the air vent.

CHAPTER 32

Fionnuaula thrust her way through whatever stood in her path, human or otherwise, thrusting the ram from left to right. She heard Paddy grunting on one side, smelled Dymphna on the other, sensed Fabrizio behind her. The foreign idiot's ram pounded into her back time and again.

The rain now pouring in buckets from the heavens battered down on her helmet, thunder echoed in the muggy chamber, and squeals of spectator delight. Her ponytails, scrunched inside the air cushion system, were like two sopping mop heads clamped to the flesh of her neck. She could see nothing but, reckless with rage and pride—her family was going to win or God help humanity!—her feet charged like galloping hooves across the deck. Or where she thought the deck was. They flew across ball bearings and sent her mass hurtling forward into black space. The crack of her helmet against some hard thing reverberated through her eardrums. The battering ram clattered to her feet. Her pruned fingers groped around the sludge until a fist clutched it tight again. Tears welled, snot dribbled, spit hung, sweat poured. Fionnuala cursed inside the hellish blind depths of the helmet. She hauled her creaking limbs and all the tonnage attached up the side of what seemed to be a funnel.

The fingers of her free hand felt around the curvature, her fingernails digging into the metal hull for dear life. Limbs and battering ram pads jolted her shoulder blades, her elbows, her left hip.

"Paddy?!" she called out. "Where the bleedin feck are ye?"

"Here!" she heard nearby.

"I'm almost at the other end, so I am! Get yer daft arse over here! Follow me voice."

"I'm here as well, Mammy!" Dymphna's shrill voice pierced Fionnuala's ears.

"I too." That must be the foreign git.

"Get yerselves over here! Now!" For once, her brash howl was put to good use.

Rounding the funnel, Fionnuala heard the chants and claps of spectators from the other side through the peals of thunder. She flipped to the side as the ship lurched over a massive wave. Her rump splat on the deck. She ground her teeth as she got upright again, tossed the useless ram into the water—now above her ankles!—and blindly felt through the lashing buckets of rain, hands grabbing air.

She groaned as her pelvic bone smashed against the side of what felt like—

"A boat! I'm at one of the lifeboats now, youse! Get yer lazy arses in gear and scoot yerselves over here! Or there'll be hell to pay!"

She felt around in the dark, located jerking shoulders and arms and heads of two people inside. Two were missing. This boat was still fair game.

"This our boat!" she heard.

"Naw, ye mindless fecking git! Not yet, so it isn't!" Fionnuala roared down into the darkness.

The arms turned to fists that battered her chest. She grabbed hair and tugged.

"C'mere, youse! Paddy! Dymphna! And you, the other one! I've found us a boat!"

They were soon by her side; she heard their labored breath, smelled their sour sweat.

"Pull them out!" Fionnuala barked. In the back of her mind, she wondered, *how the bloody feck is this meant to be fun?*

She heard the rams clatter to their feet. She felt their arms reach into the darkness beside her, heard the screams as Paddy and Dymphna and the other one clamped down on human flesh and dug in. Fingers grabbed her shoulders and sought to fling her to the deck. They were like crabs in a bucket, trying to pull each other down. Fionnuala threw off her helmet and widened her maw. Her yellow teeth gleamed in the plummeting rain. She chomped down on a shoulder.

She heard dimly from the megaphone in the background as her eyes took it all in, the two in the boat, one screaming and clutching his shoulder, Paddy and Dymphna pounding uselessly on the other, battering rams flying through the torrents of rain, clapping, jeering, cheering fools surrounding the sides, "You in the pink and gray top! You! Pink and gray top! Follow the rules!"

Letting go of the woman's neck, Fionnuala wrenched off her blindfold. She looked behind the masses gathered to see who he meant. So she could laugh along with the crowd at the clueless cow's misfortune. She was shocked that the field of eyes bored through the rain directly into hers, fingers pointing laughingly and accusingly. At her.

Startled, she looked down at her top. When she had purchased it years back it had been stripes of red and black. A thousand washings later it had faded, but even while checking herself out in the reflection of the porthole that morning, she had seen it as red and black. That's why she had chosen the earrings.

"Disqualified!" the megaphone squawked. "Team EconoLux is disqualified!"

Fionnuala bubbled with rage as the laughter rang out. She somehow sensed Paddy and Dymphna dropping their rams and tugging off their helmets at her side, but really her brain focused on the blood flooding her panting face as mortification overtook her. How could she have thought her top was still red and black?

"Aye, go on and have a good laugh, youse!" Fionnuala's furious voice rang out across the length of the deck. "God punishes them what laughs at the misery of others! Youse are all on yer way to the fiery pits of Hell!"

As the laughter increased, Fionnuala shuddered with fury. They must be non-Christians, she thought, and—

A bell rang out, and the megaphone shrilled: "We have winner! Team Czech has won!"

A roar went up from the sopping crowd.

"And, a surprise runner up, Team Golden Oldies!"

Paddy, Dymphna and Fabrizio struggled out of their helmets and glumly unwrapped their blindfolds. As the applause began to die, Fionnuala peered down the deck, past Team Czech, who were, all four in the boat, slapping one another's backs and mugging it up to the crowd. Shock attacked her skull. She stood, a woman electrocuted, and not by the lightning spearing through the sky around her.

She would know that unseemly shade of purple anywhere...like a big purple blimp, an eggplant sat atop her head. Ursula Barnett! With both feet firmly in her lifeboat, waving at the crowd and wrapping her arms around—Jed! And the walrus-type creature, Fionnuala's brain would realize hours later, his fat must have been responsible for their win, and the tiny woman with the big red glasses. As the shock permeated through her veins, Fionnuala couldn't know she wasn't thinking clearly. She was thinking that once she had asked Ursula if Lady Clairol rolled that shade of purple off the production line for her exclusive use; she had never seen anyone else with such a revolting dye job the breadth and width of Derry. Ursula retorted that Fionnuala hadn't seen all the people in the world.

Fionnuala forced her neck around and faced Paddy and Dymphna, raw, fresh rage shooting from beneath her eyelids.

"The cunt! We've only gone and been beaten by the flimmin fecking Lady of the Manor, *yer sister*, Paddy! Ursula Barnett!"

She slipped on a ball bearing and would've fallen into Paddy's arms, but he was scratching his head and staring in shock at his sister down the deck. Fionnuala dove into a pool of scabby sea water.

CHAPTER 33

Jed's tuxedo still lay spread out on the bed, but where was the man himself? They had to leave for dinner at the captain's table in half an hour. He would have to shower and shave, and it took him an eternity to wrap the cummerbund around his waist; he had to ensure his waistline couldn't be seen between it and his pants.

Ursula reached out for her handbag, which was strangely silent. In this world of surprises, few of them pleasant, he was her constant; she could always rely on Jed. Why hadn't he called? Texted, even?

After they had been presented their second place trophies, he had pecked her on the cheek and said he had somewhere to go. He had gripped her hands especially hard and stared into her eyes. He seemed to be jittering with an excitement beyond that which winning a plastic trophy or a Cleopatra penny slot might give. He would be back in time for dinner at the captain's table, he had said; he knew how much Ursula was looking forward to it. He had given her his trophy and staggered down the deck, clutching the handrails as the ship groaned from one side to the other.

Ursula opened her purse and looked inside the slot reserved for her cellphone. It was empty. Then she remembered she had thrown it overboard. She would have to call Jed. She must find a phone. But... She knew their home phone number by heart, knew the store phone, but Jed's cell...??

She wrung her hands. The little animal charms from the bracelet jingled. She took steps to the bathroom, the hem of sparkling red gown sashaying around her pantyhosed feet. She looked at herself in the bathroom mirror, and realized her makeup was only half done, lipstick on the left of her mouth. She had been too busy checking her watch— the silver Rolex left on her pillow—and trying to arrange the other accessories so that they looked like they matched. Her neck especially, the Egyptian necklace coupled with the amethyst choker, screamed out, look at me! Look at me! The staff hadn't left another pearl earring, but a large Sade-style golden hoop for her other ear. It definitely clashed with the purple of her hair and the amethyst, the silver and gold of the watch and bracelet, the pearl, the busy mess of the Egyptian necklace and the ruby of the choker.

"Oh, Jed, Jed," she murmured, thrusting the rest of the lipstick on her lips. She reached for her bottle of Xanax and was horrified to see it was empty. Empty. She would have to do this with her mind intact. She smiled at herself in the mirror. She looked like a schizophrenic's Christmas tree.

It was now quarter to eight. She squealed her frustration. There was nothing else for it. She grabbed her sparkly green clutch and slipped into her heels. She left the cabin and went next door. She looked behind her, and it wasn't to see if her heels were trailing toilet paper. She wondered what hours housekeeping worked. But she saw no sign of Casino Woman. She knocked on the door, dreading slightly what she had to do. She waited, then knocked again. And again.

Slim poked his head out. His face pink. His walrus mustache was tousled. His mounds stretched the straps of the wife-beater t-shirt to snapping point.

"Where's Louella?" Ursula asked.

"We were just, uh, she's...mmm..."

"I see," Ursula said with a quick cringe. "Anyroad, Slim, get yer laughing gear and yer tuxedo on. Jed's not surfaced, and there's no way I'm missing the captain's dinner. But I'd be mortified to go on me own. Ye're me new date."

Ursula and Slim clanged their flutes together. Champagne bubbled over and rolled down their knuckles. Ursula knew she shouldn't be drinking, but decided to throw caution to the wind. It wasn't every day you ran out of Xanax and had the privilege of dining with the captain of a cruise liner, after all, and she didn't want to waste the experience worrying about Jed's whereabouts. She feared for him, how could she not?, especially as the ship was careening inches from rocks, tossing them about in the middle of this storm, but he was ex-military and could look after himself. She hoped. She guzzled down. And, aware of the odd looks the four others invited to the table were passing her, guzzled some more.

"C'mere," she said to the bartender, "give me a refill, would ye? Och, ye're grand and lovely, so ye are."

He avoided her eye as he poured. Ursula wasn't sure if it was the tonnage of her mismatched jewelry or the tonnage of Slim in general that was the cause of the distantiation, but, with her mind numbed and getting number, she didn't care. She decided to hob nob with the crème of the crème of the passengers. She sidled down the bar away from Slim, who was filling himself up with peanuts against her advice, and smiled at a man in a bow-tie and obvious toupée.

"Hello," Ursula said, extending a hand dripping showy tat, and why her mouth was affecting a posh accent she didn't know. "I'm Mrs. Jed Barnett. And you are...?"

He took a step back.

"I work for the Department of Health and Mental Hygiene in Geneva." He stared pointedly at Ursula as if there might be something she would want to reveal. His hand disappeared into his tuxedo jacket pocket. "Perhaps you'd be interested in this." He pressed his business card into her palm.

Ursula was relieved when Slim puffed over to her and pulled her aside.

"I don't think I can do this, chipmunk," he said. "I've tried to talk about our store to these people, but they're not interested in guns or bait or hot sauce or even beef jerky. I don't even have no samples of the hot sauce to let them taste no more anyway. Those guys over there are scientists of some sort." Ursula inspected the two Slim pointed out, elbows on the bar. She had never seen a scientist before, and one was even a female scientist! "Who's this dang Higgs Boson, and why are they looking for him? That's what I wanna know! I just left them to allow them to talk about whatever junk they talk about with themselves. How is that interesting?" he sputtered.

Captain Hoe arrived, to the smiles and nods of the invited guests. He was to guide them to their table. Ursula eyed him up in her haze as he approached, tall, gray hair, immaculate white uniform. A man of power and intelligence.

She held out her hand and let it be kissed. The little animals jangled. "Mrs. Jed Barnett. And this here be's Slim Barnett, me *brother-in-law.*"

Captain Hoe's eyes seemed to do cartwheels in their sockets, so unsure were they as to what from all the glittering objects suspended from Ursula's body parts to land upon, and in what order. They chose to look behind her left shoulder instead.

"Do I detect an accent?" he asked, eyebrows raised with interest.

"I'm from Derry, Northern Ireland," Ursula said proudly.

This sentence was usually greeted with a look of sympathy, and this time was no exception. Ursula knew why. People still thought of her hometown as a war-zone. They had no idea what a handsome city Derry was now, years after the troops had finally pulled out.

"Derry's been chosen UK City of Culture for 2013," she quickly added, bristling with defensive pride. Since she had read the news, she was forever telling anyone who would listen, and many who didn't want to know, that Derry was chosen UK City Of Culture for 2013. She never mentioned the City Of Culture headquarters had already been blown up by dissident republicans twice.

Through the velvet drapes adorning the windows, crackles of lightning shot through the sky. The ship careened. Ursula fell into the captain's brass buttons, a cacophony of metal meeting metal ringing out.

"Watch it, there, my little lady," he said, straightening her, "we're going through a stormy patch of the Caribbean Sea at the moment. The turbulence should pass, but if it doesn't, we'll be docked in Puerto Rico soon, anyway."

"All this lightning," Ursula said, while Slim, who had moved to martinis, dug his fingers into the glass to scoop up the olives and gobble them down, "what will happen if it strikes the ship?"

She stiffened at Captain Hoe's chuckles.

"My dear, dear lady," he said, patting her shoulder. "Although this is a *Titanic* centennial cruise, there *have* been advances in the construction of cruise liners since then. Believe it or not. Nowadays, all modern liners are equipped with protection against lightning. Have you seen the mast on the deck outside?"

She fumed at being talked to as if she were a simpleton.

"Ye mean the sorta thinner thing than the funnels? The one that looks all electric with the two wee flags flying from it?"

"That's the one. The mast has the radar equipment on it. Radar is something that uses radio waves, which are invisible things in empty space, that means we can't see them, and radar helps us locate other things in the ocean and the air, other ships and bits of land and things. Do you understand? And in addition to the radar, there is also a lightning protector mounted on the top of the mast. And a grounding conductor in the hull. Electrical conductors run from the protector to the grounding conductor and keep us safe. Lightning won't hurt us, except maybe for some burn marks. The hull is the bottom of the ship."

The clutch twitched in Ursula's hand. But she smiled. Captain Hoe looked at his watch.

"I'm afraid Mrs. Hornington-Ffrench, she's our director of staff, has been delayed. We must start without her." He called to the other five guests at the bar to circle him and listen. "We have a very, very special meal planned for you all this evening. It's the actual meal, yes, the *actual* meal, that was served to the first class passengers on the *Titanic* on her fateful last night. All ten courses of it."

The female scientist looked stricken. "How long is this going to take?" she asked in concern.

Captain Hoe's smile was strained.

"In 1912 they dined in a rather more...leisurely manner than today. And, just like they did, we'll be offering a different wine with each course. And after the tenth, there is a selection of cheeses, and then we can have cigars and port, just like they did on the *Titanic*. It'll take some time, so we'd best get started. Mrs. Hornington-Ffrench will have to catch up with us."

As they approached the table, decked out in all its finery, Ursula was pleased to see that her gown matched the napkins.

"What a lovely choker!" the scientist cooed, but there was something about her tone Ursula didn't like.

"Aye," Ursula said, looking down and locating the amethyst amongst all that glittered below her neck. She fondled it self-consciously. "EconoLux gave it me. Left it on me pillow, so they did. All these others and all."

She sat down at the seat with her nameplate on it, trying to push the irritation to the back of her mind. She pointed at Slim to take Jed's place. The scientist was unfortunately sat to Ursula's left. As Ursula settled herself before the glittering crystal and fine bone china, the wide array of silver utensils, as she unfolded the plush napkin and settled it on her lap, trying to bask in the luxury, she saw from the corner of her eye the woman still eying the brooch.

"Really?" she said, lips like slits. "Only, my lab partner, Margo, who's also on this cruise, has one *exactly* like it. And it disappeared from her cabin a few days ago. She contacted security, but nobody could find it. And you must admit, it *is* a distinctive piece."

Unease crept around the nape of Ursula's velvet-choked neck. She cursed the empty Xanax bottle.

"Where's wer first wine, captain?" she called across the table. The captain and the others were hidden behind their very tall menus. Ursula picked up hers and shivered with excitement at all the little French accent things above the words.

First Course—Hors D'Oeuvres

Canapés à L'Amiral

Oysters à la Russe

Slim nudged her elbow and almost knocked the glass of wine out of her hand.

"Now, you know I love food as much as the next man," he hissed behind his menu. "But...what is all this stuff? I ain't heard of half of it! Vegetable Marrow Farci? What the jiminy cricket's a roast squab and what's it on *wilted* cress for? Punch Romaine?! Can't we just get pizza? Or a burger or something?"

"I'm sure ye'll scoff it all up, love," Ursula said, though she herself was particularly worried about both the Minted Green Pea Timbales and Consummé Olga. "And you must admit...ten courses be's wile exciting!"

Captain Hoe looked around the dining room. He grabbed a passing lower server who dealt with the minions' buffet.

"We're ready to begin," he said. "Where's the waitstaff for this table?"

The server nodded towards the galley.

"There they are, sir," he said.

The scientist kept peering at Ursula's choker more than her menu, and the galley doors opened wider. Ursula would have more than Consummé Olga to worry about.

CHAPTER 34

"Don't ye take one fecking step toward that jumped up bitch of a sister of yers!" Fionnuala had snapped at Paddy, though there was really no need, as he had then slipped on ball bearings and cracked his skull on the edge of the lifeboat. The looks Dymphna had launched her way as the silly girl hunched down to help her spineless wretch of husband still rankled. That wee girl needed to be put in her place, the disrespect she had for her elders and betters!

In the heat and stench of the galley, Fionnuala tottered back and forth on the writhing floor, a silver spatula in one uncertain hand, the other clutching the serving trolley out of fear and necessity. The throngs of foreign help came at her at all angles, a sizzling pan here, a glinting knife there. It was like the Tower of Babel, them yapping in their strange tongues, barking things at her she couldn't make sense of. Buckets had been set up all over the floor to catch the gray water that dripped from the rust-encrusted piped above them. Aquanetta nudged her.

"Ain't you gonna get to work? We got all them shrimp things to move from the counter to the tray, the oysters to the trolley, and those bottles of wine to open. You gotta do that. I can't with my nails."

After she and Aquanetta had forced themselves into black outfits with frilly white aprons, what Fionnuala guessed was some boss of the galley, a darkie of sorts, had tried to explain in haste and an English Fionnuala struggled to comprehend what they were supposed to do. They had then been ushered into the melée of the galley, a counter had been hastily cleared of the discarded bones and skins of food animals, the rinds of strange fruits and vegetables and gooey substances that had the drool of Fionnuala's taste buds dripping down to meet the sick shooting up her throat, so starving was she but so repulsed by the fancy foreign food they were preparing here. She had only had a few moments to throw a Cup-O-Noodles, Oriental flavored, down her throat before she hurried from the lifeboat activity to the galley for her surprise shift.

There were ten courses to serve, and they were being thrown on the counter in the order she and Aquanetta were meant to bring them to the captain's table, with the appropriate china beside them. Fionnuala was still struggling to understand how it was supposed to go.

"I know ye, love," Paddy called out to her through the hanging pots and pans that clanked against one another, "don't ye be spitting in them oysters."

"Spit?" Fionnuala scoffed. "Slipping ground glass into them, more like. Naw, but, I'll keep me spittle in me mouth. I swear to the Holy Father."

He was furiously chopping cucumbers into tiny slices, and had a mound of what looked like marrows to move on to next. Fionnuala had kept silent about knowing Ursula would be dining at the captain's table that night. She was sure her turncoat husband would plead and beg for Fionnuala to let her be.

As Aquanetta shoved a strange contraption at her, together with bottles of wine lodged between the crux of her arm and her matronly breasts, Fionnuala couldn't understand how, after all these years of holy matrimony, she hadn't realized her chosen was such a wussy. Paddy was finally showing his true color, and it wasn't Catholic green, it was yellow. He had no backbone. And he had no clue as to Fionnuala's plan which, hopefully, would send security racing to the table to haul Ursula away.

"Open them," Aquanetta barked, nodding down to the bottles.

Fionnuala was taken aback. Corks! The wine she bought at the Top-Yer-Trolly didn't have them; corks were for pretentious gacks and arse-bandits. But she supposed that's who was dining at the table with the captain. Along with Ursula.

An hour ago on the deck, when she had spied her sister-in-law in the winning boat, Fionnuala had had to fight the urge to race across and push her into something. The edge of the pool had been tantalizingly close, but it was child's play when she considered the whole of the Atlantic Ocean was there at her disposal a handrail away, and *for* the disposal of Urusla's body, if it came to it, for that matter. She had relented. Security would soon be doing all her work for her. The awakening, she thought, would be just like Ursula's personality: rude. She felt Aquanetta inspecting her motionless fingers.

"Ain't never done no work of your own?" she asked, an edge to her voice.

Fionnuala stared. Nothing could be further from the truth! She had toiled, thanklessly, since she had entered the world, and the state of her hands could prove it. Fionnuala grabbed the bottles, balanced them on the trolley as best she could, and tried to pierce the corks with the pointy curly thing of the contraption.

Aquanetta grabbed shrimp halves on little bits of bread with some orange gooey stuff on top and thrust them onto a huge silver platter. She moved it to the trolley.

Fionnuala ground the pointy thing into cork after cork, and the entire galley wailed as the ship suddenly lurched to the left. Plates and pots and glasses flew. The lights above them flickered. Fionnuala blessed herself, her fingers flying around her head and breast. Aquanetta grabbed the bottle of champagne. The cooks had been using it for the strange slushy-type thing that was course number six, the one before the strange little chicken-type birds each passenger was going to eat his own of. She took a terrified gulp.

"Lord help us!" she implored of the ceiling, "Yeah, I'm on the wagon, but this ship got me scared shitless. Gotta fall off. Gotta gulp down."

"A-ye, me and all."

Aquanetta passed the bottle to Fionnuala. She arranged her lips around the top and let the champagne flood her throat. Fionnuala wiped her mouth, then flinched as Aquanetta opened her mouth and filled the greasy depths of the galley with song: *"I'm gonna...take a trip! On that good ole...gospel ship!...And we'll go saiiiling through the aiiir! Yes, Lord!"* The black woman smiled as she sang, her faith seeming to allay her fear, and moved her hips back and forth as she hauled a massive bucket of ice onto the trolley.

Rage consumed Fionnuala. She thrust the pointy bit into the cork as if it were Aquanetta's left eye. She loved the woman, she really did, but she was treading where no non-Catholic had the right to, praising the Lord—and, worse, with an alien gospel song that Fionnuala hadn't even heard the choir at St. Molaug's sing. As if the Heavenly Father were a coon himself! *Blasphemy!*

Perhaps Aquanetta had forgotten the rest of the words, because, as she filled the bucket with oysters with tomatoes and green things on top—they might have been scallions, but Fionnuala wasn't sure—she moved to humming. To holier-than-thou her, Fionnuala began to hum a reedy *Nearer My God To Thee*. Fionnuala herself never sang at mass; she left the other faithful to that, and just moved her lips along. As she hummed, she glared at Aquanetta, and was all set to segue into *Ave Maria,* when the darkie, the one in charge, hurried over to them.

"Captain Hoe at table. Go now!"

He shoved them towards the door.

"God luck to youse!" Paddy called out, wiping sweat from his brow.

"Ta," Fionnuala said with a scowl.

She was scared of her grand entrance into the swanky dining room, but was suddenly struck with the greater fear that it might have already kicked off at the table, Yootha calling security and Ursula hauled off in handcuffs and shame. She didn't want to miss the fireworks. She grabbed the trolley, but Aquanetta forced her to the side.

"I'll serve," Aquanetta said. "You pour the wine like you were showed. We'll take turns. You serve the next, I'll pour."

Armed with the first wine bottle, Fionnuala whispered gleefully into Aquanetta's ear. "I've something to reveal to ye. Me sister-in-law be's dining with the captain, and I've—"

Aquanetta glared at her.

"Hrmph! Somehow don't surprise me!"

"What are ye saying with that?"

Aquanetta didn't answer, just took another gulp of champagne and, armed with Dutch courage and serving tongs, exited the galley. Fionnuala adjusted her ponytails under the frilly cap and pushed through the swinging doors, trembling with excitement.

CHAPTER 35—AN HOUR AND A HALF EARLIER

"Gimme two cards," the terrorist said.

Through the cracked lens of his glasses, Jed eyed the drunk old eterna-teen across the green felt of the poker table with a sense of disbelief. Sagging breasts strained her Britney Spears halter top, and she was almost hidden behind a barricade of empty wine glasses and the smog of cigarettes from two wolfish men who hovered over either side of her and who, between hands, urged more drink down her throat. Raw lipgloss carved a path along her chin. She didn't look like an Anti-American dishing out red mercury to the highest bidder; she looked like she were at the poker table to win rent. But Nigel, sitting to her right in another sharp tight shiny suit, this one brown, had nodded three times every deal since they had sat down. She was supposed to win. And she had. Thanks to Nigel and Jed. Seven times Jed had had to fold; once with a pair of aces, once with a straight, and, most agonizingly at all, once with a high full house...when all she had held was three sixes!

The fumes from Jed's cigarette joined the cloud above the poker table. Behind Nigel, Agent Matcham coughed into a frilly hanky. Jed kept gulping down the carcinogens.

Nigel threw three cards onto the table.

"Hit me," he instructed the dealer.

How Jed would love to do just that! Not only were his glasses broken and his limbs still aching from the little creep, his $50 chips had dwindled to a mere three, while the horrible woman opposite him rasped her laughter every time she scooped Jed's chips into her ever-growing mound. She didn't even have the decency to pile them on top of one another! They were spilled across the table under her breasts. The men were eying them eagerly.

As Jed tossed down a two of hearts and received a queen of clubs in return, he considered whether these two men could also be part of the cell. It didn't seem likely. It seemed they had just happened upon the table and, seeing the piles of chips and the state of the woman, had swooped down on her like vultures.

Jed checked out his hand. He now held three queens and two jacks. Another full house. He stared over at Nigel, which was difficult at this angle, but if he leaned back in his chair he could just about manage it. He was trying to tell him with his eyes he wanted to win this time. He had already handed over $1050 to the woman. Wasn't that enough to make her feel confident, or whatever this strange poker part of the mission was supposed to accomplish? Surely MI-6 wouldn't begrudge Jed a little $150 for his loyalty and silence?

Nigel nodded once, twice, three times. Jed felt the anger building under his cowboy hat. He shifted his chair forward, the rage churning through him. A gambling man like him didn't appreciate being forced to lose time and again.

"I bet $1000!" the woman squealed.

Nigel and Agent Matcham above him looked alarmed.

"I fold," Nigel said.

"I'll meet you and raise $500," said the man to Jed's right.

"I'm out," Jed said, tossing his cards in disgust on the table.

Nigel straightened his tie. Jed was grateful. He waited until Nigel had gathered the remains of his rum and coke and what few chips he also had left, stood up, and guided Agent Matcham out of the private poker room, his hand on her elbow. Jed threw back the remnants of his Bailey's, scraped his chair across the carpet and stood up. He glanced at his watch. Shocked gripped him. It was seven o'clock! He had to get to the cabin and change for the captain's dinner at eight!

He didn't care, particularly, but Ursula had been counting down the minutes, squealing with delight every afternoon when she found a new piece of jewelry on her pillow, and she had even given him an impromptu fashion show with some of the items. Ten courses of food didn't thrill him, but he didn't want to let her down.

He met Agent Matcham and Nigel where they had arranged, between the roulette and the restrooms.

"How did I do?" Jed asked, flush with the excitement of it all.

Agent Matcham gave him little claps. Nigel just looked at him.

"Brilliantly!" she cooed, pecking him on the cheek. Jed blushed. "We were certainly spot on when we chose you. Nigel and I were just discussing...we think we have that horrid woman almost in our reach now. All thanks to you."

"That's great," Jed said. "When are we gonna meet next? I didn't realize how late it is. I gotta get to my cabin. My wife's got a seat at the—"

Nigel snorted.

"You'll be doing no such thing. We are at a crossroads in the mission. We can't just leave her there at that table. We've to continue! *You've* to continue!"

"But—"

Nigel sped towards him like a ferret. Jed, hands shooting up to protect his face, backed into the water fountain. Nigel sneered into his drooping collar: "You want another round with me, old man?"

"Enough!" Agent Matcham snapped. She pulled Nigel away. He shrugged his shoulders, adjusting the cuffs of his shirt, all the while the look on his face baiting Jed.

"Anyway," Jed said, "I've only got $150 left. I don't know how much more I can do."

"*Ohhh!*"

It was one of the few times during the storm the ship *didn't* toss to one side, but it looked like Agent Matcham pretended it had, thrusting her body across the carpet and hurtling toward him, earrings flying. Jed's arms shot up—to catch her or protect himself, he didn't know—and she landed in his arms. She peered up at him, bosoms pressing against the polyester of his shirt, gratitude sparkling in her eyes, running a hand through her flips of hair and doing something subtle with them that suddenly made her even more alluring. She ran a finger up the length of his arm. Torn between an uncharacteristic desire and characteristic discomfort, Jed sought to remove her from his personal space.

"That's something we must discuss with you, dear," she said.

Jed had the sensation what would come from those strangely- and suddenly-puckered lips wasn't going to be good news.

"You see...there's been a mishap with our funds. We're on the verge of having that woman in there just where we want her, and ready to move on to the next step of the mission. Soon the red mercury will be in our possession, and the fate of the world will be secure. But a money transfer from the UK hasn't been able to get to the ship due to the inclement weather. And we need it now."

"And how am I supposed to help with that?" Jed asked, in his mind each minute ticking by ratcheting up the rage/disappointment Ursula would unleash upon him.

"We need a sub of $25,000," Nigel said. "And we know you have it, mate."

Jed saw a flash of annoyance glint in Agent Matcham's eyes for a second, then she turned to him and smiled her best come-hither smile.

"How...?" Jed wondered.

"MI-6 knows everything," Agent Matcham told him softly. She placed a hand on his and squeezed it gently. "It will only be a short-term loan. For the next and final game. Don't forget, MI-6 has unlimited funds, and you will be paid handsomely for your services."

"And we gave you that $1200," Nigel said.

This was true. Jed massaged his goatee as he thought. It seemed incredible that they needed exactly the amount he had in his special account.

"But...how would I get that much out of the ATM?" he asked. "Aren't there limits?"

"The ATMs are Russian," Nigel said. "They have no daily limit. We checked."

"And," Agent Matcham wittered on, "depending on the circumstances of the next game, it might not even be necessary to part with the money. Nigel might decide you must win it all, don't forget."

The thought of a terrorist making off with his and Ursula's nest egg and doing God only knew what with it, the time spent building up the interest to get it to $25,000, rankled Jed. But he *had* won the principal in the lottery. If that hadn't happened, he and Ursula wouldn't even have it to rely on. So it was like free money. And the British government *would* be paying him back, and he *would* be making the world a safer place...

Agent Matcham placed her briefcase on the water fountain and snapped it open. It was angled so that Jed couldn't see inside. He wondered, wondered what was in its leather-bound depths. She tugged out a sheet of embossed paper. It had the Queen's logo on top. It looked very official.

"We have here a promissory note," she said, "which, of course, I will be happy to sign, if that makes you feel more secure. I can assure you, however, the British government pays its debts in a very timely manner."

"Come on, come on!" Nigel snapped, stamping his foot. "She might be leaving the table soon. She might already have left, and then our chance will be gone. We may as well have just blown up the world ourselves! You want another round with me? Another round of training, innit?"

He glared menacingly through the cracked lens of Jed's glasses. His fists were ready for action.

Jed looked at his watch.

"Can we complete the mission, the next few hands, in a few minutes?" he asked. "I really have to go."

"A poker game doesn't take long," Agent Matcham said. Jed wondered about this. After a youth of military training, he had gotten used to split second decisions of life and death, of instant action. He hadn't actually put this skill to use on the battlefield, and the older and older he got, the more time it took to let the mission sink in before he prepared himself to the actuality of doing it. But now, with no time left for thinking, he nodded his head. He grabbed the pen she proffered and signed the paper.

Agent Matcham clapped her little claps again, the gratitude this time beaming across her entire face. Nigel deflated with relief.

"Let's go," he said, grabbing Jed's elbow and guiding him to the ATM which was, remarkably, Jed thought, right beside their meeting place.

Flanked by Nigel's menace and Agent Matcham's menopause, Jed was ushered towards the machine. Shielding the keypad with his hand, he tapped in his code. It was the year he and Ursula got married. The many dollar bills shot through the slot. And with each bill that emerged from the slot, he could see Ursula's disappointed and raging face in the place where the faces of dead presidents should be. He got a sudden cramp in his finger – his ring finger on which his band of gold was a constant reminder of the vows he'd committed to his Ursula and the undying trust she placed in their marriage.

CHAPTER 36

Serve on the right, clear on the left, serve on the right...

With her horsey teeth arranged in a smile, bottle of posh-git wine brandished in her stubby fingers, Fionnuala felt she was on display as she crossed the dining room towards the captain's table with its special table cloth. Perhaps it was the champagne on her basically-empty stomach, but she felt like Nicole Kidman on the red carpet at the Oscars in Hollywood. Aquanetta and the trolley trundled at her side, like her PA or a minion from her entourage.

Fionnuala counted the bodies around the table. Her shoulders slumped with disappointment. Six invited guests, one, two, three four, five, six, the captain and...she couldn't miss Ursula's eggplant blimp, but she couldn't see the distinctive tiki-bamboo fright of a hairdo that was Yootha's poking above the back of one of the chairs. Where was she? If she had decided to cancel, Ursula's humiliation would have to be postponed. Though, Fionnuala thought, she could always alert security herself, let them know she recognized the jewelry, and they'd haul Ursula off. Hopefully kicking and screaming, with all the ship looking on as they ate. The smile that already strained her chapped lips widened. She couldn't wait to see the look in Ursula's eyes when she slopped the wine into her glass. She hoped she choked on it.

*Serve the captain first, serve the captain first, serve **the overprivileged git!** first...*

As they got closer, Aquanetta's steps grew more wobbly, the roll of her hips more suggestive. It was more the drink, Fionnuala thought, than the passage of the ship, and the distance between them seemed to be growing. It seemed to Fionnuala as if the booze was making the woman more black.

One hand rolled the trolley, the other snapped the tongs at the backs of diners' heads as she passed, and Aquanetta was now singing a low, mournful "One Nation Under A Groove," *...getting down just for the funk of it!*

Fionnuala nudged her. "I don't think themmuns wants us singing at the table."

The glare Aquanetta bored into her with made even the unflappable Fionnuala shrink. The woman's nails flickered with menace around the tongs.

217

"You got something against Funkadelic?"

Fionnuala didn't know what this meant, nor did she want to. They reached the table. Nobody paid them a blind bit of notice. The captain was deep in conversation with the woman beside him. Ursula was pointing to her nameplate and wittering on to the manatee-type thing sat next to her. Fionnuala smiled at the backs of their heads as she raised the wine bottle and approached the starched back of the captain's collar under his jacket. She figured out which his right shoulder blade was, found the wine glass among all the many on the table, and began to pour. He looked up at her, alarmed.

"Aren't you going to let me taste it?"

Fionnuala did something with her knee that was meant to be a curtsey.

"Och, catch yerself on! Ye'll taste it when it's in yer mouth, sure!"

She moved on. Aquanetta followed her, grappling a shrimp thing and dumping it on the captain's plate, then an oyster.

Around the table they moved, wine sloshing into crystal, shellfish plopping onto china, and not a word of thanks nor a smile of gratitude from any of the self-obsessed toerags around the table did they receive. Fionnuala shuddered with rage. The servants were invisible. She and Aquanetta were sub-humans only there to satisfy their desires of hunger and thirst. While the hunger rumbled in Fionnuala's stomach! And, from the look of slowly-bubbling fury on Aquanetta's drunk face, she was feeling just the same.

After this poncey-looking git, Ursula was next. As Fionnuala poured—she realized she had given the first few too much wine; those at this end of the table were only getting dribbles as the bottle was emptying quickly—her eyes shot wildly through the chattering, dining masses from the buffet for any sign of Yootha. There were nine more courses to serve, so there was plenty of time for her to arrive, but—

There! There, across the expanse of the dining room, was Yootha, racing out of the elevator towards the table, huffing and puffing and waving a hand in greeting, though why she bothered, Fionnuala didn't know, as nobody was paying her any mind. Fionnuala stifled a giggle. And moved behind Ursula's back to the wine glass at her right, Aquanetta and her trolley serving the git to Ursula's left. As Fionnuala poured droplets of wine into Ursula's glass, the silly bitch unaware, Aquanetta approached Ursula's neck, tongs-a-clacking.

Ursula turned her head at the noise, looked up, saw the curling, sparkly fingernails, the Gothic lettering, the little ring dangling from the pinkie, pried open her horrified lips—

—and shrieked like a sow at the slaughter. The plates, her wine glass, Slim, all receded from her vision. She saw only the nails. *Casino Woman!* Coming at her with a strange weapon! Here on the ship! As shock and confusion flooded her brain, she was vaguely aware of heads shooting around, eyes inspecting her the length of the table. She grabbed Slim's hand, twice as big as Jed's but half as comforting.

Ursula focused on the pattern of her empty plate and managed to pry from her tight throat: "I-don't-want-the-likes-of-her-serving-me. I-don't-want-*her*-serving-me!"

She couldn't see the alarm flickering on the faces around her, the black woman over her staring down, confused. As if from miles away, she heard Captain Hoe gasp his disbelief.

"My dear lady! It's not 1960! You can't object to an African-American servin—"

"I don't want *her* here!" Ursula screamed into the napkin strangled in her fist. "Get *her* away from me! I'm telling youse, *get her outta me sight!*"

Somewhere above her right shoulder, she heard gleeful cackling, but couldn't force her head around on her neck to inspect the culprit. She had a vague awareness of Captain Hoe thrusting back his chair and rising. But clear as day was Casino Woman staring down at her, hand on hip, glaring her hatred into her face.

"You don't want me serving you?" shot out of her mouth, and then she seemed to grow more enraged, more a woman of conviction, as she continued, "You racist *bitch!* You ain't nothing but a...*honkey!*" The woman now took in all the white people sat before the finery, tongs snapping. "Treating me and *her,*" she nodded somewhere above Ursula's right shoulder, "like dog shit from your shoes! Can't even look at us! Can't waste your eyesight looking at us. You *all* motherfucking *honkeys!* Yeah, I know folks don't say it much no more, not since *the Jeffersons* been canceled, but they outta! Crazy-assed white *honkeys!* Who to blame for all the banks going under and the economy collapsing and people losing their homes? *Honkeys!* Who gun down all their classmates in schools across the nation, and movie theaters too? Ain't no blacks, no latins, no Chinese do that. I'll tell you who! Outta their mind *honkeys!* Who run the crack labs that churn out the shit that got my little baby

219

D'Kwon killed? Who fill up all the therapists office? Ain't no blacks in the waiting rooms. All *honkeys,* I tell you! Yeah, you too! Fireplace my *ass!* Crazy motherfuckering *honkeys!"*

As Yootha scurried over to the table, she clucked her annoyance. Severe staffing issues were billowing. That woman with the nails, she searched her brain for a name, but no, was having a meltdown at the table, and, she glanced at her watch, it was only the first course! She must be restrained and another take her place. Yootha thought wildly for a suitable replacement. She was pleased to see, at least, two security guards racing towards the table. There were two members of staff who wouldn't be getting the sack.

Just as she joined Captain Hoe at the silly fool's side, the woman roared like an unhinged beast, grabbed the edge of the trolley and toppled it over. Shrimp and oysters flew through the air. Splattered on the guests.

"Cease—"

The entire dining room screamed as a unit as the metal hull of the ship shuddered and crackled. They were thrust to the side like midnight on *the Poseidon Adventure.* Bolts up and down the length of the walls fizzled, bodies flew across tables, plates spun like Frisbees, food sailed from them and spattered faces and walls. Fionnuala was tossed into the table, the wine bottle shattering in her hand. The ship moaned, then roared. A metallic ripping pierced the air, and fingers pointed in terror at a crack that gnawed through the metal above the *Titanic Centennial* banner. Black ooze seeped from it and trickled down the wall. The lights went out. The A/C died. A stench of scorched metal filled the air.

The emergency lights were but yellow flickers from overuse. The ship seemed to settle upright.

"Calm down!" Captain Hoe yelled through the shrieking and moaning. "You've nothing to fear except yourselves! Calm down *now! I'll take care of this!"* Nobody heard him, except maybe Yootha, right beside him as she was. He raced through the staggering masses out of the dining room.

—Plucking oyster goo from her choker, Ursula turned her head.

And screamed again. Through the yellow gloom, Fionnuala Flood was brandishing a broken bottle, shards racing toward her neck. Her eyes were dancing with delight. Visions of all sorts of pub brawls from her youth sprung to Ursula's mind. Her sitting in the nook with a gin and tonic, Fionnuala, Paddy's new squeeze, center stage, broken bottle in her hand, spewing drunken abuse at all around her.

"Fionnuala!" Ursula gasped, fingers clutching the little of her neck exposed through the choker and necklace. "Here to murder me in cold blood!"

"Och, ye're talking out yer arse! Wise up, would ye?"

The sneer of her voice was like a stab in Ursula's heart. As the black woman was dragged away by one of the security guards, Slim's hand grabbed for the bottle. Fionnuala smacked it to the side.

"What...what are ye doing here on the ship...?" Ursula gasped, shuddering in shock and fear. Nothing, not even Casino Woman or a sinking ship, was worse than Fionnuala standing before her, sneering into her face.

"Eat yer own shite, you!" the sneering face spat.

"Ladies! Ladies!" Yootha said, but her voice of reason was drowned by their madness.

"That woman's trying to murder me!" Ursula appealed.

"I think we have more important things—" The woman with the hard hair, Ursula guessed she was some sort of ship official, took a startled look up and down her body.

"She be's a thieving, conniving creature, and now she's moved on to murder!" Ursula sputtered.

"Aye, and ye're a sleekit, pence-snatching, Lady of the Manor, nose in the air so the rain'll drown ye, face like a bulldog licking piss offa nettle fecking bloody slapper of a *cunt!*"

"I'm not gonny sit here and let the likes of her insult me!"

"Would ye feel better if ye stood?"

To Ursula's shock, the ship official was pointing at her, accusation flashing in her eyes.

"*You!* You're the one who's been nicking all the jewels from the cabins!" Ursula clutched at the scarabs, little animals jingling around her wrist. They were pulled from her. Clips and pins and clasps popped and sprung open. "Security!" The woman turned to the remaining guard, who had been chuckling as much as Fionnuala now did. "Take this criminal down to the brig! *Now!*"

As Slim tried to pry his body from the seat and protest, as Ursula was hauled with a rough hand through the increasingly muggy darkness of moaning, food-spattered passengers, Fionnuaula threw back her head and roared with laughter.

CHAPTER 37—TWENTY MINUTES EARLIER

"I want you guys to tell me more about all this, this plan of yours," Jed said, clutching the money to his chest. Agent Matcham and Nigel flanked him as they made their way through the slots towards the poker room. "Or am I supposed to say *our* plan? How exactly is winning this poker game going to make that woman hand over this red mercury to you? And she seems strange to be a terrorist. I don't understand. Can it really be true? And what the hell *is* red mercury again? I seem to remember something about it from the tv, some show I watched, about it not being real. Some sort of hoax...I've been thinking about it since you told me..."

"Don't worry yourself about that," Agent Matcham said. "All in good time. All will be revealed. You must put all these questions to the back of your mind and focus on the task at hand."

"For a junior agent," Nigel snarled, "you're one inquisitive bastard."

"Nigel," Agent Matcham tutted. "Manners, please."

They reached the poker room. But the Britney terrorist was gone. The two horny men were still there, hovering next to a cocktail waitress whose eyes were dancing for tips.

"Great," Jed said. "Now I can leave. I need to get to this dinner. My wife's gonna kill me."

"And MI-6 won't?" Nigel countered. "Insubordination!"

Agent Matcham smiled gaily at Jed.

"Would you please excuse me?"

She grappled Nigel by his collar and hauled him around the corner. Jed heard her hissing and Nigel whining, but couldn't make out what they were saying. Her briefcase leaned against a leg of the poker table. The players were paying him no attention. As if it were the most natural thing in the world, Jed hunched down, placed the pile of money on a hardened patch of the carpet, the remnants of sick, he supposed. He moved the bills to a cleaner spot. He clicked the briefcase open. He stared inside the leather-lined depths. There were a few manila folders, empty he saw, her notebook, the latest issue of *Hello!* celebrity gossip magazine, and a breath mint. He snapped it shut and leaned it back on the leg. He grabbed his and Ursula's nest egg again and held it tight.

His fevered thoughts were interrupted by Britney staggering through the door. From her half-zipped Daisy Dukes, she had apparently been on a comfort break. She toppled into her seat to the left of the dealer, the men surrounded her again, and seconds later Agent Matcham and Nigel reemerged. There was something strange about them now. They were staring so eagerly at the hefty pile of bills clutched in his sweaty hand, Jed half-expected to see drool. They gave him looks which said, "Well...?" Nigel twitched with menace, fists curled. Agent Matcham gave him her best 'bad boys get spanked' look. They blocked the door.

Jed moved reluctantly to an empty seat at the table beside Britney. He sat down. Nigel sat three chairs down. They waited for the game to play out. Britney, Jed noticed, was still winning. She must have thousands in chips before her. Jed wondered about the contents of Agent Matcham's briefcase. She carried it as though it held For Her Eyes Only files, yet... Perhaps the confidential files were locked in a safe in their cabin. The game was over. The man next to Jed won the pot. It looked like a few hundred dollars. He felt Agent Matcham behind his back. She gave him a little nudge between the shoulder blades. Biting his lower lip, Jed slid the piles of cash across the green felt.

"I'd like...um..."

"Hundred dollar chips," Agent Matcham instructed the dealer. "This *is* the high limits poker area, after all."

The dealer's eyes flickered towards the pit boss. Jed wondered it this were a strangely large amount of money to play at this table. Perhaps not in Vegas or Monaco, but considering the detritus of humanity slumped at the chairs around him, he supposed so. But the pit boss gave a subtle nod. Jed watch his and Ursula's security for their twilight years disappear into the little slot in the table, shoved in with a grunt. Well...the British government would soon be paying him back, along with his regular MI-6 salary. Wouldn't they...?

The chips slid across the table. Nigel changed a few hundred dollars into chips, and then the deal began.

Aware of Agent Matcham's breath on his neck, Jed looked at his hand. He felt her eyes inspecting the cards also. A two, a five, two sixes and the ace of hearts. Britney changed a card. Jed threw the two and the five face down across the table. The dealer tossed over two new cards. Jed slid them across the table and peeked at them from the top. The ace of spades and the ace of clubs! A full house! Again! Agent Matcham's excited pants were like an asthmatic perched on his collar. Jed swallowed a yelp.

Nigel changed three cards. He scooped up his new ones and jittered and squirmed in his seat, the buttons straining the shiny brown of his suit jacket.

"I bet two hundred dollars," Britney said.

She pressed her chips into the center of the table. Agent Matcham ran her fingers across Jed's shoulders and massaged gently. His head shot around for the cocktail waitress, but she was gone. One of Britney's posse leaned over and covered the woman's breasts with slobbery kisses. She squealed and jerked, and Jed caught a glimpse of the cards clutched in her writhing fingers. He was barely aware of four of them, but saw clearly the ace of diamonds. There were none left for the other players.

He jolted as Agent's Matcham's lips pressed against his ear. "Bet it all," she hissed into it. "For a free world."

She must have seen Britney's ace as well. He grappled the tops of his little piles of chips with his fingertips. His heart raced. Agent Matcham's fingernails bit into the flesh of his back. He gulped.

"I...I'll match the bid," Jed said. "And...I'll raise...$24,800."

There were gasps all around the table.

The dealer cleared his throat. If he thought Jed insane, his week of training didn't make him show it. "For an even $25,000," the dealer clarified.

"Too rich for me," said the man to the left of Jed.

"I'm out too," said the man to his left.

At least, thought Jed, staring mournfully at his chips now so far away on the green felt surface of the table, that snide little shit, Nigel, would be out of the game, what with the piddling few hundred he had left.

Nigel's manic sneer shot across the table. He banged on the edge of the table with quick slaps like a hep cat hopped up on pep pills.

"I'll..." he said, "I'll..." He shot a look above Jed's cowboy hat at Agent Matcham and motioned for her to come over. "Get over here, *mum.*"

The gasp from Agent Matcham was as surprised as Jed felt; this was a new development to the mission, letting the mark think they were mother and son. But, Jed supposed, they did need alternate personalities.

As Nigel tsked his impatience, she moved from Jed to Nigel.

"Give me your watch. Come on, come on, then!" Agent Matcham began to unshackle her Cartier watch from her wrist. Nigel snatched it off and dangled it under the light of the table.

"I'd like to use this watch as collateral," Nigel announced to the dealer. "It's worth $25,000 at least. Diamond studded, as you see."

Jed eyes bulged, and the dealer's eyes shot towards the pit boss. The pit boss seemed to consider, but then gave a barely perceptible nod.

"Most unusual," said the dealer, taking the watch and placing it beside the chips that towered around him. "But if there are no objections...?"

There were shakes of the head all around the table, including Jed in his shock. Britney shook hers as well, though she seemed not to know what was happening. The men whispered animatedly into her ear and she began a furious counting of her chips with a chipped fingernail. Nigel giggled like a mental patient as the dealer placed the necklace on top of the chips in the middle of the table.

"I'm in," Nigel said, nodding at the necklace. He turned to Jed, "$25,000." He smiled at all.

They all started as Britney squealed with excitement. "I got it! I got $25,000 here too! Count me in! Weeoh-yahoooo!"

She threw her chips to the table and did the dancing-in-her-seat-with-her-arms-held-out-and-her-elbows-thrusting-from-side-to-side. Her breasts hung unaffected.

The dealer eyed Jed. Jed shook his head. He couldn't raise any more. He had no money left. At all in the world. Until that transfer from the Queen... Agent Matcham's massage was now like talons piercing his back.

Jed slipped his eyes to the lefts of their sockets to see Nigel's nods, though he knew the deal by now. Nigel's overly-gelled head began its journey up and down. One, two, three...

So Britney was winning it all. Jed was a man resigned. His heart was racing so quickly, he feared medical assistance.

...four, *five!*

Jed's brain froze. Nigel must win. Something clicked in that frozen brain, like a crack in the ice. Under his cowboy hat, Jed's thoughts did gymnastics as he struggled to comprehend why his subconscious knew that Nigel would want to win this hand. Why, when Nigel had called her 'mum,' it had seemed natural. Why the woman clawing his back only had a breath mint in her secret aluminum government briefcase. Why he knew that Cartier was a fake. Just as fake as Agent Matcham and junior agent Nigel. Jed ground his molars. He threw his cards on the table. Face up.

"Full house!" he said.

Agent Matcham and Nigel gasped. Jed reached across and trailed the cards out of Nigel's slimy fingers.

"A two, a four, a six, an eight and a Jack. Jack shit!" Jed roared.

The cards fell from Britney's fingers. The ace, a five and three tens. They were no match for Jed's full house.

Jed roared, thrust his hands around the chips and watch and raced from the table.

"Our mission, we—!" Agent Matcham gasped.

Jed threw open her briefcase, spilled the loot inside, snapped it shut, and raced out of the poker room.

"You daft cunt!" he heard Nigel roar, but soon all he heard was the ringing of the slots as he raced through them.

Jed's feet pounded on the floor, briefcase banging against his thigh, but then there was no floor. He toppled into a slot as the ship thrust to the left and screams rang out around him. He was vaguely aware of the ship shuddering as if it had just been electrocuted, the walls crackling, but he kept thrusting his feet one in front of the other. He shoved past teetering, shrieking bodies and found himself in the hallway.

He stared around wildly for the elevator. It was probably the last amenity he should be using, the state the ship was in now, but he certainly wasn't going to tackle the stairs. He raced towards it and glanced back. The two thugs were fifty feet behind him. Agent Matcham's speed belied her age as, Jed feverishly thought, did his. His heart felt like it would thrust from his breastplate as he pounded on the button. The door pinged open at once. Jed heaved exhausted pants, the sweat lashing from his hat as the elevator seemed to crawl to the main deck. But at least it was functioning as it should, though the lights flickered and went dim. The door creaked open. He squealed at Nigel, bent over, hands on knees, wiping his brow. The enraged face, three slick hairs disheveled, dissolved into a malevolent grin.

"It's all over, pensioner!"

Jed hefted the briefcase in the air and smacked the snide shit-eating grin off his face. Nigel toppled to the floor with a groan. Jed felt his foot shoot forward and land with a satisfying splat in the depths of the little bastard's well-ironed groin.

As squeals of a tortured pig rang in Jed's ears, Agent Matcham appeared from the emergency stairs door, flush with exertion and anger. Her hands flew to her cheeks, disbelieving shock, Jed thought, at the sight of Nigel writhing on the floor. And that noise coming from his mouth! Could a human really emit—? But Jed realized it was alarms or sirens or both, filling the air with an urgency that set his teeth on edge.

There was a roar of hundreds behind Agent Matcham. Jed couldn't comprehend what his eyes were seeing. Hoards of EconoLux staff—he knew from the uniforms—were marching and cursing and swaggering mob-like down the shuddering hall, mops and brooms and strange kitchen-type things brandished like pitchforks, smashing the windows of the upmarket stores that lined the main hall.

His brain didn't have time to understand. Agent Matcham was now flinging herself towards him, her posh mask of intelligence and refinement sliding down her neck to reveal a shrieking shrew.

"You bastard! You horrid, horrid bastard! That's our money!"

The briefcase clutched to his heaving chest, Jed feverishly followed the signs that pointed to the gangway meters away. He was relieved to see the gangway was down. They had docked!

He glanced around and saw the woman wailing as she tried to extract the youthful offender's limbs from the mob of feet that enveloped them and trampled on top of his screaming body. Jed ran onto Puerto Rico. Behind him, the woman pried the young man from the floor and whoever the hell they were raced after him.

CHAPTER 38

"Hallelujah!" Aquanetta bellowed, her talons launched towards the heavens. "Lemme at them Channel bags! Thank you, sweet Lord Jesus!"

She didn't even mind that two of her nails had been broken by the security guard when he hauled her screaming mass from the dining room. As he had marched her past the dining room door to dump her in the brig, the mob in the hallway overran them. The guard's fingers had slipped from Aquanetta's bulging bicep. He had been torn from her as the sirens and alarms rang out, his hands, clutching at the air as if in the throes of drowning, disappearing through the charging, chanting masses.

Aquanetta had been thrown to the floor, screamed as another nail shattered and, brushing off the footmarks, hauled her mass up.

"What the hell?"

Aquanetta looked around and, as a standing ashtray was thrown through the Apple store window and gangs of workers poured through the shards, whooping, she hooted and praised the Heavenly Father. He had indeed pried open the pearly gates for the meek and huddled lumpen masses of the earth, the disadvantaged, the poor, the pearly gates of Prada, Gucci and Fendi, and Burberry, Coach and Chanel too, that lined the tony main passageway of the *Queen of Crabs,* showplace of the supposed luxury of the cruise liner. The trampled were doing the trampling now, trampling over any rich white, honkey, passenger that stood in their way, she now saw and, oh, but black ones and Asian too, for those with a bank balance were traitors no matter what the color of their skin. Anyone not in uniform. Except the hated security guards. They were equal opportunity tramplers. And their long-simmering rage was exploding in shattered store windows and hands grabbing only for items with price tags of three figures or more. At long last! Hallelujah! Amen!

Aquanetta's mouth, without her bidding, started chanting into the shrieking bodies around her, *"Free Rodney King! Free Rodney King!"* at nobody and everybody.

A guy from the engine room grabbed her hands, his eyeballs bouncing with joy, an X-Box under one arm, Nikes under the other, his face stretched with rage. "Been kept down by the Man too long," he babbled into her face. "It started with us in the engine room. Low pay, long hours. Fuck that shit! Some rioting going on." He giggled. "And some looting too! These Lebron X Nikes. Go for 30 grand a pop! Get you some!" He raced past the Apple store melée, down the dank, smokey hallway through a cacophony of elbows and arms and flying bodies. Aquanetta supposed he already had an iPad. But she didn't.

Fighting through the mob racing from the Apple store, she tried to squeeze her mass over the shards of glass, then realized they were all leaving.

"No iPads left?" she asked a skinny girl.

"Nope."

Aquanetta pushed her way up the crowd to Chanel. She emerged ten minutes later, panting with sweat and exertion, bags dangling up and down the lengths of her arms. She had put her talons to good use, and there were bits of blood spattered on the floor inside, but thankfully not on the bags.

"Shit!" Aquanetta moaned, spying the security at the end of the hallway, legs spread, fire hoses aimed at the crowd. Getting ready to—

There were screams through the sirens as water shot from the hoses and pinned bodies against walls. Swag flew from fingers and dropped to the ground. Aquanetta pried open a broom closet and hid inside. And was shocked to find Fionnuala already there. They crouched together in the darkness, wincing at the shrieks and wails outside, the slosh of water.

Fionnuala eyed the bags hanging from Aquanetta's arms. She clucked her tongue as her body shuddered with irritation.

"Looting! I kyanny comprehend how ye've stooped so low, hi. Looting be's for wanes of the day, sure. Smashing and grabbing whenever the whim hits them, and when they can be bothered to prise their lazy arses from their computers and video games. But c'mere til I tell ye, if everyone could afford them Channel bags ye've draped around yer arms now, they wouldn't be exclusive, so they wouldn't. I'll tell ye what I think, shall I? Lazy fecking eejits the wanes of the day be's. Not bothered to learn a skill nor a trade. And why should they? Not when everyone what was born with two hands can grab a rock and smash a window and reach in and grab. Smash and grab, the new money for the millennium. I mind in me youth the Top Yer Trolley store down the town in Derry was bombed time and again, but ye didn't see me digging through the rubble for a new pair of trainers or free mascara. As we had self-restraint and manners and we was brought up with belt buckles hammering down on wer arses if we put a foot wrong. Shoplifting, I'll grant ye, I'm all up for it, aye. Sure, women's been participating in that for yonks, and there be's times when it's dead necessary, like when them queues for the tills at the Top Yer Trolley be's winding a mile and it be's easier to lift what I need and make off with it down the street with what I need than pay for it. And what I want, and all."

"Can't understand a word you just said. But I'm guessing you wanna say you pissed you got here too late to grab yourself some stuff?"

Fionnuala scowled. How did she know? She waited for Aquanetta to offer her one of the nine, ten, eleven? bags that pressed against her various body parts. Just one. The leather smelled like money.

"Hrmph!" Fionnuala heard beside her in the gloom. "You might be wondering why I ain't offering you one of my Chanel bags. It cause you ain't told me the truth. You see that rioting out there? We was fighting against folk with money. Rich fat folk. Like you."

Fionnuaula gasped. "Are ye saying I'm fat?"

There was silence. Fionnuala grabbed Aquanetta's hand, but the woman flinched and snatched it away.

"Hands off my bags!"

"Naw, I was...trying to..."

Fionnuala trailed off in confusion. She was trying to comfort her? Who had she ever comforted? Aquanetta spoke.

"Ain't heard no screams in a while. Think the pigs with the hoses are gone. Best get ourselves outta here now."

They pried open the door and peered down the shambles of the hallway. They crawled out of the closet and sloshed their way through broken glass and discarded loot towards the main lobby. Aquanetta snorted and pointed up the main staircase.

"What the hell she doing here? Looking for the second course? What she got against me, that's what I wanna know! Rich white bitch. *Another* rich white bitch."

Through the mist and the trails of smoke, as if she were an apparition, Ursula was descending upon them, clutching a single high heel to her bosom as if it were her last Xanax, her battered handbag banging against her hip, her hair at an odd angle, welts around her neck from where the jewelry had been wrenched from her, eyes like the president of the Marilyn Manson fan club. Fionnuala couldn't have been more surprised if it were the Virgin Mary herself, with an assortment of lesser known but still beloved saints in Her wake, descending the stairs.

"Hello?" Ursula called out. "Who's there?"

She approached them, seeming shell-shocked, the stench of oysters rising from her.

"But...!" Fionnuala gasped. "Ye're locked up, ye hateful bitch!"

"The...the doors to me cell were electronic ones. Them security lads give me some tablets for to calm me nerves, and I had meself a wee lie-down, like, och, I was surprised the pillow was lovely and soft, so I was, when one of them lightning strikes that hit the ship musta done something, as the the door just popped open on its lonesome, like. And when I got outside..." She shuddered.

"Och, caught in the crossfires, were ye?" Fionnuala snapped, hand on hip. Aquanetta's Chanel bags swayed next to her elbows. "I thought ye'd be used to that, the shite that spills outta yer mouth causing all sorts of grief and misery and people lining up to take well-deserved pot shots at ye, like."

Ursula's brain was frazzled on whatever the security guards had given her. All she could think of was the book she had been reading now that her inspection of *Lotto Balls of Shame* was complete. Step 17 of *Twenty Steps To Winning Every Argument* intrigued her: Pay Your Adversary A Surprise Compliment In The Middle Of A Screaming Match. Ursula took a deep breath as the spittle sprayed her face and grasped step 17.

"Sure, I'm only noticing now...that's a grand and lovely top you've on there, but, Fionnuala."

Fionnuala spat with scorn: "Aye, and yer bloody jungle suit be's the height of fashion and all...in Hell!" But halfway though the knee-jerk spite, in the back of her mind, in one of the grottos, she sparkled with delight. She felt weird and tingly. A compliment! The last one she would recall was after that Irish dancing championship she had come third runner-up in when she was fourteen, but even those few kind words had been about her frock, not her dancing.

Ursula forced herself to look towards the other enemy's fingernails and though fear of them sparkled in her eyes, pharmaceuticals were making her stronger and she forced herself to say: "And them nails! Wile fetching, so they be's."

Smack!

Ursula didn't know which Chanel bag hit her first. She wailed and clawed the air as her body plummeted to the slosh.

"Crazy white bitch!" Aquanetta roared, bags shuddering and twitching from her arms. "Got me hauled off by security! What I ever done to you? Nothing, that's what! Like I done said, you white folks some crazy-assed *loonies!* And you the craziest I ever laid eyes on! Mama told me not to trust no white folk!"

Ursula whimpered in the sludge, holding her hands out to quell the barrage of Chanel that was about to rain down upon her.

Fionnuala took a step forward, then a step back, then a step forward again. Her left eye twitched and her left shoulder jerked and her mind swam with the madness she was about to perform. She hated Ursula, *hated* her, but... How dare this stranger, this *foreigner* roar abuse at a citizen of Derry City? How *dare* she! Irish pride brimming through her, Fionnuala grabbed what she could of the swinging bags. She shoved Aquanetta into the promotional poster for Claratin. It toppled, and so did she. Fionnuala raised her hand to strike, and she was an expert at it. But—

"Mammy! *Mammy!*"

Scampering towards them was Siofra, clothes in tatters, hair like a nest, face like a bin man at the end of a shift.

As Ursula struggled to get up and Aquanetta flapped in the water, Fionnuala looked around the empty lobby, mortified. She roared down at the trembling little form: "How dare ye show me up like that, ye daft eejit! Roaring 'mammy' at me outta ye, so's everyone knows I'm responsible for ye. What are themmuns gonny think of me parenting, like, when ye're in such a state? The bold faced cheek!"

"Auntie Ursula! Auntie Ursula! Ye've to come quick! They've me uncle Jed held prisoner!"

"Ye ungrateful wee bitch! All them years I fed and clothed ye...wasted! And an ungrateful, spiteful wee cunt, ye turned out, and pig ugly and all!"

She turned to Aquanetta to explain.

"A face begging to be smacked, that one has. Years, I've been trying to smack the ugliness offa it. Hasn't worked, but. As I'm sure ye can tell." Dymphna had finally moved up a notch on her list.

"Come, Auntie Ursula," Siofra said, grabbing her arm and pulling uselessly. "I know where they've Uncle Jed holed up, so I do! I've been following them, like."

Siofra quickly checked Ursula's hands for a gift; that was what she always expected and usually received from her minted lotto-winning aunt, and her godmother as well, but she didn't see one. Her disappointment was tempered, though, by the thought she supposed her auntie Ursula couldn't always cart sticks of rock or dolls or whatnot about on the off chance she might run into her goddaughter.

"Jed's been missing," Ursula explained to Fionnuala. "But I hadn't a clue—"

"Clattering the shite outta him, they've been, auntie! It's money themmuns is after, I think."

"Why don't ye just contact the local filth? Doesn't that be what *you lot* does anyroad? Grass people up?"

Phoning the authorities had been Ursula's first plan of action. But, somewhere in the fuzziness of her mind, she realized she couldn't. She couldn't remember why, but, oh, yes she could. She wrung her sopping fingers.

"I kyanny. Och, ye're never gonny believe this, Fionnuala, I'm on the run, but. From the coppers, like. Ye've not a clue what I've been up to. I had to take this cruise to escape them, if ye can believe that."

Then was born something Fionnuala never thought she'd have for Ursula Barnett, ever: respect. Grudging, against all her better instincts and nature, but nevertheless...respect. And, she remembered, she *had* had the hots for Jed back in the mists of time. She looked at her out of the corner of her eye, stifled a giggle and sidled up to her.

"Ye sleekit, sly bitch ye! Yer filthy sin be's safe with me, so it does."

"Help, then, Mammy!"

"Naw!" Fionnuala still snapped.

"Mammy!" Siofra squealed, stamping her foot, tears welling in her eyes. "Stop yer foolish carry-on now! We've to find Uncle Jed!"

Fionnuala was reluctant. She really, really was. But...

As the three walked off, each step of Fionnuala's dragged, Aquanetta finally forced herself upwards, filthy, sodden Chanel bags splayed across her thighs. She was crestfallen. She thought she had made a new friend, a white one. But she had been wrong. Still, she mused, she had the bitch's extra $20.

234

CHAPTER 39

Dymphna was trying to position Keanu's little fingers around the baby spoon so he could feed his little sister. But at one and a half years of age, he didn't seem to understand what he was supposed to do. He kept throwing the spoon to the floor and wailing out of him. And if he was struggling, Dymphna dreaded to think how it would go when she tried to have six-week-old Beeyonsay feed him in return.

Her father was passed out on his bunk from drink and exhaustion. When the electricity had gone out from the lightning strike, he had told her, the galley crew had thrown down their utensils and joined the looting mob. Paddy had pushed through them in the opposite direction and staggered back to the cabin.

Fabrizio hovered above Dymphna's disheveled curls, clucking his disapproval. Their furious sex session had been interrupted first by the father coming in, then the children screaming from their stroller. He stared down in ever-increasing disgust at the state of the children. Filthy, malnourished beings, tattered cloth hanging from their tiny struggling limbs, the boy's too small, the girl's too big, their eyes begging the world for mercy. He was looking for a wife to bear his children, and although this strange foreign girl had the appropriate child bearing hips and breasts that could feed an orphanage, he was realizing how his own progeny, his own little toddling gifts to the world, would be raised. Worse than cattle.

"Och!" Dymphna huffed. "Them wanes be's flimmin eejits, so they does. Kyanny make them see the sense in feeding each other. Ye know, their daddy be's a Proddy, and—"

"*Basta!*" Fabrizio snatched the spoon from her hand. Dymphna looked up at him in alarm. "Whata you do to babies? My mama and my grandmama, they teached me how to treata the child. Not likea that! You...you...mama from Hell!"

He tried to pat the head of the boy-creature, but the tufts of hair on his skull were slick with grease. Fabrizio shuddered. His hand recoiled. Dymphna's alarm dissolved into anger.

"Aye," she yelled up at him, "and if ye want some home truths being told, I'm about to tell some to *ye* right now. Shagging ye sends me to heaven, aye it does, nobody's plowed me better, like. C'mere til I tell ye, but, I just kyanny rid it of me mind that yer granny just butchered

235

the wanes of others and ate their flesh without even pausing to cook it! All of youse in yer family! Deranged, filthy-minded cannibals, the lot of youse! And ye've the bold-faced cheek to stand there and criticize me mothering skills! Feck on off outta here if ye think yer mammy and granny be's better at raising wanes. At least these two of mines won't end up down some sad old bugger's throat!"

He roared a torrent of his strange language at her, his face stretched with rage, arms flying through the air. Then he turned and stomped out of the cabin.

"Aye, off ye go! Fecking toerag *arsehole!*" Dymphna taunted, memorizing that arse for her use later on.

She ignored the shrieks from the stroller, her hunger for an appropriate husband was more important than their hunger for food. Through her tears, she tried to peer out the porthole, but even if she could have seen through the caked-on filth, she would have had difficulty distinguishing where the torrents spewing from the sky ended and the churning Caribbean Sea began. There was nothing outside but Last Judgment Gray. She expected the Four Horsemen to descend any second, reach down and drag her off to Hell.

Fabrizio was gone. Dymphna saw her future through that porthole: pints of lager thrown down her throat, staggering mateless through the pubs of Derry, shots of whiskey and tequila stretching endlessly before her bleary eyes, nobody wanting to gaze upon her goggled, unfocused face with tenderness, the years dragging by in a drunken haze, fingers pointed at her in sport, faces turned to avoid her eyes that used to sparkle, and whisper about the deadness in her features, clucking at the folly of her behavior, her faltering tongue, her tainted breath, her impaired health... All would recoil in horror from the sight of her as she staggered over the cobblestones of the city center, the sick of curry chips down her top. She would lie down, spread her legs and pop out the wanes in a row, the hooligans and loose shop floor girls, the fathers dimly remembered in an alcoholic haze, her only reason for living. She would be a slave to the bottle until she lost her manners, her shape, her beauty and, finally, her virtue. Then she would die.

Tears poured like the rain outside. The door rattled open and—Dymphna's shock was greater than the Four Horsemen would have been!

"Blessed Virgin!" Ursula said, clutching her nostrils with a handkerchief. Tears stung her eyes. "They have ye living here like...like..."

"Aye, we know, sure," Fionnuala said, marching in behind her. "Worse than slaves."

"Auntie Ursula!" Dymphna said. "And...*Mammy?!*How...why...?!"

They were with a fat man and a skinny woman Dymphna hadn't met before, but who were Yanks, she could tell. They stood outside in the hallway, unwilling to step inside. The woman in the red glasses looked like she was dry-heaving. And behind them...

"Siofra!"

As Dymphna hugged her auntie Ursula, then Siofra, even she knew from her mother's blazing eyes, the faltering of her steps and the exaggeration of the sweeps of her arms, she knew alcohol had brought them together. It was the trifecta of emotions Dymphna had lived over and over at a glance at the pillow next to her after a night on the town: first came the shock, then horror, and it was only later, over a cup of black coffee after the drink was oozing out of the brain and regular thinking began, that the shame set in. Followed by a fourth and the worst: cold, raw regret. She cringed at the thought of the rage that would accompany Fionnuala's regret once the alcohol wore off.

"We're gonny save Uncle Jed!" Siofra squealed, eyes bright with excitement. "And I've a secret weapon and all, youse!"

"Rouse yerself!" Fionnuala barked at Paddy. She shook his limbs as Ursula wrung her hands at her side. He sputtered awake. "We've to find Jed. Get yer shirt on."

"Who? Where? What?" The look up at them through his blood-veined eyes let them know he thought he had woken up roaring mad.

"And yer jacket and all," Dymphna told her daddy. "I heard on the radio in the staff room they be's forecasting a tropical storm."

Fionnuala inspected her with suspicion as she forced Paddy's arms into his shirt. Perhaps, Dymphna feared, the drink in her mother's brain was beginning to wane. It didn't bode well for the next few hours.

"Tropical storm!" Fionnuala snorted. "What's that meant to mean, ye jumped up cunt? Some fancy Yank name for 'hurricane'?"

"It's like an infant hurricane, Mammy."

"I think," the man at the door said, "half of it already hit us."

"We're probably in the eye of the storm," the woman with the glasses said. "Which means we don't have long for this calm to last."

They all jumped as Paddy yelled out, fingers playing air guitar:"*Dah! Dah-dah-dah! Dah-dah-dah! Dah-dah-daaah!*"

"Daddy," Dymphna said, patting the tattered denim of his jacket. "That be's *Eye of the* **Tiger.**"

It didn't bode well for Uncle Jed's rescue, both her mammy and daddy paladic, but they had to try. Already, she could see her mother casting Ursula looks as if to say, "What the bleeding feck am I doing with *her?*"

"It doesn't be far!" Siofra piped up, as if this knowledge would make them move quicker. She jumped up and down and twirled her greasy hair impatiently. "C'mon youse! Let's save Uncle Jed!"

Thrown from one side of the gangway to the other, clutching each other for support, they left the creaking carcass of the ship behind. Ursula, Fionnuala, Paddy, Dymphna, Siofra, Slim and Louella pressed themselves through the air of Puerto Rico.

Back in the cabin, Keanu and Beeyonsay screamed in their stroller for food. The spoon was on the floor, out of the reach of their tiny fingers.

CHAPTER 40—LA ISLA BONITA, PUERTO RICO
¡Co-quí! ¡Co-quí! ¡Co-quí!

Siofra skipped backwards before the adults who were wincing through the horizontal drizzle, and she pointed eagerly behind her. "It's just down this wee dirt footpath of sorts a bit, and then through a patch of jungle sorta garden thingy. Get a move on, youse!"

"Eh?" Paddy called out; they were all straining to hear. Their ears had been attacked by the sound the moment they staggered off the gangway. Yes, there was the usual squawking of birds, the chirping of crickets, perhaps even the shriek of a monkey, the definite roar of drunken locals somewhere in the distance, but there was also a strange two-part whistle which pierced the air, filling it like a living thing and coming at their ears at all angles.

Louella, trapped between the twin evils of Ursula's diligent hairdressing and Fionnuaula's delinquent hygiene, tilted her head, then clapped her hands with glee. "I know this sound! I know it from my *Ambient Sounds Of The Rainforest* CD! It's the mating call of the coquí, a small frog that belongs only to Puerto Rico. You hear the whistles it's making?"

"How can we not?" Paddy muttered, holding his head and wincing.

"That's why they called the frog that, the coquí, because it makes a noise like that. Co-*quí!* Co-*quí!* Try it with me, little girl! *Co-quí, co-quí!*"

Slim gave it a half-hearted try, "co-*koo!*" but the dirty little girl ahead, wavering between excitement and nervousness, seemed to have other things on her mind. Perhaps she wondered how these adults, two of them drunk, one of them sightseeing, one of them fat, one of them dear but dim-witted, Dymphna, could possibly save her Uncle Jed. She had seen him struggling through the window, tied up to a chair and yelping every time the horrible man in the suit smacked him in the face, yelling "Where's the briefcase? Where's the briefcase, innit?" and the old woman did nothing but stand there and watch them like it was her favorite show on the telly. If Siofra hadn't been sat down time and again on the settee at home and warned by her mother never, ever to speak to the Filth, she might have sought out someone in uniform to help free Uncle Jed. But that was forbidden by the Floods.

In her drunken haze, which *was* fading fast, Fionnuala couldn't understand the air around her. It was like what her hands felt when, after a load set on 'boil', she reached into the washing machine at home to retrieve the underwear. And Fionnuala also couldn't understand how the air could be like that if it was raining. Surely it should be cold if it was raining? She had never encountered anything like it in Derry. And she knew, *knew* there were beautiful places in Puerto Rico; she had seen photos of a tropical paradise, though with scantily-clad slags, in the brochures at the travel agent's down Shipquay Street. But this wasn't it. Far from it.

They weren't on Puerto Rico proper, but on a little island to the south which maybe belonged to it. It seemed the government had forgotten about it. They were in a scattered collection of dwellings that time and the local police had passed by. There seemed to be no sidewalks, just a few crooked footpaths, which were also used for garbage disposal. They stumbled over old milk cartons, kicked through tin cans, sopping wrappers clinging to the soles of their shoes. Each garbage can they passed was empty.

"The stench offa the ground here be's something terrible, hi," Dymphna said, her own sick threatening to join the piles she minced through.

As they squelched after Siofra through the muck, they cast furtive glances across the panorama of overgrown weeds and ramshackle shacks with many boarded up windows that had long ago been painted bright primary colors but were now glum, some riddled with bullet-holes. They forced their way past discarded refrigerators and over squashed iguanas and bicycles with no wheels.

The only person was sat outside the scary-looking store with the faded, tattered "Grand Opening" banner trying to flap in the wind, a grizzled, menacing man, ancient, with a straw hat and one leg who tried to sell them drugs from his wheelchair as they passed.

"This way, youse!" Siofra bubbled in excitement. She pointed to a sign which promised they would soon be at La Villa Boracha.

They hurried toward the jungle-garden-area. Their faces were smacked by the sopping, oversized leaves and twisting vines they had last seen the likes of when watching *Jurassic Park* and which hung glumly in the humidity from tired, graffiti-defaced trees, trunks sullied with bizarre fruit rotting where it had fallen, colonies of flies the size of golf balls devouring the mushy piles. They stared in fear at the buzzing masses as they passed.

"Would ye look at the state of them bananas!" Fionnuala marveled in disgust. "And I thought they only came in yellow."

"Those are plantains," Louella said, pointing. "And those are avocados and those are mangos. Not worth the prices they charge in our supermarket in Wisconsin."

Fionnuala, Paddy and Dymphna exchanged a look which said 'intellectual twat.'

"No need to rub it in wer faces that ye know foreign languages," Fionnuala said.

"But...they're called plantains and avocados and mangos in *English*."

Fionnuala gave her a look which said she didn't believe it, and that she knew all the words in the English language.

"Naw, them be's bananas, but you be's calling them some other foreign name."

Louella didn't know how she could explain it.

"Come on, youse!" Siofra said, her face red from the squealing. "Och, youse are dead slow! Put a bit of spring in yer steps!"

"We—we're twice as big as ye, love," Paddy said through the vines, panting up against the bark of a tree. Slim lumbered past him. "Most of us, anyroad. It takes us longer to get through these vines and whatnot."

"Shall we not just concentrate on the task at hand?" Ursula wondered with a worried look up at the quickly darkening sky. She missed the look Fionnuala passed her which said she would soon be unleashing her tongue on her and worse if she didn't shut up.

Slim was proving surprisingly nimble in the jungle, traipsing through the vines like he had been born a wolf-child, while the others tripped and cursed and toppled. Actually, Slim's mass was remarkably pliable for its size. Flight attendants frequently marveled at how he could configure his folds so that they didn't ooze over the armrests. He always fit in his seat, though usually to the chagrin of the passenger in the next seat, but that usually was Louella.

"The hunger's pure gnawing a hole in me stomach, so it is," Paddy said.

"Aye, mine and all," Fionnuala snapped grumpily. "And them flimmin sounds be's driving me mental! Shut the feck up! Shut the feck up, youse frogs and whatever flimmin godless insects youse be's! What the bloody feck am I doing here anyroad? With *her?!* Deranged, imbecilic with drink, I musta been to allow meself to be dragged along

241

on this trip through Hell! I swear, heavenly Father and blessed Virgin, to never press a bottle to me lips ever again!"

Ursula was disappointed. She thought a truce had been called between her and Fionnuala, their own personal Peace Process, but the more time passed, and the more sober she became, Fionnuala was reverting back to form. But Ursula had to push it to the back of her mind and focus on saving Jed. That was the important thing right now.

They came to a clearing. A sign, splinters rising from it, told them this was La Villa Baracha. They peered through the gloom, which was now approaching pitch black, at the main house, where they supposed the offices were. From the yellowish glow of the few lights around, it looked relatively new, but the bungalows that stretched out from it on the grounds beyond looked like there was a permanent vacancy for a maintenance man on the premises. And a landscaper and exterminator.

"Here, here!" Siofra hissed, pointing eagerly at a bungalow that back in the mists of time must have been flamingo pink and Caribbean aqua. "Number 12!"

"What is this place?" Slim asked as they tiptoed toward it.

"Used to be some sort of swanky hotel, looks like," Louella answered.

"Who in their right mind would want to vacation on this island?"

Nobody had the answer to this question. With the chirping of the coquís around them, the angry black sky pressing down, the sopping air being sucked with difficulty down their throats, their hair frizzy and their clothing stuck to their exhausted limbs, they approached, hunched down, with little steps. Rats and lizards scattered through their feet. There was a light in the main window.

Louella took off her glasses, Slim his bifocals, and they wiped the raindrops from them. All eyes peered through filth of the window to the scene beyond. A few gasped at the sight of Jed splayed on the chair next to the old fashioned square tv, bedsheets wrapped around him, an impromptu rope, they supposed. A mournful mew rose from Ursula's throat, and she tried to stifle it with a fist to her lips. Jed was either passed out or dead. The thugs who held him captive were sitting at the kitchenette table, looking exhausted and at a loss, taking sips from mugs that read "Welcome to Paradise! Stay a while..."

"Oh, Jed," Ursula moaned against the pane, "Please be alive and...*dear God!*" She clutched the arm closest to her. "It be's Frank the

Faith Man! With his beard shaved off and wearing different clothing, aye, but Frank the Faith Man plain as day!" They all stared at her for an explanation; nobody knew who this Frank the Faith Man was. They got none. The thoughts were like bullets shooting through Ursula's brain: after her confession, Frank the Faith Man not interested in giving her penance, more interested in asking about the lotto win, how much they had won, what they had bought, how much they had left, how much interest the bank gave them. She had spewed out the information, and had even lied a bit, telling him they had won much more. Then the money slipping through their fingers, in no small measure due to Jed's gambling and drinking, and the loss on selling the dream house and moving to Wisconsin. But she had told him about the special account, and how she kept checking it to make sure the $25,000 was still there. It had been the last time she checked.

"Distract them gits," Siofra said. "One of youse knock on the door or something. I seen things like that done on the telly all the time. And I'll slip through this wee window here."

"How can you do that?"

"Och, I've been climbing through them vents on the ship for the better part of the journey, so I have," Siofra said.

Ursula looked alarmed, but not surprised.

"Has she really...?" Ursula looked accusingly at Fionnuala. Fionnuala wrapped her arms around herself.

"Mind yer own business, Ursula. Or themmuns in there can slaughter yer Jed for all I care."

"Mammy! Show some, uh," Dymphna struggled for the word. "contrition, does it be called?"

"I think you mean 'compassion'," Louella said.

The Floods glared at her.

"It's too dangerous to put a little girl through that," Louella said. "How old are you, sweetie pie? Six?"

"Nine!"

"But...what are you going to do when you get inside, love?" Ursula asked. How she wanted to run her fingers through Siofra's hair, to show her gratitude and give the trembling, malnourished girl a bit of comfort. But...she felt queasy at the sight of the ratty, muck-caked throngs of greasy black filth that passed for her hair. And she thought she saw little things jumping around on the scalp. Och, to hell with it! Siofra was her goddaughter after all! As Siofra answered, Ursula reached out and touched the alternately slick and hardened locks.

"I've me special weapon, don't youse forget!" she said. After a few tentative strokes, Ursula moved her fingers off her head to safety, her stomach churning and finally now understanding the Yanks' love of disinfectant wipes.

"What is that weapon ye've been yammering on about?" Fionnuala asked. "Are ye planning on spreading yer cheeks and spewing yer shite all over themmuns? Is that yer special weapon? Yer shite?"

Siofra stamped her foot, enraged. "Naw!" she hissed up at her mammy. "Don't be an eejit! This!"

She reached into her unicorn jeans and tugged out a bottle.

"My Liquid Death triple X!" Slim gasped. "It's a controlled substance! Where did you get that?"

"Ye left it in the place ye met me," Siofra said. "And piles more of them wile burny sauces. A wile craic, them sauces of yers be's. I've been making me way to the dining room and staff canteen and pouring them into people's tea. Ye should see the looks on their faces! And that many of them had to race to the toilet afterwards! Aye, a wile craic. This one, but, be's the worst. Or the best, if ye get what I'm saying. I figure I can slip through the window and pour some into whatever they be's drinking from them swanky mugs of theirs. Tea, I'm guessing."

Fionnuala inspected the mugs through the window.

"Only an eighth of a drop will do the job," Slim said. "Watch how much you put in. They might sue us."

"Aye, I know sure. Now," Siofra continued, as they formed a little circle around her, the light from the window shining on their heads. "Who's gonny go knocking on themmuns' door to distract them? Mammy and Daddy, I don't think it should be youse."

"Why not?" they chorused, looking put out but relieved.

"As yer eyes be's goggled with drink, and there be's an awful stench rising from youse...And, Dymphna, I love ye dearly, but...Well..."

She turned to Slim and singled him out.

"You! Ye seem wile civil and a good craic. Are ye up for it?"

Slim looked chuffed. He rubbed his face with his filthy handkerchief, and Louella eyed him with jealousy, but also with relief.

"Well, okay!" he said. "Let's go!"

Ursula, Louella, Paddy, Fionnuala and Dymphna hunched in the fronds under the window, the fronds which were beginning to whip in the wind, as Slim approached the door and Siofra shimmied up to the window sill. She unscrewed the top of the hot sauce and brandished it in her little hand. She pressed her other hand to the filthy glass. One push and she would be able to open the window wider and scamper inside. Slim raised his massive hand before the door, knuckles ready. Ursula and Fionnuala blessed themselves in unison.

Knock! Knock! Knock!

They saw the two at the table jolt with alarm and their heads whip towards the door.

"Who...?" the youth asked.

The woman placed her hand on his and, eyes glinting, placed her finger to her mouth to warn him to be silent. "Who is it?" she called out in a posh voice, shooting glances over at Jed's body.

Slim cleared his throat.

"Uh, I've got to check the AC. I'm from the hotel."

"It's working fine." They saw the youth remove himself from the table and sidle towards the door. Jed remained either passed out or dead.

"Um, after that first part of the hurricane, there's been some complaints." Siofra poised at the window, ready to drop down and scamper across the floor to the table and the mugs.

"Well, ours is working fine! Please leave us in peace!" The woman, wringing her hands, got up and tiptoed beside the youth.

"Ma'am! If you don't let me in to inspect the AC, we'll have to add an extra charge to your room!"

"Fine! Charge us, then!" the woman spat, while beside Ursula, Louella bristled. That would certainly make *her* fling the door open wide. "Do you not see the Do Not Disturb sign on the door?"

From the window sill, Siofra poked her head into the room and saw the two on the other side of the door, clutching at it and trying to peer through the peephole. She poked her head back out. Slim wiped his brow, struggling for something else to say. He looked across the heads under the window to Siofra for support. She motioned for him to break down the door. Slim looked uncertain. Siofra hopped down from the ledge and ran over to him.

"Break it down! Ye've the mass to do so, so ye have!"

Slim took a step back, geared his shoulder and...

Agent Matcham and Nigel screamed as the door thrust inwards. They were propelled into the wall, their heads clanking together. They groaned, eyes rolling, bodies slumping to the floor. Their eyes flickered and they passed out. Siofra raced between the mountains of Slim's legs, screaming, "I'm not looking at yer faces! *I'm not looking at yer faces!*" just in case they caught her and would use that as an excuse to kill her. But they were passed out.

Siofra fought the urge to pry open their eyelids and squirt the Liquid Death into their eyes. The others raced past her and Slim towards Jed.

"Quickly, quickly," Dymphna said, hopping up and down with nerves. "Themmuns is going to wake up soon!"

"Och, Jed," Ursula said, feeling for a pulse. "Don't be dead."

Paddy knelt down and began to fiddle with the knots. "Christ, themmuns have tied them tight! Hours, it's gonny take to undo them!"

"Maybe, uh, Fionnuala, I think your name is?" Louella said, "You can just lick the knots and the acid of your tongue will dissolve them off."

"Jed, what use are ye to me dead?" Ursula wailed, shaking his body as Paddy managed to undo a knot and Fionnuala just stood, arms folded. "If ye die, I'll fecking kill ye!"

But Jed sputtered and was awake.

"What...?" he asked.

"These guys are coming to!" Slim called from the passed out bodies. As Louella, Dymphna and Ursula joined Paddy in trailing the knotted bedsheet from Jed's limbs, Siofra raced over the quickly-wakening bodies.

She pried apart the lips of the guy, took aim and poured gooey Liquid Death down his gaping throat. As the guy sputtered and jerked like he had been electrocuted, Siofra forced the bottle between the woman's lips and forced her to drink down.

Their howls filled the room.

They seemed unable to speak, coughing and sputtering and gasping, their faces beet red, hands clawing at the bulging veins of their necks. Siofra giggled and clapped and jumped from one foot to the other. They clutched each other for support, their bodies writhing on the floor in torrents of pain.

"Scalded!" the woman managed to scream. "My mouth's been

scalded! Medic! Call a medic!"

Jed, his legs buckling, was being carted past them, one arm around Paddy, the other around Dymphna. He paused over Agent Matcham.

"Maybe MI-6 is coptering in their own doctor for you," he said. Then he spat in their faces.

Even as Ursula's heart sang the praises of the Lord and Virgin Mary for Their help, she sought to contain her rage and feelings of betrayal as Frank the Faith Man jerked on the floor before her. She grit her teeth. Her right foot twitched. How it longed to shoot out and stomp time and again against his hateful, sinful body. But that would be another sin chalked up to her, and another confession. She had had enough confessions. She headed to the door.

Fionnuala swiftly grabbed the paradise mugs and spilled out their liquid contents. She was going to bag a souvenir from this trip to flaunt to her neighbors no matter what. She quickly inspected the sputtering, roaring woman for any fancy jewelry or accessories on her way out. She froze in shock. That necklace jerking atop the bulging veins of the woman's neck! A sparkling, intoxicating dark blue and shaped like a—it was the Heart of the Ocean! Just like in the film! The one that went overboard and sunk to the depths! Eyes still shining their disbelief, Fionnuala trailed it off the woman's neck, shoved it in her pocket and raced outside.

"H-how are ye getting yer hair to do that?" she wondered of Dymphna, all the while thinking how supremely worldly she was going to look blessing the cobblestones of the Moorside with her presence, the necklace displayed on her décolletage, though she didn't use that word in her mind.

"What are ye on about?" Dymphna asked, groaning at the weight of Jed on her shoulder.

"Making it look all alive like that. How...?" Fionnuala was aware of her ponytails hanging, glum, dead.

"Och, mammy, it be's the wind, so it is," Dymphna explained.

"The tropical storm! The eye has passed!" Louella squealed.

"Hurricane!" Paddy corrected.

Indeed it was. Rain bit into their faces, shard-like, in the whipping wind. Jed was carted outside, and his hat was wrenched from his head. It disappeared into the enraged sky. Their hair smacked against their faces, even Fionnuala's ponytails, their bodies were buffeted by the fury of Mother Nature, unleashed in all her rage and barreling down upon them. All around them, trees and signs and vertical things creaked and shuddered and strained to stay put.

They could see the furious wind now, carving paths through the air and battering everything in its path. Massive leaves slapped faces, shrieking iguanas, eyes agog, sailed past, garbage and filth swirled into mini-tornadoes and ripped into their tender exposed flesh. They screamed and clutched for something stable, but there was nothing. They slit their eyes as flying bits of grit threatened to spear them. They were ten steps from the door of bungalow 12.

Jed seemed to strengthen with every thrust of the foot forward. The battered little group seemed all to be gravitating toward Slim and grabbing onto his various parts of his body for leverage. He seemed unaffected by the wind, his mass a levee.

"How," Ursula screamed through howling wind, "How are we meant to make it back to the ship?"

She glanced back through the door that was smacking open and shut. She saw the bodies of the kidnappers running around in a frenzy. The hot sauce wouldn't keep them non compos mentis forever. They couldn't go back. They had to go forward. Into the jaws of the hurricane.

Louella screamed and stumbled to the ground, elbow cracking into her handbag. She looked down and roared out of her, clutching her side.

"*Arrghhh!!* I've been shot! They've gone and shot me! I'm bleeding! Bleeding to *death!*"

They forced their heads around on their necks to look at her in alarm. Nobody had recalled seeing a gun on the kitchen table. Ursula staggered across to Louella and fell on top of her.

"*Look!* Look at the blood!" Louella squealed through the whipping wind and Ursula's bulk.

Ursula lifted herself as best she could and winced at the red mucus-like mess that was slowly oozing down Louella's side. Her eyes narrowed in the wind.

"Wait a wee minute."

She dipped her finger into the red and slurped it as if she had suddenly developed a taste for human blood.

"Pomegranate!" she yelled down at Louella's screaming face. "Tastes like them jelly sticks from—"

"Dunkin Donuts!" Louella spat, disbelieving. "Still in my bag!"

She and Ursula gripped each other as they struggled upright and pushed their drenched bodies on through the swirling trash out of the compound.

Siofra, her tiny, infirm legs unable to stand the force of the wind any longer, stumbled forward, buffeted through the air, tiny fingers trailing vines and leaves, heading towards the maws of a bottomless pit of muck.

"Uncle Jed!" Siofra screamed in fear, as he was the closest to her. *"Uncle JEDDDDD!"*

Jed clomped towards her shrieking form. She was thrust against a tree and clung onto it tight. Jed pried her body from the bark and wrapped her in his arms, shielding her as best he could. Quid pro quo.

On they trudged, past the store, towards the harbor.

Out of the corner of her slitted eye, Fionnuala watched in amazement as the roof of a shack shuddered and pried itself from the house proper. The planks of wood soared through the air as a unit, racing downwards. Straight for Ursula. She was struck with a thought, and it surprised her. She didn't want Ursula to die, she thought. She wanted her to live.

"Ursula! Watch yerself!" Fionnuala screamed out. "Bloody watch yerself!"

As the wood propelled towards her blimp, Ursula twisted her head at Fionnuala, confusion on her face. She tripped and fell into lake of mud. The wood sailed past her head.

A trash can was barreling towards Fionnuala. She put her hands out to stop it. The mugs fell. She screamed. The can slammed into her screaming face. They watched in amazement as Fionnuala was lifted into the air with the can. Twenty, forty feet she flew. Sixty, seventy. She toppled into the sea.

And then, as suddenly as the hurricane had begun, it stopped. They flung their bodies in exhaustion to the mucky ground. Rain still bucketed down upon their heads, but they were safe. Even Fionnuala, as they saw her fingers clawing over the edge of the dock, and heard the effing and blinding raging out of her parched throat. Nobody helped hoist her body to shore. They would tell her later they had been too exhausted. Ursula put her arm around Jed's shoulder, Siofra looked up at her aunt and uncle with love, Louella and Slim exchanged a sloppy kiss, Dymphna and Paddy stood there, dreading Fionnuala's arrival. Then they staggered up the creaking gangway onto the *Queen of Crabs.*

Limping towards the ship ten minutes later, cursing Paddy and Dymphna for not pulling her out, ponytails like dead things, Fionnuala reached into her pocket and draped the showy bitch-lady's loot around her sopping, soggy breasts as if she was born to wear it. She ascended the *Queen of Crabs,* plotting her revenge, almost smiling genuinely. She softly hummed "My Heart Will Go On,'" imagining she was Celine Dion herself. Life was good. Or it would be once she had dished out to her family what was due them. And that would happen soon.

"Neaaaar..." ¡Co-quí! "Faaaar...!"

CHAPTER 41

Jed had downloaded two weeks' worth of *Coronation Street,* and Ursula's eyes were bleary from trying to catch up, her head spinning from trying to keep up with the twists in all the different storylines. She switched off the computer, deciding to live in the real world, scratched Muffins on the head, and the dog padded after her as she headed out of the bedroom. Jed was at the store, taking stock.

As she went down the hallway, she looked at the head of the woman from Mali she had gotten from the dirty laundry basket in the basement and hung back up. She would never forget Fionnuala coming to her defense like that with Casino Woman. Nor would she forget Fionnuala warning her about the roof about to smash into her skull. They might never be able to exchange a civil word with each other, but at least now Ursula *knew.* She knew.

Ursula felt like celebrating, so she mixed herself a little gin and tonic in the kitchen. She could drink now, as she was off the Xanax. She and Louella had passed the statue of whatever, and, she thought, she felt better than all those immigrants to the US who had passed the Statue of Liberty in the 1880s on their way to Ellis Island. Giving up the love of their families, everything that was familiar to them, packing up and coming to the land of the free. To be free. Even Jed had said when they had gotten home and he had kissed the asphalt of their driveway (Ursula had been mortified) that it was the 'best damn country in the world. I'm happy to be home.'

And Ursula, the immigrant, was starting to grudgingly feel it was home as well.

Her heart had frozen with fear when Detective Scarrey had, yet again, called her the day after they came back home. But in the back of her mind, she knew she and Louella were now safe.

"Mrs. Barnett!" he said. "I've been trying to get in touch with you. I've left you many messages. Why didn't you call back?"

"I...we were on a cruise, sure," Ursula said, nibbling on her lower lip. "Me cell phone wouldn't pick up messages so far away."

There was a moment of silence, and visions of coppers knocking on the door, throwing on the handcuffs, danced in her mind.

"I thought I told you and your sister-in-law that you were still under investigation about the missing $100,000. I thought I told you not to leave the jurisdiction."

"It was me and me husband's anniversary, so it was. I wasn't gonny spend it here. Would yer wife be pleased to spend yer 35th anniversary here in Wisconsin?"

"No I guess you're right. Anyway, the reason I was calling..."

Ursula gripped the handset.

"First, all charges have been dropped. The statute of limitations has passed anyway, but we were struggling to find the money trail in any event. Actually, and this is strictly off the records, I think that if anything did go down with the church funds, your sister-in-law was more to blame than you. So, you're off the hook. And, second, I was calling because you left your umbrella in my office during your last interview. It's a Mark Cross, I see, and my wife's told me they're expensive. I wanted to make sure it got to you."

Ursula's pounding heart stilled. And, oh, the price of that Mark Cross umbrella, bought in the heady post-lottery-win days. She could never afford one now. "Sure, that's wile civil of ye, Detective. I think, but, I've had enough of that cop shop of yers. I don't mind telling ye I'd rather never step foot on yer premises again. Why don't ye give it to yer wife as a wee gift? A lovely little surprise for her to come home to, so it'll be."

"Er, I guess, yeah. Well, and there was another reason I was calling you so many times."

He cleared his throat. Ursula waited for him to speak.

"Aye?" she finally said.

"Now that you're no longer a suspect in an ongoing investigation..."

"Aye??"

"Me and my wife, well, I don't think we're getting along so well lately. I wonder if you'd like to have a drink with me some night?"

Ursula grinned into the phone. "That's dead nice of ye, Detective. But I love me husband, ye see."

"Oh. Well. Sorry to have disturbed you."

"Ach, go on away a that! I've not given it a second thought. No problem at all. Cheerio, then, Detective Scarrey."

"Uh, yeah, bye."

The moment she hung up, Jed rang.

"Hey, Ursula, what about us going to the movies tonight?"

"Shall we not invite Slim and Louella over for cribbage instead? That movie theater in town be's wile noisy, so it does. Or perhaps a wee game of poker?"

"Absolutely not!"

As the conversation continued, Ursula kept smiling to herself. Jed seemed to have left gambling behind. And Wisconsin was becoming her home.

Louella was clipping coupons at the kitchen table. Slim was at the store, taking stock. She had been behind in her couponing, and was looking forward to all the money she'd be saving.

As she clipped, she glanced over at the postcard clamped under the fridge magnet from Morocco, the one with the pointy red shoes. The postcard was from her cousin Wanda, who was eighteen and trying to make it big as an actress in Hollywood. Wanda was currently a waitress.

Louella didn't know how, after all those times in the interview room with Detective Scarrey, she had managed to keep up her lie to Ursula. She was lucky the police had always interrogated them separately. And now had been cleared, the statue of limitations had passed, and Ursula need never know exactly what she had done with that $100,000.

Yes, her friend Daisy Flynster had succumbed to mesophelioma, and it had been a crying shame, and she had died. But...the real reason Louella needed the money was very different. Wanda had called her up one night and told her she was putting herself up for auditions for a movie. But, oh, not any movie. It was a Christian musical. And she wanted to play the role of Mary Magdalene. Christian as Louella was, she was excited that Hollywood was even considering a religious movie. She did wonder, however, how Wanda, who was dumpy and grotesque—she was Slim's sister's daughter—could every play statuesque Mary Magdalene. Wanda told her she had met the casting director and wowed him with her portrayal of Mary crying at the garden of Gethsemane. But he told her nobody would want to watch her on the screen looking like that; it wasn't horror movie, after all. If she underwent liposuction, breast implants and a bit of light facial cosmetic surgery, then the part was hers. It would cost almost $100,000. Wanda promised her, if she got the part, she'd give Louella a portion of her paycheck. Louella had haggled it up to 30%, and then only had been too happy to promise her the money. The only problem was getting to money. So Louella had. The postcard, lying on the floor amongst the bills when they got home, told her it had worked; Wanda had gotten the part! They would start shooting in two weeks.

Louella took a bite out of a Munchin and smiled as the scissors clipped through the newsprint, each clack saving her that little bit more.

CHAPTER 42—SEVEN MONTHS LATER

Fionnuala dragged her hands through the dishwater, her fingers landing on whatever spoons or plates or she didn't really know what lurked in the dank water. She gave the mystery items little rubs with her fingers and balanced them on the top of the towering mass in the draining tray. With Lorcan and Eoin back home, and her mother Maureen now living permanently with them, and, of course, Seamus and Siofra, there were always many things to wash that the Floods had fed off of, and they fed often.

Fionnuala tugged the dingy clump of hair, hanging before her bleary eyes, with dripping fingers and flung it over her left ear. *"Cheer up sleepy Jean...!"* sang the song from the radio. She snapped it off, then her hand aimed again for the dingy water with its few tired bubbles left.

"Does this really be how I live, merciful Jesus?"

The rain was pelting down outside. She could hear it, but couldn't see it, as Paddy still hadn't replaced the board at the scullery window with glass. Lazy git. But at least this was the cold rain she had grown up with, not the unseemly hot drops as if from Hell she had encountered on that godless foreign land. It seemed a dream.

She looked down at her hand. Yellowish, chipped fingernails, knuckles like walnuts, a wedding ring now two sizes too small, the flab of her finger almost hiding the tarnished metal, whatever it was. Gold, Paddy had told her at the time. Fecking liar! She had caught a glimpse of a show about cosmetic surgery Dymphna had been glued to, and remembered the narky little toerag in the flash suit saying that the only thing they couldn't help were the hands. They would always show the age. The bulging veins she looked down on now, the wrinkles crisscrossing like— She flung her fingers back into the water. She gulped more poisons into her lungs, the cigarette clamped to her lower lip.

She shouldn't have lost it with that woman on the boat, her name letters on a nametag Fionnuala's brain could no longer conjure up. The black woman. She had promised to do her nails a fancy Yank way. Swanky colors and letters and what not. MARY MOTHER OF GOD, was it? Och, naw, not enough fingers for that. Fionnuala's heart gave a little lurch of regret, then anger. That flimmin Ursula! Why in the name of God had she sided with Her Ladyship the Cunt? Had she been deranged? She wondered what would have happened if—

The front door clattered open.

"Mammy, Mammy!" Dymphna called from the hallway, breathless.

Fionnuala clenched her jaw at the inhuman shrieks of Keanu and Beeyonsay from their stroller. Her fingernails scraped down the length of a plate. This was the last thing she needed! The tart and her two half-Orange bastards, paying her a visit. Well, Dymphna wouldn't be getting an offer of a cup of tea, as the Lord was her witne—

"Mammy! Ye'll never guess what I just came upon at the Mountains of Mourne market! Och, I even splurged on a mini-cab to get up here to show ye!"

Fionnuala turned from the sink and wiped her hands on her top. Dymphna was barreling towards her, a look of joy on her face as if she had just woken up in the men's side of a Turkish prison. She held something ratty in her hands, and it was coming closer to an alarmed Fionnuala.

"Would ye have a look? I couldn't believe me eyes!"

"I haven't the time to—"

Fionnuala's eyes widened, the scorn dissolving from her face.

"It's me satchel!" she gasped. "Me Celine Dion-*Titanic* satchel!"

She snatched it from her daughter, held it out before her disbelieving eyes and felt the lump in her throat as Dymphna babbled on. Fionnuala paid her no mind.

"I didn't know if ye were still mad into the *Titanic*. After wer trip and all. I've seen ye wearing that necklace, but, and drinking from them mugs, so I thought, maybe ye still love it. And I know how much ye loved that satchel."

Celine's face on one side, frozen singing into her microphone, was hidden behind muck, and on the other side, the ship was hidden, only the smoke stacks poking out of the waves. Fionnuala shook the bag up and down furiously, but the *Titanic* was permanently sunk. She pressed the mesh to her face and cried into it.

"I meant to tell ye, aye. The wee mechanism that allows the ship to sink when ye place items in it be's broken, like. And it be's wile minging, I had to clench me nose shut, but I'm sure ye can get it cleaned. Maybe at the dry cleaners. I know it's terrible dear, but to get clothes dry-cleaned, but Zoë swears by—"

Fionnuala's face reappeared.

"Och, must be water from the sink," Fionnuala said, wiping at her eyes and staring down at her treasure, inspecting every tired seam, every hanging thread. The cells of her brain trundled as they figured out how to put it back like new with the aid of the sewing machine. "Months, I scoured that market trying to find this. I knew in me heart of hearts it'd eventually find its way there. All nicked goods does, sooner or later. Och, Dymphna..." The kindness on Fionnuala's face, though she still couldn't look in her daughter's eyes, turned to sudden horror. Her eyes narrowed as they zoomed in on the mesh. "Wait a wee moment there...!"

Dymphna flinched as her mother shrieked and tossed the bag the length of the kitchen. It smacked against the broken ice cream machine and fluttered to the top of the garbage pail piled with rotting potato peels. Dymphna feared her mother had taken leave of her senses. Again. She took a step towards the door.

"Ye hateful slag, ye!" Fionnuala roared. "Lice-ridden, so it be's! Crawling with the filthy wee creatures! So help me God, Dymphna, if ye somehow infested that bag yerself and this be's some type of joke, Lord help ye when ye feel the force of me hand on yer—"

Fionnuala silenced herself. Dymphna had long since fled the house, taking the shrieking bastard wanes with her. Fionnuala glared around the misery of her scullery, and again she blinked back tears. But these were not tears of joy. She bit her wrinkled fist with its bland, unadorned fingernails. She glanced at the garbage can. She took a little step towards it and...

CHAPTER 43—TWO YEARS LATER

Anthea Planck rolled her cart from the frozen foods, where she had stocked up on a wide array of meals for one, to the fresh fruits and vegetables. She hummed along to the Black Eyed Peas from the speakers. She was feeling marvelous, though her head still ached a bit. The night before, she had gone out with the girls from the office to celebrate her first year there. Anthea had quit EconoLux, signed up for a six-month training course, and was now a medical biller. She loved her job.

She paused before the celery. All the bundles looked a bit grim, their stalks brownish, their fronds wilted. Except for that bunch in the back. She reached out—

—and jumped as a manly hand shot in and snatched it from the pile. Her fingers clawed at air. Anthea looked up, annoyed. *What rude arsehole would—Oh!* Her lips disappeared.

It was Richard the Dick. Looking disheveled, Anthea was happy to see, an unironed shirt ill-fitting, the buttons straining from a newly-forming beer gut, his face in need of a shave and his body even maybe a bath.

"Richard!" She eyed the celery clutched triumphantly in his fist.

"Oh! Did you want this?" He attempted a sheepish look down at the vegetable, but he was crap at it. Anthea could tell he was annoyed she was claiming the celery as her own. Which it was; she had seen it first, reached for it first. He pushed it reluctantly towards her, the corners of his lips tight with anger. "Go ahead and take it then."

He seemed surprised she did, and a bit alarmed at the speed with which she snatched it to her breasts. She held it like a Miss Universe trophy.

"So how have you been?" Anthea asked. "How's the, what did you call her? Snarling beast?"

Richard fiddled with the leaf of a cabbage.

"Silly woman filed for divorce."

It was all Anthea could do to hide her glee behind the fronds of the celery.

"Oh, I'm so sorry for you."

Richard inspected her with his eyes.

"You look...refreshed," he said. "Happy."

"I am. Very."

"I wonder..." He ran his fingernail over the top of a turnip. "Would you like to meet for a drink? Maybe rekindle—"

He shrunk at the laughter that spilled from her throat, and looked around the aisles, annoyed.

"Please, Anthea," he hissed. "Show some basic human civility!"

"And why should I?" she retorted, forcing the celery into her cart. "You never showed *me* any!"

She calmed down quickly. He was looking shocked at what she had said. Poor, doltish, ignorant Richard with his puny little...career going nowhere. He shouldn't anger her. She should pity him. She placed a hand on his shoulder. She felt the tufts of back hair under his shirt.

"I'm sorry, Richard. I shouldn't have behaved like that. I'm over it. Especially with the new man in my life."

Richard looked at her askew.

"Who—?"

"*Anyway!* Let's not dwell on the past. Unless..."

"Yes?" He was eager, gagging for it.

"Unless you want to tell me something I've wondered for years now."

"Yes?"

"I read all about it in the papers, of course, and on the Internet," she said. "But I had left EconoLux by that time, of course. If you recall, right when I broke up with you," she quenched the little smile that begged to be set free on her lips, "I just rang in ill the next day and never returned. So I never got the inside scoop. But what on earth happened on the *Queen of Crabs?* The rioting staff? The looting? The MI-6 scam artists? Bloody typical, I work for that company for a decade and each day was a misery of boredom. The moment I quit," she snapped her fingers, "fireworks!"

Richard shrugged. "It's not our policy to discuss the details with those who aren't EconoLux employees. Any more."

"But surely you can tell me, Richard?" She moved a bit closer to the kiwis where he had now taken root. "For old times' sake? Oh, I did read that quite a few of the staff were hauled into court for the looting and that EconoLux got most of the goods back. And, of course, there were a few heavy sentences for the leaders of the riot, I believe they were the engineers? But what I'm really interested in is the mother and son scam artist team. What happened to them? How many innocent passengers did they manage to scam?"

Richard pried a cherry from its stem as he considered. He shrugged nonchalantly. "Not many," he said. "The guy, he started in the Faith Center. We realized afterwards that the minister who was supposed to be there had been fired, and a replacement was never found. So, there were a few lonely women he cheated out of a few hundred pounds. But the biggest loser was this Yank. He believed they were agents from MI-6! They tried to take him for $25,000 at some poker scam or another. God knows how he ever fell for it. Anyway, they were caught by Interpol. They picked them up in some Puerto Rican hospital. They were in for gastro-intestinal disorders brought on by extremely hot hot sauce. Apparently, the niece of the man..." He shuddered suddenly with anger. "I don't want to talk about it any more. Take your celery and go. Leave me be."

Anthea smiled.

"With pleasure," she said. "Have a nice life, won't you, Richard?"

And off down the aisle she rolled the cart, towards the selection of international wines. It was time, yet again, to celebrate.

Fleeing The Jurisdiction

If you enjoyed this book, try Gerald Hansen's others:

An Embarrassment of Riches

Hand In The Till

www.geraldhansenbooks.com

18440596R00155

Made in the USA
Lexington, KY
04 November 2012